I0700119

Every Rule Worth Breaking

AMANDA CHAPERON

ON THE EVENING OF February 13, 2023, a shooter opened fire on Michigan State University students. That night, the safety and sanctity of the campus and city I once called home—and still consider as such—was ripped away from the current students, faculty, staff, and residents. One senseless act from a cowardly man changed millions of lives in an instant.

The Spartan community is a strong one, including a tight-knit alumni community spread across the globe. I've always been proud to be a Spartan; receiving my degree from MSU's school of journalism is one of my greatest and proudest accomplishments. In the days that followed this horrific night, it was of great comfort to me to see our alumni community band together. It became more and more evident why the phrase "Spartans Will" is so commonly spoken in MSU circles. Typically, it's reserved for successes. But in the wake of this tragedy, it's taken on a new meaning, at least for me.

Spartans Will protect each other.

Spartans Will mourn together.

Spartans Will be strong.

From the near-immediate response of law enforcement officials and medical personnel to the scene and nearby Sparrow Hospital where victims were rushed and treated, and not just locally but from agencies across the state, to the outpouring of love, support, grief, devastation, sadness, and anger from not only our community but those of our rivals, "Spartan Strong" became a rally cry. As an alum, it means to the world to see so many standing with us. Because we *are* strong. And we will endure. I just wish it wasn't necessary.

We'll never understand why this happened, or what was going through the shooter's mind when he decided to end the lives of three young adults before they'd even really begun—and critically injure five more—and that's something I think all of us will struggle with for the rest of our own lives.

On these pages, Kenzie and Aiden are lucky enough to live in a universe where MSU is safe, where the buildings and sidewalks and dorms and classrooms aren't tainted with the memories of gunshots or students hiding under desks to protect themselves. They are able to walk into the Union and Berkey Hall without thinking of their fallen classmates. They don't have to think, "it could've been me."

Unfortunately, the same cannot be said for those on campus that fateful night, and three members of my Spartan family lost their lives far too soon.

Brian Fraser, Alexandria Verner, and Arielle Anderson—I'm sorry we failed you. I remember you, today and every day. I hope and pray that your deaths will not be in vain. I hope another community will not have to endure the life-altering shockwaves of a similar tragedy.

Before you read, whether it's an early copy, on release day, or in the days, months, and years that follow, I hope you'll take a second to send a prayer and good thoughts to the families of these three. If you're reading this and you're a Spartan like me, please reach out. It would make me so happy to hear from you.

As always, Go Green, forever and ever.

EVERY RULE WORTH BREAKING is a steamy college hockey romance full of explicit language and sexual content. To avoid—or locate—the open door chapters, please flip to the Dicktionary I've provided in the back. For the complete list of *Every Rule Worth Breaking* content warnings, please visit my website at www.achaperonauthor.com.

*For anyone who's ever felt like a prisoner in their own mind.
Breathe. You got this.*

MACKENZIE JEAN'S HANDS SHOOK as she withdrew the oversized envelope from her mailbox and raced to the elevator bank. It took her several tries of stabbing at the up button before she managed to call the car, and when the doors slid open, she rushed inside and punched the number for her floor.

She wanted to tear into the envelope right where she stood, but she forced herself to wait. To occupy her hands and mind, she flipped through the other pieces of mail in the stack, ripping open some bills from utility companies and mentally reminding herself to enroll in paperless billing.

Finally, what seemed like eons later, the elevator lurched to a stop and the doors parted with a *ding*, spitting her out onto the grey carpeted hallway that led to her condo.

Once she was safely ensconced inside, she tossed the remainder of her mail on her large kitchen island and sat on a bar stool.

The tremors in her fingers grew with each inch she opened the envelope. The contents shook like leaves on a particularly windy day as she withdrew them.

She closed her eyes, sent up a silent prayer, took a deep, steadying breath, and began to read.

Dear Ms. Jean:

After careful review of your application, we are pleased to grant you transfer admission to Michigan State University starting the Fall of 2023...

With a huge sigh of relief, Kenzie threw the papers in the air in celebration and let out an excited yell as they floated down to the floor around her.

She'd done it.

She was going back to college.

The idea to complete her degree had taken root the previous fall, when Berkley, her big brother Brent's wife, had decided to go back to school and fully pursue her dream of becoming a sports agent.

Since she'd moved to Detroit, FLEX had grown from a mom-and-pop business she and Brent operated out of the office in his condo to a nationally-recognized brand, thanks in no small part to her. As a woman in her early-twenties, she certainly had her finger on the pulse of what was trendy, and social media marketing played a huge role in generating sales. Once she'd convinced Brent to bring on a select group of influencers to act as brand ambassadors instead of spending an ungodly amount of money on advertising campaigns people would ignore, FLEX became a top-tier activewear brand.

The real-world, hands-on experience she'd gained by working

full-time on FLEX with her brother's genius business mind at her side was irreplaceable. Sure, a lot of the success was because her brother was *Brent Jean*, but Kenzie had also worked endless hours with designers, textile companies, website designers, and marketing representatives to launch FLEX into the stratosphere. Brent's name may have been the reason people gave their company a second look, but Kenzie's dogged promotion of their products converted those looks to sales. She was of the mind that if people saw something enough times, they'd be intrigued enough to try it for themselves. And what one man or woman had, others wanted. It became a domino effect, when one sale led to two more, led to five more, led to ten more, and so on and so forth, until the Jean siblings had been able to rent out a small office space and hire help.

Kenzie loved the advertising and marketing aspects of business, and quickly realized it was something for which she had a knack. Suddenly, after two years in this role that had been incredibly lucrative for her, and had given her ten times the experience her peers had at her age, she felt pulled in a new direction, compelled to take a new path.

A path that, maybe, no longer included FLEX.

But she didn't want to get ahead of herself.

Quietly, without telling anyone, Kenzie had set about gathering her transcripts from NYU, filling out the application, and submitting it to her brother's alma mater.

And she'd done it. She'd been accepted.

It wasn't exactly surprising, but it was a weight off her shoulders.

However, going back to school meant she'd have to make some lifestyle changes. For starters, while she was focusing on school, that would leave less time for FLEX, which in her opinion wasn't a bad thing. In fact, it was the *best* thing. Kenzie felt urged to turn the page and enter a new chapter of her life.

Without thinking twice, Kenzie lifted her phone and dialed a number, hoping the person she called wasn't with a patient.

"Hello, Mackenzie."

No matter how hard she tried, she couldn't get her therapist to call her *Kenzie*.

"I got in," she said, feigning calm.

"That's wonderful!" Dr. Mathews said. "I knew you would. But why don't you sound more excited?"

"I have to tell Brent," Kenzie said with a sigh.

"I think you need to give your brother more credit, Mackenzie. I know it's going to be an adjustment, but he's your brother. He loves you and wants what's best for you."

"I think he *will* be happy for me...eventually. But when I tell him I'm leaving FLEX? He won't take that well."

The simple thought of telling her brother she wanted to leave the company they'd poured so much blood, sweat, and tears into had Kenzie's skin breaking out in hives. Her breath hitched, shadows appearing at the edges of her vision.

She was quiet for long enough that Dr. Mathews understood what was happening, because she said, "It's okay, Mackenzie. Just breathe."

Kenzie did as she was told, in and out slowly, making her inhales longer than her exhales until she no longer felt like she was suffocating.

Anxiety was such a bitch.

"Look," Dr. Mathews said, and Kenzie perked up, ready for the wisdom the woman was about to drop. "I know I'm an advocate for always speaking your truth, but I know how heavily this weighs on you, and we're trying to combat your anxiety, not contribute to it. What if, for now, you simply tell him you want to step back from FLEX while in school? That gives you some freedom, gets him used to the idea that you're leaving, and gives you time to figure out how to fully break from the company. Plus, who knows. Maybe in two years, you won't actually want to leave."

Kenzie considered this, considered saying it was a terrible idea and that she would fight through her nerves to tell Brent now. But...she couldn't ignore the weight that suddenly lifted off her chest with Dr. Mathews' suggestion, and she found herself agreeing with the idea.

For now, she'd make due with a half-truth.

***

"I'm going back to school," Kenzie announced at dinner that night, then braced herself for the explosion.

She, Brent, Berkley, and Berkley's best friend Lexie were gathered around the table in Brent and Berkley's dining room, a spread of chicken alfredo, garlic bread, salad, and soup laid out in front of them.

The three of them stared at Kenzie as though she'd sprouted a second head, and to her surprise, it was Lexie who recovered first.

"That's great, Kenz! Where are you going to go?"

"Your alma mater," she said proudly.

"You got into State?" Berkley asked, her smile growing to match the one stretching across Kenzie's face.

"Sure did," she said. "I start classes in the fall."

"That's amazing, Kenz!" Berkley said, popping up from her seat and rushing around the table to wrap her arms around Kenzie's shoulders.

Lexie grinned. "You're going to *love* it. Not only is it the best university in the world, but East Lansing is uh-may-zing," she said, drawing out the last word dramatically.

Kenzie giggled, but sobered when she glanced at her brother, who still had not spoken, his face a carefully constructed mask of calm.

Kenzie knew that look, knew that something was churning below the surface, waiting to spout free like Old Faithful, taking them all by surprise.

"Bee?" Kenzie asked quietly.

"Why didn't you tell me?"

Kenzie rolled her eyes. Leave it to her brother to jump right past, "I'm proud of you, kid," or, "Congratulations, little sis," and straight into accusations.

"I didn't want to make a big deal out of it until it was a sure thing."

"What if you hadn't gotten in?" Brent asked. "Would you have said anything then?"

Kenzie considered that. Would she have mentioned it? Probably not. The problem with her brother—both of them, actually—was that they were overachievers. Brent had known he wanted to be a professional hockey player since he was a teenager, and he'd worked his ass off in the intervening years to become one of the NHL's top forwards. In comparison, around the same time Brent realized he was good at hockey, her other brother Nate had discovered he wanted to be a doctor—and was currently an orthopedic surgery resident at the University of Michigan.

So if Kenzie had failed to gain admission? No, she wouldn't have said anything. As the baby and only female among her siblings, she felt like the odd one out frequently enough that she'd rather avoid having *that* conversation with her family.

Berkley saved them all by saying, "Well, that doesn't matter, does it? Because she got in!" She raised her glass of wine above the table and said, "To Mackenzie!"

Everyone followed suit, although Kenzie didn't miss the way her brother hesitated before lifting his own to clink against the other three.

After dinner, Brent and Kenzie sat in Brent's office, him behind the desk, her in the plush armchair across from him. With the walls lined with shelves filled to capacity with books and awards, she felt more like she was in some grand library than an office in a suburban Detroit home.

All her life, her brother had been a master at maintaining his silence and composure in tense situations until Kenzie was squirming and eventually blurted out whatever he wanted to hear.

Tonight was no different.

"I'm sorry I didn't tell you I was applying to school," she said finally.

"You know you can talk to me about anything," he said, his gaze softening. "I don't understand why you kept this from me."

"It's exactly like I said. I didn't want to make it a thing until I was sure I got in."

Brent studied her for a moment, then said, "I am proud of you, you know."

She gave him a small smile. "Thanks, Bee."

"But we're going to have to figure out what this means for your role with FLEX. If you're going back to college, you're finishing your degree this time."

Kenzie knew he was right—she had obviously given that particular dilemma a fair amount of consideration herself—but his tone still chafed. "Okay, *dad.*"

Brent glared. "I'm serious. What do you want to do? Do you want to work part time, full time? Completely remove yourself from the picture until you're done with school? I'm good with whatever you want, Kenz."

As someone who suffered from pretty severe anxiety—often exacerbated by taking on too much at once—Kenzie knew the only way she'd survive was to make a clean break. And after her earlier conversation with Dr. Mathews, her path forward was crystal clear. The fact that Brent had offered it up as an option of his own free will made having this conversation much easier than she'd anticipated.

"I want to take an administrative leave," she said. Brent's mouth dropped open and his eyes darkened to the color of a storm surge. He clearly hadn't expected her to take him up on the offer of leaving, and she felt compelled to soften the blow by tacking on, "At least during the school year. But I think, if I'm going to do this whole college thing, I need to give it my full attention."

Brent was familiar with her mental health struggles. She'd long suspected he suffered from some of his own but was too afraid, or too *manly*, to admit it. She knew he'd understand her desire to step back, to lessen her load.

Her brother nodded. "Then that's what we'll do."

She'd gotten exactly what she wanted, but still she frowned. "Are you going to be able to handle everything?"

"We're going to have to bring a couple more people on," he said. "But yes, I can handle it."

Kenzie sighed, her shoulders drooping in relief.

"What exactly are you going to study?" he asked.

"Marketing…" she said, and he nodded approvingly. "And advertising."

Brent may approve now, but he wouldn't take so kindly to the real motivation behind those majors. On the surface, they seemed ideal for her work with FLEX. The truth, however, was rooted in the fact that her time with FLEX was quickly coming to an end—*and* in what she wanted to do next. If she were honest with him, this conversation would take a sharp southern turn, and she didn't have the mental capacity to deal with it right now; her nerves were already completely frayed.

Later. She would tell him everything *later*.

Brent raised an eyebrow. "Dual major? That's a lot of work."

And he would know, considering he'd managed to graduate on time with degrees in business and finance, all while playing hockey at the collegiate level.

Kenzie shrugged. "Go big or go home."

A niggling voice in the back of her mind whispered, *Famous last words.*

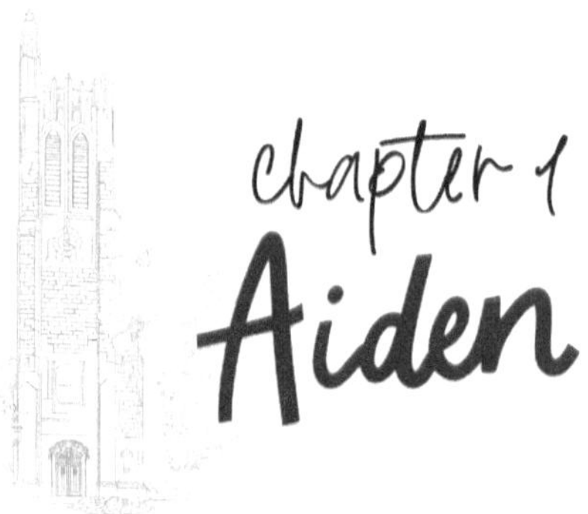

chapter 1
Aiden

THE NUMBER ONE RULE of Michigan State University hockey was simple: never turn down a dare.

That was the first thing Aiden Fuller learned the second he stepped foot on campus four years ago. Dares were always to be obeyed, whether one wanted to or not.

And right now, Aiden definitely did *not*.

Aiden and his teammates were gathered at the south entrance of Munn Arena, the names of all the Spartan greats that had come before them staring down from the walls.

Briefly, he wondered how many of them had done dumb shit like what he was about to do.

"Just go out there and give them a show," his classmate and Spartans' starting goaltender Jack DeLuca said. "You're a hot ass college hockey player. Time to act like it."

Aiden glared at Jack. "You are so fucking weird."

Jack tilted his head to the side and gave Aiden a smile. "I know."

"Where exactly do I have to run again?" Aiden asked.

Jack detailed the route, a loop that would take him through a small—but busy—section of this side of campus, and Aiden groaned.

"That's so fucking far, dude."

Jack shrugged and looked over his shoulder at their other teammates, who had gathered behind him. "Too late to back out now, unless you want to suffer the consequences. We can give you your punishment right now."

Aiden vigorously shook his head; he had never in his entire tenure as a member of this hockey team refused a dare, and he wasn't about to start today. "And we agreed, no cameras, right?"

Each of his teammates patted themselves down as if to prove they left their phones in the locker room. Half of them were shirtless anyway, thanks to the sticky, late-August weather.

Jack raised three fingers and said, "Scout's honor. No one has their phones."

"Let's go, Fuller," Captain Lucas Hayes said, tapping his Apple Watch. "We don't have all day."

He was right, as usual. They'd arrived early for training today so Aiden could complete this dare.

Running a loop through one of the busiest parts of campus might not seem like much of a dare to some people.

But doing it naked? *That* was Aiden's worst nightmare.

At Luke's prodding, and with a resigned sigh, Aiden shucked his t-shirt and dropped his shorts and boxers to his ankles before stepping out of them and kicking them away. Instinctively, he covered his junk with his hand, but his ass remained bare, and his teammates instantly erupted into obnoxious catcalls and whistles of appreciation.

Thankfully, Jack was right about him being a hot ass hockey player. He might only be twenty-three, but after nearly fifteen years of competitive hockey, his body detailed his hard work and commitment to his sport. He stood six feet, three inches tall, with thick, blue-black hair that waved across his head. After spending most of his summer outside, working construction with his uncle and boating on Lake Michigan with his friends, his skin was perfectly bronzed, making the muscles he'd worked so hard for look even better. Not to mention his entire left arm was engulfed in ink, from chest to wrist. He'd heard from several viable sources—a.k.a. hookups—that his tattoos made him infinitely more attractive.

"Alright, Fuller," he said quietly, pumping himself up. "Let's do this."

And he was off.

Running across the expanse of Munn Field was the easy part. The field hockey team was indeed on Forest Akers practice field, running drills in preparation of their upcoming season. Aiden ran by, not turning his attention in their direction, trying to keep his balance as his sandals slipped and slid along the dewy grass.

Then he came upon Shaw Lane, where he'd have to cross four lanes of traffic to reach the other side. He stood, bouncing on the balls of his feet with his dick cupped in his hand, waiting for a break in the cars whizzing past. A cherry-red Bronco sped by, the girl behind the wheel honking and giggling with her friend in the passenger seat, both shouting sexually suggestive comments at him. Aiden responded in kind...by raising one hand and flipping them a middle finger.

Finally, traffic paused long enough that he was able to sprint across the road and onto the sidewalk in front of the fire station before taking a left.

This was where Aiden had protested this chosen route the most. Case was a residence hall, but it also housed one of the campus cafeterias. As it was centrally located to all of the sports complexes, most Spartan athletes ate either here or at Brody, which was now at Aiden's back.

He wasn't even remotely surprised to find a mass of people milling about the sidewalks, coming in and out of the building, and every last one of them stopped and stared.

Upon realizing what was happening, the cell phones emerged.

Did he mention it was Welcome Weekend? And campus was crawling with new and returning students in the process of moving in?

I am so fucked.

He made it past Case and stood on the corner of Shaw and Chestnut, waiting for the walk sign to change so he could begin his loop back toward the arena.

"Hey, Fuller!" someone yelled from behind him. A *female* someone. "Nice ass!"

Another said, "I want to lick your tattoos!"

Creepy.

And honestly, *fuck* his teammates.

Well, mostly Jack. This dare had been all his idea.

Aiden ignored the group gathered at his back as they laughed, hooting and hollering and catcalling, until the light blessedly turned green and he hustled across the road. In front of the Skandalaris Football Center, the crowd was much thinner, and Aiden's burning cheeks cooled a bit as he once again waited to cross Shaw.

When the light changed again, he took off at a dead sprint, bobbing and weaving between people on the sidewalks, not slowing until he could once again cross Chestnut near the side entrance to Munn.

The group of his teammates who had followed his streak raced up and followed through the door, where they walked along the concourse until they reached Aiden's pile of clothes.

"I didn't think there were going to be that many people out there!" Jack said, bending at the waist to catch his breath after running and laughing so hard.

Aiden angrily pulled on his boxers, then shorts, before picking up his t-shirt and snapping it in Jack's direction. "Did you see how many people there were in front of Case? If Coach sees a video, I'm screwed."

"Don't worry," Jack said, dropping a sweat-sticky palm on Aiden's naked shoulder. "Coach isn't on any social media, remember? How would he ever see it?"

Jack had a point, but that didn't loosen the ball of nerves and anxiety in Aiden's chest.

Welcome Weekend at MSU was in full swing, and the last thing Aiden wanted to do after showing off every inch of his body to campus was go out Friday night with the boys.

But Jack had made it impossible to say no.

"All I'm saying is the last thing I need right now is a bunch of puck bunnies all up in my business because they got a good look at what's under all the gear," Aiden had said, gesturing to his body, where his cut-off tee clung to his sweaty chest and his dark green athletic shorts hung low on his hips. After a hellish afternoon of training, his skin had glistened with sweat, making his tattoos stand out in stark relief. "I want to enjoy a quiet night in."

Jack had rolled his eyes. "Bro, it's Welcome Weekend. You *have* to come out. In fact..." His goalie had paused for dramatic effect, and Aiden knew exactly what that glint in his eyes meant. "I dare you."

"Fuck you," Aiden had said on an exhale, and Jack had cackled.

That's how Aiden found himself at Rick's that evening, a bottle of Bud Light sweating in his hand.

Rick's had been an East Lansing staple for over four decades. It wasn't the classiest bar or club in the city, but it was the most popular. Separated into two sides—one well-lit with booths and a full-length bar, the other dim with more booths and random tables, the dance floor, and the bathrooms—Rick's was unassuming. The floors were sticky, the drinks inexpensive. It was a no frills kind of place, the perfect spot for athletes to unwind without being mobbed by adoring fans.

Tucked into an alcove near the bathrooms, the MSU hockey players held court. They weren't as popular as the football or basketball players, but they spent enough time at Rick's to be easily recognized.

Tonight's group was small. It was relatively early yet, but Jack liked to go out earlier than normal people. His philosophy was, "The earlier I go out, the sooner I can start drinking, and the sooner I start drinking, the sooner I get drunk."

Aiden found it hard to argue.

He was squeezed onto a padded bench with a deep tear that had been duct taped over several times. On his left sat one of the team's best defenseman, Asher Rhodes. Asher had curly, dirty-blond hair and pale green eyes. When he first arrived on campus three years ago as a true freshman, his arms and legs were toothpick thin, his torso long and skinny. They'd all been lanky in those days. Thanks to their rigorous training regimen, the kid had filled out nicely, going from a dorky freshman to a senior who had the attention of several females around campus.

On Aiden's right sat Luke and Jack, the former taking a shot with a group of girls standing across from them and the latter with his face buried in the neck of the big-breasted brunette on his lap.

"I'm going to get another drink," he said to no one in particular. None of them would miss him anyway.

Aiden pushed his way through the crowd until he was belly up to the bar, draining the remainder of his Bud Light before setting the empty on the counter and signaling for another. The girl working—a slim blonde with a high ponytail long enough to swish between her shoulder blades as she moved—winked and spun toward the beer fridge. A moment later she set the bottle in front of him and said, "On the house."

Aiden grinned widely before bringing the bottle to his lips.

"Men," a feminine voice to his left groaned. It was loud enough in the bar that Aiden knew she purposely said it with enough volume to reach his ears.

He turned toward her, and found himself looking down at an average-height, athletically-built brunette with piercing blue eyes. The girl reminded Aiden vaguely of someone he'd seen before, but he couldn't quite put his finger on who.

It didn't matter, because the second their gazes locked, Aiden knew he'd do whatever it took to find out.

"Why am I the bad guy in this scenario?" he asked, grinning down at her.

"You just buy right into the stereotype!" she said. "You don't even feel a little bit bad about using all of this—" she gestured at his entire person "—to get what you want."

"I would gladly pay," Aiden said. "But why mess with a good thing?"

"You're disgusting," she said, but he didn't miss the way her lips tilted up slightly before she flattened them again.

"You know, you could easily get your own free drinks," he said, eyes scanning her from head to toe.

"And how would I do that?" she asked, arching an eyebrow.

Did this girl really have no idea?

"Use your feminine wiles, of course. I mean, you're sexy as hell, so it shouldn't be too hard."

A blush crept into her cheeks at his compliment, and Aiden's pulse sped as his fingers itched to feel that heat against his skin.

He desperately wanted to learn what else he could do or say to elicit the same reaction.

"I don't think—"

"I dare you," Aiden blurted, cutting her off mid-sentence. Something told Aiden this girl wouldn't back down from a direct challenge. He may not even know her name yet, but he'd seen a glint of fire in her eyes.

He was rewarded a moment later when she determinedly set her jaw and turned her body to the bar, catching the eye of the male bartender.

Aiden watched with rapt attention as the girl worked her magic, the blush receding from her cheeks as she turned on the charm, flirting shamelessly with the guy—whose name Aiden knew was, ironically, Rick.

The guy practically had hearts in his eyes as he asked, "What can I get you to drink?"

"A vodka cranberry would be great," she said, batting her lashes and biting seductively on her lower lip.

That attention wasn't even turned on Aiden and suddenly he was sporting a halfie. What would she do to him if she turned that charm his way?

This girl was a mystery Aiden wanted to unravel.

A moment later, the bartender returned with her drink and slid it across the bar with a wink, his number scrawled on the napkin underneath.

Aiden smirked knowingly. "One of those girls, huh?"

The brunette looked at him quizzically. "One of those girls? What's that supposed to mean?"

"You're drinking vodka cranberry because you're counting calories or because of some other dumb health-related reason that I can *assure* you—" he gave her another obvious head-to-toe appraisal "—you do *not* need to be worried about."

The girl leaned an elbow against the bar top and folded her arms over her chest, pinning him with a glare. "Did it ever occur to you that maybe I just don't like the taste of beer? Or that I'm allergic?"

Aiden gave her a wide grin. "Not for a second. Girls with bodies like yours do not get them by not caring about what they eat."

"I'll have you know I've worked my ass off for this body," she said with an edge to her words that had Aiden cowering a little under her gaze. "But even if I hadn't, it's not up to you to make comments on what I do or do not put into it."

Now it was Aiden's turn to blush.

Briefly, he considered apologizing, but he had a feeling it wouldn't win him any points.

The pair stood in fraught silence for a long moment before Aiden cracked.

After taking a fortifying sip of beer, hoping the cool liquid would soothe his burning skin, he asked, "What's your name?"

"Kenzie," she said.

"Aiden," he replied. "Are you new here?"

"That obvious?" A nervous laugh escaped her.

Aiden studied her again. As an athlete of one of the big three sports at this university, and as someone who had been running around this town and campus going on four years now, he'd interacted with his fair share of the student population. One thing he had quickly learned was that every weekend at Rick's was filled with the same people. New faces rarely made their way down the stairs into the basement bar, and if they did, it wasn't without a good fake ID and an older friend dragging them along. Aiden could tell this was Kenzie's first time here based on the way her eyes darted around, widening at the debauchery surrounding them.

"I've never seen you around before," he said with a shrug.

"Would you have remembered if you had?"

"I never forget a pretty face."

That blush crept back, and this time, Aiden reached out and trailed his fingers over her cheekbone, tucking an errant lock of hair behind her ear. It was a bold move, far more forward than he typically ever was—or ever had to be—with women. But something about this girl intrigued him.

"Well, yes," Kenzie finally said after a large gulp of her drink. "It's my first year here."

"You should give me your number," Aiden said, withdrawing his phone from his pocket and unlocking it before holding it out to her.

"Oh, I should?"

Aiden grinned. He liked this girl, liked that she wasn't tripping all over herself to get on his good side. "Sure," he said. "I can show you around."

"What makes you think I need a tour guide?"

"You just said it's your first year here. This campus is huge and it's easy to get lost."

Kenzie looked as though she wanted to argue, but snatched his phone and quickly punched in her information.

"No last name?" Aiden asked when she handed it back.

"Nah," she said, taking a long pull of her drink, and Aiden found himself fixated on her lips—painted in a matte lipstick several shades darker than what he guessed was her natural color—as they wrapped around the two skinny red straws. "I'm like Cher. Or Madonna."

Aiden snorted, considering it a win that she'd given him her number at all. Well, he thought she had. To be sure, he tapped the call button on her contact, satisfied when her phone lit up with his number.

"Alright, *Kenzie*," he said. "What are you planning to study?"

"Advertising and marketing," she said quickly, but didn't elaborate.

Aiden smiled. "I'm in journalism."

"So what, you want to be a writer?"

"More like a broadcast personality."

"Radio or TV?"

"Definitely TV."

Kenzie studied him for a moment, turning her head this way and that as though viewing him from different angles. Finally, she said, "I thought broadcasters were supposed to be at least semi-good looking."

Aiden boomed out a laugh and stepped closer, leaning into her. "That wasn't very nice," he whispered.

He didn't miss the way she shivered when his lips brushed the shell of her ear, and he grinned wider.

"Maybe I'm not a nice girl," she said.

Aiden pulled away, studying her face for an indication of how he should react to that statement. But Kenzie's cool, calm, collected exterior remained in place, her face passive under his scrutiny.

"Be honest," he said. "Would you kick me out of bed?"

Without hesitation, Kenzie said, "Definitely." Aiden frowned, and Kenzie laughed, adding, "But not before we had a little fun first."

HA! he thought. *She* is *attracted to me. I can work with that.*

"So let's get out of here," he said, low enough for only her to hear.

It wouldn't be the first time Aiden picked a girl up in this very bar and brought her home. After all, he had a well-earned reputation as a lady's man. Or, what was the term they used nowadays? Fuckboy? Playboy? Aiden wasn't always proud of it, but either one would describe him perfectly.

Although, it had been several months since he'd taken anyone home. Between his summer job and summer training, sex had been the last thing on his mind.

Now, though? With this girl standing in front of him? It was all he could think about.

"What did you have in mind?" she asked, teeth sawing at her bottom lip. Aiden was gripped by the urge to pull her flush against him and run his tongue over that spot.

"I only live a few blocks away," he said, reaching out to settle his hands on her hips.

"I just met you," she said, but her pulse tripped in her throat, a deep inhale brushing the tips of her breasts against his chest. She wasn't wearing a bra, and her nipples hardened under his gaze—a lot like his dick under hers.

Women rarely played hard to get with him. As a rule, Aiden never chased girls; *they* pursued *him*. But something about this girl had him wanting to break his rules. Like some invisible string was pulling them together.

On a whim, and simply because he couldn't hold himself back, he bent and brushed his mouth against hers, a barely-there slide of his lips, an appetizer of things to come, running his tongue along her full bottom lip. Then he backed away to study her, gauge her reaction, and found her pupils blown wide, ocean-blue eyes now dark and stormy.

"Come on, you know you want—"

His sentence was cut off as Jack stumbled through the crowd and plowed into him, bumping Aiden's side painfully into the bar. Aiden released his grip on Kenzie's hips to shove Jack away.

By the time he turned back to apologize for his teammate's rudeness, Kenzie was gone.

Aiden raised onto the tips of his toes and searched the crowd for a flash of brunette hair and a white tank top, but found none.

"What're you looking for?" Jack asked.

"That girl I was talking to before you so rudely interrupted," Aiden said, shrugging off the arm Jack had slung around his shoulders.

"Was she hot?"

Aiden rolled his eyes. "Yes, she was hot. She seemed...innocent, but not? That doesn't make any sense. She flirted with me, and I asked her to come home with me, but she seemed unsure. She told me she's a freshman studying business or something."

"And let me guess," Jack said, taking a slug of beer. "You were going to give her the business?"

Jack gave Aiden a suggestive eyebrow wiggle, and Aiden punched him playfully in the shoulder.

Aiden ignored the implication, though Jack was spot-on. "Maybe I just wanted to get to know her better. She didn't seem to recognize me."

Jack raised an eyebrow. "You say that like it's a good thing."

"It *is* a good thing," Aiden insisted. "When was the last time you met a female who wasn't trying to get in your pants because you play hockey for this university?"

Jack squinted his eyes and scrunched his nose up in an exaggerated thinking face before he said, "I honestly couldn't tell you."

"Exactly."

"It's cute that you're interested in this girl after a single ten minute conversation and all, but I think you're forgetting something here."

Aiden hadn't mentioned the kiss. Jack didn't need more ammunition to chirp him.

"What's that?"

"She disappeared," Jack pointed out. "And you have no way of finding out who she is. Did you even get her name?"

"Kenzie," Aiden said immediately. "And I have her phone number."

"Okay, we have a name and a number. But only a first name. And chances are high it's a nickname for something like Mackenzie or Kensington. And there's no chance she'll respond to your messages if you reach out."

"Kensington?" Aiden asked with an arched brow.

"Okay, I'll admit that's a stretch," Jack said with a laugh. "The point is, this campus is huge. And if she's a freshman, the chances of you bumping into her again are slim."

"It can't be that hard to find her," Aiden protested. "We live in the social media age. I guarantee I find her before the end of the week."

Jack rolled his eyes. "Christ, you're about to go all Prince Charming with that fucking glass slipper, aren't you? Only that girl was less Cinderella and more...runaway puck bunny."

"Dude, I just told you she didn't even recognize me. I think it's safe to say she's not a puck bunny."

Jack shrugged, unbothered. "It sounds good though, doesn't it?"

Aiden glared at his teammate, who held up his hands in surrender. "Consider it a working title, then. Project Runaway Puck Bunny."

Aiden snorted a laugh and hooked his arm around Jack's neck. "I'll take it under advisement."

chapter 2
Kenzie

"Why exactly couldn't you continue to commute from Detroit?" Brent asked his sister as he and their brother Nate hauled her couch up a short flight of stairs from the elevator en route to her new apartment.

Because, naturally, Kenzie had leased the penthouse.

She stood in the open doorway of her rental, arms crossed over her chest as she watched her brothers—one of whom was a professional athlete—struggle with half of her large, cushy sectional. The other half was still in the back of the illegally parked U-Haul.

A cop had already come by to tell them to move it or they'd be fined, but Brent Jean, being who he was, talked him out of giving them a ticket.

Kenzie's first week of classes at Michigan State were wrapped, and though she'd only made the drive from Detroit to East Lansing and back twice, it had been enough. She didn't even want to consider what that stretch would be like in the winter.

25

"I want the full college experience," Kenzie said, finally responding to her brother's question.

"You already had two years of the *full college experience*," Nate reminded her through labored breaths.

"That was in New York City," she reminded him, moving out of the way so he and Brent could move the couch through the door. "It's impossible to feel like you're in college when the campus isn't all in one spot, and that city is massive. Here I can walk from one end to the other in a half hour if I hit every crosswalk light perfectly."

"What does that have to do with living in East Lansing?" Brent asked as he and Nate dropped the piece of furniture in the center of Kenzie's large living room, where she'd already unrolled a shaggy area rug to go underneath.

"You've lived here," she said. "You tell me."

Brent studied her for a moment, and Kenzie resisted the urge to squirm. The eight years between them often felt like millions when he turned what she referred to as his *dad gaze* on her.

"You're here to study and finish your degree," he said with a pointed finger. "You're not here to fuck around and party."

Nate and Kenzie let out matching sighs of exasperation, and Brent's glare darted between the two of them. "Cut her some slack, Brent," Nate said. "She's not a kid anymore, and it's not like you were a saint while you were in school."

"I was in a serious relationship for over half my time here," Brent said.

"That may be true, but you were still a fuckboy before Ashley came around. And you were a fuckboy after."

Brent's cheeks reddened with anger and embarrassment, and

Kenzie wouldn't be surprised if steam started pouring from his ears any second now. With only two years separating them, her brothers tended to butt heads more often than not. As much as Kenzie hated to admit it—and refused to think about it—Brent's antics as a bachelor had been well-documented, especially after he became an NHL phenom.

"I'm not here to *fuck around*, as you so eloquently put it," she said to Brent. "But I'm also not here to be some nerd who spends all of her time holed up within these four walls, studying and not having any kind of social life. I want to finish my degree, but I want to have fun, too." Brent opened his mouth to speak, but she raised a hand to cut him off. "Those things are true, whether you think it's necessary or not. When I dropped out of NYU and moved to Detroit, I was only twenty. I hadn't given myself the chance to truly experience the things I *should* have been experiencing at that stage of my life. This is my opportunity to right some of those wrongs."

"Such as?" Nate asked.

"Such as going to a real college party," she said, avoiding Brent's gaze. "And going to football, hockey, and basketball games with friends. Going on day trips to wineries or cider mills. All of those quintessential Midwest college experiences."

Brent looked unconvinced, but before he could rebut, Nate elbowed him and said, "Let's go get the other half of this couch."

Kenzie mouthed *thank you* to him as they left.

What she didn't—and wouldn't—tell her brothers was that she wanted a chance to let loose in very real and messy ways. Owning FLEX was great, but some of the shine had worn off, and she'd spent the last year feeling like she was dying, both creatively and emotionally. Kenzie had felt caged, and it was time she pried the gate open and set herself free.

Up until now, her anxiety had marshaled her life. It was high time she took back the power.

Earlier in the week, when Kenzie and Dr. Mathews had discussed her nerves over starting over in a place where no one knew her, and how terrified she was about walking into her first class, Dr. Mathews said something that struck a major chord with her: "Your comfort zone will kill you."

It was time to get uncomfortable.

Last weekend, Kenzie had gone out to the bars with Berkley's younger sister, Jessica, and crashed at her place after. The night life in East Lansing was worlds away from what she'd experienced in NYC, and she'd immediately known she'd made the right decision coming back to school and choosing Michigan State.

All her life, Kenzie had struggled with anxiety. During her senior year of high school, she had a mental breakdown that necessitated completing her final semester from home.

That was how she met Dr. Mathews.

Dropping out of college had been a rash decision, but ultimately a good one for the sake of her mental health. Her family hadn't entirely understood the motivation behind it, but they had supported her.

But Kenzie was once again on the precipice of losing her mind, and coming back to school was her way of taking the heat off herself. The itch to completely overhaul her life had started, exactly as it had two years before.

The time from when she'd moved to Detroit until now had been spent in the company of real adults, attending business meetings, attending dinners and outings with potential partners, and generally living inside the FLEX bubble. She hadn't made friends outside of Brent and Berkley's social circle, and had spent the bulk of her time holed up in her condo, eyes glued to her computer screen or phone, exercising when she needed a break and then getting right back to it.

Movement was medicine for her, and the hours she'd spent strength training and doing cardio had done wonders for her, not only physically but also mentally. To her, a healthy body equaled a healthy mind, and after the episode at the end of high school had left her down and out of it for months, she had needed all the help she could get. It was only after a friend had suggested she join him at the gym one day—and then another and another, until she began looking forward to it—that she started to feel like herself again.

She wasn't sure when her role at FLEX had started to feel more like a chore she dreaded than something she genuinely enjoyed participating in, but she saw it for what it was: a sign that things needed to change.

Her brothers returned with the other half of her sectional five minutes later, pulling her from her reverie.

Once the couch was perfectly positioned—after Kenzie made her brothers shift it around several times, prompting a ridiculous number of expletives from them both—the three of them dropped onto the deep cushions. At opposite ends—Brent on one and she and Nate on the other—the Jean siblings silently chugged the bottles of water Kenzie had passed around.

"I'm all for you getting the college experience you dream of, Kenz," Nate said after several long moments, wiping his mouth with the back of his hand, "but I can't understand why you gave up your condo with that stunning view of the Detroit River for…this."

Nate lazily swept his arm out at the view. Kenzie didn't see what the problem was. Her apartment faced south, looking out across downtown East Lansing, Grand River, and the fringes of campus beyond. The view, though not as stellar as the one from her condo in Detroit, was still pretty incredible. But it wasn't why she'd leased this place. No, she'd leased it because it was located at the epicenter of East Lansing nightlife, and campus was only a few blocks away.

"I wanted to be within walking distance to classes," she said. "Besides, I didn't give up my Detroit condo. I'm subletting it."

She likely would never move back in, but again…that was a conversation for another day.

"I'm sure that's it," Nate replied. "It has nothing to do with the fact that there are like ten bars within spitting distance, one of which is on the main floor of this building."

"You should have told me this was where you found a place," Brent said.

"Why, so you could've talked me out of it?"

"Exactly," her oldest brother replied. "The last thing I need is to be worried about some creep trailing you home from the bar and knowing exactly where you live because it's so damn close. I have enough going on."

Kenzie's sister senses perked up. Brent and Berkley had gotten married the previous month. For all intents and purposes, they should still be in the honeymoon phase.

"What's going on?" Nate asked, picking up on the same note of something fishy as Kenzie.

"I…" Brent trailed off and carded his fingers through his thick brown hair.

"Are you okay? Is it Berkley?" Kenzie prompted.

"I'm sure you'll feel better if you just let it out," Nate said.

"Berkley's pregnant!" Brent blurted.

Nate let out a whoop of laughter and launched himself at their brother. Nate, their stoic, avoid-touchy-feely-shit-at-all-costs brother, willingly hugging Brent, compounded by the bomb Brent had just dropped on them, had Kenzie rooted to her spot on the couch, mouth gaping in shock.

When Nate broke away from Brent, he sat next to him with his arm slung across Brent's shoulders, both of them staring at Kenzie, smiling—Nate's broad and unchecked, Brent's small and sheepish.

"Well? What do you think, kid?" Brent asked. "You ready to be an aunt?"

"Holy fuck," she said quietly. "I'm going to be an aunt."

"Damn, that kid hit the genetic lottery," Nate said with a laugh. "Whatever it is, you're going to have your hands full."

As if understanding that Kenzie needed some time to process, and that she would catch up eventually, Brent and Nate began chatting about what this new life would mean for all of them.

Kenzie was undeniably excited for her brother, and Berkley, who was the sweetest girl alive and had somehow managed to turn her overbearing, overprotective big brother into a giant cinnamon roll. But she couldn't help wondering what becoming a dad would mean for Brent and his relationship with FLEX. Hockey already took up a vast majority of his time from August through May—and then beyond if the Warriors made a deep playoff run like they had this past summer.

While he and Berkley had been dating, he'd still been very

hands-on. Now that he was married, though? With a child on the way? Kenzie was worried her plans to pull back from FLEX and leave the company entirely wouldn't be so easy now that Baby Jean had entered the picture. She may currently be lying to him about her wants and needs and intentions, but she couldn't leave her brother in the lurch.

Her chest tightened as her pulse spiked, adrenaline coating her veins like ice as her anxiety ratcheted up several notches. She'd barely started school and things were already far more messy than she wanted or needed them to be.

Kenzie took deep breaths, inhaling for six seconds, holding for two, and exhaling for five, exactly as Dr. Mathews had taught her. Across the room, Brent glanced at her quickly before returning his attention to Nate, and Kenzie silently thanked him for not drawing more attention to her freak out.

A few more breathing exercises had her heart rate slowing to normal, the spots receding from the edges of her vision.

The baby wouldn't be here for several months yet, which was plenty of time for her, Brent, and Berkley to sit down and come up with some sort of plan that worked for everyone. Maybe in that time, she'd find a way to be truthful with her brother. For now, though, it was business as usual. Which meant, for the time being, Kenzie wouldn't be involved with FLEX at all. She *wanted* to help, and knew her brother well enough to know he expected her offer of such, but she couldn't make herself speak the words. Not when the mere thought threatened to send her into a tailspin once again.

Finally, Kenzie stood on shaky legs and walked to her brothers, climbing onto their laps exactly as she had when she was a child. Their arms and legs entangled until they were one giant ball of Jean siblings twisted together on Kenzie's couch.

"I'm so happy for you, Bee," Kenzie told him honestly, pressing a kiss to his cheek. "I can't wait to be Auntie Kenz!"

"You guys can't tell anyone you know yet," he said. "We just found out."

"How far along is she?" Nate asked.

"Three months..." Brent said, trailing off.

Kenzie and Nate were quiet as they did the math.

"Holy shit," Nate breathed. "She was pregnant at your wedding?"

Brent nodded solemnly. "She was really sick after. Like...more than a normal hangover. So she decided to take a test, and surprised me with the results on our honeymoon."

Brent's grin grew as he told them the story of how, on their last night in Croatia, they had a quiet dinner on the balcony of their room, and Berkley had presented him with a tissue wrapped pregnancy test.

"She started crying before I could even open it," he said with a laugh. "So I stopped opening it to comfort her, and she yelled at me!"

Kenzie and Nate chuckled, both easily able to picture their sister-in-law yelling at Brent for wanting to hold her while she cried, when in fact she was crying because she was afraid of his reaction upon seeing the positive test.

"Are you excited?" Nate asked.

"Of course I am!" Brent said. "I hope we have a little girl just like her mother."

Nate reached around Kenzie and gave Brent's shoulder a squeeze. "Whatever it is, you're going to be the best dad."

Kenzie nodded in emphatic agreement. If there was one thing Brent had been good at his entire life, it was taking care of people. His teammates, his siblings, their parents, Berkley and her friends. Fatherhood would come naturally to him.

Later, Kenzie stood in the middle of her closet, surrounded by boxes filled with clothes, when her phone trilled from somewhere in her bedroom. She stumbled into the space, which currently sat in disarray, with a desk and chair haphazardly pushed against one wall, her bed frame—thankfully put together but without the mattresses stacked on top—leaning against the opposite wall, and her nightstand several feet away in front of the window.

When she finally reached her phone, which had been buried under a stack of sheets on the floor, Kenzie found a missed call from Jessica.

"Hey!" Jessica shouted when Kenzie's return call connected. "What are you doing?"

Kenzie could barely hear her over the noise in the background, so she said loudly, "I could ask you the same thing!"

"I'm at HopCat and then we're going bar hopping!"

"But it's like...early still!" Kenzie protested.

"Girlfriend, it's nine o'clock."

Kenzie whipped her gaze to the window, surprised to find that dusk had indeed settled over the city. Several blocks away, campus glowed under the street lights, and on the road below her building, masses of people moved from one place to the next, enjoying the East Lansing nightlife.

"Holy shit," Kenzie said with a laugh. "I've been so busy unpacking I hadn't even realized."

The noise level behind Jessica suddenly cut off, as though she'd stepped outside. In fact...Jessica stood on the street corner in front of the bar/restaurant that occupied the main floors of Kenzie's building.

"Get your cute butt down here!" Jessica said, craning her neck to look up at the residences over her head, as though she could see Kenzie.

"Oh, Jess," Kenzie said. "I'm a wreck. I've spent all day moving!"

"I don't care," Jessica said, turning her teacher voice on. "It's hot and sweaty out here anyway, so no one is going to give a damn. You survived your first week of classes, Kenz! It's time to come out, meet some new people, and celebrate. Put some dry shampoo in your hair, change your clothes, swipe on some deodorant, and meet me down here. I'm giving you five minutes!"

"Five minutes!" Kenzie protested. "Have you met me? I can't pick out an outfit in five minutes!"

Jessica sighed and said, "Okay, fair. Buzz me up, and I'll help you."

Kenzie walked into the living room and pressed the button on the panel next to her front door, unlocking the one in the lobby for Jessica. "I'm on the top floor," she said. "The door is unlocked!"

Jessica disconnected, and Kenzie hurried into her bathroom, unzipping bags and digging through boxes, searching for her makeup, dry shampoo, and a hair tie. It was the first weekend of September, and now that she was in the city and—mostly—settled, it was time to start enjoying herself. This was what she'd come here for, wasn't it? To experience life as a run-of-the-mill college student, in a place where no one knew her.

Your comfort zone will kill you.

She couldn't live her life holed up in her room, pretending the outside world didn't exist. In order to master her anxiety, she had to go out and experience life. Every day, she had to actively force herself into stressful situations in order to overcome them. At first, Kenzie struggled with Dr. Mathews' advice, unsure of how sound it was to intentionally trigger her anxiety. But, as usual, her doctor was right.

As she whipped her milk-chocolate brown hair into a sleek pony—after coating her roots in a pound of dry shampoo and using one of those little sticks to tame her fly-aways—she considered the taste of college life she'd gotten the weekend before. The girls in East Lansing were stunning, and the boys were the very definition of eye candy. Since high school, Kenzie hadn't been in a serious relationship. It was difficult to find the courage to open her heart to someone when her own mind constantly rebelled against her. She'd had a few flings, but nothing worth mentioning. At the moment, she wasn't looking, but if the right boy came along...

Jessica burst into Kenzie's apartment as she was putting the finishing touches on her makeup, which was really only a swipe of mascara and gel through her eyebrows, topped with a bit of bronzer and tinted lip balm. As Jess chattered about who was waiting for them downstairs—her boyfriend, for one, who Kenzie was excited to finally meet after hearing so much about him—Kenzie couldn't help the way her mind drifted back to the boy she'd met at Rick's the weekend before, and the way he'd had her wanting to do things completely at odds with the good girl reputation she typically maintained.

With Aiden, she'd been bold, explicitly telling him what she wanted with no fear of judgement. The reaction he'd elicited within her body was unlike anything she'd ever experienced before, and she'd been more than ready to take their instant, mutual attraction from the crowded bar to quieter, more private places.

Then his teammate had walked up, and Kenzie had instantly sobered.

Because Mackenzie Jean's number one rule? *Don't date hockey players.*

chapter 3
Aiden

Several videos of Aiden had circulated around the campus gossip scene, but a few weeks had gone by now, and none of his coaches had found out about his streaking escapade. He was flying high as he walked into Munn on Tuesday morning for strength and conditioning. Classes had started, so of course the team's practice and training schedules were incredibly hectic, bogged down with tutoring sessions and media engagements in addition to keeping on top of their game. Aiden felt amazing physically, and he was itching for the season to start.

Not to mention, he couldn't stop thinking about Kenzie. He'd been texting her at irregular intervals since the night they met, but he had yet to receive a response. If she had stuck around, she would've learned he was a hockey player, and thus had the ability to doggedly pursue the things that interested him.

And Kenzie certainly interested him.

He'd wear her down. It was simply a matter of time.

All that to say, things were looking pretty good from where he was standing.

So of course, the absolute last thing he expected was for Coach to come out of his office as soon as Aiden set foot in the locker room and crook a menacing finger in his direction.

Aiden's heart sank as he glanced around the room at his teammates, who all suddenly found their shoes or the ceiling far more interesting than him.

"What's up, Coach?" Aiden asked as he sat down in the creaky chair across from him.

"I don't exactly know how to say this, Fuller, but...well, it's come to my attention that you were videotaped streaking across campus a few weeks ago."

Fuck. How had he found out?

"My daughter showed me the video, in case you were wondering. My *seventeen-year-old* daughter."

Aiden hung his head. This was bad. *Very* bad.

"So what happens now?" he asked, raising his head to look his coach in the eye.

"The university wanted to come down hard on you. I'm talking pressing charges, police involvement, the works. Thankfully, I talked them off that ledge. But, of course, we can't let you get away with this without some sort of punishment."

Aiden nodded and swallowed hard. "Whatever it is, sir, I can take it."

"We've agreed to suspend you."

"How long?"

"The first five weekends of the season."

Aiden ground his teeth together, mentally flipping through

their schedule. Five weekends meant he wouldn't be able to play until their first series in November. That meant ten games of his senior season, lost to his stupidity.

"Fine," he said finally.

"I know this isn't ideal," Coach said. "It's your senior season, and you've got your future to think about. But I promise, if you keep your head down and don't fuck up anymore, your talent will more than speak for itself. I don't have a player that works harder than you, Fuller. And we're going to be hurting without you out there. But that's the price you have to pay."

"I understand," he said, standing to shake Coach's hand before exiting to the locker room.

He quietly padded over to his stall and sat hard on the seat in front of it, dropping his head into his hands.

"How long?" Jack asked quietly as he sat next to him, echoing Aiden's words to their coach minutes before.

Aiden didn't have to ask what he meant, only replied, "Five weekends."

A collective groan went up from his teammates. "Fuck, man, I'm sorry," Jack said. "I can go in there right now and take some of the heat off you if you want."

Aiden lifted his head and gave Jack a wobbly but grateful smile. "That's the dumbest idea you've ever had. We can't leave the boys without our starting goalie."

Jack surprised Aiden by not making some self-indulgent comment about how talented he was.

"Five weekends," Aiden said. "I feel like that means I can basically kiss any shot at a rookie contract goodbye."

His chest tightened with the thought; everything he'd been

working for, gone in an instant, all because he couldn't turn down some ridiculous fucking dare.

During his senior season of high school, Aiden had entered the NHL Draft. That summer, he'd been selected in the third round by the Detroit Warriors, and every single day since had been spent in preparation of going pro once he graduated college.

At the end of the previous season, he'd been approached to join the Warriors' farm team in Toledo, but had turned them down. While he was eager to start his professional career—which would hopefully be long and successful—he'd felt he still had a lot to learn by playing college for another year. Plus, he wasn't ready to leave his teammates, and he wanted to complete his degree.

"Not so fast, Fuller," Luke said, walking up to drop a reassuring hand on Aiden's shoulder. "Your career thus far speaks for itself. And once we get you back out there, you'll have plenty of chances to show the Warriors just how stupid they'd be not to sign you."

"He's right," Jack said, walking into the middle of the room and positioning himself so he was dead center below the Spartan helmet on the ceiling. "We're all to blame for Aiden getting suspended," he said loudly. "Which means now we're all paying for it. With him out for the first five weekends of the season, we're going to have to work extra hard to make up for that loss in offensive output. And off the ice, we're going to make sure we do everything possible to keep him out of more trouble. So I'm instituting a rule: Aiden Fuller does not get dared for the entire season."

Everyone gasped. Dares were a cornerstone of MSU hockey, and players didn't simply get a free pass without a damn good reason.

Aiden supposed being suspended as the result of one of those dares *was* a damn good reason.

"What if it's something super small?" one of the freshmen asked. "Something that won't cause a scene or get him in any more trouble?"

Jack placed his forefinger in the cleft at the center of his chin, the picture of thoughtfulness as he considered the rookie's question. "Fair enough. So we'll make an amendment: Fuller can take dares that won't get him in trouble with the powers that be." Jack cut his gaze to Aiden. "You on board with that?"

"Am I on board with not having to show my cock and balls and ass to the entire campus again? Fuck yeah, I am."

His teammates laughed, and Jack raised his arm, a silent command for everyone to gather around him.

"Go Green, on three," he said when they'd all assembled.

"One, two, three, GO GREEN!" they shouted in unison, then dispersed.

That afternoon, as Aiden sat in his advertising class, his mind was decidedly absent, his professor's lecture no more than the dull buzz of a bug in his ear.

Ten games was nearly a quarter of the season. It wasn't simply that Aiden would miss out on playing time–and all those chances to learn and grow as a player–that was tripping him up. It was also the fact that once he finally *could* play again, he'd have to catch up in the stats rankings not only with his teammates, but with the entire country.

Mentally, he began a checklist of everything he needed to do in order to return at the top of his game, if such a thing was possible.

That list included, but was not limited to, extra time in the weight room, two-a-day skating sessions, keeping a very strict diet, and being there for his teammates every step of the way, even if he couldn't contribute how he wanted. On top of it all, he had to keep his ass out of trouble, and that started with paying attention in class.

Aiden shook his head and refocused on the room in front of him. Student-athletes at Michigan State were required to sit in the first three rows of lecture halls and the front two of smaller classrooms. Aiden was in the third row, flanked on one side by Jack and the other by Asher. The professor droned on about some sort of project they would each need to complete before the semester ended. Aiden had a feeling he hadn't missed much.

Still, he turned to Jack and whispered, "What is he talking about?"

"Big semester-long project," Jack, who was also a senior and preparing to graduate in May, said. "He said he's going to email us the specifics, but it sounds pretty grueling. Bet you're happy you don't have to worry about hockey until November."

Aiden glared daggers at Jack out of the corner of his eye and, through clenched teeth, said, "I will always worry about hockey. And in case you forgot, your dumbass is the reason I'm in this mess." Aiden paused for a moment, then narrowed his gaze on his goalie. "Why am I even in this class? I'm not even an ad major."

Jack raised his hands in surrender. "Sorry, bro," he said. "I offered to take some of the heat off you, in case you forgot. And you're here because you waited too long to fill this requirement, and I talked you into it."

"You have a habit of talking me into doing stupid shit," Aiden pointed out. "And I hate you for all of it."

"Boys!" The professor called in their direction, pulling them from their conversation. "I understand you athletes think you're gods around here, but in my class there is no special treatment. I suggest you pay attention if you wish to pass and keep playing whatever precious sport ball game it is that gained you admission to this university."

Aiden's cheeks heated as he nodded his acquiescence. "Sorry," he and Jack mumbled together.

The professor speared them with one last withering glance before resuming his lecture.

When class was over, as Aiden joined the queue of students filtering from the room, he caught a flash of brunette hair hurrying through the crowd and out of the room.

Hair he thought he recognized, though he'd only spent ten minutes in the girl's presence three weeks ago.

After class, he had a break before evening practice, so Aiden headed to the Case cafeteria to read over the specifics of his advertising project.

Mostly, he wanted to stalk the class list to see if he shared it with a girl named Kenzie.

Once he settled at a table tucked into the corner of the dining hall, away from prying eyes, and settled his oversized Beats headphones over his ears, he logged into his advertising class's online platform.

The online platform was exactly as it sounded: a place where their professor could upload pertinent class information such as the syllabus, and make announcements to his students about things such as cancellations and due dates. And, luckily for Aiden, it was also where he could view the class roster.

His eyes darted back and forth across the screen as he scrolled through, scanning the names.

Finally, he came across one that held promise: *Mackenzie Jean.*

Mackenzie *Jean*? She couldn't possibly be...

Well, there was only one way to find out. Aiden swiped his phone off the table, tapped into his Instagram app, and typed the name into the search bar.

There she was, the top result.

As Aiden thumbed through Kenzie's pictures, he paused on one of her standing between two tall, incredibly good-looking men. The group was posed on the deck of a boat, the three all dark hair and bronzed skin, a sparkling body of water spreading out around them. Aiden couldn't help zooming in, studying the contours of Kenzie's abdominal muscles, the rounded edges of her quads, the long, sleek column of her throat. How her breasts filled out her bikini top perfectly, the high-cut leg holes of her bottoms accentuating her lean legs.

She hadn't been lying; she'd worked hard for her body. Muscles like that didn't come from only good genes.

Then he studied the men bracketing her. The one to Kenzie's left was slimmer than the other; still chiseled, but softer. His hair was shorn close to his scalp on the sides and longer on the top, flopping onto his forehead and into crystal blue eyes that were squinted against the sun.

The other man? Aiden recognized him quite well, as he passed by his picture every time he walked into Munn.

Boat day with my bros, the caption read, followed by a string of summer-related emojis.

Mackenzie Jean, his runaway puck bunny, was the younger sister of the legendary Spartan, Brent Jean.

"Holy fuck," Aiden breathed.

"What?" Jack asked as he dropped his body onto the chair across from Aiden.

"I figured out who she is."

"Who? Your runaway puck bunny?"

"Yeah, and I was right about her not being a puck bunny, so you can stop calling her that."

"I'll bite," Jack said, resting his elbows on the table and steepling his fingers under his chin, waiting. "Who is she?"

"Mackenzie Jean."

The world stilled a beat as Jack connected the dots.

"As in…"

"Brent Jean," Aiden confirmed. "Yeah."

"Holy fuck," Jack said, leaning back and sifting his fingers through his floppy blond hair.

"Exactly," Aiden said.

"I didn't even know Jean had a sister," Jack said, and they were momentarily joined by Asher and Luke.

The four of them typically met on campus in between classes and evening skate, liking to have what they referred to as *family dinner.*

Not only were they his teammates, but they were also Aiden's best friends, and if he was going to figure out what to do about Mackenzie Jean, he needed their advice, no matter how bad or stupid it was sure to be.

"What're you two talking about?" Asher asked as he sat in the seat next to Aiden, his dinner tray falling hard onto the table as his backpack dropped onto Aiden's foot.

"God," Aiden grumbled, kicking the offending bag out of the way. "What do you have in there, bricks?"

"No," Asher responded, shoveling some sort of quinoa salad into his mouth. "Although my Econ textbook is quite heavy."

Aiden rolled his eyes, and Jack and Luke chuckled.

"For real, though," Luke said. "What were you guys talking about? You looked sort of shaken up when we got here."

"Remember Fuller's runaway puck bunny?" Jack asked.

Asher and Luke both nodded.

"You'll never guess her last name."

"Lewinsky!" Asher shouted, a piece of steamed broccoli falling from his mouth and bouncing across the table.

"Manners, Rhodes," Jack said. "And really? Lewinsky? As in Monica?"

Asher shrugged and swallowed. "I was watching a documentary on the Clinton administration the other day."

Aiden chuckled. Even after four years with these guys, they still managed to surprise him.

"No, dipshit, her last name isn't Lewinsky," Aiden said. "It's Jean."

He paused, gaze flitting back and forth between Luke and Asher, studying their expressions, waiting for the moment when understanding dawned.

It was Luke who caught on first. "As in...Brent?"

Aiden and Jack nodded solemnly.

"Holy shit. *That* girl is Brent Jean's little sister?"

"The very same," Aiden confirmed.

"Damn..." Asher said. "I've seen mentions of her in press about him and stuff, but when you think *little* sister, you certainly don't think of some college hottie."

"How old is she?" Jack asked.

"I'm not sure," Aiden said, shrugging. "She told me it's her first year here, so she's either a freshman or a transfer."

"My bet is transfer," Luke said. "I can't imagine Fuller going all googly-eyed over some freshman."

"I'm not googly-eyed," Aiden protested, reclining in his chair to cross his arms over his chest and level each of his teammates with a glare.

Jack barked out a laugh. "Fuller, get real. You're so googly-eyed, you're practically that scene in *The Mask* where Jim Carrey's eyes literally bulge out of his head."

Aiden smacked Jack upside the head and leaned forward, resting his elbows on the table and his head in his hands.

"It doesn't matter," he said, flipping his hat onto the table and tunneling his fingers into his hair.

"And why is that?" Asher mumbled through what sounded like a mouthful of food...again.

Aiden lifted his head and locked eyes with him. "Because I can't even get her to text me back."

"Send her a dick pic," Jack suggested. "That'll get a reaction out of her."

"You do realize that public nudity is what got me suspended, right?"

"Yeah, but this wouldn't be public," Luke pointed out. When Aiden narrowed his eyes at his captain, Luke added, "I'm not saying it's a good idea. Just stating a fact."

"It's *not* a good idea," Aiden said with a laugh. "It's terrible."

"How many texts have you sent her?"

Aiden's cheeks heated. "A few…"

"How many is a few?" Jack asked.

"Like…twenty?"

"Fuck."

"Shit."

"You're an idiot."

"Thanks, guys," Aiden said. "Really appreciate the confidence."

"It's just…" Jack trailed off. "You know there's texting etiquette in place for a reason, Fuller!"

"I know, I know," Aiden said, returning his head to his hands. "But I can't take them back now."

"You just have to give her something to make it worth her while. Figure out why she ran away from you at the bar, why she's avoiding you now, and either fix the problem, or find a way to make her see there isn't one."

Aiden looked up at Luke, surprised by the helpfulness and normalcy of that bit of advice.

Aiden turned his attention inward as his teammates carried on a conversation around him, giving him space to mull over his options.

It didn't make sense, his fixation on this girl. She'd run away from him, leaving him with nothing more than a nickname and a phone number. Now that he knew her full name, he could get to know more about her from her social media, but where was the fun in that?

No, Aiden wanted to get to know Kenzie in the flesh, where he could look her in the eye when he asked her questions, where he could touch her.

The fact that she had the upper hand in this situation didn't sit well with Aiden, who was used to being the one in control in all of his relationships. This girl, who was related to one of the National Hockey League's biggest stars, wasn't even remotely impressed by Aiden Fuller, and why should she be?

Of course, his *relationships* never amounted to anything more than a string of one and two night stands. Aside from his family, hockey had been—and always would be—his top priority. It was a hard and fast rule of his that he didn't do relationships. There was only room for one great love in his life, and it required skates. A long-term, committed relationship with any sort of emotional intimacy wasn't even on the table.

The simple fact of the matter was that he was extremely good looking, with an impressive physical presence and a hockey player's stamina. He was no slouch in bed, and the women of Michigan State knew it.

But Aiden was also a nice guy, and always upfront with girls every time he hooked up. There were boundaries, and both parties always knew what they were. They'd have a few nights of fun together then go their separate ways. No drama, no focus being pulled away from hockey.

Satisfaction all around.

It was a rule he'd set for himself years ago and never broken.

But Mackenzie Jean might prove to be an exception, if only because Aiden never walked away from a challenge.

"Well, well," Jack said, emitting a low whistle. "Look who just walked in."

Aiden's head snapped up, gaze instantly zeroing in on the brunette who was walking across the cafeteria.

"Are you going to go talk to her?" Asher asked Aiden.

"You totally should," Luke said.

"I agree," Jack said, turning a borderline-sadistic grin on Aiden as he raised a finger in the air, like a conductor ready to begin a concert. "In fact, I have an idea."

Before the words even left his mouth, Aiden knew what was coming, and he groaned as Jack said, "I dare you to get Mackenzie Jean to go on a date with you."

chapter 4
Kenzie

KENZIE MOVED FROM THE lecture hall as quickly as the crowd would allow, hoping the crush of bodies would keep her hidden until she could get outside and away from the building.

"Hey!"

The voice rang out behind her, but Kenzie kept moving, positive they weren't speaking to her.

"Hey!" the voice said again, this time louder, more insistent, and Kenzie glanced over her shoulder to see a girl rushing after her, holding Kenzie's leather-bound date planner out.

When Kenzie stopped and the girl reached her side, she said, "You forgot this," through labored breaths. "Damn girl, you move fast."

Kenzie laughed and took her proffered planner. "I'm sorry," she said. "Thank you so much for rushing after me. I would've been so lost without this."

The girl patted her bag. "Trust me, I get it."

Kenzie thrust out her hand. "Mackenzie Jean," she said.

The girl slid her hand into Kenzie's. "Sofia Kinsey," she said.

"I love your bag," Kenzie gushed, eyeing up the tote resting on the girl's slim shoulder.

Sofia looked down, surprised, and gave Kenzie a small smile. "Thanks! T.J. Maxx is my favorite."

Kenzie nodded. "Me, too. And thrift stores." She glanced down at her outfit, which featured high-waisted Levi's shorts and an oversized Def Leppard tee she'd thrifted back in New York. It may have been early October, but the heat of summer still clung to the city like glue, and Kenzie would enjoy every second until fall took hold.

"Thrift stores are the *best*," Sofia agreed.

"I haven't had a chance to go anywhere around here," Kenzie said sadly, realizing how much time situating herself in East Lansing had consumed.

"Oh my gosh, really?" Sofia asked with a gasp. "There's this one in Old Town you absolutely *have* to check out. We should go together sometime!"

"That would be amazing!" Kenzie said.

They continued to walk in the same direction, chatting about their favorite pieces.

Sofia was, in a word, stunning. With deep brown hair and skin the color of a cup of coffee with a splash of cream in it, she turned heads everywhere she went. Kenzie had seen her on campus before, and she'd been mesmerized every time. Sofia practically floated along the sidewalks, her amber eyes missing nothing, always dressed to kill. Though, she and Kenzie had very different styles. Where Kenzie favored oversized band tees and men's flannels with tight shorts and leggings, feet usually stuffed into combat boots or her favorite sandals, Sofia preferred pastels, each shade in a rainbow of colors complementing her dark skin perfectly. Today, she wore a short, cream-colored skirt and a pale-blue crop top with cute little cap sleeves. An assortment of golden chains adorned her neck, and platform wedges showcased her bright-pink toenail polish.

Where Kenzie was comfort personified, Sofie screamed *fashionista.*

Kenzie immediately liked her.

"So wait, your last name is Jean? As in *Brent Jean*?" Sofia asked. "He is like...so hot."

Kenzie's smile turned down. "Gross, that's my brother."

Sofia laughed, a high, melodic note. "Okay, sorry," she said. "But aren't you like twenty-three? Shouldn't you have graduated by now?"

Kenzie took a deep breath, her mind racing, searching for a response. Telling people she'd dropped out of college at twenty wasn't the best way to make a good impression, so she settled for, "I took some time off to get FLEX off the ground. Brent and I decided now was a good time for me to come back."

It was close enough to the truth that it rolled easily off her tongue.

"I love FLEX," Sofia said wistfully. "It's basically my entire workout wardrobe."

Kenzie was caught off guard by this admission, and infinitely flattered. "Thank you," she said with a smile. "That's wonderful to hear."

They reached a crosswalk, and Sofia nodded toward the right, saying, "Well, I'm heading this way. Another class to get to. See you around!"

And she was gone, breezing across the street, apparently unaware that people watched her every move.

Kenzie shook her head, a small smile on her lips as she paused to take in her surroundings.

Despite the balmy air, the leaves had started to change on the towering maples, the deep green of the pine trees growing bolder, readying for the colder months when it was their time to shine.

For a moment, she dropped onto a nearby bench and simply breathed.

Coming back to college was no joke, and she waged a daily battle between letting her anxiety pull her under and fighting through to swim ashore. Lists had always been important to her, and these days they were her best friend. Sofia couldn't understand what returning her date planner truly meant to Kenzie.

Her stomach grumbled, and she checked her watch, confirming she had another hour and a half before her next class. Kenzie pulled out her phone to consult the campus map, orienting herself. Much to her surprise and pleasure, she discovered she was across the street from Case Hall and its attached cafeteria. When she'd signed up for classes and moved to East Lansing, she'd sprung for a campus meal plan, deciding it was a necessary expense with her chaotic schedule.

East Lansing and Michigan State's campus couldn't be more different from NYU and everything she'd left behind in New York City. Kenzie shouldn't be surprised by this, and yet, she was. While campus was still bustling with thousands of people from all walks of life, hurrying in and out of buildings to classes and meetings, things moved slower here. There wasn't that same sense of urgency she'd experienced every time she walked the streets of Greenwich

Village, where NYU's main campus was located. Living in Brooklyn had been a nice respite from the fast-paced lifestyle of the city, but it still hadn't given her what she wanted.

In New York, she'd constantly been compelled to keep *moving*, which wasn't ideal for someone who suffered from anxiety. Even on bad mental health days, she hadn't been comfortable enough with her "friends" to tell them that what she *really* needed was to indulge in her well-practiced routine of spending all day in bed with a book. Those people hadn't discussed mental health struggles; they simply powered through as though nothing bothered them. It had been exhausting for a number of reasons.

It was understandable that, in a fit of desperation, she'd moved clear across the country.

Coming back to school was her chance to finally live out her college fantasies. She'd grown up listening to Brent talk endlessly about how much he'd loved it here, how amazing the campus and East Lansing were, and how his four years as a Spartan were some of the best of his life.

She wanted some of that magic for herself.

As she rose from her bench, her phone buzzed in her pocket, and Berkley's name showed on the screen.

"Hi, Berk."

"Hi!" Berkley said. "Just calling to check in. How are you holding up?"

"I'm...okay," Kenzie said honestly.

"That's...good?"

Kenzie laughed at her sister-in-law's confusion. "Yes, it's good. I'm still adjusting, but I love it here."

"It really is the best place on the planet. Although, I'm still shocked you wanted to go back to school. You were set for life with FLEX."

Kenzie sighed heavily. "When I had that…episode…and missed the last half of my senior year, I felt so untethered. I was terrified to show my face in town. Everyone thought I was crazy, and a lot of the time, I believed them. You've only known me as this anxious version of myself, but I wasn't always like this. I used to be so much more carefree and confident. And I have my good days now, but…NYU should've been a fresh start, free from the Albany drama. Somehow, I curled in on myself. Physically, I was out doing all these things with my friends. Getting tattoos and nose piercings in Williamsburg, and hitting the clubs in SoHo on the weekends. But all of it just made me feel so empty. I was always bracing myself for the thing that would trigger my next attack. Moving to Detroit helped a lot, and you and Brent and your friends welcoming me with open arms means more to me than I can ever say. But I never saw myself as some corporate type, spending my whole life co-owning a company with my brother, always in his shadow.

"I guess what I'm trying to say is I'm giving myself another chance at a fresh start. I'm hoping being here will help me find myself again. That girl I used to be is trapped inside me somewhere, and I miss her. I think it's time we reunited."

Berkley was silent for so long, Kenzie was worried she'd hung up. Then a sniffle filtered through the line, and finally Berkley said, "That's beautiful, Kenz. And I'm so proud of you. I know your brother is, too."

Kenzie smiled, the edges of her lips wobbling. "Thanks, Berk." Her stomach groaned again, and desperate for a change of subject, she said, "Hey, is Case any good?"

"It's one of the best cafs on campus, next to Brody. Why?"

"I'm across the street, and I'm starving."

Berkley laughed and said, "Well, go eat! I'll talk to you later."

Before her sister-in-law could hang up, Kenzie said, "Hey, Berk?"

"Yes?"

"Thank you."

"Anytime, little sis." And then she hung up.

Walking into Case cafeteria was a bit of a shock to her senses; it was loud, brightly lit, and *very* crowded. Tables and booths were spread out around the centrally located food counters. The options included classic American cuisine like burgers and fries, pizza, pasta bowls, sushi, soups, and dessert. After she'd swiped her student ID to gain entrance—the guy working the computer gave her a little smirk, and whether it was because he recognized her last name or because he found her attractive, she'd never know—she took a moment to wander around and take it all in.

Finally, she settled on a black bean burger and fries from Brimstone, and a chocolate chip cookie from Bliss. Once she'd scanned the room and found an empty two-person table, she set up camp and dug into her food.

She inhaled her burger in record time, leaving only her fries. She pulled her laptop from her backpack and looked over the homework schedule for the advertising class she'd had that morning.

The advertising class whose roster happened to include Aiden Fuller.

Kenzie groaned under her breath, thoughts drifting back to when she'd first met him at Rick's.

Right off the bat, she should've known he was a hockey player, or at the very least, an athlete. She had spent the bulk of her life around both, thanks to her brothers. Average twenty-something men didn't look the way Aiden looked. They didn't fill out a simple black t-shirt the way he had, his biceps testing the limits of the sleeves when he'd folded his arms over his chest, studying her from head to toe.

They certainly weren't *ridiculously* tall with wavy, blue-black hair and deep, chocolate-brown eyes.

And they *definitely* didn't make Kenzie's toes curl against the flimsy material of her sandals when they grinned, dimples deep enough to dig her fingers into appearing in both cheeks.

The instant attraction, the way she'd felt like she was glowing under the attention he'd given her...she shuddered at the direction her thoughts had turned that night.

Kenzie had never done one night stands, could only imagine the havoc her anxiety would wreak in retribution if she did. It scared her that, for him, she'd been about to make an exception.

If his teammate hadn't run up, broadcasting to the entire bar exactly who he was in the form of a ball cap nestled atop his blonde hair, with SPARTAN HOCKEY and a jersey number on it...Kenzie didn't want to consider where the night would've taken her and Aiden Fuller.

And then discovering she had a class with him?

Because *of course* she would.

She should've known that night at the bar. The swagger, the hair and the face and the *body*. Aiden was a walking, talking billboard advertising one thing and one thing only: *heartbreaker.*

In truth, Kenzie's steadfast vehemence against dating hockey players had been inspired less by her own experiences with the type and more by the things she'd witnessed her brother say and do. Not to mention, Brent Jean could be an overprotective asshole, especially with the women in his life.

All that to say, Aiden Fuller had trouble written all over him. The way she'd been drawn to him that night at the bar was dangerous, an urge she must resist at all costs. She'd tried to convince herself it was nothing more than a fluke, a trick of the alcohol and the heady combination of dim bar lights and being the new girl on campus. After living under the Brent Jean umbrella of attention and protection for the last couple of years, that change had been nice. Typically, once guys realized who she was, they quickly looked the other way, in search of someone who wasn't the younger sister of the Warriors' star forward.

She'd had flings, of course. After all, she wasn't a prude, and she had urges like every other twenty-something girl. But they were more of the go-on-a-couple-dates, hook-up-a-few-times-and-move-on variety. She hadn't been in a serious relationship since high school, when her mental breakdown precipitated her then-boyfriend to leave her in favor of greener pastures.

Namely, her best friend.

At a party.

Where they were caught making out.

On video.

While she'd been home, attempting to keep her brain from leaking out through her ears.

How was that for adding insult to injury?

"Hey," a voice said, and Kenzie blinked rapidly, clearing the memories and focusing on the mass of dark green in front of her.

She trailed her eyes up, across a flat stomach and an incredible set of pecs, snagging on biceps she vaguely recognized.

When her gaze connected with the man in front of her, she gasped.

"Surprise!" Aiden said with cheery little jazz hands, then pulled out the chair across from her, dropped her backpack unceremoniously onto the floor, and sat.

"What…" Kenzie trailed off, unsure how she wanted to finish that sentence. What was he doing here? What did he want? What right did he have to look that good, like a snack she wanted to unwrap and take a bite out of?

And woah…where had *that* come from?

"I know, you're surprised to see me, aren't you?" he asked, the corner of his mouth tipping up so the ghost of one of his dimples appeared. "You wouldn't be if you'd bothered to answer any one of my texts."

"Surprised is one word for it," she said, sitting back in her chair and crossing her arms, blatantly ignoring the comment about his texts. She planned to pretend she'd never gotten them. "What do you want?"

Aiden leaned back and mimicked her body language. "What's with the animosity?" he asked. "I thought we really hit it off at Rick's. Then you ran away and have spent the last three weeks ignoring me."

"I had somewhere to be," she said. "And I'm too busy for you."

Aiden smirked. "I don't believe you."

She gestured to her laptop and the notes fanned out around her. "I don't care. It's the truth."

Sort of, but he didn't need to know that. And what was it about this guy that instantly set her on the defensive? Like flipping a switch, her usually-even-keeled demeanor became antagonistic in a heartbeat. With two older brothers, she'd always been good at standing up for herself, but never like this. Never with someone she barely knew.

It was kind of empowering, turning this guy down. Maybe that version of herself she'd told Berkley about was already coming back.

A myriad of emotions flicked across Aiden's face before he said, "How has your first semester at our fine institution been so far?"

Kenzie raised an eyebrow. "That's what you want to know?"

"Sure," he said with a shrug.

Kenzie considered how easy it would be to get rid of him quickly—and decided the answer was *not very*. So she chose to humor him. "It's been good. I'm still settling in, but I'm enjoying my classes and the city."

"It can be a lot at first," Aiden said, and she actually detected a hint of sympathy in his voice, but it was quickly obliterated by his next comment. "But those freshman gen eds are a breeze. If you ever need someone to study with, you should call me."

"Why would I do that? Don't athletes have someone who does their homework for them?"

Kenzie knew she was playing with fire. If Aiden was anything like her brother, the comment would strike a nerve.

When he leaned forward and settled his elbows on the table, bringing himself down to eye level with her, she knew she'd hit her mark.

"Listen here, bunny," he said, lifting an arm to wag a finger at her. "My teammates and I, and every other athlete on this campus, work our asses off in mandatory tutoring sessions every week to make sure we get our homework done and turned in on time, despite our grueling practice and game schedules."

"Don't call me 'bunny,'" Kenzie said, then leaned forward herself, mimicking his pose like he'd done to her earlier.

And God, had that only been a few minutes ago? Kenzie flicked her wrist up to check the time on her watch right as it vibrated with a text from Berkley. She picked up her phone and found a picture of her sister-in-law's still-flat stomach, the accompanying message complaining about how this baby was already ruining her figure.

Kenzie barked out a laugh.

"What's so funny?" Aiden asked.

Kenzie clutched her phone to her chest and said, "Nothing," before quickly typing out a response to Berkley.

Faster than she could fathom, Aiden reached across the table and plucked her phone from her hands.

"Hey!" she protested. "That's not yours."

Thankfully, she'd learned the hard way to keep pictures of her brother off her home and lock screens. Instead, her home screen was a picture of her and Jessica posing at the end of the dock at the family cabin this past summer, when the Jean and Daniels families had gathered to celebrate Independence Day. All you could see was Jessica's damp blonde hair pooling around her shoulders next to Kenzie's brunette waves, their tanned arms wrapped around each other as they faced away from the camera.

"I want to make sure you have my number saved," Aiden said, not bothering to look up as he presumably navigated to her contacts and added his information. "So you can't blow me off anymore."

"What if I don't want it? And you do realize I could just delete it as soon as you leave, right? Which I'm hoping will be any second. Plus, I can blow you off with or without your number."

Aiden glanced up at her, his criminally-long eyelashes brushing those thick brows of his, and said, "Is that a promise?"

"You're disgusting" Kenzie said as she snatched her phone back, and his grin turned wolfish.

Although, his suggestive tone sent shivers skittering along her skin. Secretly, she wondered what it would be like to get between the sheets with Aiden Fuller.

"No, I'm not disgusting. I'm sexy, and you think so, too."

And damnit, she did.

"Awfully full of yourself."

"Bunny, when you look like this, it's hard not to be," he said, gesturing to his entire being. Kenzie struggled but succeeded in not removing her gaze from his face to scan that delicious body.

"Well, this has been fun," she said as she closed her laptop and shoved it back into her bag.

"Go out with me," Aiden blurted as she stood and gathered her trash.

Kenzie gave him a pitying smile. "Sorry, lover boy. No can do."

She moved away from him, hoping he'd leave her alone.

Of course, she wasn't that lucky.

"And why exactly can't you? I'm not proposing marriage. It's just a date. Don't you know who I am?"

Kenzie emptied her tray into the garbage, then stacked it and her dirty dishes on the table next to it before whirling on Aiden. "Oh, I know exactly who you are. Do you know who *I* am?"

Aiden studied her, dragging his gaze from her face to the tips of her toes and back up. Kenzie had to work hard not to squirm under the attention. "I know your name is Kenzie Jean, and—"

"Technically, my name is *Mackenzie*. Strike one," she told him, not even pausing to consider how he'd figured her last name out. That was a problem for a different day. But if he knew *that*, he definitely knew who her brother was, which made his refusal to back down from her rejection ballsy as hell. Then again, whether by ignorance or sheer lack of fucks to give, his attitude toward her *was* refreshing.

Turned out, she liked *not* being treated like somebody's little sister.

"I know you're a freshman, so that probably makes you, like, eighteen or nineteen."

"I'm twenty-three," she said flatly. "Strike two."

Aiden huffed out an exasperated sigh, blowing the inky strands of his shaggy hair off his forehead. "How are you twenty-three and a freshman?"

"I never said I was a freshman," she said with a shrug, then turned and walked out of the cafeteria, knowing full well he'd follow.

When she reached the lobby, Aiden caught up and curled a palm around her upper arm, spinning her to face him. "Damnit, Kenzie. Why do you keep running away from me?"

"I'm not running from you," she said, pointedly glancing down at her watch. "I have class in twenty in Kedzie, so I need to start walking if I don't want to be late."

His grip on her arm didn't loosen, and Kenzie glared at him, eyes darting between his face and his arm in a universal expression of *get your hands off me.*

Still, she couldn't quite ignore the way the heat from his palm spread across her skin in a truly spectacular way. She hoped he didn't notice how her breath ticked up a notch, or how goosebumps had risen on her flesh.

"Just agree to go on a date with me and I'll let you go," he said, moving further into her personal space, sliding his other hand up to mirror the one already wrapped around her. "Do you know how many women would fall all over themselves to go on a date with a hockey player?"

The cocky smile he gave her had Kenzie letting out a derisive laugh as she yanked her arms from his grasp. Then she stepped even closer so she was toe to toe with him, her chest brushing his with each inhale and exhale. Meeting his eyes was surely a bad idea, but unavoidable if she wanted him to hear and understand the weight of her next words. Kenzie proved herself correct a moment later when their gazes collided and held, when she discovered the deep brown of his irises were ringed around the pupil by a band of gold. They reminded her of melted chocolate and gooey caramel she wanted to dip her finger into and savor.

Blinking several times to gather her thoughts from where they'd so rudely wandered, she finally said, "Aiden, you know what my last name is."

It wasn't a question, and he didn't treat it as such.

"Yes," he said, full mouth curling into a broad grin that showed off his straight white teeth, and the reappearance of those clefts in his cheeks nearly had Kenzie caving and giving him what he'd asked for.

Nearly.

But she wasn't in the habit of dating hockey players, and she certainly wasn't about to agree to go out with a fuckboy like Aiden Fuller. His *I'm-hot-and-I-know-it* attitude grated on her, and she wanted no part in his particular brand of egotism.

"So you're familiar with my big brother. If you ever put your hands on me like that again, it won't be me you'll be dealing with. It'll be *him*, and he's not nearly as nice."

She paused for a beat, biting off a grin at his stunned expression. She leaned closer still and rose onto her tippy toes so her mouth brushed the shell of his ear, palms resting on those ridiculous pecs. She resisted the urge to dig her fingers into them, to clutch his shirt, shift her head, and slant her mouth over his. What the hell was happening to her?

"As for the fact that you're a hockey player? Strike three."

IN A DAZE, AIDEN shuffled back into the cafeteria and made his way to the table his teammates were seated at, each of them tracking his return with shit-eating grins on their faces.

"She turned you down, didn't she?" Jack asked.

Aiden ignored him, staring down at his half-eaten lunch while his other teammates proceeded to rib him.

"Maybe Fuller isn't the ladies' man everything thinks he is," Luke said with a smirk.

"Fuck you, Hayes," Aiden said half-heartedly.

Brent Jean was a god around here. Inside Munn Arena, there was an entire wall dedicated to Spartans in the NHL, and Brent's larger-than-life photo was situated smack dab in the middle. When he had played here, he'd served as captain for two seasons and had taken his team to two Frozen Fours. After graduating—with two degrees, no less—he'd quickly made a name for himself with the Detroit Warriors, and had finished every season since going pro near the top of the league in points.

All that to say, Brent Jean was a hell of a hockey player and a legend in MSU hockey circles. And he was a stand-up guy to boot. He and his long-time girlfriend, also an MSU grad, had recently gotten married.

And now Aiden had set his sights on his baby sister.

This was going to end badly.

"Okay, forget about the fact that she's Brent Jean's little sister," Jack said. "Did she agree to go out with you? Or did your little bunny get away again?"

"She blew me off," Aiden mumbled, and his teammates erupted into laughter loud enough to attract the stares of diners around them.

"Fuller is losing his touch," Luke said with a smirk.

Aiden flung a piece of broccoli at him.

"I'm not losing my touch, you assholes. But her brother is *Brent Jean*," he said with a disbelieving laugh. "There's nothing about me that's all that impressive when you're related to *that*. But never fear, my friends."

"Oh no," Jack said, studying Aiden. "He's got that look in his eyes."

"What look?" Asher asked dumbly, bringing his head closer to Aiden, eyes squinted.

Aiden pushed him away with a palm to the face and said, "I'm going to get her to go out with me. I don't know how yet, but I'm not backing down from this dare."

Visions of Mackenzie Jean swirled relentlessly in Aiden's mind, always pushing at the edges of conscious thought when he should've been paying attention to his homework and mentally preparing for that night's training session.

When he got to Munn that evening for practice, half of his teammates were already in the locker room, each in various stages of undress. Jack, in particular, was sitting at his stall clad in nothing but black boxers, the bulk of his tan skin on display, his blond locks falling into his eyes as he laced his skates.

Aiden walked past him and ruffled the hair on top of his head like he would a little kid.

"Put some clothes on, DeLuca," Aiden said when he reached his own stall and whipped his shirt off.

"And deprive everyone of all this?" Jack said, waving a hand at his body. "No thanks."

Aiden removed a sock and tossed it at Jack's head. "You're an idiot. Plus, I'm better looking than you."

Jack studied him for a moment, eyes roving over Aiden's body as if seriously considering this, then said, "No you're not."

"Aiden's not what?" Asher asked as he walked into the room.

"Better looking than me," Jack replied.

Asher looked between them, as if weighing whether or not he should insert himself into this debate, then said, "This is a trap, isn't it? Some sort of dare?"

"No, it's science." Aiden walked toward Jack and pulled him off his stool to tow him into the center of the room. "For starters, my biceps are bigger," he said, flexing the muscles in question. Jack raised his arms to mirror the pose.

Their display of masculinity quickly gained the attention of the rest of their teammates, and soon the bulk of the MSU hockey team was gathered in a semi-circle around Aiden and Jack, voices rising as the forward and goalie compared physiques.

"What in the fresh hell are you idiots up to now?" Coach's voice boomed across the room. The team parted around Jack—still in nothing but his black boxers, one hand propped on his hip while the other arm flexed in a traditional body-builder pose—and Aiden and Asher, who stood next to each other, the latter's hands wrapped around the biceps of the former.

Everyone dispersed quickly to their stalls, and Aiden's cheeks heated as he turned away from Coach and took two steps in the direction of his own.

"Fuller!" Coach called.

"Fuck," Aiden swore under his breath before spinning toward his coach and saying, "Yeah?"

"My office," Coach said with a jerk of his head.

Aiden avoided the gazes of his teammates as he shuffled his feet toward Coach's office, still shirtless, the rock in his stomach sinking further with each step.

What could he possibly have done wrong this time?

When Aiden stepped inside, the last thing he expected to see was Mitch Frambough seated across the room from him.

"Fuller, have a seat," Coach said, gesturing to the chair next to Mitch.

What the fuck was *Mitch Frambough* doing here? And why was Aiden in this room right now?

"I'm sure you know this guy," Coach said, hooking a thumb in Mitch's direction.

"Mitch Frambough," Mitch said, extending a hand, which Aiden shook in a daze.

Aiden cleared his throat. "Aiden Fuller," he said as he sat down. "Great to meet you. I'm a big fan."

Mitch gave him a tight smile, and Aiden was suddenly reminded that Mitch didn't play anymore.

About a year and a half ago, in a move that had rocked the hockey world, Mitch had been traded from the Detroit Warriors to the Los Angeles Knights. Aiden and his teammates had sat around for days, discussing at length what possible reason the Warriors could have had for trading him, which team had gotten the better and worse ends of the deal—LA and Detroit respectively—and what the Warriors would do without one half of their top defensive pair.

As it turned out, the Warriors had gone on to win a championship the following season, but that was only after Mitch had gone to California and had broken his back in a game. That injury, coupled with previous spinal trauma, had effectively ended his career. After returning to Michigan for rehab, Mitch rejoined the Warriors as a consultant, and had been forced to watch his old team win a championship without him.

That had to have been a tough pill to swallow.

"I was sorry to hear about your injury," Aiden added quickly, and then mentally smacked himself for the word vomit. "You were a hell of a player."

"Thanks, kid," Mitch said. "Now let's talk about *you*."

"Me?" Aiden said, stabbing himself in the chest with a finger.

"What about me?"

"You were drafted by the Warriors in the..." Mitch pulled a sheaf of papers from the bag by his feet and shuffled through. "The 2018 draft, right?"

"Yes..."

"And then you played two years of juniors with the Chicago Steel after graduating from high school. Before that, you were with the NTDP, right?"

"Yes..." Aiden said again, mind spinning.

"I played in Ann Arbor in high school too, you know."

Aiden hadn't known that, but the United States Team Development Program had a habit of pumping out star players, so he wasn't entirely surprised.

"What's this all about?" Aiden asked suddenly, glancing between Mitch and his coach, wishing somebody would get to the fucking point already.

Aiden prided himself on being unflappable in high-stress situations, but right now, he was moments away from snapping.

"This year, my role with the Warriors is changing a bit," Mitch said. "I've enjoyed my time as a defensive consultant, but thanks to my other business ventures, I'm traveling a lot more—which isn't conducive to working with the team the way I'd like. So I'm transitioning away from coaching and into scouting."

Scouting? Aiden thought. *And he's here meeting with* me?

"The Warriors have been keeping an eye on you over the last three years," Mitch said. "Personally, I've watched several hours' worth of game tape on you. You were really impressive in that game against Wisconsin in Madison last season."

Aiden remembered the game well; that was the night he'd scored his first collegiate hat trick, but it had been a bittersweet. Being the visiting team meant the celebration hadn't been as big as Aiden would've liked, but it was still a major accomplishment and a night he looked back on fondly.

"Thank you," he croaked out.

"Look...I'm just going to cut to the chase here."

Finally, Aiden thought, but kept his mouth shut.

"We're interested in giving you a rookie contract in the spring once your season is over," Mitch said. "But I have to say...the Warriors franchise has always taken its reputation for molding young players into upstanding men on and off the ice very seriously. We're aware of your...antics, shall we say, and we have some concerns."

Aiden cut his gaze to Coach, who gave a slight shake of his head, urging Aiden to keep quiet.

"In reference to the recent incident of Aiden's public nudity, I can assure you that I and the university have already leveled punishment against Fuller. He's out for the first five weekends of the season, and it won't happen again. Right, Fuller?"

"Right, Coach," Aiden said, then turned his attention back to Mitch. "Look, I know I messed up. As a team, we've always had this thing about dares and—"

"I'm aware," Mitch said, and Aiden looked at him quizzically. "Brent Jean is my best friend."

Of *course* he and Brent were close. Which meant he also knew Mackenzie.

"So you understand why we just...can't say no," Aiden continued. "I don't personally know anyone who's ever turned one down and had to suffer the punishment, but I've heard horror stories from the guys who came before me. The point is, we got a little carried away with that one. The boys are under strict instructions that I'm exempt from dares for the rest of the season."

Well, most *dares, but semantics.*

Coach sighed deeply and pinched the bridge of his nose, his entire demeanor broadcasting his thoughts, which were clearly, *my players are idiots.*

"I get it," Mitch said. "We've all been young and dumb. But you have the opportunity here to represent the greatest franchise in the NHL. And you're also representing this university, your teammates, and yourself. So here's what I'm asking: keep your head down and yourself out of trouble. When you get back on the ice, play the game the way you know how. The Warriors want to sign you because you're a stud on offense and one of the best defensive forwards in the NCAA. Ten games isn't going to change that."

Aiden tried not to preen at that confidence in his abilities coming from a player of Mitch's caliber.

"I appreciate that more than you know," Aiden told him honestly. "I'll be on my best behavior."

Mitch stood and Aiden followed suit. Mitch was only two inches taller than Aiden, but he seemed larger than life in this office, his big body taking up more space than Aiden was used to from his own teammates. He understood why opponents hated playing against him; the man was a giant, and had been deceptively fast despite his size.

Aiden stuck out his hand and Mitch grabbed it, pumping it a few times. "Nice to meet you, Aiden. We're looking forward to seeing you back out there."

When Mitch had gone, Aiden fixed his gaze on his coach and

said, "Did that just happen?"

Coach smiled indulgently. "I don't quite understand it myself after the shit you pulled a few weeks ago, but the man's not wrong: you are a hell of a player."

"Thanks, Coach," Aiden said with a grin.

Coach nodded his head toward the door. "Now go get changed."

Aiden saluted him and spun on his heel, but only managed two steps before Coach called him back.

"What's up?" Aiden said.

"You haven't RSVP'd to the alumni dinner," Coach said. He fished a creamy, rectangular piece of cardstock with the Spartan helmet logo on the back out of his desk and handed it over.

Aiden had an identical one buried at the bottom of his bag.

"Isn't it mandatory?" he asked with a raised brow.

"Just fill out the damn card."

Resigned, and without really thinking, Aiden checked some boxes and handed it back, then turned to get suited up for practice.

"You're bringing a plus one?" Coach asked incredulously.

"I...what?" Aiden asked, once again pivoting to face the man.

"You checked the box for a plus one."

"Oh...I...uhh..."

Fuck. Think, Fuller.

"I recently started seeing someone," he blurted. "I wanted to bring her with me."

One of Coach's eyebrows rose, and Aiden steeled himself for the man to call him on his bullshit. He surprised Aiden by saying, "Well...I'm excited to meet her."

Aiden gave him a tight smile and finally exited the office, mumbling, "Yeah, me too," under his breath.

The locker room was empty when he reentered it, his teammates already on the ice warming up.

Aiden suited up quickly and shuffled down the tunnel on his skates, then pushed off onto the ice and sprinted to the end where Jack was in net, scooping up a loose puck and shooting it at him.

"Did you get in trouble again?" Jack asked once he'd stopped Aiden's shot.

"The opposite, actually," Aiden said, showering him as he came to a stop on the goal line. "When I walked in, Mitch Frambough was there."

Asher, who was a defenseman and practically idolized Mitch despite the fact that he no longer played, skated closer, eyes wide and mouth dropped comically open. "Mitch Frambough?" he whispered reverently.

"What did he want?" Luke asked, gliding over to join them.

"The Warriors want to offer me a contract in the spring."

"Holy shit, dude!" Jack yelled, and the three of them clapped Aiden on the shoulders, tossing around words of congratulations.

"I just have to keep my head down and have my best season yet once I actually get playing time."

"Dude, you could be playing with Brent Jean this time next year," Luke said, eyes wide.

"Maybe then you'll be dating his sister, too," Jack said with a wink.

And wouldn't that be something?

Coach skated onto the ice and blew his whistle, signaling for them to gather at center ice.

Physically, Aiden was with his teammates, but mentally he was a million miles away. In the excitement of telling them about the meeting with Mitch, he had forgotten that he was apparently bringing a date to the alumni dinner...which was happening at the end of next week. Where was he going to find a girlfriend in ten days? He couldn't bring just anyone. None of his previous casual hookups would do.

No, Aiden needed someone classy and sweet. Someone who would convince his coach and everyone else that he was trying to get his shit together. Someone beautiful and funny, who would be confident and comfortable surrounded by the who's who of Michigan State hockey alumni and donors.

Someone like Mackenzie Jean.

chapter 6
Kenzie

"WHAT THE FUCK IS this?" Brent asked Kenzie the second she walked into his and Berkley's house on Saturday morning, three days after the encounter with Aiden.

It had been a few weeks since she'd seen her brother, so she'd decided to show up unannounced this morning to catch up and see how Berkley was feeling in the midst of her second trimester. Every Saturday, her brother and sister-in-law prepared a massive breakfast buffet and invited Lexie and Mitch over. Of course, both Kenzie and Jessica had standing invites, and Kenzie had come over every week when she'd still lived in the city. Now that she'd moved away, this was the first time she'd been back. Jessica, as far as Kenzie knew, had never attended.

"You're gonna have to be more specific, big bro," she said, making her way into the massive kitchen for a cup of coffee. Kenzie loved coming here because Brent and Berkley had the fanciest coffee maker, meaning she could whip up any type of drink she was in the mood for without paying Starbucks prices.

Brent stalked closer to her, the ocean-blue gaze that usually matched her own turned grey with whatever fit he'd worked himself into.

"This," he said, holding his phone inches from her face. Kenzie backed away and studied his screen. It took her brain a few moments to process what her eyes were seeing, but when it did, she let out a low groan.

Unbidden, her heart rate kicked up.

This was *not* good.

Half of what Brent ranted about next was lost to the roaring in her ears. She pulled out a barstool and sat, nearly missing completely and falling to the floor. As she wiped her clammy palms on her pants and worked through her breathing exercises, her brother continued to yell.

A comforting hand settled on her spine, and Kenzie swallowed hard, her heart slowing.

"Brent," Berkley said, sliding onto the seat next to Kenzie. "Chill out. Can't you see she had nothing to do with this?"

Finally, her brother shut up, and in the silence, Kenzie's mind ceased spinning.

"Shit, Kenz. I'm sorry," Brent said.

His apology lowered her heart rate further, but she sat with her head bowed for a few beats longer, letting memories—more like nightmares—wash over her before letting them go.

In the wake of Kenzie's mental breakdown nearly six years ago now, her then-boyfriend had grown distant. She hadn't really blamed him, his disinterest in being connected to the town freak not all that surprising.

What *had* been surprising was that, instead of breaking up with her, he'd gone to a party and had made out with her best friend in front of a crowd full of people.

Kenzie had found out because someone had captured it on video and sent it to her.

Suffice to say, she wasn't a fan of everyone knowing the particulars of her relationships, especially when she wasn't in control of the narrative.

Not that she was in a relationship with Aiden Fuller. But...that's what it looked like.

"It's not what it looks like," Kenzie said finally, lifting her head.

"It *looks like* you're awfully cozy with some fuckboy," Brent said through gritted teeth, her episode apparently doing nothing to bank his rage.

The picture in question showed Kenzie and Aiden at Case, his massive hands curled around her upper arms. She had to admit, they looked...cozy.

Once again stable now that the worst of the episode had passed, Kenzie glanced at Berkley and said, "I can't believe you're having a child with this guy. That poor kid is going to be so sheltered."

Berkley snorted, and Brent said, "Don't change the subject, Kenz. Who is this guy?"

It shouldn't have surprised Kenzie that someone had submitted the picture to The Green, or that it had made its way into her brother's hands.

The Green was Michigan State's version of an online tabloid. Mostly, it was a place where students could submit juicy gossip for the consumption of their peers, and more often than not, that gossip featured athletes.

Athletes were, after all, the celebrities of college campuses. She knew for a fact her brother had been a common fixture on the site during his tenure at MSU.

"Why are you even on The Green?" Kenzie asked her brother. "Are you stalking me?"

"Someone has to keep an eye on you," he said, brandishing his phone like a weapon. "You haven't even been on campus a month and you're already pulling this shit?"

"Brent..." Berkley warned. "She's not doing anything wrong."

"Berk's right. Besides, he's nobody," Kenzie said.

"Really?" Brent said. "Because he looks an awful lot like Aiden Fuller."

"What about Aiden Fuller?" Mitch asked as he and Lexie walked into the kitchen.

"Uncle Mitch!" Kenzie yelled, hopping off her stool to run at him. True to form, Mitch scooped her up and swung her around in a bone-crushing hug. Lexie pecked her on the cheek before making a beeline toward the coffee maker.

Of Brent and Berkley's friends, Mitch and Lexie were her favorites. Mitch appeared menacing at first glance, and certainly had been on the ice when he was still playing as a defenseman, but inside he was a giant teddy bear. And Lexie encapsulated the term *resting bitch face*, but Kenzie had seen over the years how loyal she was to the people she cared about most. Both of them had been instrumental in getting Brent and Berkley back together after their breakup, and had been their maid of honor and best man when they'd gotten married in July.

Not to mention, their own love story was the stuff of legends. Neither time nor distance could've kept them away from each other, and when they finally reunited at Brent and Berkley's wedding, everything had seemed to click back into place.

Was it strange to be so heavily invested in someone else's relationship? Possibly. But Brent's little found family in Detroit had, by extension and association, become Kenzie's when she'd moved to Michigan. It made her happy to see these people happy and in love, especially Lexie and Mitch, who had each suffered so much heartbreak. They deserved a win.

And maybe...maybe Kenzie hoped some of that good luck would rub off on her.

Not that she'd ever admit that to anyone. She hadn't been in a serious relationship in ages, and while some people were lucky enough to meet the loves of their lives in college, Kenzie wasn't delusional enough to think she'd be one of them.

Plus, her anxiety made things difficult. When life became too overwhelming, she had a bad habit of retreating into herself, becoming a hermit until the dark clouds that had settled over her passed. In truth, there were stretches of time when she struggled to take care of herself, often missing meals because she was working too hard, or going days without exercising simply because she couldn't be bothered to get out of bed. It seemed unfathomable to add a second personality to the mix, someone whose feelings she had to consider when making decisions, someone who wanted to spend time with her and could potentially react negatively when she needed time for herself.

The day Kenzie found a man willing to adapt to her messy little brain and the physical manifestations of her chemical imbalance would surely be the day hell froze over.

"This picture popped up on The Green of Kenzie and Aiden

having what looks like an intimate moment," Brent said, voice dripping with disdain as he passed his phone to Mitch, snapping Kenzie back to the present.

"The Green?" Lexie asked. "I can't believe that stupid site still exists."

"That's what I said!" Berkley exclaimed. "I'm surprised the university hasn't found some way to shut it down."

"Ladies," Brent growled. "Not the point."

"Then what *is* the point, big brother?"

"The point, Mackenzie Elizabeth Jean," her brother said, and Kenzie crawled back onto the barstool next to Berkley, preparing to be fully and embarrassingly reprimanded in front of his friends, "is that Aiden Fuller is a bad guy."

"Actually," Mitch piped up, dropping down onto a stool next to Mackenzie and nudging her with his shoulder, as if to say, *I've got you, kid,* "I just met with him yesterday, and I wouldn't say he's all bad. He's a hell of a hockey player, and he seems like he's got a good head on his shoulders. I think he just got swept up in all the status and attention that comes with being a collegiate athlete–especially a hockey player with a program as storied as Michigan State's."

"You lived it," Berkley reminded her husband. "What was it you told me once? That you couldn't turn down dares even if you wanted to because the punishment would be worse than the actual dare? If you ask me, Aiden's little streak through campus has *dare gone wrong* written all over it."

"Whose side are you on here?" Brent asked Berkley, narrowing his eyes at her.

"I'm not on any side," she said. "I'm reminding you that you were young and dumb once. Cut Kenz some slack, babe. If she says it's not what it looks like, you owe it to her to take that statement at face value."

Kenzie sat up straighter and grinned broadly at her brother, whose narrowed gaze continued to dart between her, his best friend, and his wife.

"I feel like I lost this one," he finally said quietly.

"Get used to it, honey," Berkley said, standing to move around the island toward him. When she reached his side, she stretched onto her tiptoes and kissed him on the cheek, a hand settling on her abdomen. "Me and this baby are about to outnumber you."

"Unless it's a boy," Lexie said.

Berkley cut her best friend with a look. "Even if it *is* a boy, he will always take his mama's side."

Brent placed his hand atop Berkley's and said, "It doesn't matter what it is, as long as both it and my girl are healthy."

"Gross," Kenzie said with a gag.

Brent pointed a finger at her. "I don't care what these guys say," he told her, gesturing to Mitch, Lexie, and Berkley. "You will stay away from that kid. If I see you pop up on The Green again, there will be hell to pay."

"You are insufferable," Kenzie said to her brother. "Why are you being such an asshole about this? It's just a picture!"

"Because I know how college hockey players are, Mackenzie. And I know the type of feelings that accompany two people standing that close. That kid only wants one thing, and you won't be the one to give it to him."

Kenzie opened her mouth to protest, but clamped her jaw shut. Arguing with him wouldn't get her anywhere.

"Wait," she said, circling back to something Mitch had said

earlier, before her brother had gone for the jugular. She turned to the blond. "Did you say you met with him yesterday? Where? Why?"

"I went to campus," Mitch said. "You know I'm transitioning into a scouting role this season, right?"

"Bee mentioned it," she said, and although she generally tried to tune her brother out, she did vaguely remember a passing comment about the change in Mitch's job title.

"So I'm in charge of keeping track of our draft prospects," he said. "And scouting new talent. Free agents, guys playing internationally—that sort of thing."

Kenzie frowned. "So you're going to be traveling more?"

"We already travel a lot as it is," Mitch reminded her, sharing a small smile with his girlfriend. "But that's not the point, Little Jean. The *point* is that Aiden is a Warriors' draft prospect, and I met with him yesterday to tell him if he keeps his head on straight and stays out of trouble, he'll have a rookie contract waiting for him in the spring when his season wraps."

"You have got to be fucking kidding me," Brent muttered.

Kenzie beamed, positively gleeful over this new development. "So if Aiden stays out of trouble and has a good season, this time next year he could be playing with Bee?"

"I mean, there are a lot of contributing factors to whether or not Aiden ever makes it to the show," Mitch said. "But if everything goes right, yeah, he could be."

She turned to her brother, her small smile splitting into a full-blown grin. "You better get used to the kid, big bro."

Brent made a disgusted sound in the back of his throat. "Never."

"I don't know, Jean..." Mitch said, curving his shoulders in a bit, as if bracing himself for Brent's reaction to what he was about to say. "I've watched endless hours of tape on the kid. He's good. *Really* good. He reminds me of this guy I know. Quick, great read on the ice, hell of a defensive forward, natural goal-scorer."

"That kid is nothing like me," Brent said, sounding for all the world like a petulant child.

"He's a little raw yet," Mitch continued, "but a few years in Grand Rapids? He could turn into an absolute stud. Brent Jean caliber for sure."

"Get out of my house," Brent told his best friend.

Kenzie laughed, and Berkley said, "Brent!"

Mitch held up his hands defensively and said, "You'd be saying the same things if you hadn't caught him in a compromising position with your little sister."

"It wasn't 'compromising,'" Kenzie protested, but everyone ignored her. "And I'm going on a date with him anyway."

The conversation around her came to a screeching halt, like tires burning on asphalt.

And...*fuck.* Why had she said that? The problem with her brother was that he always elicited certain reactions from her, where she reverted from the adult she was now into the sullen teenager she'd been when Brent was her age. She didn't like being told what to do, and she certainly wasn't going to take relationship advice from her brother, the ruler of Fuckboydom before he'd met Berkley.

The thing that angered her the most was that her brother couldn't simply take her at her word. At the slightest provocation, the smallest mention of a perceived romantic attachment to someone, he blew a gasket. And she tended to respond in kind.

The double standard was exhausting. He was allowed to get

married and start a family, and Nate was allowed to run around New York, then Boston, and now Ann Arbor, fucking anyone he wanted—including Lexie, by the way—and no one batted an eye.

But Kenzie was *the baby*, and a *girl*. Of course *she* couldn't even look at a guy without Brent doing...well, what he was doing right now, which was trying to control her.

"I'm sorry," Brent said, breaking the uncomfortable silence that had settled over the room. "Did you say you're going on a date with him?"

Kenzie nodded, swallowing hard around the lump in her throat. She was committed now, refusing to back down. Willing her voice to remain steady, she said, "That's what was happening in the picture. He was asking me out."

"You can't be serious," Brent said.

Kenzie's phone buzzed on the counter. She lifted it, nearly dropping it in surprise when she saw the name on the screen, which she should have changed the first time he'd texted her. But, for reasons yet unknown, she hadn't.

Besides, it wasn't exactly a lie. The boy *was* sexy.

Kenzie barked out a laugh. "Sorry," she said, an irrepressible smile tipping up the corners of her mouth. "Aiden just texted me."

Her brother's eyes narrowed, but Kenzie turned away from him, a plan forming in her mind.

Because she *did* need a plan. She'd told her brother Aiden was taking her on a date, and now she needed to make that happen.

After all, as far as her brother was concerned, she was already—what were his words? *Awfully cozy with some fuckboy.*

Kenzie hadn't done anything wrong; she'd been trying to get *away* from Aiden, not closer. But of course, in her short time on campus, she'd learned that The Green could take even the most innocent of interactions and put a nefarious or explicit spin on them. Now, she'd dug herself into a hole, using the photo as evidence, and was dragging Aiden down with her.

It wasn't often she put her foot in it like now, having long since mastered the ability to filter her thoughts before they left her mouth. As a product of her anxiety, Kenzie carefully considered everything she did and said. She didn't like disrupting the status quo.

People with anxiety understood the importance of routines. Kenzie didn't like change, which had made the cross-country move from New York to Detroit all the more puzzling to her family. It had been a big step, to uproot her life and start over somewhere new at twenty years old. So while she didn't like change, she always trusted her gut, and her gut had told her it was the right path to take. The opportunity had called, and she'd answered.

The same thing had happened when a little seed had taken root in her brain and sprouted, telling her to go back to school. The longer she'd considered it, and the bigger the idea had grown—eventually blooming into a full-fledged plan—the more at peace she had felt.

The same could be said of the pull to leave FLEX behind, which tugged harder and became more insistent by the day.

Coming back to school had been the right decision, and she knew leaving FLEX would be too, but she could only accomplish what she wanted to accomplish if she took some risks. Broke a few rules. Shook up her life a bit.

Maybe her outburst had been her subconscious telling her Aiden was the guy to help her out with that. And, she realized with a jolt, he *wanted* to go out with her, had been begging for exactly that for weeks. This was already a done deal. All she had to do now was put the poor guy out of his misery.

Her fingers flew across the screen of her phone, typing out a message to Aiden. As she pressed send, a crash echoed in her brain. She couldn't help thinking it was the sound of her number one rule—don't date hockey players—hitting the floor and shattering into a thousand pieces.

chapter 7
Aiden

Sunday night, Aiden lay awake well past the time he should've been asleep.

Morning skate would be a bitch.

Rolling onto his side, a glance at his clock alerted him to the fact that it was well after three in the morning. Flipping onto his back, he sighed, thoughts swirling.

Aiden had been prepared to do whatever it took to get Mackenzie to attend the alumni dinner as his date. Especially since, after the boys dared him to ask her out and she blew him off, he'd suddenly started viewing her as a challenge. And getting her to go out with him was how he won.

So when she'd texted him to meet her in the Union after class the next morning, she'd taken him by surprise. Maybe she'd decided to stop playing hard to get, and he fully intended to take this opportunity to shoot his shot.

He would get down on his knees and beg if that's what she

wanted.

Which, admittedly, would be a bit much, but he didn't give a fuck. He wanted this girl.

One big question remained: what could she possibly want from him? After the amount of shit she'd given him about being a hockey player, and how she'd never go out with him, there had to be something that had prompted her to arrange this meeting.

Eventually, Aiden drifted off into a fitful sleep, his dreams full of chestnut hair and piercing blue eyes.

After what felt like five seconds, his alarm blared, causing him to jolt upright in bed. Feeling like a zombie, he shuffled into the kitchen to chug a mug of coffee. Asher was already there, elbows bent on the counter, stuffing a banana in his mouth.

The scent of coffee filled the air, drawing Jack and Luke into the kitchen like a siren luring a ship to a rocky shore.

"Morning," Luke said, bright-eyed and bushy-tailed as always. Of the four of them, Luke was the only one who could stomach being awake this early, and Aiden supposed that was one of the reasons why he was the captain. It didn't matter how many years he'd been playing hockey at a highly competitive level, or how long this had been his reality: Aiden would *never* be a morning person.

His sleeplessness also meant he was a deadweight at practice, and unfortunately, Coach took notice.

"Look, I know you're not going to be playing for a few months yet," he reminded Aiden, who was well aware of this fact, "but that doesn't mean you can slack off. As an alternate captain, you're one of the leaders of this team, and I expect you to act as such. Got it?"

"Got it," Aiden mumbled, then skated away to join his teammates as they lined up on the goal line to do suicides before practice wrapped for the morning.

Coach stood at center ice, surveying them. "Well..." he finally said. "I've seen worse."

Then he blew the whistle.

When Aiden arrived at his eight a.m. after morning skate, his mind was completely consumed by thoughts of Mackenzie Jean. This particular class—College Sports in the United States—didn't require a ton of brainpower from him considering his status as a college athlete. Instead, he mentally spun his wheels, cooking up all sorts of schemes and scenarios that grew more and more improbable the longer he sat there. The professor finally dismissed them, and Aiden looked at his desk to gather his things, realizing he'd spent the whole class period without even removing his laptop from his bag.

However, that ended up working in his favor, because his advertising class started immediately afterward, and he had to haul ass across campus to get there in time. Thankfully, the university provided him with a moped to zip around campus.

When he reached the lecture hall in the Communication Arts and Sciences building, he spotted Kenzie immediately, as if she were one of those blinking red lights atop a skyscraper.

While he wanted to sit next to her and get their meeting started a little earlier, he didn't. First, because she sat near the back of the room, which went against his requirements as an athlete, and second, because Jack stood up, windmilling his arms to attract Aiden's attention.

"Why are you out of breath?" Asher asked when Aiden dropped into the seat between him and Jack.

"No parking out front," Aiden said. "Had to run from the ramp across the street."

"I would've just parked on the sidewalk," Jack said.

"And get a ticket? Or worse yet, get the moped towed and not be able to use it anymore? No thanks."

Contrary to popular belief, athletes had to follow the rules like everyone else, and Aiden was already in too much shit with the university to risk something as silly as a ticket when he could park in a lot or ramp like a normal student.

If Aiden thought his attention span had been nonexistent at practice and in his earlier class, he'd been sorely mistaken. Now, being in the same room as Kenzie, it wasn't only his mind that had checked out; his entire body was now focused on her presence at the back of the room, despite the several rows and mass of people between them.

And, honestly, what the fuck was wrong with him? Was he nervous about their meeting, or was it something else? No, that had to be it. Aiden didn't get nervous around girls; he had no reason to. For starters, they always came to him, making their intentions so clear that there was no mistaking what they were asking from him.

Everything with Kenzie was different. Whatever she wanted, it wasn't any sort of physical relationship. It was blatantly obvious that she wasn't interested in him in that kind of way, no matter how badly he wished the opposite were true.

He barely knew the girl, and somehow she'd managed to get him all twisted up. He was definitely going to have to do something about that.

When their professor ended class, Aiden wanted to follow Kenzie out and trail behind her like a lost puppy all the way to the Union. Instead, he forced himself to hold back, waiting for the room to completely clear out before he collected his things and made his way up the ramp to where his moped was parked.

But he'd be damned if he didn't speed all the way back across campus.

The MSU Union was a stately building on West Circle Drive, located in what was affectionately referred to by students as the Harry Potter Campus but more commonly known as North Neighborhood. Inside, students could find the Spartan Spirit Shop, a Sparty's Mini Market, and three food court stations. It also contained studying spaces, an art gallery, the University Activities Board office, and meeting areas for student groups.

Aiden entered after he'd parked his moped, and was instantly confronted with one of his favorite things on campus: a bench with a bronzed and green statue of Michigan State's mascot, Sparty, smack dab in the center of it.

When Aiden was a boy, his father, who had grown up in the Lansing area, always brought him here to get a picture with the statue anytime they were on campus. It became a fun tradition of sorts, getting a new one each year as he grew, and eventually adding his younger sister to the photos once she came along.

Though his father was gone, Aiden could stand here, staring at the statue, and remember those days fondly. He was reminded why he was here, and who and what he was working so hard for.

"What are you doing?" a voice asked, and Aiden looked up into the cold blue gaze of Mackenzie Jean.

"Reminiscing."

She jerked her head in the direction of the stairs that led down into the main lounge space and said, "Come on, I've got a table over here," indicating to an alcove that provided some modicum of privacy.

"You afraid to be seen with me, bunny?" Aiden asked, a cloud of floral perfume enveloping him as he moved down the short flight behind her.

She glanced over her shoulder. "Absolutely."

Okay then.

"You know, bunny," Aiden said as he took a seat, "if you wanted to get me alone, all you had to do was ask."

"Does that smarmy attitude of yours ever actually work on girls? And stop calling me that."

"All the time," he said, grinning. "Most of them aren't nearly as smart as you."

"Obviously not," she said, sitting down across from him and flipping her long hair over her shoulder.

"Why am I here?" he asked. His skin tightened under her unrelenting gaze, and anticipation buzzed in his chest.

He had been obsessing over this meeting for the last twenty-four hours, and though his mind had conjured a hundred different scenarios for its necessity, he hadn't once considered he might hear the words that came out of Kenzie's mouth next.

"I have a favor to ask."

"So do I," he blurted.

A delicate crease formed between her brows as they scrunched up in confusion. "You do?"

"I need you to be my fake girlfriend for this alumni dinner

thing on Friday night," he said in a rush, then added, "Please. I accidentally told my coach I was bringing a date because I was really distracted when I filled out the RSVP card, and I'm really trying to look like I have my shit together, so I can't say I'm bringing someone then show up alone. That would be so lame, and make me look *so* bad."

"Why can't you ask one of the other girls who can stand to be around you?"

"None of them are you," Aiden said without thinking, instantly wishing he could rewind time and suck the words back into his throat. "What I mean is that...your brother is Brent Jean. Surely you're used to these kinds of things."

She remained skeptical, arms crossed in a defensive, unimpressed stance, one eyebrow arched dubiously.

"What's it going to take to get you to agree to this?" Aiden asked when she didn't respond. He hadn't even thought to ask what the favor she needed was. He had a one track mind for not making himself look like a fucking chump in front of his coach and whoever else saw his RSVP card. "Do you want me to get on my knees and beg you? I'll get down on the floor right now." Aiden slid out of his chair and lowered to a knee.

"Get up," Kenzie hissed at him, reaching out and gripping his bicep with her hand, as if to pull him up. "Don't make a scene, Fuller. That's the last thing we need right now."

"We?" he asked when he was once again seated. And he'd be damned if his dick hadn't twitched when she'd called him by his last name.

"That picture of us," she said flippantly.

"What picture?"

She narrowed her eyes, as if gauging whether or not he was fucking with her. When she decided he wasn't, she said, "You really haven't seen it?"

"No!" he said loudly, and she cut him with a glare when a few students turned to look in their direction.

Kenzie pulled out her phone and tapped around on the screen before flipping it in his direction.

There was a picture of...them. Outside Case cafeteria, standing too close for comfort—Aiden remembered the way his body had reacted to her nearness—his hands wrapped around her upper arms as she cut him down a few pegs with her words.

The caption read: AIDEN FULLER'S LATEST CON-QUEST?

"Damn, bunny, I'm sorry," he said. "You know that's not how I see you."

"I do?" she asked, an eyebrow rising doubtfully.

"You *should*." And he didn't know where his next words came from, because he wasn't entirely sure they were true. But they seemed like something she'd want to hear, so he continued with, "You're not some game to me. I'll admit, you're hot, and you want absolutely nothing to do with me, which only adds to the allure, but that's not what this is about. You'd really just be doing me a favor by going to this alumni thing with me. I realize you owe me nothing, and it's probably the last thing you want to do, but...I could really use your help."

And, okay, *some* of it was true, but mostly he was trying to save his own ass, *and* he still hadn't gotten over the sting of her rejecting him the week before. His teammates had ribbed him endlessly for failing that dare, and his suspension was the only thing that had saved him from suffering the consequences.

That and his absolute vehemence that he could still make it happen.

He was *so* fucked if it backfired.

Kenzie studied him for several long moments, lifting her coffee and taking a long pull from the cup before she answered. "I'll do it."

Aiden sat frozen, unsure he'd heard her correctly. "You will?"

"Yes."

Now it was Aiden's turn to narrow his eyes at her. "What exactly are you getting out of this?"

She hesitated. "I kind of already accidentally told my brother I was going on a date with you to piss him off."

Aiden stilled, completely at a loss for words, but Kenzie obliviously plowed ahead.

"The way I see it, this is beneficial for both of us. You need to rehab your image a bit, and as far as anyone else knows, I'm the good-girl younger sister of a professional hockey player. *And* I have a sparkling reputation. You won't look like an ass in front of your coach and these alumni people, and I'll get to annoy my brother. It's a win-win."

"Are you saying you're not a good girl?" Aiden asked, voice low as he leaned forward.

Kenzie mirrored him, resting her elbows on the table so their faces were mere inches apart. "That is for me to know and you to never find out."

This girl, Aiden thought. The fire in her eyes, the confident way she moved through the world, her absolute refusal to want anything to do with him.

Even now, when she was asking for his help, her reticence, her stubbornness, the I-know-this-is-a-bad-idea-but-I'm-going-to-do-it-anyway expression, clinging to the delicate bones and muscles of her face—it was sexy as fuck.

Aiden's first instinct was to say no. He needed to, to use her words, "rehab his image," certainly. But badly enough to...what? Pretend to date Brent Jean's baby sister, even if only for one night? That had *bad idea* written all over it.

Then again, they both needed each other. He needed a date to this alumni dinner, and she'd lied to her brother about going on a date with him. He supposed he could throw her a bone and make an honest woman out of her. He'd simply ignore the fact that he needed this more than she did. He was the clear winner in this scenario, and what was it they said about looking gift horses in the mouth?

Oh yeah.

Don't.

And, damn the consequences, he wanted an excuse to spend time with this girl.

"Okay, bunny," he finally said. "You've got yourself a deal."

Chapter 8
Kenzie

"WHAT ARE YOU DOING Friday night?" Jessica asked Kenzie.

It was Wednesday night, and the pair were at Dublin Square, another East Lansing bar only a few blocks away from Kenzie's apartment. She and Jessica hadn't seen each other since the weekend after classes had started, when Jessica had dragged Kenzie away from packing, introduced her to some friends, and convinced her to spend the whole night dancing their feet off in this very bar.

Jessica had texted that morning, asking if they could get drinks, saying she'd had a hellish week of student-teaching and that she needed a night off from her boyfriend, Silas, who was "one overreaction away from being single."

Yikes.

Kenzie choked on a sip of tequila-heavy margarita. "Why, did someone say something?" she asked. Going on a...could it even be considered a date if they were both getting something out of the arrangement that had nothing to do with companionship?

Probably not, but for lack of a better word, going on a date with Aiden wasn't a big deal—in theory. Kenzie simply didn't need people asking questions she didn't have the answers to.

Honestly, she had no clue what she was actually doing with Aiden. Surely this little agreement they'd come to was a disastrous idea when Kenzie *could* have just told Brent she'd lied, but...it was too late to back out now. In truth, something about Aiden brought out a different side of her. Some long-forgotten piece of her personality clicked into place in his presence. Around Aiden, she felt confident and powerful and sexy—things she hadn't experienced in a long time.

"What?" Jessica asked, confused. "No, I'm just curious. Some friends, Silas, and I are going to a show at this event space downtown, and I was going to invite you along."

Kenzie's shoulders relaxed. "Oh, I'd love to, but I have other plans." She didn't elaborate, but she also knew Jessica wouldn't let it go that easily.

"What kind of plans?"

"FLEX stuff," she said automatically. Though Jessica knew she'd taken a step back from the company, Kenzie hoped she wouldn't question it.

Jessica rolled her eyes but let Kenzie's slip go, then lifted her own drink to her mouth, taking a dainty sip. She had never been much of a drinker, and she'd surprised Kenzie tonight by ordering a rum and Coke. Things with Silas must've been weighing on her more than she'd let on.

"Sometimes I think you and Berkley should've been sisters," Jessica said. "You're both workaholics."

Kenzie snorted. "Have you met my brothers?"

Jessica laughed with her. "Okay, you have a point there. Do you ever feel like a major slacker compared to them?"

"Every day," Kenzie said without hesitation.

This was a frequent discussion of theirs. Both of Jessica's older siblings—Berkley and their brother Logan—were well-established attorneys. On top of that, Berkley was currently in school completing the classes necessary to open her own sports agency. Jessica often thought her decision to be a school teacher made her a slacker in the eyes of her family, but anyone who knew Jessica could see how passionate she was about educating, and Kenzie had heard Berkley gush about her little sister enough to know that the Daniels family was very proud of her.

As for Kenzie, well...obviously, everyone knew Brent had built a beautiful life for himself in Detroit with his hockey team and with Berkley. And Nate was in his fourth year of residency in orthopedic medicine at the University of Michigan's hospital in Ann Arbor.

"It's hard being the youngest," Jessica said with a sigh, and Kenzie nodded in agreement.

Being the youngest had its perks, of course. Growing up, her parents and brothers had rarely denied Kenzie anything, and the four of them were her biggest cheerleaders. She loved her brothers dearly, more than she could ever say, and was insanely proud of them both. But on the flip side of that pride, Kenzie often felt like the black sheep, the one who was dragging down the image of the uber successful Jean siblings by not living up to her full potential.

The problem was, both of her brothers had figured out early on exactly what they wanted to do with their lives. Unfortunately for Kenzie, she was still searching for that *thing*. She had yet to find her calling, and it was a constant source of anxiety for her, like a low-level hum in the back of her mind, whispering, *Figure it out, Kenzie; when are you going to get your shit together?*

For someone who already suffered from depression and high-functioning anxiety, the added pressure to live up to the standards her brothers had set often made matters worse.

Truthfully, she often felt like a prisoner inside her own mind.

Jessica snapped her fingers in front of Kenzie's face, pulling her back to the present. "Dude, where did you go?"

Kenzie shook her head and took a long, fortifying gulp of her drink. "Thinking about my brothers."

Jessica lifted her glass and clinked it against Kenzie's. "To overachieving older siblings."

Though she'd tried everything she could to remain calm, after her conversation with Jessica on Wednesday, Kenzie's anxiety was at an all-time high.

Not ideal when she was about to go on her first "date" with Aiden Fuller, who embodied the phrase *calm, cool, and collected.*

As she didn't have any classes on Fridays, she spent the bulk of the day catching up on homework so she wouldn't have to worry about it over the weekend.

Unfortunately, her brain had other ideas, and after an hour of thought-spiraling over what she had planned that evening, she called Dr. Mathews.

"Hello, Mackenzie."

"I'm going on a date tonight," she blurted.

"Really?" Dr. Mathews responded. "With who?"

"His name is Aiden. He's a hockey player here at MSU. But it's not a real date. I'm just doing him a favor."

Concisely, she filled Dr. Mathews in on the last few weeks, surprised this was the first time since school had started that she'd really needed her therapist's guidance.

"So let me get this straight," the woman said, and Kenzie could easily picture her in her warm, creamy office behind the mammoth walnut desk, reclining in her plush leather chair as she considered how to approach this session. "You're going on a date with a hockey player, the kind of guy you've repeatedly said you'd never date, because you want to piss your brother off? Mackenzie, that's not—"

Kenzie knew what was coming, and cut off Dr. Mathews' admonishment. "I know, I know," she said. "He just makes me so mad!"

"We've talked about this."

"I know!" Kenzie barked, and Dr. Mathews remained silent on the other end of the line. "I'm sorry. I know this is a bad idea."

"Is it really, though? Or do you only think so because Aiden is the kind of guy you've never pictured yourself with?"

"I..."

Kenzie trailed off. She'd never considered that before. Aiden definitely wasn't the kind of guy she'd ever imagined herself with, but she had to admit his attention was flattering. He was, after all, MSU hockey's golden boy, much like her brother had been. Aiden was ridiculously good looking, funny, *and* physically attracted to her. Attending a fancy alumni dinner on his arm wouldn't exactly be a hardship.

Maybe tonight wouldn't be all bad.

Her chest loosened, heart pumping freely, lungs once again accepting unrestricted air. She hadn't realized how worked up she'd been until Dr. Mathews had given her permission to enjoy herself tonight.

As if her thoughts had conjured him, her phone beeped, alerting her to another incoming call.

"Sorry, Dr. Mathews," she said. "That's him calling. I have to take this."

"Have fun tonight, Mackenzie," her doctor said before Kenzie connected with Aiden.

"Fuller," she said in greeting.

"Hi, bunny." She could practically hear the grin in his voice.

"What do you want?"

"Just calling to make sure you're ready."

Unable to resist fucking with him, she said, "For what?"

"Don't play with me. Alumni dinner? You scratch my back, I scratch yours? Our deal?"

"I've been studying," she said, as though that explained everything.

Aiden let out a disgusted snort. "Who studies on a Friday?"

"Someone who doesn't like putting it off until the last minute," she said, putting her phone on speaker as she moved through her apartment and into her bedroom.

"Fair enough," he said. "Where do you live again? I'll pick you up."

"Not necessary," she said as she set her phone on her dresser and rifled through her clothes, looking for something to wear.

"Bunny," Aiden said again, this time sounding exasperated. "If we're doing this whole pretend-dating thing for tonight, I'm going to pick you up at your place like a gentleman. I'll open any and all doors for you, and maybe I'll even give you a goodnight kiss when I drop you off later."

"You are insufferable," she said, pulling a dress out and whipping her t-shirt and shorts off to try it on. "I really don't need a ride, Aiden. I can find my way there all by myself. I'm a big girl."

"I think that's the first time you've called me by my first name," he said. "I don't like it."

Kenzie snorted. "I'm sorry, *Fuller*," she said, then pulled the dress off with a frustrated groan.

"Better," he said. "But I'm picking you up, and that's the end of this discussion. If I'm going to be your fake boyfriend, I'm going full send here. Picking you up and holding your door open for you, giving you my suit jacket when you're cold, holding your purse when you go to the bathroom. That kind of shit."

"You're not my fake boyfriend," she said. "This is *a* date. A one-time thing. A singular occurrence. And where do you get your ideas from? *The Brady Bunch*?"

Aiden huffed out a laugh. "Consider it wishful thinking for when you finally stop pretending you hate me and give into this thing between us. And don't knock *The Brady Bunch*. Did you ever stop to consider that maybe I'm old-fashioned?"

Aiden Fuller, old-fashioned? Fat chance.

"I can assure you *that* will never happen."

"Never say never," he said. When she didn't respond, he asked, "What're you doing?"

"Trying to find something to wear. What are you wearing?"

"Charcoal suit, white shirt, deep-green bow tie," he said. "Though it's sticky out, so I'll probably ditch the jacket at some point."

Kenzie rolled her eyes, irritated by how easily men dressed themselves. Not to mention, Aiden probably looked good in everything he owned. And she couldn't help imagining what he'd look like with those sleeves rolled up, revealing that full arm of tattoos...

She shook her head, clearing the mental image of Aiden's ink before it could take her dangerous places.

"Maybe this one..." she said, pulling on the hem of a black dress and immediately dismissing the idea. "No, that won't work."

"Kenzie," Aiden said, tone belying his exasperation, "I do not give a fuck what you wear. You'll be hot in anything. Throw something on, put on some perfume, and let's go. I'll be there in fifteen minutes."

Kenzie's face blanched. "I'm sorry, did you say *fifteen*?"

Aiden snorted at her panicked tone. "Yep. Where do you live again?"

"Above HopCat."

"Tick-tock, bunny," he said, then hung up.

"Fuck," Kenzie said to her empty apartment.

She finally settled on an emerald-green dress made of a silky material so thin she could've easily scrunched it up and stuffed it into a clutch the size of her hand. She paired it with some strappy nude stilettos and delicate gold jewelry, then quickly sprayed some dry shampoo on her roots and swept her heavy locks to the side with some bobby pins the same dark brown as her hair.

Fourteen and a half minutes later, as she put a final coat of bronzer on her cheeks, Aiden texted that he had arrived.

Kenzie straightened in front of the full-length mirror hanging on her bedroom wall, turning this way and that to survey her appearance. Satisfied, she quickly shoved her ID, key, powder, and lipstick into a clutch and rushed downstairs.

Aiden had parked illegally in front of her building, and an East Lansing public safety officer parked right behind him. The two men stood near Aiden's back bumper, apparently shooting the shit. Kenzie was hit by the sudden force of déjà vu, remembering Brent in this exact same position the day she'd moved into the building.

And that was an image she absolutely didn't need right now. Comparing Aiden to her brother wouldn't end well for anyone; the two men were *not* the same.

Kenzie made her way toward him, waiting for Aiden to look up and catch her gaze. When he did, she could've laughed at his expression.

"I'm sorry," he said to the officer, extending a hand and drawing the guy in for a bro hug like they were old friends. "I won't park here next time I pick my girl up."

"No problem, man," the officer said, glancing over his shoulder at Kenzie. "It's all good."

Aiden winked at him, then stepped toward Kenzie and pulled her in for a hug, sliding his hands along the exposed skin of her back.

Kenzie stiffened under his unexpected touch, and Aiden said, "Sorry, bunny. We've gotta make it look good for that guy."

Kenzie nodded and leaned closer, slipping her fingers into the waves at the base of his skull and pressing a kiss to his cheek. She pulled away as quickly as she'd come to him and brushed her thumb over the lipstick she'd left on his skin.

Aiden cleared his throat and said, "You're beautiful."

"Thank you," she replied, a blush creeping into her cheeks. "Can we go now?"

"Oh, sure," he said, moving around her to open the passenger door of his Jeep. She climbed in, the hem of her dress clutched tightly in her hand.

Once safely ensconced in the car, they began the slow crawl through East Lansing traffic to get to the interstate connection that would take them south to Holt. It was a short trip to the suburb—only about ten miles—but it was a Friday night. Football was home the next day, taking on their first conference opponent, and the summer heat still clung to the city, the hot days giving way to comfortable nights, where the college girls could go out in their short skirts and crop tops and not freeze to death. As Aiden maneuvered the car out of the city, Kenzie studied the crush of bodies outside Dublin, then Harper's and Rick's, as they passed. It was barely five-thirty, and East Lansing nightlife was in full swing.

"So, bunny," Aiden said as he turned onto Grand River. "Tell me about yourself."

"What do you want to know?"

"Where are you from?"

"New York," she said. "Near Albany."

"I should've known that," Aiden said. "Your brother is basically a god inside the walls of Munn."

Kenzie snorted. "Don't let him hear you say that. The last thing Brent needs is any more inflation to his ego."

"I'm sensing some animosity here."

Kenzie sighed heavily. "He's my big brother. And there's eight years between us. He has a habit of acting more like my dad than my sibling, and it really gets on my nerves."

Aiden didn't respond, and the silence was uncomfortable enough that Kenzie kept speaking. "He saw that picture of us on The Green and told me in no uncertain terms that I needed to stay away from you."

"And that's how you ended up telling him you're going on a date with me, right? You're only doing this to piss him off?"

Something about being in Aiden's presence brought out things in her that she'd sooner keep hidden, had her wanting to spill all her secrets. It would be so easy to tell him that she was on a mission of self-discovery, and she couldn't accomplish her objectives alone.

But as she'd told Aiden earlier, this was a one-time thing, so it didn't make sense to dump all her drama on him. For now, he was simply her unwitting accomplice.

"I'm doing this because you need my help, and I'm a charitable girl. Pissing my brother off is just an added bonus."

"Charitable?" Aiden said with a snort. "Not exactly the word I'd use."

Ignoring him, she turned her attention inward as she finally, *fully* confronted this mess she'd landed in.

Kenzie had dropped out of college when she was twenty. Living in New York, and being so far away from her brother and their business, basically forcing him to run everything while also maintaining an incredibly busy career, had stopped making sense. And once she'd gotten that bug in her ear, there was nothing that could've stopped her.

At the time, she hadn't thought there was anything college could teach that she couldn't learn from Brent and real world experience.

The first year was great. But she'd quickly realized there were some things she could still learn in school.

In particular, she needed to learn how to have fun again.

New York City wasn't exactly a college town, and she'd never really been able to do the quintessential college thing there. She'd loved NYU, mostly because she'd only been a few hours away from her parents. But it hadn't been what she'd pictured when she imagined her college experience.

As cheesy as it sounded, Kenzie wanted to go out to the bars with friends, have all-night study sessions, and binge junk food during movie marathons. She wanted to go to football, basketball, and hockey games. And maybe she wanted to go on fall-themed dates, and have someone to hold hands with as they strolled through campus, and post cute coupley photos on Instagram.

The better part of the last two years had been spent being anything but a young, early-twenties girl.

Aiden glanced at her quickly, then returned his gaze to the road, suddenly breaking the heavy silence in the Jeep.

"I'm not a bad guy," he said quietly. "These dares my teammates and I do…they're dumb, but we're not hurting anyone. And, usually, we're not hurting ourselves. This last one…it was incredibly stupid, and I tried to get out of it, but the punishment for saying no is usually far worse than the dare itself. I wouldn't know because no one in my entire four years here has ever turned one down, but your brother probably knows someone who did."

Kenzie had heard her brother mention in passing the shit he got up to with his college teammates, but she wasn't aware of specifics. When Brent was in college, Kenzie had been young, barely a teenager; she'd had her own drama to worry about.

"He's mentioned it, but I try not to stick my nose in his business," she said. "I wish he'd extend me the same courtesy."

"I have a little sister," Aiden said suddenly, and Kenzie turned to him, surprised. "She's only twelve. So…I can understand where Brent is coming from. Being a big brother is an important job, and if my sister grows up to be anything like you…like I said, I understand."

Kenzie fell silent, face heating with Aiden's words. She knew her brother loved her, and everything he did where she was concerned was born of that love. Sometimes, she simply wished he would let her live her life, make her own mistakes, and suffer the consequences of her actions without breathing down her neck, trying to direct her every move.

"I know he means well," she said finally. "But he's not my dad, and I wish he wouldn't act like it."

"I don't think that's too much to ask," Aiden said. "You seem to be doing pretty well for yourself. You're the co-owner of a successful activewear brand, and you're going back to school to finish your degree. Most girls in your position would coast on Brent's success and money."

"My brothers are driven and successful. They've both worked their asses off for everything they have. I could never take advantage of either of them like that. And anyway, I'm leaving FLEX."

It was the first time she'd said the words aloud to anyone besides Dr. Mathews, and her shoulders felt lighter.

Aiden appeared stunned. "We'll revisit that," he said. "Your other brother is Nate, right?"

Kenzie nodded, looking out the window as the trees lining the freeway rushed by. "He's currently in residency at Michigan to become an orthopedic surgeon."

Aiden let out a low whistle. "A professional athlete and a doctor?

No wonder you feel like the black sheep."

Kenzie's face reddened with embarrassment. "Yeah."

She felt more than saw Aiden glance at her. "Sorry," he said quietly. "Sore subject. I understand. Tell me why you're leaving FLEX."

"My gut is telling me it's the right move. I feel...stifled, creatively and socially. Owning a company is hard work, and I'm just not enjoying it anymore. But I've always loved the marketing and advertising side of running FLEX, so coming back to school to major in both while I figure my shit out made sense."

"Couldn't you just stay with FLEX and do only the marketing and advertising stuff? Relinquish your ownership rights?"

"I mean, yes, I could. But I don't want to."

"Why?"

"It's like you said earlier. Most girls would coast on their famous sibling's success, but I can't do that. My brothers are stupid smart and crazy successful. I don't think it's too much to ask that I find *my* thing. My hockey. My medicine."

"So what do you want to do instead?"

"My sister-in-law's best friend is a successful influencer, and I'm fascinated by it. I keep thinking maybe it's something I might like to get into."

Becoming an influencer was something Kenzie had only recently begun to consider. One thing FLEX had taught her was that she loved being her own boss, but she also wasn't great at managing people. So she'd been thinking about ways she could work for herself.

"I think you'd be amazing at that," Aiden said earnestly, shooting a grin her way.

The conversation suddenly had Kenzie wanting to turn the attention away from herself, to peel back some of Aiden's layers.

"Let's say hockey wasn't an option anymore," Kenzie said suddenly, smiling when Aiden's thick brows scrunched in confusion. "What would your dream job be after college?"

"Hockey will always be an option," Aiden said through gritted teeth, and Kenzie knew from experience that this was a sore spot for most top-tier athletes.

"You met Mitch last week, didn't you?"

"I did..."

"He thought he'd be playing into his forties," Kenzie told him. "Instead, he took one bad hit, broke his back, and now he's tasked with flying around the country scouting cocky assholes like you."

Aiden's face blanched, his knuckles going white as he gripped the steering wheel tighter. Kenzie sat still, silent, waiting for him to reply.

"I'd like to be an on-air personality for one of the major networks," he said, at last answering her question. "Or even call games. Like Doc Emerick."

Kenzie was surprised. Most of the hockey players she knew, especially ones at the professional level, like her brother and his teammates, had majored in something practical—or never finished their degrees at all. It seemed rare to find someone who wanted to be a journalist of sorts, but she supposed nobody was better suited to comment on the sport of hockey than someone who had dedicated so much of their life to it.

"I think you'd be amazing at that, Fuller." I smiled as I parroted his words back at him.

"You think so?" he asked, turning a breathtaking grin on her.

She couldn't help once again fucking with him. "But maybe stick to radio. You've certainly got the face for it."

Aiden growled low in his throat, and Kenzie laughed. A moment later, he pulled up alongside the curb on a quiet suburban street lined with cars, putting his Jeep in park and turning the key, the tick of the engine as it cooled filling the quiet between them.

"It's cute how you're pretending you wouldn't do unspeakable things to me if given the chance," Aiden said finally, breaking the silence, his voice low and dangerous.

Kenzie shivered. "I'd definitely do something to you," she muttered.

"Careful what you wish for, bunny."

And Kenzie would be damned if the words didn't feel like a caress, igniting every nerve on the surface of her skin like a live wire. Even that damned nickname was growing on her.

She swallowed hard and looked away, gesturing at the house up the street where the dinner was taking place. "Shall we?"

"We shall," Aiden replied, then jumped out of the car and came around to her side to open the door before she could even unbuckle her seatbelt.

"So what should I expect from this thing?" she asked. Aiden reached for her hand and laced his fingers with hers, beginning a casual stroll up the sidewalk like this was an everyday occurrence for him.

Kenzie, meanwhile, had to surreptitiously take steadying breaths and will her skin not to sweat against his.

"My teammates will be here," he said. "But it's also an alumni dinner. A way for guys from the past to come back and schmooze with donors. Give the old fucks with money a reason to donate."

Kenzie choked on a laugh and said, "Don't let them hear you call them 'old fucks.' They pay for your equipment, and travel, and literally every brick of that arena you call home."

"I wouldn't dream of it," he said with a cheeky grin as he tugged her down a path around the side of the house. Rounding a corner, an expansive backyard opened in front of them, where two large white tents were set up and over a hundred people mingled on the lawn.

Kenzie's gaze swept the crowd, eventually meeting a pair of blue eyes that mirrored her own.

"Oh fuck."

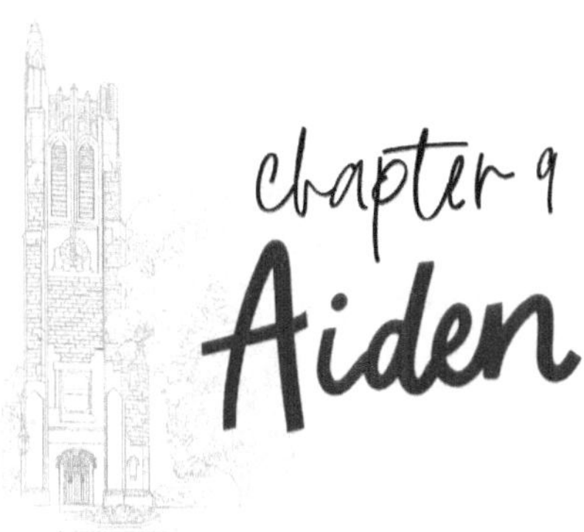

chapter 9
Aiden

"OH FUCK," AIDEN SAID when he laid eyes on Brent Jean, who glared daggers at him and his baby sister from across the lawn, a pretty and petite blonde woman standing arm-in-arm with him.

"You took the words right out of my mouth," Kenzie said, then heaved a massive, world-weary sigh. "*Alumni* dinner, Fuller. Why did neither of us consider that my brother, arguably the most famous alumni this place has, would be here?"

"I truly don't know," he said. "I know things between you two are tense right now, but please, just...don't cause a scene. I can't afford that right now."

Hurt flashed in Kenzie's eyes, and Aiden nearly apologized. But he was in deep enough shit as it was; the last thing he needed was his girlfriend-for-the-night getting into an argument with her brother—her *super famous, very recognizable* brother—in front of people who potentially controlled Aiden's destiny. His only focus right now was getting back on the ice.

"I promise I'll be on my best behavior," she snapped, then grabbed a flute of champagne from a passing waiter, downed it in one gulp, and returned it to the tray before the waiter could fully move away.

"Okay," he said. "I'm sorry, but I have a lot on the line here."

Kenzie sighed and reached down to thread her fingers through his. "I know," she said. "Let's get a drink and you can introduce me to your teammates."

Aiden grinned and let Kenzie tow him across the grass, over to a bar that had been set up along the fence separating this yard from the next. Aiden ordered a beer, while Kenzie ordered a vodka soda.

"Mackenzie," a voice at their backs said, and Aiden stiffened. He'd heard that voice in interviews more times than he could count.

"Brent," Kenzie said when she turned to face her brother.

"Fancy seeing you here." Brent Jean turned that steely blue gaze on Aiden, which would have been unsettling enough on its own had his eyes not matched the exact shape and shade as his sister's. "You must be Aiden Fuller," Brent said, extending a hand. "Brent Jean."

Aiden shook it, refusing to wince when Brent attempted to crush his fingers like they were in a vise grip.

"I know who you are," Aiden said. "Great to meet you. Kenzie's told me so much about you."

Brent raised a skeptical brow at his sister, voice flat when he said, "Has she now."

Kenzie reached up and patted him on the cheek. "Only good things, big brother."

"I'm sure," he said drily.

A moment later, the small blonde woman Aiden had seen Brent with earlier joined their little powwow.

This must be Berkley, Aiden thought.

Damn, she was stunning—which wasn't surprising considering how good looking her husband was.

"Babe, have you tried these?" Berkley said, holding up a handful of puff pastries that appeared to be filled with cheese and topped with jam. "They're incredible."

"I haven't," Brent said, then leaned forward with his mouth open so Berkley could pop one in. "Oh, damn, those are good."

Berkley smirked. "Told you." Then she turned to Kenzie and pulled her into her side. "Hey little sis."

"Hey, Berk," Kenzie said, the tension in her face dissipating as she looked down at her sister-in-law. "How's my niece or nephew?"

Berkley patted her belly and said, "Good. Sucking the life from me, and I'm barely out of my first trimester. I'm not sure how I'm going to keep up with school."

Brent snaked an arm across her shoulders. "We'll figure it out."

Aiden stood, staring down at the tiny blonde who apparently carried the next Jean heir.

Kenzie glanced up at him, as if suddenly remembering he was there. "Oh gosh, sorry, Fuller. Berkley is, as I'm sure you've guessed, my brother's wife. And is currently pregnant with his spawn."

"Don't call him that," Brent growled.

"You don't even know if it is a *he*," Kenzie said. "You could end up with a little girl just like your wife. Or worse, your baby sister."

"Oh, Kenz," Berkley said, reaching up to place a hand on Kenzie's cheek. "That wouldn't be worse. If we have a little girl who's anything like you, I'll consider us very lucky."

"If only my brother felt the same," Kenzie said quietly, so low only Aiden heart her, turning away from them and grabbing his arm. Aiden's eyes met Brent's, which were narrowed in displeasure.

"This conversation isn't over, Mackenzie," Brent said quietly.

Kenzie looked at her brother over her shoulder. "What conversation?" she asked sweetly, then pulled Aiden away.

"Your brother *really* doesn't like me," he said.

"I think it has less to do with you and more to do with me ignoring a direct order from King Brent," she said, voice laced with venom. "He can never just let me live my life. Everything I do, he's gotta go all overprotective-big-brother on me, like I'm not perfectly capable of making my own choices. It's exhausting."

"I told you in the car," Aiden said, "and I'll say it again: he loves you, and he only wants you to be safe and happy."

Kenzie's shoulders drooped, and she glanced up at him through the thick fringe of her eyelashes. "I know," she said with a sigh. "I just wish he'd trust me more is all."

Aiden trailed his fingers down her arm and laced his fingers with hers, giving her hand a squeeze. "I get it. But look, we're here at this fancy pants party with free booze and good food, so what do you say we snag something to eat and go sit with my teammates?"

"Deal," Kenzie said, giving him a grin that Aiden would kill to see on her face all the time.

Dazed by that blinding smile, Aiden followed her to the buffet table and filled a plate, mindful of his meal plan. Kenzie, meanwhile, loaded up on finger foods and sweets.

"Sweet tooth?" he asked her.

"I love chocolate," she said, gesturing to the plate in her left hand that was loaded with mini eclairs.

"Duly noted," Aiden said.

"Well well well," Jack said when they approached. "If it isn't Fuller's runaway puck bunny. I'm surprised he got you to go out with him."

Kenzie placed her hand on Aiden's chest, right over his heart, which picked up speed under her touch. "How could I resist this face?" she said. "And I'm sure you guys realize by now that I'm not a puck bunny, right?"

"Sure do," Jack replied.

"Then will you stop calling me that?"

Jack paused a beat, as though considering, before happily saying, "Nope."

Kenzie groaned. "You know my brother is here, right? One word and he'd rough you up."

Jack turned to Aiden, an eyebrow quirked. "Meeting the fam already? You move fast."

Aiden heaved a world-weary sigh and ignored them.

His teammates burst out laughing at his expression, drawing stares from people nearby. Aiden shushed them and sat down, pulling out the chair next to him for Kenzie.

"You know," he said quietly against her ear, "if the nickname bugs you that much, I can tell them to knock it off."

Kenzie shook her head. "I appreciate the thought, Fuller, but honestly? It's kind of growing on me. Makes me feel like part of some secret club. I like the irony of it. Plus, bunnies are cute, right?"

"You are a lot more than *cute*, Mackenzie Jean."

Kenzie's cheeks deepened to a glowing pink, and Aiden grinned in response, wondering what else he could say to keep that color in her face. He was growing addicted to that blush.

As his teammates turned their attention to Kenzie, Aiden dropped his to his food.

Unsurprisingly, Kenzie ate that shit up.

Aiden knew she would be an asset on a night like tonight. Her brother was living proof that she had spent plenty of time around important people in fancy, professional-type settings. But witnessing her charm his boys was impressive. With him, Kenzie was sassy and stubborn and sarcastic. With his boys, she was sweet and effervescent and almost...soft. It was an entirely new side of her, and Aiden had to admit, he enjoyed discovering this new facet.

He finished eating before she did, and sat back in his chair while she continued to pick at her own food, chatting with Jack, Asher, Luke, and a few of the freshmen who had wandered over.

Absently, Aiden lifted his hand and toyed with the ends of Kenzie's hair where they brushed her spine. Briefly, she stiffened, but settled into the touch quickly.

"You okay here?" he asked eventually. His leg bounced, nerves thrumming.

"Yeah," she said, peeling her eyes away from Asher, who was animatedly telling a story about one of their many dares gone awry. "Where are you going?"

"I want to mingle. You know, image rehab and all that," he said, standing and shrugging off his suit jacket and hanging it on the back of Kenzie's chair. He'd had enough of playing the buttoned-up hockey player. The sweat trapped on his back and arms by the heavy material of his jacket made his skin crawl, and he needed to breathe.

Slowly, he rolled the sleeves of his button down up to his elbows, not missing the way Kenzie's eyes widened and sparked with heat as they settled on the corded muscles of his forearms. First, he revealed the golden, unmarred expanse of skin on his right, then the swirls of ink on his left. Their gazes locked, Kenzie licked her lips, and Aiden smirked, knowing exactly where her mind had gone.

Kenzie smiled shyly, clearing her throat. "Do you want me to come?" she asked, her voice hoarse.

He bent and dropped a chaste kiss on her cheek, that smooth skin against his lips sending a jolt through him, the innocence of it so at odds with his next words. "Maybe later."

A sharp inhale followed, and Aiden backed away with a laugh. "Stay here with the boys, bunny. I can fight my own battles."

"If you're sure," she said roughly.

"I'm sure. I'll find you later."

Aiden walked across the lawn, beelining for his coach.

"Fuller!" Coach said loudly. Apparently he'd already hit the free alcohol a little harder than was probably socially acceptable, but Aiden wasn't going to be the one to call him on it.

"Hey, Coach," he said, reaching out to shake his proffered hand.

"You know these guys, right?" Coach said, gesturing to the other men forming their little circle. Coach rattled off the names of a few big donors, people Aiden did in fact recognize. He thanked them all in turn.

"And of course you know Jean," Coach said finally, pointing the neck of his beer bottle in Brent's direction.

Aiden turned slowly and met Brent's chilly gaze, reminiscent of

Lake Michigan on frigid February days, when white caps dotted its surface, sending cold winds blowing through the Windy City.

"I do," Aiden said, shaking Brent's hand for the second time that evening.

"He does," Brent responded. "In fact, my little sister is his date tonight."

Aiden checked his urge to wince, instead glancing at Coach for his reaction. The man's eyes comically bugged out of his head. He opened his mouth to respond, seemed to think better of it, and instead took a giant slug of his beer before he said, "Cute kid."

Several of the other men chuckled, and Brent looked murderous. "She's definitely something," he said through clenched teeth.

"I can't believe you didn't tell me you were dating Jean's little sister," Coach said to Aiden, punching him softly on the shoulder.

Aiden shrugged, eyes locking with Brent's again. "We're not really *dating*," he said. "This is actually our first date."

Looking irate, Brent opened his mouth to say something, but one of Aiden's former teammates—a guy named Simmons who had been a senior when Aiden was a freshman—called his name from across the grass, and Aiden gratefully exited the uncomfortable situation.

The next few hours passed in much the same way, with Aiden making his way around the party, interacting with old teammates and new, donors he recognized and ones he didn't. All the while, he was acutely aware of the positions of the two Jean siblings, mentally bracing himself for the moment when they'd openly clash and this entire facade he and Kenzie had crafted would go up in smoke.

Only...it never happened. Brent and Kenzie avoided each other all night, though Aiden *did* notice Berkley flitting back and forth between the two like a tiny blonde messenger. Aiden was grateful, at least, that Kenzie had heeded his warning about not making a scene.

Aiden stood in the corner of one of the tents, bullshitting with Jack, Luke, and Asher. Without a word, Kenzie, who had been standing on the fringes of their group tapping away on her phone, backed away, retreated across the yard, and walked inside the house.

Moments later, her brother followed.

"I'll be right back," Aiden told his teammates, then took off after them.

The second he walked inside, he heard raised voices.

"What the fuck are you doing here?" Brent hissed.

"I was invited by my boyfriend," Kenzie responded.

Brent let out a derisive snort. "That little shit is not your boyfriend."

"Yes he is."

Brent was right; Aiden was *not* Kenzie's boyfriend, but he couldn't begrudge her the chance to piss her brother off a bit, not after the way he'd reacted to seeing them together. It was the prerogative of younger siblings to antagonize their older counterparts. Aiden was used to the same treatment from his little sister, Eloise.

However, when the time came for her to start dating, or when boys started noticing her, Aiden liked to think he wouldn't treat Eloise the way Brent was treating Kenzie, but he couldn't be sure. What he *did* know was he hadn't liked the way Brent had looked at him, like he'd be better served as scum on the bottom of Kenzie's shoe than someone worthy of being on her arm.

Aiden tiptoed forward and peeked around an archway, finding

Brent and Kenzie standing in the middle of what appeared to be a well-appointed study, the walls lined with walnut shelves filled with heavy, leather-bound tomes.

Kenzie's arms crossed defensively over her chest, a stance Aiden had seen her take on countless occasions in the short time they'd known each other. Her brother mirrored her.

"I told you to stay away from him," Brent said. "What about that didn't you understand?"

"The part where you thought you could tell me what to do," she said. Her ocean blue eyes narrowed, her mouth set in a firm line, and Aiden decided the expression was sexy as hell when it wasn't turned on him.

"Kenzie..." Brent trailed off, the two syllables of her name dripping with exasperation. "I only want what's best for you." He reached out and settled a hand on her shoulder in a placating, fatherly gesture.

Kenzie shrugged him off. "You don't even know what that is!" she yelled, and Aiden was thankful they'd waited until they were away from prying eyes to hash this out. "*I* don't even know what that is! I'm only twenty-three, Brent. Can't you just...let me live my life without trying to micromanage everything? Did you treat Nate like this when he was my age?"

"When Nate was your age, he was fucking his way through his final year of undergrad and preparing to do the same in med school."

"What if *I* want to do the same?"

I volunteer as tribute, Aiden thought.

"That's not the kind of girl you are."

"You don't know what kind of girl I actually am, Bee. When

you look at me, all you see is the awkward, freckle-faced preteen who followed you and Nate around like a puppy dog. I worshiped you both. My big brothers, these insanely smart, talented, larger-than-life men. And now...I'm not that little girl anymore. You have to let me make my own decisions and mistakes, free from judgement. Your job as my brother is to support me and love me. No more and no less. That's all I'm asking."

Brent was silent for several long, tense moments, carding his fingers through his hair—one of Aiden's own nervous ticks.

Finally, he reached out and hauled Kenzie in for a hug, saying into her hair, "I don't like that Fuller kid."

Kenzie curled her lips between her teeth, clearly biting back a grin. "You don't have to. I doubt he'll last long."

A pang of hurt lanced Aiden's chest. This thing between them *wasn't* real, and Kenzie was right, it *wouldn't* last long. But that didn't make it any easier to hear. In that moment, he felt...disposable.

He didn't like it.

The siblings hugged it out, and Aiden turned away, sprinting outside before they discovered him eavesdropping.

As Aiden set foot on the lawn, Berkley met him on the path and asked, "Where's my husband?"

Aiden hooked a thumb over his shoulder as Kenzie and Brent exited the house. Kenzie's face lit up when she saw him, and she hurried over, gripping his hand in hers and towing him away from her brother and sister-in-law.

"You were gone a long time," Aiden said conversationally, wondering if Kenzie would share any of her conversation with Brent.

"I got lost," she said simply, and Aiden's heart sank. He didn't expect her to always be honest with him given the precarious nature of their relationship, but he didn't appreciate the outright lie, either.

When they rejoined his teammates, Jack, who was well on his way to a blackout, pointed a finger at Kenzie and said, "Bunny, we're having a house party tonight and you're coming."

"What if I don't want to?"

Jack shrugged. "I don't care what you want."

"Jack..." Aiden warned.

Jack raised his hands in surrender. "Okay, okay, I'm sorry. How about this..."

Too late, Aiden saw the gleam in Jack's eyes and realized what he was going to say next.

"Fuller, I dare you to bring Kenzie to the party tonight."

Son of a bitch.

Aiden turned to Kenzie, fully expecting her to tell Jack to fuck off and leave.

For reasons still unknown—or perhaps, ones he simply wasn't ready to admit to—he couldn't let that happen. He wanted to stretch this night out like a piece of taffy and savor it.

As he readied to launch his argument for her coming over, Kenzie surprised him by saying, "I'll do it, but only because you assholes will never let me hear the end of it if I don't."

"That's the spirit!" Jack said. "And you're absolutely right. We'd think you were too cool to hang out with us."

"I am too cool to hang out with you," Kenzie deadpanned. "I'm really slumming it here."

His teammates burst into laughter, but Aiden narrowed his gaze. "Are you sure?" he asked her quietly.

"Positive."

His grin unfurled slowly, excitement over keeping this girl by his side a little longer blooming in his chest.

Aiden, Asher, Jack, and Luke had been roommates for the last three years, since they'd been allowed, by university rules, to seek lodging outside of the dorms. They'd found a house on the corner of Charles and Linden, close enough to downtown and campus that they could get there easily, but far enough away that they got some peace and quiet.

The fact that there were four sorority houses within two blocks had absolutely *nothing* to do with signing the lease.

"Do you want to stop at home and change first?" Aiden asked Kenzie as they drove back to East Lansing.

"What's wrong with this?" she asked, frowning down at her dress.

"Absolutely nothing," Aiden assured her. "I just don't want you to be uncomfortable."

"I appreciate the concern," Kenzie said, flipping down the visor and checking her appearance in the mirror, the weak lights casting a warm glow on her skin. "But I'm good."

Aiden tracked her movements from the corner of his eye as she pulled a compact from her clutch, along with a small brush, and dabbed powder onto her cheeks, chin, and forehead. Once she replaced them, she removed a tube of lipstick, uncapped it, puckered her lips, and dabbed on the liquid.

"Don't get all made up on account of the boys," he said. "This isn't like going to the bar, or the party we just left. It's chill."

Kenzie turned to him and blinked slowly. "I know that."

Aiden exited the freeway and pulled up to a light, glancing at Kenzie once the car was stopped. "Don't take this the wrong way, but...have you ever been to a house party?"

"Yes!" she replied, too quickly, then tipped her head down.

"Bunny..."

"Okay, fine. No, I haven't."

Aiden laughed. "How is that even possible? Don't people have houses in New York?"

"Of course they do," she said. "Just not anyone I was friends with. Our apartments were basically shoeboxes, so we preferred to go out to the clubs."

Moments later, he pulled into his driveway and killed the engine, waiting for Kenzie's reaction. It wasn't a top floor condo that overlooked the entire campus, but...it was home.

The house itself was a two-story Craftsman, painted custard yellow with white trim and a massive front porch. The open-concept main level included the kitchen, dining, and living room, along with a half bath. The master bedroom with its en suite was situated off the kitchen. Upstairs were three more bedrooms and another full bath.

They had drawn straws for who got the master, and Aiden had ended up winning. He had come to look at it as both a blessing and a curse. A blessing, because he had his own bathroom, plus enough room for a desk, his large flat screen TV, and a small weight setup. A curse, because after they'd first moved in, he kept finding couples hooking up in his bed when parties got too rowdy. After one too many times of walking in on half-naked people, he'd smartened up and put a lock on the door, keeping the key on a chain around his neck.

"This is not what I was expecting," Kenzie said finally.

"And what exactly were you expecting?"

"I'm not really sure. Certainly not something that looks so...normal."

Aiden snorted and opened his door. "I'll take that as a compliment. C'mon, let me show you around."

He shuffled across the lawn and onto the porch, then shoved the heavy oak door open and shouted, "Honeys, I'm home!"

"Back here, shithead!" Asher yelled, and Aiden followed the sound of heavy bass thumping from the general direction of the kitchen. When he and Kenzie stepped through the wide entrance, he found all three of his roommates gathered around the worn, round dining table, methodically pouring bottles of liquor and Sprite into a plastic tub already half-filled with liquid colored a dubious shade of orange, pieces of fruit bobbing on the surface.

Kenzie leaned closer and wrinkled her nose. "What the hell is that?"

"Jungle juice!" Jack said, dumping more watermelon chunks into the mix.

A moment later, Sofia appeared in the kitchen, and said, "I tried to talk him out of it, but he wouldn't listen."

"Sofia!" Kenzie said. "I didn't know you'd be here!"

Sofia smiled and pulled Kenzie into a brief but warm hug.

"I live right up the block," she said. "I'm always here for hockey house parties unless I have a sorority conflict!"

Jack interrupted by asking, "Will you grab the peach vodka from the freezer?"

Sofia did as she was asked, and Kenzie turned to Jack, saying, "I will not be drinking that."

Next to her, Aiden laughed and said, "Don't worry, you don't have to. If you want, you can put your bag in my room. I'm going to change out of this suit."

Kenzie nodded and followed him around the corner, then down a short hall to his bedroom. He stepped inside, shrugging out of his suit jacket and peeling off his button-up—which clung to his skin courtesy of the high temps—and tossing it in the direction of his hamper. Then he toed off his shoes, kicked them into his closet, and undid his belt and zipper before dropping his pants to the floor.

"You do know I'm still here, right?"

Aiden whirled on Kenzie, having indeed forgotten for the moment that she was with him. Clad only in his boxers, he resisted the urge to cover his body. Entering his room and immediately undressing after a function or game was so deeply ingrained in him that somehow, not even Kenzie's presence had pulled him from the routine.

He wasn't ashamed or embarrassed of himself. As a college athlete, he was in ridiculously good shape. But he never wanted Kenzie to feel uncomfortable around him; he enjoyed her company too much for that. So he spun back to his dresser, grabbed a t-shirt and a pair of khaki shorts, and rushed into the bathroom to get dressed.

"Sorry!" he yelled once he was behind the closed door. "I hate wearing suits, and I was sweating my ass off tonight."

"You hate wearing suits?" she asked, tone shocked.

"I really do," he said a moment later when he came out of the bathroom fully clothed. Kenzie stood near his desk, heels dangling from the fingertips of her right hand, clutch in her left. Aiden reached over her shoulder to the hooks on the wall and snagged one of his Spartan hockey baseball caps, settling it backwards atop the blue-black waves of his hair.

"That's...ridiculous."

"And why is that?"

"I thought all hockey players loved them. Girls everywhere are obsessed with you all in suits."

"I do look pretty fucking hot in a suit, bunny; you're right about that. Doesn't mean I like wearing them."

"Fuller!" Luke hollered from the kitchen. "Get your ass out here! Bunny, you too!"

"I'm never getting rid of that nickname, am I?" Kenzie asked, sounding resigned.

"Nope," Aiden said, grinning down at her. "You can leave your stuff here. I lock the door during parties, so nobody is going to steal it or anything."

"Paranoid much?" she asked, one corner of her mouth tipping up into a smirk.

"More like I've walked in here at the end of the night to find people fucking in my bed way too many times."

Kenzie's face blanched, but she nodded. "Makes sense."

Aiden nodded and extended his hand. "Shall we?"

She laced her fingers through his. "We shall."

Less than an hour later, the house and backyard were packed wall-to-wall with bodies.

Aiden and Kenzie were in the living room, sunk side-by-side into the low couch while Jack held court, regaling the room with one of his own dare stories.

"And that's how I found myself missing both of my eyebrows two days before roster pictures. I had to ask one of the sorority girls to come draw them on for me."

The entire room burst out laughing, cheers floating to the ceiling as they toasted Jack's fearlessness.

"Speaking of dares," Jack said, gaze zeroing in on Kenzie and Aiden. "I think it's time we initiate Kenzie into the club."

"Jack, no," Aiden said firmly, though his words were swallowed up by shouts of affirmation from various teammates.

Louder, he said, "Girlfriends are supposed to be exempt from this bullshit!"

As previously stated, Kenzie wasn't his girlfriend. But Aiden was willing to fudge the truth a little if it meant sparing Kenzie from whatever Jack was cooking up.

Jack's grin turned wicked. "Under normal circumstances, you're absolutely right. But you're a mostly dare-free zone for the season. Which means your girl has to step up to the plate."

Aiden turned to Kenzie, who met his gaze with wide eyes. Her pulse tripped in her neck. Without looking away from him, she said to Jack, "What's the dare?"

"I'm glad you asked."

"Kenzie, you don't have to do this—"

"—we'll give you an easy one," Jack was saying.

"—we can leave right now and forget this whole thing," Aiden told her.

"I want you to kiss your boy in front of everyone."

Both of them turned to Jack at the same time, and said in unison, "What?"

Aiden had not been expecting that. He remembered that innocent brush he'd given her at the bar the night they met, the appetizer to a main course he desperately wanted to devour. But as badly as he wanted to kiss the lipstick right off of her, getting physical hadn't been part of the deal. Plus, he wouldn't subject her to the whims of his sadistic teammates.

Kenzie pushed herself up and scooted to the edge of the couch, her shoulders rising and falling as she deeply inhaled and exhaled before standing. Then, much to Aiden's surprise, she turned to him and reached for his hand.

Her fingers shook against his as she pulled him to his feet.

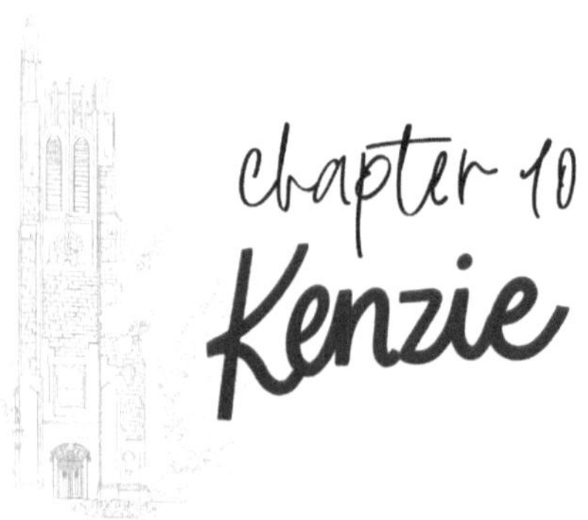

chapter 10
Kenzie

WITH A CONFIDENCE SHE didn't feel, Kenzie held her hand out to Aiden.

This was what she'd wanted, right? Experiences like this were why she'd come back to college, and why she'd approached Aiden with this crazy ass plan. If those experiences included being dared to kiss this smoking hot hockey player in front of a room of people...so be it.

Before the episode that had taken her out of commission her senior year, she'd always been a flirt. Some girls grew up sheltered and innocent under the watchful eyes of their older brothers.

Not her.

She'd always been...adventurous. She'd lost her virginity at sixteen and, while she'd certainly been more reserved in recent years, that flirty, confident girl still lived somewhere inside her. Being near Aiden had that version of herself slowly undoing the locks and chains on the cage in which she'd barricaded herself.

Aiden slipped his hand into hers as she attempted to pull him to a standing position—though his quads did the bulk of the work. Standing this close, he towered over her, his oversized frame making her average one seem petite in comparison.

When they were toe to toe in the center of the room, Aiden pulled her close with a tug on her wrist and settled his hands low on her hips, his long fingers curving around and brushing that spot where her back met her ass.

He leaned down, pressed his mouth against her ear, and said, "We don't have to do this. I can walk you home right now. We can even stop and get ice cream on the way."

Kenzie pulled back to look at him, momentarily losing herself in the depths of his molten-chocolate eyes. She reached up to brush her fingertips along his sharp jaw, the stubble there scratching her skin. "It's okay, Fuller," she said quietly. "I want to."

"You two have kissed before, haven't you?" Jack asked, breaking the spell they'd been wrapped in.

Aiden's stricken expression surely mirrored her own, and he shook his head once, twice. Obviously, that teasing contact the night they'd met didn't count.

Jack cackled. "Even better!" he said. "What better time than now?"

Kenzie's eyes darted around the room, noticing for the first time all of the cameras pointed in their direction. "Fuck," she breathed, anxiety rising. "We're going to end up on The Green again."

This was surely a terrible idea, and it would take Kenzie days to list all the reasons why. Reflexively, she dug her fingertips into Aiden's biceps, attempting to both anchor herself and quell the shaking in her hands in equal measure.

Aiden's head shot up, eyes sweeping the crowd. Then he said, "DeLuca, you know the rules," gesturing to all the phones.

"Ahh, yes, thank you for reminding me." Jack ran into the kitchen and came back with a wicker basket Kenzie had seen holding various fruits earlier. "Ladies and gentlemen, all phones into the basket, please! Dares are a phone-free zone."

A collective groan rose to the ceiling, but the group complied, dropping their devices into the basket as Jack made his way around.

"Are you sure about this?" Aiden asked quietly.

Kenzie took a deep breath, the tips of her breasts brushing Aiden's chest. A jolt of heat shot straight between her legs. God, it had been an embarrassingly long time since she'd been this close to a guy.

Finally, she whispered, "Yes."

Aiden nodded, and Kenzie swallowed around the lump in her throat, a ball of anxiety remaining tangled in her chest. It spread down her arms to her fingers, which trembled as she slid them to Aiden's shoulders.

When Aiden raised his hand to tuck a lock of hair behind her ear, she noticed his fingers also shook. Some of her nerves eased. He gave her a small, wobbly smile, and said, "It'll be over before you know it."

And then, he pressed his mouth to hers.

In a room full of people, Kenzie should've been uncomfortable with the PDA. Only, the moment Aiden's lips met hers, all other thoughts fled her mind.

His full mouth was soft, softer than she'd imagined—and she *had* imagined it. He was tentative at first, but when she reached up to brush her fingers through his hair, accidentally knocking the hat from his head, all restraint seemed to go out the window. One moment the kiss was soft and sweet, and the next he was opening up for her, running his tongue along the seam of her mouth, then thrusting it inside when she gasped at the sensation.

It had been too damn long since she'd been kissed, and his strong hands on her waist seemed to be the only thing keeping her on her feet. When he moved one up to tilt her chin back with his thumb, tangling those long fingers in her hair, he came to her from a new angle, kissing her harder, their breaths shortening.

Kenzie was moments away from ripping his clothes off right there when he pulled away, eyes nearly black with desire. A cheer went up from the crowd.

"Not bad for the first time!" one of his teammates yelled, and Kenzie blinked rapidly, clearing the haze Aiden's kiss had painted around her.

"Shut up, Luke," Aiden growled, and the crowd laughed.

Kenzie raised a hand to her mouth, which felt swollen and bruised.

"Are you okay?" Aiden asked, curling his hands around her upper arms, much like he'd done that day outside the cafeteria when she'd been trying to get away from him.

Now...now she desperately wanted to get him alone, to get closer and closer until no space remained between them.

"I'm fine," she said, her voice hoarse. "Can we go now?"

"Yes," Aiden said without hesitation, trailing a hand down to hers and tugging her from the living room, through the kitchen, and to his bedroom. True to his word, he removed a key from a chain around his neck and unlocked the door, then pulled her in and closed the door behind them.

Once it was closed, he leaned back against it, loosing a sigh.

Kenzie moved away from him and sat down hard on his bed, bass from the music and voices from the partygoers drifting in from the backyard. Aiden's eyes popped open when the springs squeaked, and he straightened but stayed where he was.

"I'm so sorry, Kenzie," he said quietly.

Kenzie huffed out a laugh. "It's okay, Aiden. Seriously."

"Are you sure?"

"Positive. Kissing you...wasn't exactly a hardship."

A grin spread across his face. "Ditto."

Kenzie stood and walked over to her shoes and bag. "Will you walk me home now?"

"Of course," he said, then gestured to her shoes. "Are you going to wear those, or do you want to borrow a pair of socks or something?"

Kenzie hadn't even considered putting her shoes back on, but she also wasn't keen on walking the few blocks home totally barefoot, so she said, "Socks would be great."

Aiden took two long steps toward his dresser, pulled open a drawer, and tossed her a balled up pair of black socks over his shoulder. She quickly slipped them on, and they exited the room once again, pausing only so Aiden could lock up.

By Friday night in East Lansing standards, it was still relatively early. The clock had struck twelve only a few minutes before, and even two blocks off Grand River, Kenzie didn't miss the sounds of drunken revelers floating on the balmy midnight air.

Aiden stuck close by her side as they traversed the darkened sidewalks along Linden Street before cutting up M.A.C. and joining the crowds shuffling in and out of bars and restaurants along

Albert.

Aiden stayed with her the entire way back to her building. When they came to a stop at the tenant entrance, Kenzie laughed, sure they made quite the pair—her in socks that were clearly not her size, him with his hands shoved into his shorts pockets—but unable to find it within herself to care. Not to mention, her fellow students were too wrapped up in their own drama and enjoyment to pay her and Aiden any attention.

"Well," Aiden said. "I hope you don't hate me too much after tonight."

"I don't hate you." *Not at all*, she added to herself. "But we can't do that again."

"We can't?"

"This," she said, gesturing between them, "isn't real, remember? This date is supposed to be a one-time thing."

Aiden stared at her for several long moments, blinking slowly like an owl. A few times, he opened his mouth, as though he wanted to argue, before ultimately snapping it closed again. Then he said, "Okay, I understand."

He appeared sincere, and Kenzie breathed a sigh of relief. Her explanation was valid, but not the whole picture.

What she didn't say was that she couldn't do it again because she'd enjoyed it too much. Did she want to kiss him again? Absolutely. That kiss was...hot. Hot enough that she'd likely be thinking about it later, when she was alone in bed with a toy.

But that was beside the point.

Aiden's kiss was intoxicating, the kind of thing she could become addicted to. Kenzie had already broken her number one rule by agreeing to be his date tonight. Getting attached to this boy was a bad idea on so many levels, and she refused to let herself be sucked into his orbit any further.

She refused to be another one of his conquests.

Aiden didn't seem like that kind of guy—not yet, anyway. But Kenzie had learned the hard way that even the best on paper sometimes ended up being the worst in real life. That those blissful early days, when things were shiny and new and perfect, would eventually give way to knock-down, drag-out fights, insecurities, and heartbreak.

"But I'll see you soon, right?" Aiden asked, breaking through her thought spiral.

"Of course," she said instantly, though not entirely sure she meant it.

Impulsively, Kenzie stepped forward and rose on her tiptoes to peck him on the cheek. "Good night, Fuller."

Aiden grinned down at her. "Night, bunny."

Then he turned on his heel and disappeared into the night.

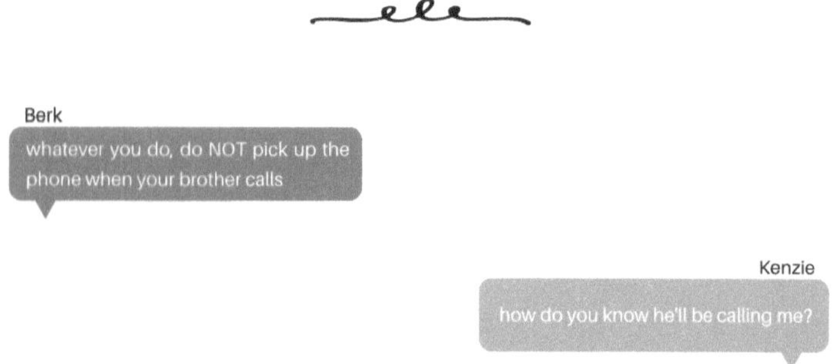

Seconds later, her phone buzzed in her hand, and her brother's face appeared on the screen. She pressed the side button to silence it, shooting him a quick text to say she was in class—even though she wasn't, and he probably knew that—then called Berkley.

"What is going on?" she asked her sister-in-law by way of greeting.

"Have you looked at The Green yet today?"

"No," Kenzie said, clamping her phone between her ear and her shoulder as she continued typing a paper for her marketing class. "Why, what's on there?"

Berkley heaved a world-weary sigh and said, "Just go look at it. I'm too damn old for this shit," before abruptly hanging up.

Kenzie let her phone fall to the couch cushion she was perched on, finishing the paragraph she was working on before pausing to look at The Green.

Suddenly, she wished Berkley had warned her.

That all too familiar wave of dread washed over her.

Before she had the chance to go into a full-blown meltdown, her phone rang again.

"Bunny."

"Fuller."

"I take it you saw The Green," he said.

"I did," she replied.

"I am so, *so* sorry. We took everyone's phones; you saw that. Someone must have snuck in after and shot that video. I don't even know what to say other than I'm so sorry."

Kenzie bit off the grin that threatened to break free at his ramblings. Ending up on The Green wasn't the end of the world for her—although her anxiety disagreed—but for him...

The video showed them at Aiden's house the previous Friday, a crowd gathered around as they stood in the middle of the living room, lips and limbs locked together in an intimate embrace. The headline read: FEEL HER UP, FULLER [VIDEO], and the caption below said, *Aiden Fuller and his new girlfriend, who teammates referred to as "bunny," share a steamy makeout at a hockey house party on Friday night.*

Kenzie had lived it, but watching a replay of it brought all of those feelings she'd experienced rushing back to the surface of her consciousness. The way her skin had burned in all the places he'd touched her. How a low groan had vibrated through his chest—and hers—when he'd slipped his tongue into her mouth the first time. The silken strands of his hair, the initial soft press of his lips, then the harder, more insistent way he'd kissed her.

It was, quite honestly, the most incredible kiss she'd ever had. Having this video in front of her now was better than any porn she could find.

"Aiden, seriously, it's okay. I'm more worried about you than me."

And that was the truth. They'd reached their little agreement as a way to help his image, and here she was, making things worse.

"What do you mean?"

"I mean, what if your coach sees this video? Or Mitch, or someone else in the organization? I don't want you getting in trouble."

Aiden was quiet on the other end of the line for so long that Kenzie had to check to make sure he hadn't hung up. Eons later, he said, "This is tame compared to streaking across campus, but I appreciate the concern."

Kenzie watched the video again. In the moment, the kiss had felt like it'd lasted for hours. According to the time stamp, it had really only been a few minutes.

A few minutes with their mouths fused together, and Kenzie

was already in her feelings over this guy.

God save her.

"Do you or the guys have any idea who took it?"

"It honestly could've been anyone," he said, resigned. "We took phones from everyone who had been in the room, obviously, but there were still plenty of people outside. Any asshole could've walked in and decided to record and send that video to The Green. I'm just sorry you ended up as collateral damage."

"Collateral damage? Hardly," Kenzie said. "Being seen making out with you is going to do wonders for my image."

Aiden snorted. "Okay, smartass."

"So we're good then?"

"Of course," he said. "But hey, I just walked into the rink for a training session. I'll talk to you later?"

"Sure," she said. "I'm apparently your girlfriend after all."

Another laugh, and then, "Bye, bunny."

chapter 11
Aiden

"CAN I COME OVER?"

The week after the kiss, Aiden was holed up in his room, the sounds of his roommates rearranging the living room, dining, and kitchen furniture filtering in beneath his door.

"Why?"

"Jack and Asher decided to host a beer pong tournament."

"On a Wednesday night?" Kenzie asked, tone incredulous, and Aiden smirked. On the assumption that she would say yes, Aiden put her on speaker and walked to his desk, unzipping his backpack to shove his laptop and textbooks into it.

"My thoughts exactly," he told her as he slung the bag over his shoulder and grabbed his keys. "So what do you say? I really need a quiet place to study."

The line was silent for a long moment until Kenzie said, "Sure, come on over. But all we're doing is studying."

"Scout's honor."

"Yeah, you're a real Boy Scout alright," she said quietly before the line went dead.

Aiden barked out a laugh. *This girl.*

After the kiss the week before, he'd struggled to clear her from his mind and focus on things that mattered, like hockey and his classes, even if the former was in a bit of a tailspin at the moment. Unfortunately, that had been easier said than done.

And that wasn't to say Kenzie didn't matter. He enjoyed spending time with her, and he cared about her...as a friend.

Okay, and he definitely wanted to get in her pants, but he respected her boundaries.

Even if their kiss *had* been incredible. Aiden wasn't a romantic by any stretch of the imagination, but that was the kind of kiss that could make a man weak in the knees. The kind that could easily send his mind spinning with a thousand thoughts of the future, and how he could make sure his included her.

The kind that nearly made him want to drop to the floor and worship at her feet.

Yeah, he had to get his shit together. Kenzie had made it perfectly clear that nothing would ever happen again; they'd simply had a mutually beneficial arrangement, and now he had to keep his head on straight. Hockey, and that contract waiting for him in the spring, *had* to be his main focus right now. He couldn't afford to get all turned around by a pretty girl and lose sight of what was most important.

Ten minutes later, Kenzie buzzed him into her building, greeting him at the door in a pair of grey sleep shorts that made her ass look *obscene,* and an oversized Warriors t-shirt with her brother's last name and number on the back.

Which, he supposed, was also *her* last name.

That was going to take some getting used to.

"Hi," he said as he stepped inside, taking in the space. To his right was a large living room with a sectional and coffee table—both littered with books and papers—positioned in front of a big wall-mounted TV. To his left sat the kitchen, with bright white cabinets, stainless steel appliances, and an impressive island lined with four bar stools. Straight ahead was a wall of glass, the windows affording a view out across campus two blocks away. A hallway branched off from the kitchen, which Aiden assumed led to her bedroom.

"Sorry about the mess," she said, gesturing to her work spread out across the living room.

She walked away from him, her long ponytail swishing across her upper back, but Aiden remained rooted to the spot.

Now that he was here, he was unsure what to do. He was rarely ever alone with a girl in a purely platonic situation. This was territory he didn't know how to navigate.

"Aiden?" Kenzie asked. "Are you okay?"

"Yes?" he said, the word more question than answer.

"Then why are you standing there like a statue?"

"Sorry," he said, stepping forward and dropping his bag on the light hardwood floors next to the arm of her couch, where a small end table held a box of tissues and a small framed photo of three children. He picked it up, taking in the subjects. In the middle was clearly Kenzie, her hair a wild tangle around her shoulders, sand below her and a body of water behind her. On either side of her, towering over her and bracketing her like bookends, were two good-looking boys with chocolate-brown hair and ocean-blue eyes that matched hers.

"You were a cute kid," he said, waving the frame at her.

"Yeah," Kenzie said, stepping up next to him to look at the picture. "That's at our cabin up in New York." She pointed at one boy, then the other. "Brent, and Nate."

Even without her help, Aiden could've picked out Brent. In the photo, he was probably in his late-teens, already tall, but lanky, not yet having filled out into the man Aiden knew today. Nate, in comparison, was a few inches shorter and more delicately built. Whereas Brent was all angles and sharpness, the shadows of defined muscles visible under his skin, Nate was softer, as though someone had taken Brent and blurred him slightly out of focus.

With their arms hooked under her thighs, Kenzie beamed crookedly at whoever was behind the camera, showcasing a missing front tooth. Brent and Nate grinned widely as well, Nate preening for the shot while Brent's gaze was turned on his little sister.

"What an ugly family," Aiden said with mock disgust, setting the frame down.

Kenzie gave him a shove but laughed. "I know, right? You've seen Brent. It's a wonder Berkley never kicked him out of bed. And don't even get me started on Nate."

"He can't be any worse than Brent," Aiden said, continuing the joke.

Kenzie raised a finger at him. "Hey, that's my brother you're talking about. He may be a jackass sometimes, but he's *my* jackass."

Aiden raised his hands placatingly. "Okay, okay."

"Nate isn't worse than Brent, exactly," Kenzie said. "Both are way too handsome for their own good, and they know it. They're both incredibly driven, not to mention smart, charming, and protective of me—just in different ways."

"How so?"

"Brent is the oldest, so he's always been the leader, the father fig-ure, even though we have a perfectly amazing one of those already. Nate was wild in high school, smoking pot, doing drugs, staying out drinking and partying all night, while Brent was busy working his ass off to make a career out of hockey. And me…" She shoveled a stack of cloth samples onto the floor and sat on the couch, patting the seat next to her, which Aiden took. "I'm the baby. Brent was eight when I was born, and legend says he rarely let me out of his sight or let anyone else near me in those early months. I love how close we are, and how much he loves me, but sometimes it's…"

"Suffocating?" Aiden supplied, giving her a small smile when she nodded. "I have a little sister, too, remember? She's twelve, so the age gap between us is actually bigger than the one between you and Brent. I understand feeling protective."

Aiden never expected to find he had anything in common with Brent Jean. The man was a legend, both on and off the ice, and Aiden was a semi-talented kid from Chicago who apparently had a proclivity for fucking up in epic, public ways.

But when it came to his little sister? Eloise had been the light of his life since the day she was born. Aiden was nearly twice her age, having turned twelve four months after she was born, and he had made the conscious decision, even as a pre-teen, to always look out for her and do whatever he could to save her from unnecessary pain.

Unfortunately, he hadn't been able to protect her from every-thing.

Kenzie hadn't spoken, as though sensing Aiden was about to

share something difficult with her. And for some reason, he *wanted* to tell her. He'd never been compelled to share with anyone before, save for his teammates. As a rule, Aiden didn't do emotional relationships. From watching his teammates and his family and friends go through it, he knew they only bred drama and heartbreak. Why did he now feel urged to share such a raw, vital piece of his heart?

Aiden swallowed around the lump in his throat and said, "My dad died when I was fifteen."

Kenzie gasped and settled a hand on his forearm. "I'm so sorry, Fuller."

Aiden sniffed, somehow not embarrassed to be emotional in front of this girl. "I don't think I've told you this, but I'm from Chicago. I grew up in Naperville, which is about thirty miles outside of the city. My dad was an executive in the Redhawks organization, and my mom is a loan specialist at one of the big downtown banks. In the summers, when it was nice out, my dad would ride his motorcycle to work. Chicago winters can be harsh, so he liked to enjoy the good weather whenever he could. The day he died, it was the off season, and he was at the rink for some contract negotiations. Afterward, he and some of his colleagues went to dinner, and by the time Dad headed home, it was dark."

Kenzie's grip tightened on his arm, and Aiden covered her hand with his own, grateful for the support. "My dad didn't drink. Like...ever. In my entire life, I saw him drink maybe two beers. On the way home that night, he was plowed into at a four-way-stop intersection. A big Bronco mowed him down right there in the middle of the road. My dad died at the scene."

Kenzie shocked Aiden by climbing into his lap and throwing her arms around his neck. He squeezed her tight, surprised to find they were both crying. "I'm so sorry, Aiden," she whispered against his neck.

"The guy who hit him *was* drunk," he said. "But he tried to blame the accident on my dad. Said my dad ran a stop sign when he didn't have the right-of-way."

"Well fuck that guy," Kenzie said, tone nasally from her tears.

Aiden choked out a laugh and said, "He's in prison, so he probably gets fucked daily."

Kenzie pulled away and smiled down at him, moisture glittering on her long eyelashes. And then, as if realizing how close they were, how precarious their position, she pushed off him and scrambled to her own side of the couch, instantly putting three feet of space between them and taking all the warmth that had settled on Aiden's chest with her.

And honestly, what the fuck was happening to him?

"Really, Fuller, I'm sorry about your dad. But I can see why you're extra protective of your sister."

"Damn, that's really what started this whole conversation, isn't it? Overprotective big brothers," he said with a laugh as he swiped at his eyes.

Kenzie nodded solemnly. "And in light of this conversation, I'll try to cut my brother some slack."

Aiden nodded back, then tugged his backpack toward him and withdrew his laptop.

"Can I ask you a question?"

"You just did, Fuller."

"So, little confession: I eavesdropped on you and Brent at the alumni dinner, and I have to know...is that really how you see me?

That I'm just some fuckboy with no redeeming qualities?"

Kenzie sat motionless, eyes blinking in slowly. "Of course not," she said. "I mean, at first...yeah, I definitely thought you were a fuckboy. But that's only because you let me believe you were. Now that I'm getting to know you better, you're the furthest thing from that. I told my brother that stuff because it was easier to act like you don't matter and save face with him than to tell the truth."

"Which is?" Aiden prompted.

"That I like being around you way more than I care to admit."

An irrepressible smile stretched across Aiden's face. "Except you just did, and I'm never going to let you forget it."

Kenzie groaned and tossed her head back, dramatically covering her face with her hands. Aiden chuckled.

"My turn to ask you a question," she said through her fingers.

"Shoot."

"Do you play hockey because you actually love it, or because your dad loved it?"

Aiden stared at her in shocked silence. How was it possible that this girl could so easily cut right to the heart of him, despite the fact that they barely knew each other? Aiden himself had considered the same question countless times over the course of the last eight years. Did he keep playing because he loved it? Or did he keep playing because his father loved the game so much, and it was something they had shared when he'd still been alive?

"My dad was actually born in Michigan," Aiden said finally. "He grew up not far from here, in Mason, and went to the University of Illinois for college. That's where he and my mom met, and she was a Chicago girl. He would've followed her anywhere, and when she told him she wanted to start their family in her home city, my dad didn't argue. My first real memory with him is us driving up to Detroit so he could take me to a Warriors game. Back then he was working within the Chicago Steel organization, so he had a lot more time on his hands. I must have been six or seven, but I was hooked. The speed of the game, the hits, the finesse, the crowds, the theatrics of it all. When we went home the next day, I asked to be enrolled in whatever skating or hockey program he could find, and the rest is history.

"So to answer your question, it's a bit of both. I started playing because it was common ground for my dad and me. He loved the game so much that he made a career out of it. He got hired by the Redhawks when I was ten. By the time Eloise was born, I'd turned into quite the player, and by the time Dad died, I was already garnering a lot of attention from scouts in the juniors and colleges. I signed with the National Team Development Program in Ann Arbor not long after he died, actually. Moving away so soon after his loss was insane, but it saved me. Then I entered the draft in 2018, and the Warriors picked me in the fourth round. It felt like a sign...not just a sign that I could keep playing if I continued to develop my game, but a sign from my dad that he was proud of me and he was right there with me."

And that was the truth of it. Aiden played hockey for two people: himself, and his dad. When the day came that his career was over, he'd part from the game happily—if a bit melancholic—but not before he exhausted every last avenue available in order to stay as long as possible.

There was nothing as intoxicating to him, no drug or drink that could give him the same high, as stepping onto the ice. The chilly bite to the air, driven away the moment he skated a few laps and set his heart pumping harder. The roar of the thousands of fans, whether he was on home or away ice, shooting adrenaline straight into his veins. The crush of his teammates after a goal or a win. The bus rides and plane rides, endless hours of practice and weights and media obligations.

All of it. Every last second was worth it to play the game he loved. The game his dad had loved.

Kenzie, apparently processing everything he'd dumped on her, remained silent. Aiden, who didn't handle fraught pauses in conversation well, opened his computer and pulled up the paper he'd been working on that was due the next day.

Sometime later, Kenzie finally said, "The Warriors is a great organization."

Aiden stared at her for a beat, then burst out laughing.

"I pour my entire heart out to you," he said through a chuckle, wiping different kinds of tears from his eyes, "and that's the best you can come up with?"

Kenzie smiled sheepishly and, on a giggle, said, "I'm sorry. I don't know what else to say. I appreciate you trusting me with all of that, though."

Aiden shrugged. "You're easy to talk to."

"You say that like it's a surprise," Kenzie said with a little smirk. A smirk he wanted to kiss away. A moment later, her expression turned solemn. "You remind me a lot of Brent. Before Berkley, he was a workaholic. Hockey and his family were his entire life. And they still are. But when that family expanded to include Berkley, his priorities shifted. *She* became his number one priority. And now that they've got a baby on the way..."

"Bunny..." Aiden said, reaching for her. She swatted his hands away.

"It's okay. I know he's my brother and he'll always love me. Things are just changing, and I don't do great with change. But I have to face it head on."

Aiden quirked an eyebrow at her. "You moved clear across the country on a whim."

"It wasn't on a whim," she said, standing from the couch and moving past him into the kitchen, where she rummaged around in the fridge until she extracted a bottle of water. "Want one?"

"Sure."

She grabbed another and walked back, dropping one in his lap, where it narrowly avoided clipping his dick.

"I didn't move on a whim," she said. "I moved to be closer to my brother and our business. They are not the same."

"That's still a big change, from New York to Michigan."

Kenzie shrugged. "I like changes I can control. My brother getting married and starting a family and treating me like some rebellious teenager instead of the adult I am? That's completely out of my hands."

Aiden sensed there was more to it than that, a reason why she was so concerned about her brother's happiness and bringing a new life into the world—a life that would be her niece or nephew. He wanted to press her, to crack her open and spill all her secrets onto the floor where he could sift through them and find out exactly what made this woman tick.

And with *that* ridiculous thought, Aiden returned his attention to his laptop.

"I'm sure your dad is really, really proud of you," she said into the silence sometime later.

"Thanks," Aiden said. "I appreciate it."

"No problem," she replied, gaze downcast, and the air thickened around them.

How would she react if he reached for her right now, settled his hands on her hips and dragged her back onto his lap? If he buried his nose in that soft spot where her shoulder sloped up to meet her neck, where the pretty floral blend of her perfume lingered? If he ground her onto his lap, showing her exactly what those little shorts and her kindness had done to him?

He opened his mouth to say something, to cross that barrier and break all the fucking rules...and his phone rang.

Anyone else and Aiden would've ignored it, but the readout showed his little sister's name, and he never passed up the chance to talk to her.

"Hey, kiddo!" he said when he answered.

"Hi, Den," she said in her soft, sweet voice, and Aiden smiled at the nickname. As a toddler, she'd struggled to pronounce his full name, shortening it to "Den," and had called him such ever since.

"What are you doing?"

"I just got home from dance," she said. "Now Mom and Dan are making me do my homework, but I told them I would only do it if I got to talk to you first."

Aiden chuckled and pulled his phone from his ear, tapping the speakerphone button. "What kind of homework?"

"Math," she said. "And I have a book report to write."

"On which book?"

"Well, I get to pick," she said, her voice muffled as though she had her hand over the speaker. "It's a summer reading book report. Which I think is so silly, considering we're already several weeks into the school year."

"Ahh, I see." It amazed him sometimes, how smart Eloise was, and how quickly she was growing. "What book are you going to choose?"

"Harry Potter," she replied matter-of-factly.

"That was my favorite growing up," Kenzie said absently, then lifted her head and clapped a hand over her mouth.

"Who was that?" Eloise shrieked.

"Calm down, El," he said. "That was just my friend, Kenzie. We're studying together."

"Excuse you, Aiden," another voice said, and Aiden cringed as his mom entered the chat. "Since when do you *study* with girls?"

Aiden winced and shot Kenzie an apologetic look. The problem with suffering through adolescence without a father was that he'd had to rely on his mother during the awkward stages of maturing. When his body had started changing, when he'd started having...urges, when he began noticing girls in more than a friendly kind of way, he'd gone to his mother for advice and guidance. She hadn't married his stepfather until a few years ago and, by then, the deeply personal bond between mother and son had solidified.

All that to say, his mother was well aware of his antics. He'd never kept secrets from her, not after the loss they'd suffered together.

"She's just a friend, Mom, seriously."

"I don't believe you," his mother said. "But I'll let it slide. El, hang up the phone and get started on that report."

His sister *hmphed* and Aiden could practically see her pout. "I have to go," she said. "Bye, Den. Love you."

"Bye, kiddo. Love you, too."

Aiden glanced up at Kenzie to apologize for his mom, finding instead a stricken look on her face, eyes brimming with tears.

"What's the matter?" he asked in alarm.

"Nothing," she said, attempting a smile that wobbled at the edges. "You two just remind me a lot of how me and Bee used to be."

"Oh, bunny," Aiden said, scooting next to her and throwing an arm around her shoulders, curling her into his side. Surprisingly, she came willingly, and Aiden settled them against the cushions. "You should talk to him. You're his sister. I'm sure he'll want to know that you're hurting."

Kenzie was quiet for a long moment, then abruptly pushed away from him and swiped at her cheeks. "No, it's fine," she said. "I'm just being emotional."

She leaned over the coffee table and gathered up a stack of papers, shuffling them into order and reclining into the corner of the couch, away from Aiden. "Now, I'd hate to make a liar out of you. You told your mom you're here studying, so let's study."

Dumbstruck, Aiden stared as she busied herself with whatever was on those sheets in her hands. Eventually, when he finally accepted that was the end of whatever sharing circle they'd found themselves in, he turned to his computer, pulled up his online class materials, and got to work.

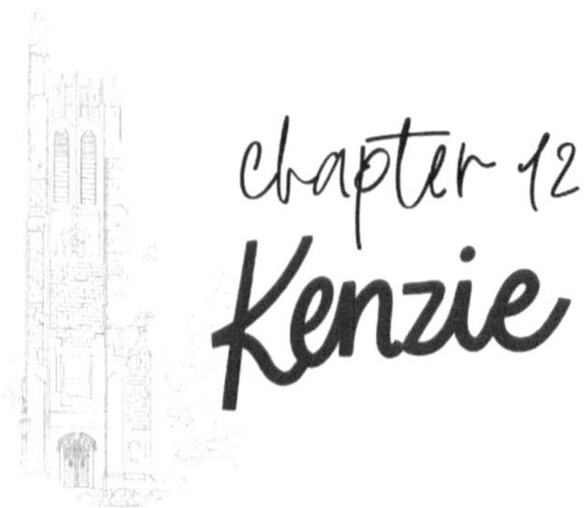

chapter 12
Kenzie

KENZIE WASN'T PROUD OF herself, but for the week after she and Aiden had spilled their guts to each other, she avoided him like the plague.

There were simply too many things about his relationship with his sister that struck chords with Kenzie, and she'd found it difficult to look Aiden in the eye after he'd unintentionally broken down some of her walls. Truth be told, she didn't like the way he made her feel—not only about Brent and the way she would fit into his life going forward, but in general.

Aiden Fuller was sex on a stick, and those moments she'd spent curled in his lap while he poured his heart out to her? That wasn't what she'd signed on for. Physical intimacy for the sake of keeping up appearances was one thing. But emotional intimacy? That was more than Kenzie had bargained for, and she needed to distance herself from him and all the long-slumbering emotions he'd stirred.

Like she said, she wasn't proud of herself.

For an entire week, she purposely avoided anywhere he might be. She either showed up to their class late, well after he'd already arrived, or sat far enough back that university requirements wouldn't allow him to sit with her anyway. And as soon as their professor called time on the session, she bolted, power walking away from the building, taking a different route every day so he couldn't track her down on his stupid little moped. She didn't eat at any of the campus cafeterias, especially not Case, choosing instead to DoorDash her meals, or go down to HopCat when she was craving crack fries and a beer.

Avoiding him allowed her to clear her head a bit.

On Wednesday afternoon, Kenzie and Sofia exited the Communication Arts and Sciences building together, intent on getting lunch somewhere on campus.

"So are you going to the football game on Saturday?" Sofia asked as they trekked down the sidewalk, heading toward the center of campus.

The concrete pathways were dusted with fallen leaves, too fresh to crunch satisfyingly under her feet but pretty in their kaleidoscope of autumnal shades. Halting Sofia by throwing out an arm, she withdrew her phone and snapped a picture of their feet—Kenzie's thick-soled vinyl boots and Sofia's beige canvas platform sandals—to post on Instagram.

"I hadn't planned on it," Kenzie said when they resumed walking. "I have a lot of work to get done."

"What, like...homework?"

Kenzie laughed. "Well, yes," she said sheepishly.

"Girl, no."

"Why not? I hate leaving things until the last minute."

"You're way too hot to spend a Saturday alone *doing homework*." Sofia spoke the last two words as though they were some kind of disease.

"I don't even have a ticket," Kenzie said.

Sofia waved her hand, dismissing the protest. "Those are easy to get. C'mon, Kenzie. You can take a day off to enjoy yourself. Come to the game with me and my sisters. The student section is insane, and I think you'd love it."

Kenzie hesitated, quickly realizing she had no legitimate reason to bow out. Hadn't her reasons for coming back to college included doing typical college things like attending football games? And making friends? Thus far, the only person she'd really managed to befriend, other than Jessica—who hardly counted because they were practically sisters—was Aiden. And if their study session the week before was any indication, Aiden Fuller was not the kind of person she could befriend. Not with the way her body reacted to him, like a magnet being pulled toward an iron surface whenever he was near.

No, she needed to put some much needed distance between them, and this was the perfect opportunity.

"Are there like assigned seats, or is it a first come, first served type of thing?"

Sofia laughed again. "It's more like the Hunger Games. Some people get to the gates hella early so they can be closer to the field. Some tailgate until kickoff and roll in around the start of the second quarter."

"Which one are you?" Kenzie asked as Sofia steered them down the path in front of Shaw, heading in the direction of the sports campus, where Spartan Stadium loomed like a mountain in the distance.

Sofia smirked. "I'm the kind of girl to get there hella early," she said, and Kenzie wasn't surprised by the admission. "I need to get as close to the front as possible. It increases my chances of getting on TV during the game."

After they'd met during the first month of classes, Kenzie may have Instagram stalked Sofia and had found one of the most beautifully curated feeds she'd ever seen. It featured fashion, beauty, college, and sorority life, with enough of her family mixed in to balance it all out. Kenzie was surprised—but also not—to find Sofia had well over one hundred thousand followers.

Her nine thousand seemed paltry in comparison.

Kenzie wanted to pick Sofia's brain, ask how she got into influencing and what kind of compensation she received.

Kenzie always had the option to ask Lexie these questions, but she didn't want to seem like that younger hanger-on sibling trying to be like the big kids. Sofia was the perfect person to ask, their budding friendship giving her more than enough reason to be curious.

Tugging Sofia along, Kenzie said, "Come on. We can go get lunch and you can tell me all about football game etiquette, and give me some pointers on growing my Instagram following."

They continued along the path and crossed the street, bypassing the traffic near the International Center and coming out in front of the football practice field.

"First rule is always go for cute over comfort," Sofia said. "You never know who you're going to run into, or whether or not you'll be featured in the broadcast."

"Even if it's freezing outside?" Kenzie asked as they passed the Daugherty Football Building. Unwittingly, Sofia had led them right to the doors of Case cafeteria, and Kenzie's blood ran cold.

What were the chances Aiden would be in there right now with his teammates? And what were the chances he'd even see her if he was? Slim, she figured, but then again, the chances that the guy she'd met at the bar during Welcome Weekend would end up in one of her classes, and then track her down a short while later in the same building they were about to enter had also been slim, and yet...

"Even if it's freezing outside," Sofia confirmed, still caught up in the conversation at hand, oblivious to Kenzie's inner turmoil.

"I'm going to be honest, Sofia," she told her as they swiped into the cafeteria, "I have very little Michigan State gear."

Sofia spun on her heels, hair flying around her head like a sleek black curtain. "But your brother went to school here."

Kenzie laughed at Sofia's confusion. "I'm aware."

"So you should have tons of stuff," Sofia said, like it made all the sense in the world.

"When Brent was in school, I was barely a teenager," Kenzie reminded her. "My tastes, and my chest, have changed a lot since then."

Sofia laughed as they sidled up to a counter for rice bowls. "Okay, fair enough. But that's perfect, because now I can take you thrifting!"

"You think we'll be able to find gear at thrift stores?"

Sofia gave her a look that said, *girl please*, and responded with, "You're supposed to be a fellow thrifter, Mackenzie Jean! You should already know the answer to that. Of *course* we'll be able to find some gear."

The girls got their food and settled at a two-person table in the middle of the dining space. Kenzie immediately clocked the number of eyes on them.

Before she could ask Sofia if the attention ever bothered her—she guessed the answer was *no*, anyway—Sofia yelled across the cafeteria.

"Jack!" Sofia said, standing from her seat and waving her hand in the air like a marshaller directing a taxiing plane out to the runway.

With a wide smile, Jack, who had just walked in with Asher, Luke, and, of course, Aiden in tow, headed straight for their table.

"Bunny!" Jack shouted when he spotted her. "We've missed you around the house this week."

At that moment, Kenzie wanted to crawl into a hole and die.

Aiden sidled up and dragged Kenzie from her chair, wrapping his arms possessively around her waist and planting a smacking kiss on her cheek.

"Kenzie is my girlfriend," Aiden said proudly.

Kenzie wanted to punch him in the throat.

Sofia's confusion turned to outright surprise in an instant, her eyebrows raising impossibly higher, forehead scrunching like an accordion.

"You're dating Aiden Fuller," Sofia said, awestruck. "I thought that kiss was just a dare? I didn't think there was anything actually going on?"

Kenzie stifled a groan and turned to Sofia, a broad, fake smile pasted on her face. "We went on *one* date," Kenzie said. "It's nothing serious. We're just hanging out."

Kenzie felt more than saw Aiden's gaze turn to the top of her head, and he whispered, "And you shouldn't avoid the person you're hanging out with for an entire week."

Shit, he was mad.

"It doesn't look like *hanging out*," Sofia said, lips turning up at the corners as she waved a hand at Kenzie and Aiden's embrace. "You work fast, Mackenzie Jean."

Kenzie smiled tightly, uncomfortable under such scrutiny. There was absolutely nothing happening between her and Aiden, but he'd walked in here and made it seem as though the opposite were true. Somehow, the thought didn't bother her nearly as much as it should have.

"Mind if we join you?" Jack asked, grabbing two more tables and pushing them together before either girl could respond.

"Sure!" Sofia said brightly, then turned her gaze to Kenzie. "Jack and I are just *hanging out*, too," she added with a wink.

"Walk with me?" Aiden asked, not giving Kenzie the chance to answer before tugging her away from the group.

He stepped into line for the same meal Kenzie had on her own tray back at the table and spun on her while the cooks prepared it.

"Why have you been ignoring me?"

Kenzie sighed, knowing there was no way she was getting out of this without providing a semi-believable response. But this was Aiden, the guy who had opened up to her in a way she was sure he'd never done before with a girl. The least she owed him was honesty.

"We got too close last week," she said.

"What's that supposed to mean?"

"It means this thing—" she gestured between them "—was never meant to be more than a surface level, mutually beneficial arrangement for one night. There weren't supposed to be cozy, soul-baring hang out sessions in my living room."

As she spoke, Aiden's expression morphed from confusion to glee. "You like me, don't you?"

Kenzie scoffed. *Yes.* "No."

Aiden leaned in, his lips brushing the shell of her ear in an echo of the move she'd pulled on him the last time they'd found themselves in this building together. "It's okay to admit it, Kenz. I like you, too."

A shiver raced down Kenzie's spine, and she pushed him away, turning her head in the direction of Sofia and the boys.

The boys appeared to have dispersed to get food of their own, so only Sofia remained at the table. When their gazes connected, Sofia gave her a wide grin and thumbs up.

"I don't like you, Aiden. Not like that, anyway," Kenzie said, surprised by the firmness of her tone. "I just don't want either of us to get confused and turn this into something it's not."

Aiden smirked, unfazed. "Whatever you say."

"I've just been busy," she added, compelled to explain herself.

"Suuuuuure," Aiden said with a look that told her he didn't believe her. "Look..." he continued, lowering his voice to a whisper. "We might not actually be dating, but I thought we really were becoming friends. I don't open up to anyone, let alone girls, and then you disappeared for a week right after? That hurt, and I'm man enough to admit it."

Kenzie was taken aback by his admission. In her desire to spare herself from pain, she'd wound up hurting him in the process.

"I didn't mean to," she said quietly, giving his arm a squeeze.

"Then why?"

She knew what he was asking, and she didn't have a good explanation for him that didn't involve her spilling her guts on the floor in front of him. And that had been the entire point of going radio silent—to avoid having to share things with him, things she wasn't meant to be sharing with someone who wouldn't be a part of her life long term.

Although, it was getting harder and harder to imagine her life without Aiden in it.

What if...what if she could keep him?

No, she told herself firmly. That kind of thinking wouldn't do either of them any good.

Aiden stared at her expectantly, his bowl of food clasped between his hands, those long fingers making the china look even more delicate.

"I don't know," she said finally.

Aiden blinked once, twice, and something Kenzie could've sworn was irritation flitted across his features, there and gone in a flash.

"Okay," he said finally, and shifted his bowl to one hand, grabbing hers with the other.

"So are you guys going to the football game on Saturday?" Sofia asked once Kenzie and Aiden rejoined the table.

"Duh," said Jack, who had scooted closer to her and slung an arm along her seat back.

"You should sit with us!" Sofia said. "I convinced Kenzie to go with me."

Aiden slid his arm around her shoulders and twirled a lock of her hair around his fingers. "I thought you were going to tailgate with me and the boys beforehand?"

"I was?" Kenzie asked.

"Yes," he said. "You promised me last week."

She had done no such thing, and she really wanted to hang out with Sofia. But when she opened her mouth to say so, her friend cut her off.

"We would love to join the hockey tailgate," Sofia practically purred, turning a sultry glance at each of the players gathered around them, lingering on Jack.

In response, Jack leaned close and whispered in her ear. Sofia giggled, a high, musical sound.

When he pulled away, Jack said, "We'll pick you up, bunny."

Sofia tilted her head to the side, reminding Kenzie of a puppy when asked if it wanted a treat. "Why do you keep calling her that?"

"Bunny?" Aiden asked, turning to smirk at Kenzie. He didn't break eye contact with her as he said, "She ran away from me the first two times I asked her out. The guys started calling her my runaway puck bunny, and it stuck."

"That's so sweet!" Sofia gushed.

If only she knew.

"It's definitely something," Kenzie said under her breath, and Aiden pinched her thigh under the table.

"What did you say to get her to finally agree?" Sofia asked.

Aiden's grin widened, that ever-present twinkle in his chocolate eyes turning mischievous. "I made her an offer she couldn't refuse."

"You two are adorable," Sofia said.

"That reminds me," Aiden said. "What are you doing Sunday?"

Aiden's palm burned a brand onto her skin, short circuiting her brain, and he expected her to know what she was doing four days from now?

"Oh!" Sofia cut in before Kenzie could conjure up a response. "I was just talking to Jack here about an outing I'm going on with my sorority sisters to Uncle John's. I asked him to be my date, and he said he'd only go if Aiden did. Why don't we make it a double date?"

Sofia looked at them expectantly, a smile spread across her face, showcasing her perfectly straight white teeth.

Kenzie couldn't outright say no, and Aiden was apparently all for it, because he said, "That sounds perfect. That's actually where I wanted to take Kenzie, but this sounds way more fun."

Cutting her gaze to Jack, Kenzie noted that he looked pained, and she guessed he'd been hoping Aiden would say no so he could get out of it, too.

And the only reason Jack had probably agreed in the first place was so he could get laid.

Aiden had no such motivation, so what exactly was he getting out of this?

Jack, Sofia, and Aiden all stared at her expectantly, so she quickly said, "Yeah, sure, that sounds amazing! Can't wait."

Everybody ignored her forced cheer.

This was going to be bad.

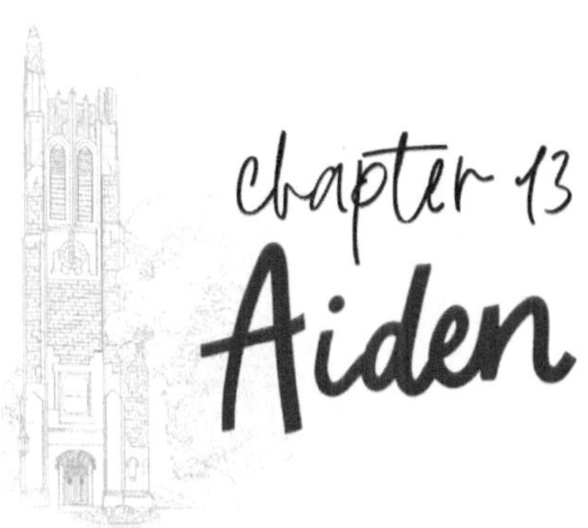

chapter 13
Aiden

THE SUBSEQUENT THREE DAYS between asking Kenzie on a date and meeting her outside Munn for the hockey tailgate on Saturday passed in a rush of classes, rink sessions, and far too many butterflies in his stomach for a guy who wanted to perform in front of thousands of people for a living.

Saturday morning, Aiden woke early when the vibrating of his phone on the nightstand dragged him from sleep.

"Hi, Mom," he said around a yawn.

"Did I wake you?" she asked.

"Yeah, but it's fine."

"Maybe you should stop staying out so late drinking and get more sleep."

"I stayed in last night."

"You still had a party, didn't you?"

Aiden laughed. "Okay, yes, we had a party. It's fine, Mom. We're all of age and we're not in season. We're allowed to have friends over for drinks."

He could practically hear the eye-roll in her silence before she said, "So what's new, kid? I feel like I've hardly talked to you since school started."

"You mean other than the fact that I'm suspended for ten games?"

"Yes, other than that."

"Well...we're tailgating today, and I'm excited for the game. And...I'm going on a date tomorrow."

"You're *what*?"

Aiden winced at the shrill tone his mother had adopted. "It's not a big deal," he said.

"Aiden, you've never brought a girlfriend home, and in high school the only dates you had were to dances. This is a *very* big deal. Who is she? That girl you were *studying* with last week?"

"That's the one," he said, sitting up in bed and reclining against his headboard. "Her name is Kenzie and she's...The night I met her, she ran away from me, and the first time I asked her out, she handed me my ass."

His mom laughed, wanting to know more.

Succinctly, he told her about the alumni dinner and their study session, but how exactly did he accurately describe Mackenzie Jean? How exactly did he capture the precise color of her eyes? The way his entire body tightened in anticipation whenever she touched him, even if by accident? How he wanted to be around her all the time?

It was insanity.

"I told her about dad," he said. "And you know what? I liked sharing that with someone."

"Sharing his loss doesn't make it hurt any less, but it does ease the weight of it a little bit," she reminded him, repeating her favorite mantra from the time she'd spent with her widow/widower support group.

"I really like her, Mom, and it freaks me out."

"Why?"

"Because I can't afford any distractions from hockey right now, especially not when I can't even play until next month. And this girl..."

Aiden swallowed hard, cutting off that thought before it escaped.

He'd been about to say that this girl could become his entire world if he let her, and he refused to admit that. Not yet, maybe not ever, and definitely not to his mom, who needled him endlessly about settling down with a nice girl and giving her grandbabies. Which was ridiculous considering he was only twenty-three and still in college.

"You can have both," was all his mom said.

"I don't know how." His voice was quiet, resigned.

"Well, if you're serious about this girl, you'll figure it out."

A few minutes later, he and his mom disconnected, and Aiden dropped his head back against the solid wooden frame of his bed, scrubbing a hand over his face.

Where Mackenzie Jean was concerned, Aiden found himself wanting things that had never crossed his mind before. He'd become surprisingly attached to the girl over the course of the last month, but he couldn't get ahead of himself. Their date could go a number of different ways, and he needed to keep his expectations low.

Tailgating for football games was serious business. Everyone had their spot on campus where they'd set up tents and grills, bars and games, and spent hours leading up to the game drinking, playing, and socializing. The hockey team's spot was, of course, the ice arena, which was only a block or so away from the stadium.

After the boys roused themselves, showered, and got ready, Aiden and Jack made a Meijer run, stocking up on burgers and brats, chips and dip, cheese, crackers, meats, and an obscene amount of beer, seltzers, and liquor.

Even at ten in the morning, with kickoff still six hours away, campus was already clogged with game day traffic, and the boys crawled along, inching ever closer to their destination. Finally, they turned onto campus and took an immediate left into the Breslin Center parking lot, using their athlete passes to gain entrance. Aiden steered his Jeep to the far eastern side of the lot, which would allow them to hop over Birch Road and right onto the steps of Munn.

"We're going to have to take a few trips," Aiden said when he popped open the hatch and surveyed the damage they'd done at Meijer.

Jack shook his head. "Already texted the boys," he said, and nodded behind Aiden at the mass of Spartan hockey players making their way toward them.

The group made quick work of setting up on the patio outside the new addition to the arena, which faced Breslin.

The addition had been added to finally expand and upgrade

the Spartan hockey locker facilities. Thanks to the generous contributions of many donors, all of their equipment was now state-of-the-art. For the current players, it made a huge difference in their training, and for prospects, completely modernizing *everything* was a huge draw.

Aiden manned the grill, methodically flipping burgers and rotating brats and hot dogs. He was humming along to the Kenny Chesney song blasting from someone's speaker, when his phone buzzed.

"Hey, bunny!" he practically shouted when he pulled it out and answered. "Where are you?"

"I was just about to ask you the same thing!"

"We're at Munn," he said, walking inside and taking a seat in one of the meeting rooms where it was quiet.

"Okay," she said. "We're walking by the Spartan statue now, so we'll be there in a few minutes!"

"Sounds good," he said. "Walk to the Munn Field entrance and I'll meet you over there."

Aiden poked his head back outside. "Pascoe!" he yelled, and the sophomore whipped his head around. "You're on grill duty until I get back."

"Sure thing," Pascoe said, and Aiden headed back inside, weaving his way around people milling in the hallways as they checked out the new digs. Finally, he stepped out into the atrium at the south entrance, now named after the long-tenured basketball coach who had contributed so much to Michigan State athletics over his nearly four decades with the university.

Aiden turned in a circle, taking in the names of players who had come before him, a small smile tipping up the corners of his lips when his eyes scanned over *Brent Jean* on the wall above his head, and then again on the video screen below, where the Spartans who had made it to the NHL were showcased on an endlessly looping slideshow.

And when he spun toward the doors, looking out over the expanse of Munn Field and the tailgates set up there, Kenzie stepped into his field of vision.

He was struck, then, why she'd looked so familiar that night at Rick's when he'd first met her; from a distance, she and Brent looked eerily similar. It was only upon closer inspection that their differences took shape.

Before he went to her, he took the opportunity to study her. Mother Nature had yet to box up summer and put her away until next year, and the temperature outside was unseasonably warm for early October. Kenzie wore a pair of high-waisted, black denim shorts and a tight, white, ribbed tank top underneath a deep-green button-down that hung to mid-thigh. Her dark-brown hair was twisted into space buns atop her head and adorned with green and white ribbons. A blonde girl joined her, and Kenzie glanced at her phone, then around her as though looking for someone.

Looking for *him*.

And he couldn't keep her waiting any longer.

"Kenzie!" he said brightly as he pushed out of the arena.

The smile she turned on him could've lit the entire city, and Aiden's grew in response. "Hey you," she said.

"Where's Sofia?"

"One of her sister's had a last minute crisis, so she headed right to the stadium. She said she'd try to meet up later." Kenzie shrugged, then lit up when she looked at her friend. "This is Jessica, though.

Berkley's sister."

Aiden stuck his hand out. "Aiden," he said.

"I know." Jessica smirked. "I've heard a lot about you."

"All good things, I hope."

Kenzie's eyes sparkled mischievously as they turned on him. "Not even close."

He boomed out a laugh. "I'd expect nothing less."

"So these are the new digs?" Kenzie asked, craning her neck to look at the soaring wall of glass and the metal MUNN ICE ARENA affixed right above the doors.

"Well, not completely new," Aiden said. "It's just an addition. Do you want to see?"

"Can we do that?" Kenzie asked, surprised.

"Of course," he said, reaching for her hand. She threaded their fingers together without hesitation, and Aiden bit back a contented grin. "I play here, remember? Plus, your brother is a god around here. Nobody is going to bat an eye at you being inside when they hear your last name."

Without waiting for a response, Aiden tugged her through the doors, Jessica following behind, and pulled them to a stop right inside the entrance, where they could take in the full scope of the vaulted ceilings, the video board straight ahead featuring him and his teammates, and the history adorning every inch of the walls.

Aiden released her hand and stood back as she spun in a circle, exactly as he had while he'd been waiting for her. The names of every Spartan from the 1950s onward ringed the space, which was now known as the Ron Mason Hall of History—after the great coach who had sat at the helm of Michigan State hockey for over twenty years, and remained one of the winningest coaches in the history of the NCAA.

"Are you a hockey fan?" Aiden asked Jessica as Kenzie considered her surroundings.

"Not really," she admitted. "That's always been more of Berk's area of expertise. I love football, and haven't missed a home game in my entire time here, but this is only the third time in four years I've set foot inside this building."

Aiden's eyes widened, probably damn near bulging out of his head. "We're going to have to change that. Are you a senior?" Jessica nodded. "Yeah, we're definitely changing that. I expect Kenzie at every home game, so you can come cheer us on with her. Our first game is next weekend."

"I'll consider it," Jessica said.

"Bee," Kenzie said quietly, pulling Aiden and Jessica from their conversation. Head tipped back, Aiden deduced she must have found Brent's name on the wall.

He stepped to her, placing a hand on the small of her back and turning her to the video screen on the opposite wall. "Watch," he said.

In groups of four or five, all of the Spartan hockey players who had gone on to have NHL careers were featured in photos, first from their time at MSU, and then with their pro team. Aiden studied Kenzie, knowing the instant Brent's face appeared without looking for himself. Her hand shot to her mouth with a little gasp, and her cheeks spread in a giant grin.

"Your family must be really proud," Aiden said.

She turned to him then, eyes shining with emotion. "We are. Even when he pisses me off, I couldn't be *more* proud."

Aiden smiled at that, hoping his little sister felt the same about him, and hoping that Eloise would get the chance to see him skate on NHL ice one day.

After leading the girls through the locker, meeting, and video rooms, as well as the training stations and everything else downstairs, Aiden finally brought them back out to the patio.

As soon as they stepped outside and Jack laid eyes on them, all the blood drained from the blond's face.

"Jessica?" he asked, tone incredulous.

Aiden and Kenzie stopped dead in their tracks, turning on each other with identical astonished expressions on their faces.

"Jack?" Jessica responded, voice small and unsure.

"Holy shit," Jack said. "It is you."

Jack and Jessica stood ten feet apart, gazes locked, the moment stretching.

Finally, Jessica shook her head and spun on her heel, disappearing inside.

"I'll be right back," Kenzie said quickly, then followed her.

Aiden turned to Jack and opened his mouth to ask what the fuck just happened, but Jack cut him off with a raised hand. "I'm not talking about this here."

Okay then.

"Look," Aiden said later as they walked over to the stadium. "It's going to be impossible to find Sofia in this mess, and even if you did, people aren't going to take too kindly to you shoving your way into a seat near her. So I suggest you just stay with us."

Jack shuffled up and hooked an arm around Kenzie's shoulders.

Both had matching swatches of pink on their cheeks, flushed from a particularly competitive game of beer pong that had pitted them against Aiden and Jessica.

After the awkward and weird initial reunion between Jack and Jessica, both had settled into each other's presence ...mainly by avoiding one another.

At one point, Aiden had followed Jack to the bathroom in an attempt to pump him for information.

"It's...I can't do this right now, Fuller," Jack had said. "Maybe not ever. Just let it go."

"Okay," Aiden had said, and dropped it.

He had his own girl problems to deal with.

In the present, Jack said to Kenzie, "Yeah, sit with us, bunny! I promise we're a good time."

On the walk over, Jessica had disappeared to meet some other friends, so Kenzie was kind of stuck with them anyway.

Kenzie reached out her hand, wiggling her fingers back and forth, and Aiden grasped it in his. Looking up at him, eyes glassy from alcohol, she gave him a small smile. "I *am* having fun with you guys," she said, sounding surprised.

"We're having fun with you, too," Aiden said, and Jack made a disgusted choking sound next to them as he withdrew his arm from Kenzie's shoulders.

"Get a room, you two," he said, picking up his pace to catch up with Asher and Luke.

"Maybe we will," Kenzie said quietly, casting her gaze down.

Aiden figured it was the gallon of High Noon seltzers she'd consumed that was doing the talking and not actually her, that she didn't really mean it, but his dick twitched anyway, his hand tightening around hers in response.

"You're playing with fire, my dear," he said quietly.

"Maybe I want to get burned."

And, okay. Aiden wasn't touching *that* right now, but his dick had other ideas, and he surreptitiously adjusted himself as they walked. He pretended not to notice when Kenzie chuckled next to him.

"Hurry up, love birds!" Jack shouted back as they approached the gates, the crush of bodies bottlenecking through the security entrances threatening to separate them all.

Their group withdrew their phones so the admittance staffers could scan their digital tickets and wave them through.

"I've never been here before," Kenzie admitted.

Aiden wasn't surprised; she'd only been on campus for a little over a month, and anytime she'd been to East Lansing before, surely it had only been inside Munn, its immediate vicinity, and wherever Brent had lived.

"It's going to be hot as shit up there," Aiden said, thankful he'd worn a pair of dark-green athletic shorts and a black tee with "Michigan State Hockey" emblazoned in white block letters stretching across his pecs. "And we're likely to win this game, so shit is going to get crazy. Stick close to me, and follow my lead for the chants and cheers and stuff."

"Did you learn the fight song?" Jack asked, dropping unwelcomed into their conversation.

Kenzie's brow furrowed in irritation, but she said, "Yes."

"Good," Jack told her. "Then you'll do fine."

And Kenzie did fine. In fact, she did better than fine. She caught onto the cheers and chants quickly, and when she didn't know what was going on, she watched Aiden.

He had to admit, he loved having her eyes on him. Her gaze sweeping over his body, those ocean eyes missing nothing, had his skin tightening in the most delicious of ways. More than ever, he was thankful his shorts were loose enough to hide the rock hard cock he'd been sporting all evening.

While the Spartans should have won the game handedly, as the final seconds of regulation ticked off the clock, the score sat tied at twenty-one all. The refs conducted another coin toss to enter overtime, which the visiting team won, and they elected to receive the ball. The Spartans elected to defend the end zone near the student section.

In college football, overtime rules were simple: each team got a possession, which started at the twenty-five yard line. Teams kept the ball until they scored, failed to score, failed to reach a first down, or turned the ball over.

The volume of the student section rose from excited chatter to a deafening roar as the visiting team lined up and snapped the ball. The first play was a pass, caught near the ten yard line, giving the Spartans' opponent a first down and goal to go.

Aiden gripped Kenzie's hand in his, holding on for dear life as the rival quarterback caught the snap and dropped back once again to pass...and ended up sacked.

The student section lost their minds, but the opponent chose to run it on the next play, for a gain of about six yards, which put them at third down and nine yards to go.

The student section's shouts and yells reached a crescendo, and once again the visiting quarterback dropped back to pass, this time floating one over the top of the defense into the far corner of the end zone, where not a single one of his teammates was in sight. Instead, the ball was intercepted by one of the Spartans' cornerbacks, and the stadium collectively lost its mind.

All they needed to do was score, and they'd win.

On the sideline across from them, Michigan State's head coach bounced around, waving his arms in the air in the universal gesture for GET LOUD.

And so they did. When the offensive line stacked themselves at scrimmage, the quarterback's cadence was lost in the din of the sold-out crowd cheering on the home team.

The play developed in slow motion, or maybe that's how it seemed to Aiden. The center snapped the ball, and the QB caught it, dropping back three steps, eyes shifting right to left, watching, waiting.

When the pocket collapsed around him, Aiden was sure he'd been sacked, until the quarterback rushed forward, narrowly avoiding the outstretched hands of a particularly meaty-looking linebacker.

The quarterback got to the edge, legs pumping for all they were worth, his teammates blocking ahead for him.

Twenty.

Fifteen.

Ten.

Five.

"TOUCHDOWN MSU!" the stadium announcer shouted as the band struck up the opening chords of the fight song, and everyone in the vicinity screamed themselves hoarse.

Aiden, however, found himself in a kind of trance. Without hesitating, without sparing the potential consequences a single

second of consideration, he pulled Kenzie to his chest, cupped a
hand around the back of her neck, and sealed his mouth over hers.

chapter 14
Kenzie

THE REST OF THE world dropped away the second Aiden pressed his lips to hers. For all Kenzie knew or cared, they were completely alone, not making out in front of the packed house of Spartan Stadium.

And they *were* making out. What had started as a tentative slide of his mouth against hers increased in pressure and intensity until Kenzie was moments away from jumping into his arms and wrapping her legs around his waist.

As it was, a piece of paper wouldn't fit between them. Aiden's fingertips dug so hard into her hips, pulling her flush against him and the hard ridge of his cock, that she'd surely have bruises tomorrow. For her part, Kenzie had tunneled her hands in his hair, and her calves strained from raising onto her tiptoes to meet every exquisite thrust of his tongue into her mouth, every scrape of his teeth against her lips.

Kenzie could've lived in that moment forever, and taken it much further, had Jack not wrapped them in a bear hug and yelled, "GO GREEN!" at the top of his lungs, forcing them apart.

To his credit, Jack didn't make a comment on the position he'd found them in, only smirked and turned to join the football team and the rest of the stadium in a raucous, celebratory version of the fight song.

"We should..." Aiden trailed off, directing his gaze away from Kenzie, as though embarrassed.

"Yeah," she said, swallowing around the lump that had formed in her throat.

Slowly, they followed the throng as fans trickled out of the stadium, eventually being spit out into the parking lot on the Shaw Avenue side.

"I'm going out," Asher said when they found some room to breathe. "I'll see you guys tomorrow."

Kenzie glanced at Aiden questioningly.

"We agreed we weren't having a party tonight," he said by way of explanation. "We're all exhausted. Asher was the only one against the idea, so he's off to get rowdy elsewhere."

Kenzie nodded, and she and Aiden turned in the direction of Munn. Why were things between them suddenly so strained and awkward? When minutes before, arousal had coursed through her, urging her to throw all caution to the wind? And he had been feeling it, too, hadn't he? Judging by the thick line of him pressed against her stomach, she could confidently say he had.

In silence, they moved away from the stadium and the crowds, walking in front of Munn and then past it. Kenzie didn't know where they were going; she was simply following Aiden's lead. But when they reached Birch Road, she decided it was time for them to part ways.

She cleared her throat and said, "Well, I'm gonna head home." She nodded down the road, indicating she planned to walk in that direction. "I'll see you tomorrow for our date."

Date. The word sounded foreign in her mouth, and suddenly tasted like acid after how he'd been acting these last ten minutes.

"Wait," he said, wrapping his large hand around her significantly more delicate wrist. "Let me give you a ride."

Sit in a car with him when the air around them currently vibrated with negative energy? No thanks.

"That's okay," she said. "I don't mind walking, and it's not that far."

"Kenzie, please," he said, voice anxious, bordering on pleading.

She studied him for several long moments as cars, lined bumper-to-bumper on the road in front of them, inched forward, their passengers surely wondering what the hell they were doing standing here, staring at each other.

"Fine," she said finally, if only because being alone with him for a while longer gave her the opportunity to ask him what in the fresh hell he had been thinking, kissing her like that.

Their short trek to his Jeep was tense, Kenzie growing more and more angry by the second.

Had she liked kissing Aiden? Yes. Loved it, in fact. It had been too long since she'd had the kind of instant physical chemistry with someone as she had with Aiden. And more than that, he was so damn easy to talk to. It wasn't fair that he should be appealing on so many levels. At this point, she wasn't sure why she'd even bothered to turn him down in the first place. Ending up here had been inevitable.

But she had told him repeatedly that there would be no physical relationship between them. Aiden may have checked several—okay, pretty much all—of the boxes on her list of things she liked in a guy, but unfortunately, he also exhibited quite a few of her red flags. Namely, he was a hockey player, and to her that spelled trouble. She wasn't naive enough to think that Aiden could be the exception to the rule.

By the time they'd safely ensconced themselves in his car, Kenzie's skin flamed, tingling with simmering rage. Blood pounded in her veins, and her armpits prickled uncomfortably with an excess of adrenaline.

Aiden didn't bother turning the engine over, as though sensing Kenzie was about to blow, like a can of soda that had been shaken too hard and needed to relieve the pressure.

"Kenzie—" Aiden started, but she cut him off.

"What the hell, Fuller?" she yelled, her voice reverberating through the small space.

"I know," he said, hanging his head. "I'm sorry. You specifically told me after that dare that it wasn't going to happen again, and I totally ignored that tonight. I just...I was so excited about the win. For some reason, kissing you seemed like the best way to celebrate."

"That's sweet and all," she said, blood pressure lowering a bit, "but we've had this conversation, Aiden. You can't just go around kissing people because you feel like it."

"And why the hell not?" he asked, turning his full attention on her, chest rising and falling rapidly. "I want to kiss you. It's all I think about."

The admission took Kenzie by surprise, but she plowed ahead.

"I've told you this. I don't want either of us getting the wrong idea here. We had an agreement. You scratch my back, I scratch yours, remember? We're just friends, Aiden. You don't get to go breaking the rules just because you feel like it!"

"And what if we weren't?" he asked, and Kenzie gasped, feeling as though all the air had been sucked from the car. "What if we weren't just friends?"

"No," she said firmly.

"But we could be, bunny," he said, reaching out. He hesitated before lifting her hand from her lap and grasping it in both of his.

"No," she repeated, trying to withdraw from his grasp, but he held fast. What exactly was he playing at here? Was he messing with her? Trying to fuck with her head? Because if that was his plan, it was working.

"I don't see why not," he said. "Look, we have a good time together, right?"

"Yes..." she said hesitantly.

"And you've already agreed to go on a date with me tomorrow."

"Technically not a date," she reminded him, "since Sofia invited us. So spit it out, Aiden. What are you talking about?"

"I'm saying I know we both had reasons for starting this whole thing, and that neither of us planned on it becoming anything real or serious. But...I want that now. I want to try. With you. If that's something you're interested in, we can quit pretending right now and take a real shot at this. I don't have anyone else like you in my life, Kenz. Someone I have this much fun with and can talk to so easily about anything. And I think you feel the same."

He moved toward her, angling his body over the console between them, reaching up to anchor his hand in the hair at the base of her neck, then hesitated.

Giving her the chance to pull away.

"Before you answer, there's something you need to know. I didn't just ask you out at Case that one day because I think you're hot. The boys dared me to."

"Wait, what?"

"They dared me to get you to go out with me. And admittedly, when you kept blowing me off, you became a bit of a challenge for me. But I swear to you, Kenzie, the dare hasn't mattered to me for a long time. Even without it, I would have pursued you. That night we met, I knew there was something here. Something about you pulled me in, and I've been entranced ever since.

"But if you don't feel the same, and you don't want to give a relationship with me a chance, then say so. I'll take you home right now and we won't talk about this again. We'll go out with Jack and Sofia and her sorority sisters tomorrow, business as usual."

Kenzie's mind spun. He actually wanted this? He actually wanted *her*? She was unsure how to respond. Every single brain cell told her—no, *screamed*—at her to run. To get out of this car, take off down the block, and not look back until she was safe in her apartment.

But every nerve along her skin begged to lean into his touch, to fuse her mouth to his again and see what happened now that they were alone and couldn't be interrupted.

Ultimately, she did neither.

"Take me home, Fuller," she said, and her stomach sank as hurt swam to the surface of his eyes and remained.

He pulled away, Adam's apple bobbing as he swallowed hard and nodded.

Aiden joined the queue snaking from the parking lot, and Kenzie withdrew her phone from her pocket, fingers trembling as she frantically texted Jessica.

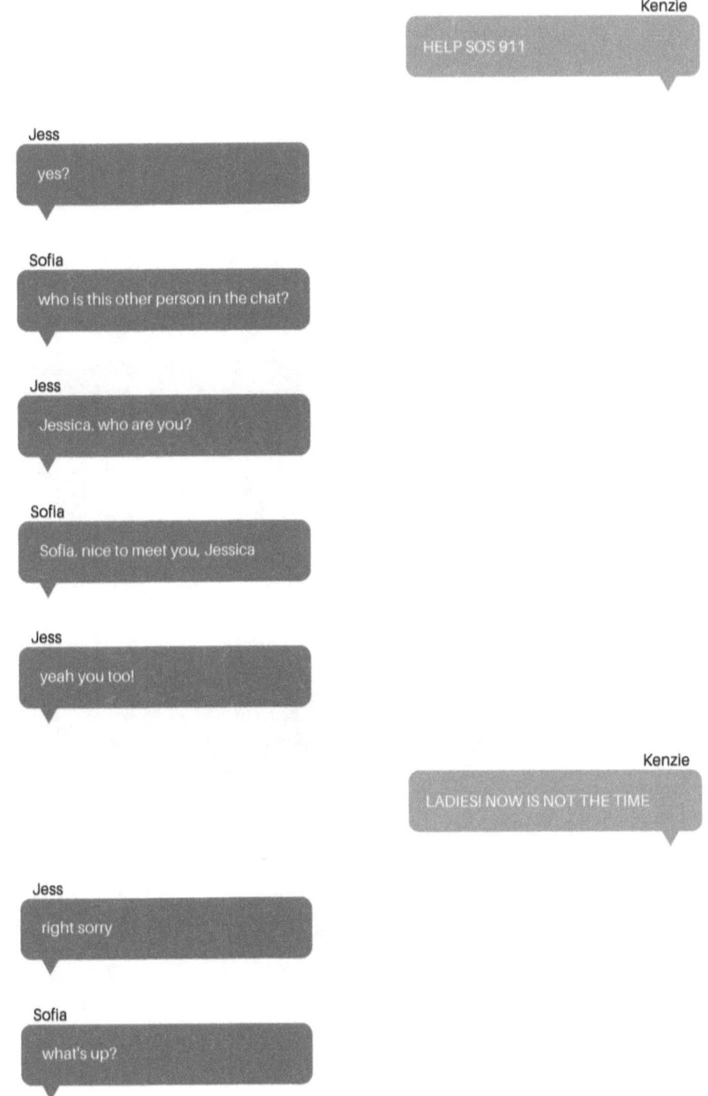

Kenzie

Aiden asked me out. he also told me the only reason he asked me out the first time is because the boys dared him

Jess

I'm failing to see why that's a problem

Sofia

what Jessica said. a hot guy asked you out and you're freaking because...?

Kenzie

he's a hockey player. a total fuckboy. I'd be an idiot to fall for his charm

Jess

I've seen you two together, Kenz, and I can assure you that boy is smitten

Sofia

yeah I've only be around you guys a few times but he's definitely obsessed

Kenzie

no he probably just wants to get in my pants

Sofia

I mean duh. you're hot

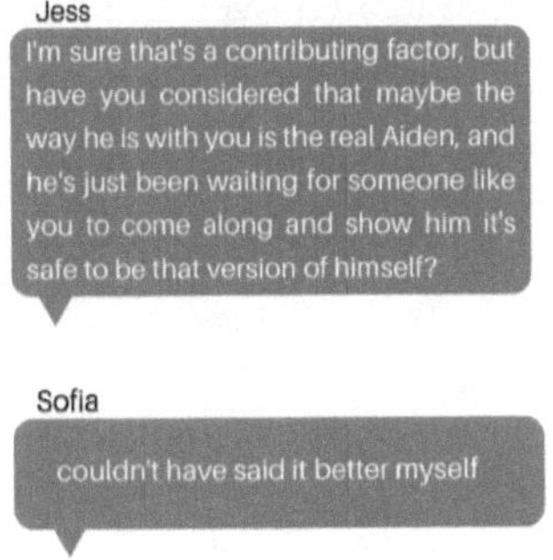

Kenzie's eyes strained as she read and reread Jessica's text.

Could it really be that simple?

There was only one way to find out.

What felt like hours later, Aiden pulled up in front of Kenzie's building. She reached for the door handle, needing to escape this car, to breathe some Aiden-free air into her lungs, and get her head back on straight.

"Do you..." Aiden trailed off, and Kenzie's gaze snapped to him.

She remained silent, waiting for him to ask whatever he had started to.

"Do you still want to go to the cider mill with me tomorrow?"

Kenzie grinned widely at him, and he blinked at her, clearly confused by the shift in her expression.

"Consider tomorrow our first date," she said. "I...I want all the same things you do. And I'm not mad about the dare. But I *am* afraid, and I think we should take it slow. Somehow, we've become friends amidst this craziness, and I don't want to throw that away just because we're both a little hormonal after a pretty hot makeout session."

"You thought it was hot?" Aiden asked, perking up, and Kenzie laughed.

"You know it was," she said. Then she leaned over and pecked him on the cheek. "Good night, Fuller. I'll see you tomorrow."

Without giving him the chance to respond, she exited the car and strode into her building.

Uncle John's Cider Mill was located on US-127 about thirty miles north of East Lansing, in a town called St. John's. The owners offered a variety of activities, everything from wagon rides and a pumpkin patch, to gemstone mining and a trail that looped the entire farm.

As much as Jack begged and pleaded with them to ride the bus the sorority had rented for the occasion up with him, Kenzie and Aiden had both agreed there was no way that was happening.

After they'd arrived and parked, Aiden took her hand as they made their way to the group gathered in the parking lot.

"We're heeeeeeere!" Sofia yelled, spreading her arms wide and spinning in a circle, her unbuttoned, oversized flannel ballooning out around her, her heeled booties digging holes in the gravel.

Jack stood nearby, also in a flannel, the limits of which were tested by his bulging biceps as he crossed his arms over his chest.

The girls sent a cheer to the heavens, then started across the lawn. Sofia walked up and linked her arm through Kenzie's.

"We're going to walk through the farm first," she said. "We've done this a hundred times before, so we're old pros. Just follow me."

Off they went on the two-mile trail, tailing the sorority sisters. Luckily for Jack, Sofia stuck close to Kenzie, so he and Aiden could shoot the shit. Kenzie felt bad that Jack was basically ignoring Sofia, but she didn't seem to mind, too intent on posing for Instagram-worthy photos.

During one of those photo shoots, Kenzie stood off to the side, waiting for her to wrap up so they could continue, when Aiden walked up and immediately reached for Kenzie's hand. She fought the urge to withdraw, reminding herself she'd agreed to give him a real chance.

And if the boy wanted to hold her hand? She'd let him.

Sofia turned from where she was miming taking a bite of an apple, her heel kicked up behind her. Her gaze brightened when it landed on Kenzie and Aiden.

"You guys are so freaking cute," she said. "You should let me take some pictures of you."

Aiden tipped his chin down to look at Kenzie, and she blushed under the attention. No amount of looking into this boy's eyes would ever condition her to their molten depths, would never not make her knees weak.

"What do you think?" he asked Kenzie. "In the interest of going full send on this thing."

And this was what she'd signed up for when she agreed to go on a date with him last night, hadn't she? It wasn't like she could back out now, especially not with Sofia's eagle eyes focused solely on them.

So she handed her phone to Sofia and tugged Aiden forward until they stood exactly where Sofia had, and Aiden tucked her close to his side, snaking an arm behind her back to rest on her opposite hip. She placed one of hers around his waist, planting the other in the center of the solid expanse of his chest.

"Smile pretty!" Sofia called as she snapped photos, the camera shutter audible between them.

Sofia directed them through a few different poses, then released them.

Kenzie walked to her side, and Sofia relinquished her phone. Kenzie scrolled through the shots, Aiden studying them over her shoulder.

She had to admit, she and Aiden looked good together. Like...really good. Kenzie had always known she was pretty. Objectively speaking, the Jean siblings had hit the genetic lottery. And she was more than aware that Aiden was practically a Greek god with his dark, wavy hair, perfectly sculpted body, and olive skin.

But together?

"Damn," Sofia said, echoing Kenzie's thoughts. "It's disgusting how hot you two are."

Kenzie blushed, mumbling a quiet thank you, then looking up at Aiden to gauge his reaction. She was surprised to find his cheeks were as red as hers felt, but something told her it wasn't due to embarrassment.

"You should post them on Insta!" Sofia said, taking Kenzie's phone back and flipping quickly through her camera roll, tapping the heart button to add a select bunch to favorites. "That one, this one, this one, aaaaaaaand this one." She handed the phone back to Kenzie, adding, "Don't forget to filter them!"

Then Sofia bounded off to join her sisters, towing Jack along behind her, who shot them a *help me* look over his shoulder.

"What do you think?" she asked Aiden, studying the photos Sofia had suggested she post. "Should we post them?"

"That's up to you," Aiden said, then placed a finger under her chin and tipped her head back until she met his eyes. "Do you want to let the world know you're dating me?"

"Is that what we're doing? Dating?"

He nodded. "I think so. I *hope* so."

Kenzie smiled. "Me, too."

This had never been part of the plan, coming back to college and immediately falling into a relationship. But she couldn't deny Aiden's presence in her life was a welcome one.

"What are you going to caption it?" he asked.

Kenzie considered that, feeling the moment warranted something super cheesy.

"*I picked a good one,*" she said as she typed, then tapped the share button, sending the photo onto the feeds of her nine thousand followers.

Immediately, she closed the app and locked her phone, shoving it deep into her pocket.

"No going back now," Aiden said, grinning down at her, his teeth glowing brightly in the midday sun, eyes sparkling like amber.

She shot him an easy smile and slid her hand into his.

"What's your favorite apple?" Kenzie asked as they walked up and down the rows of the orchard. The fruit had already been harvested, and the leaves were beginning to turn with the changing of the seasons, some already littering the ground at the roots of the trees.

"I don't think I have a favorite apple," Aiden said.

"Sure you do," she told him. "Everyone does. Mine is Golden Delicious."

"Why?" Aiden asked. She paused in front of a tree that flamed golden, and handed Aiden her phone. Without question, he lifted it, she posed, and he snapped the picture. Then he stepped up next to her and wrapped an arm around her, angling the camera for a selfie.

Now that they had sent coupley photos out into the ether, it amazed Kenzie how easily Aiden touched her, and how quickly she softened into that touch. It was surprising how comfortable she already felt around him, as though they'd known each other forever—when it had really only been about six weeks.

"Golden Delicious apples are really soft," she said when they moved on. "Kind of like a pear, but not. And they're not overly tart. They're just...perfect."

Aiden looked thoughtful for a moment, once again lacing his fingers through hers and towing her along the path between the trees. Sofia and her sisters had disappeared, leaving her and Aiden all alone out here, wrapped up entirely in the sights and sounds of nature.

Already, this was the best date of Kenzie's life.

"I think I just like the big red ones," Aiden said finally, and Kenzie snorted.

"Okay, fair enough."

They reached the end of the row and turned right, where the barns sprawled across the property came into view at the end of the lane.

"What do you want to do next?" he asked. "Pumpkin patch? Wagon ride? Check out what's going on in the barns?"

"Shouldn't we wait for the group?"

Aiden shook his head. "Hell no. I was only doing Jack a favor by agreeing to come with them. The only person I want to be here with is *you*."

Kenzie blushed, unable to formulate a response around the butterflies that had taken up residence in her stomach. Finally, she answered his earlier question. "Definitely the barns," she said. "I want to check out the tap room and get some cider. Then we can get pumpkins before we head back?"

Aiden grinned at her. "I think that's an excellent idea."

Despite the fact that it was barely one in the afternoon, they entered the taproom, bellied up to the bar, and ordered a flight of ciders. Groups of Sofia's sisters gathered around tables, sipping on glasses of cider and taking photos, filling the barn with the sounds of laughter and raised voices.

While they waited for their drinks, Kenzie took the opportunity to study Aiden, who stared out the window at the rolling green fields beyond the barns and surrounding yard spaces.

The boy was a study in Greek architecture, with a long, straight nose, eyebrows thick, dark slashes over his chocolate eyes, high cheekbones, and a square jaw sharp enough to cut glass. He had a tiny little cleft in the center of his chin, and a wide, full mouth she knew was as soft as it looked.

When he turned to her and caught her staring, he grinned, faint laugh lines appearing at the corners of his eyes, those lips stretching and parting to reveal his perfectly straight smile.

"Like what you see?"

Kenzie considered her answer, then said, "I wouldn't kick you out of bed."

"That's funny, because I distinctly remember you telling me the opposite the night we met."

Kenzie's face burned as she remembered their flirty banter and suggestive comments that night. Something about this man had turned her into a more brazen version of herself, someone who'd considered throwing caution to the wind, saying *fuck all the rules*, and letting him show her pleasure she somehow inherently knew only he could.

The bartender appearing with their drinks spared her from formulating a response.

The flight consisted of six samples—one for each of Uncle John's homemade cider flavors. Included were apple, apple blueberry, apple cherry, cranberry apple, apple pear, and apricot apple.

Kenzie had already guessed that Aiden wasn't a sweet and fruity drink kind of guy, but the fact that he'd agreed to do this for her sake earned him major brownie points.

They each took a side of the board to start with and decided to meet in the middle. Kenzie sampled the apricot, pear, and cranberry first before shifting to the other three.

"Okay, I know this isn't really your thing," she said to Aiden after they'd tried them all, gesturing at the drinks, "but which was your favorite?"

Aiden wrinkled his nose before he answered. "Honestly? I hated all of them."

Kenzie barked out a laugh, and Aiden shot her a sheepish grin. "I'm really trying here. For you. But I just cannot do the fruity shit. I can feel my stomach lining burning away under all the sugar."

Kenzie laughed harder. "I didn't know I was out with someone so picky!"

"I'm not picky," Aiden said, leaning back in his chair. "You don't get a body like mine by consuming things that are bad for you. I have a very strict meal plan I follow year round to be in the best shape I can to play."

"To be fair, they're way too sweet for me, too," she said with a laugh, then sobered at the stern set of Aiden's jaw. Unwittingly, she'd struck a nerve.

Settling a hand over his on the bar top, she said, "I was just kidding, you know."

Aiden smiled. "I know. Honestly, I wouldn't like these even if I wasn't such a control freak about what goes into my body."

"Well," she said. "I appreciate you humoring me."

Aiden squeezed back and said, "Finish these and I'll take you on a wagon ride."

Kenzie downed the remainder of each sample like a shot, then stood and reached for Aiden.

He raised a quizzical brow at her.

"I really love wagon rides," she said by way of explanation.

They walked back out into the yard and made their way toward the pumpkin patch, where people milled about, waiting for the tractor pulling a red tent-covered wagon to arrive. When it did, Kenzie and Aiden loaded up, choosing a seat on the outer edge near the front of the wagon. As though it were the most natural thing in the world, Aiden scooted close, the length of his hard-as-a-rock quad pressed against hers, his arm coming to settle around her shoulders.

With the familiarity of a long-term boyfriend and not a couple on their first date, Aiden hooked his arm around her neck and pulled her closer, planting a soft kiss on the hair at her temple. She was still getting used to this, the fact that he already understood physical touch was her love language. Her body's initial reaction was to stiffen and shrink away, but this was *Aiden*. She *wanted* his hands on her body. Soon, she relaxed into his embrace.

"This is nice," she said quietly, tilting her chin to look up at him.

"You're going to have to be more specific."

Kenzie glowered at him, and he smirked. "Being here," she said.

"With me? Or just in general?"

"You are insufferable," she told him. Still, she smiled and added, "With you."

"I thought so," he said, a blissful smile stretching his mouth as he looked away from her and out over the fields as they rolled past.

Conversation buzzed around them as the tractor carved its path around the farm, the sorority girls and their dates louder than most, but Kenzie and Aiden remained quiet, soaking in the gorgeous fall day and each other's company.

When the tractor pulled to a stop in front of the pumpkin patch, Aiden grabbed her hand and dragged her off.

He led her through the winding field, careful not to trample any of the orange globes as they searched for ones to take home.

They finally settled on two near-perfect pumpkins, plus some gourds to dress up the hockey house's front porch, before loading back onto the wagon to continue the tour.

Kenzie was surprised by how easy it was to be with Aiden. She expected to be nervous, or at the very least awkward, given how long it had been since she'd been on a proper date. Even in the best of social situations, Kenzie's anxiety hummed right below the surface of her skin, waiting to take over. For reasons unknown to her, that didn't happen with Aiden.

With him, she was calm. At peace. Content.

When she spoke, he focused all of his attention on her, letting her know he was listening to every word. His gaze never wavered, and some part of his body—arm, leg, shoulder, head—was usually always in contact with hers.

Aiden was...surprising. How sweet he was under his cocky, fuckboy, hockey player exterior, how protective he was of his little sister, how he knew exactly what to say in any situation to put Kenzie at ease.

The way his thumb lightly traced circles on the back of her hand where it rested on his thigh. How, without even trying, he turned Kenzie on simply by being himself.

She could write a book about all the things this man made her feel.

"What're you thinking about?" he asked quietly when they settled in his Jeep to head home. Guilt that she hadn't said goodbye to Sofia stabbed Kenzie in the chest, but she'd been too focused on Aiden to even consider it as they'd departed.

"You," she answered honestly.

"What about me?" He leaned that big body of his over the center console, his face close enough now that she could easily tip her head forward and kiss him.

Angling herself, she faced him, his hand sweeping up her thigh and coming to rest on her hip. "You continue to surprise me," she said, looking into his eyes, the exact color of rich hot chocolate made with a splash of milk.

"How?"

She bit her lip, weighing how much to reveal. But if they were doing this, if he was serious about giving a real relationship a try, she owed both of them complete candor.

"I never expected to feel like this. Before I met you, I had a rule that I'd never date a hockey player. I've been around the game too long, seen too much. I love my brother, but he wasn't always the family man he is now. When I met you at Rick's and realized who you were, *what* you were, I ran because I was scared. I had way too much fun talking to you, and even then you made me feel things and act in a way completely at odds with who I usually am. I panicked. But the more I get to know you, the more I realize you're nothing like I expected."

"Is that a good thing or a bad thing?" Aiden asked, mouth turning down into a small frown.

"A good thing," she assured him, reaching up to cup his face in her hands. "The *best* thing."

The frown instantly flipped into a devastating grin, and he leaned forward to kiss her. When his lips met hers in that exquisite soft and slow slide she'd been replaying on a loop since last night, her fingers anchored themselves in his hair. And when the kiss turned more insistent, her toes curling and stomach flipping as he deepened the pressure and licked his way into her mouth, Kenzie realized something.

She was falling for him, hard and fast, with no idea when she'd meet the bottom.

I am in deep shit.

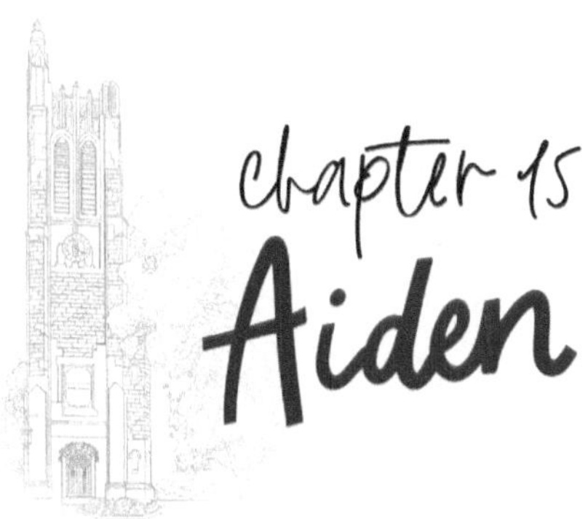

chapter 15
Aiden

AIDEN WAS IN DEEP shit.

Mackenzie Jean had him hopelessly wrapped around her little finger, and he wasn't sure he could untangle himself.

In fact, he wasn't sure he *wanted* to.

But he also didn't have the time or mental capacity to devote to falling head over heels for this girl, because it was opening weekend of the season, and while he wasn't playing for over a month yet, as alternate captain, it was his job to psych the team up and prepare them for a win against a very solid Princeton team.

"Is your friend coming to your game?" Eloise asked on the phone that Friday morning.

Aiden didn't have classes that day, so he'd woken up and decided to make breakfast for his roommates, pulling out the recipe book their nutritionist had provided and selecting something at random.

When his sister called, he was shirtless at the stove, watching the

207

eggs in the pan bubble and firm up.

"What friend?" Aiden asked absently, trying and failing to split his focus between cooking and conversing.

"The one you were *studying* with," she said, and he could practically see the air quotes she used around *studying*.

"Oh, Kenzie," Aiden said, glad his sister couldn't see him. Eloise was at that age where she would mercilessly tease him for the splotches of color that appeared on his cheeks. "I think she'll be there."

"I want to meet her, so she better be!"

Aiden chuckled, already lifting his phone off the counter to text Kenzie. "I'll see what I can do, bug, but she might be busy."

Eloise *hmphed* and said, "Fine," then unceremoniously hung up.

"Can't wait to see you, too!" Aiden said to nobody.

Aiden laughed at her vehemence. He could picture her, sitting on her couch, thumbs angrily tapping at her screen as she meted out her response.

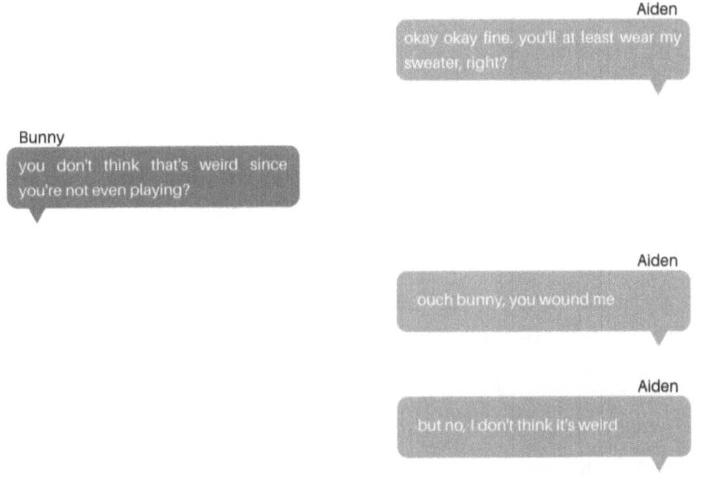

A second later, his phone buzzed with an incoming call.

"I don't know if that's a good idea," Kenzie said as soon as he answered her call.

"Why not?"

"Females are vicious and I don't want to cause a bunch of drama by sitting in the student section wearing your sweater."

"You could always sit with my family," he reminded her.

"Ugh," she said. "No, that's even worse."

"Didn't you ever do that in high school?"

"Do what?"

"Wear your boyfriend's jersey to his games?" He didn't really want to know the answer, not too keen on picturing her with another guy, but he desperately wanted her to support him in this way.

"Well, yeah," she said. "But I didn't realize it was a thing that graduated high school with you. It seems kinda...silly."

Aiden sighed and set his phone down, stirring the eggs one last time before removing them from the heat and dividing them equally onto four plates. Overhead, the floorboards creaked as his roommates stirred.

"Trust me, bunny," he said as he moved the plates from the counter to the table. "There's nothing hotter to a guy than seeing his last name on his girl's back."

"You know I'm not like...your property, right?" she asked.

"Of course I know that," Aiden scoffed. "But tell me something: does your sister-in-law wear Brent's jersey to his games?"

"Well yeah," Kenzie said. "But technically, Jean is her last name now, too."

"I mean before they got married, and you know it," Aiden said with an eye roll.

Truth be told, Aiden was a little afraid of what seeing her in his jersey would do to him. He'd never had a serious girlfriend before. She'd warned him she wasn't his property, but what if he went all neanderthal at the sight of FULLER on her back? He couldn't be held responsible for his baser instincts.

Kenzie was silent for several long moments. By the time she responded, Jack, Asher, and Luke had shuffled into the kitchen and sank down at the table, unceremoniously digging into the meal Aiden had prepared.

"Fine, Fuller," she said, her voice surprising the boys as it echoed through the room. Aiden had forgotten to take her off speaker. "I will wear your jersey tonight."

Aiden grinned. "The boys and I just sat down to eat, but I'll bring it over after."

"K bye," she said, and hung up.

Aiden tucked into his food, aware of the gazes his friends settled on him but choosing to ignore them.

He might not be able to play tonight, but he felt like he'd already won something more valuable than a hockey game.

It had been an incredibly long time since Aiden had last attended a game where he wasn't suited up to play.

He didn't like it. In fact, he downright hated it.

As a scratch, he wasn't even allowed on the bench with his teammates, so he was relegated to finding an empty seat in the stands or watching from the press box.

He'd opted for the press box, deciding he'd get fewer dirty looks and blend in better in his suit and tie than he would surrounded by fans.

The second he stepped through the door, someone yelled his name.

Aiden whipped his head around to find Jeff Flash, who had been the voice of Spartan hockey since before Aiden was even born.

"Jeff," Aiden said, stepping forward to shake the man's hand.

"How you been, man?"

"Good, good," Jeff said, patting Aiden roughly on the back. The man came up to Aiden's shoulders, his face dominated by a massive white beard, blue eyes crinkling at the corners when he smiled behind Coke bottle glasses. "Shame about what happened, though. We all wish you were out there."

"Me, too," Aiden said. "But I'll be back before you know it."

Jeff nodded, then squinted up at him. "Hey, you wanna join us for a period? We can get another headset up here, and there's plenty of room. Could be fun!"

Aiden considered the offer. He was two semesters away from getting his journalism degree, and had embarrassingly little experience in the field thanks to his grueling training, game, and class schedules. Coach probably wouldn't like it, but he wouldn't know until it was too late.

Plus, the man could hardly fault Aiden for doing a little job shadowing, right?

"You know what, I think I will," Aiden said. "Just tell me where you want me."

Jeff clapped excitedly, like a little kid who had been gifted exactly what they'd asked for, and Aiden smiled.

"We'll put you in between me and Rico," Jeff said, gesturing to the front row of the press box, where Jeff's broadcast partner was already seated.

Aiden descended the steps and Rico stood, extending a hand. "Fuller! Good to see you, man."

Rico Playfair was a legend at Michigan State, much like Brent Jean. He had been an enforcer for four years in the eighties, when the Spartans had gone to eight Final Fours—and had won a National Championship in 1987 when Rico was a senior. He'd gone soft around the middle with age, but still stood tall enough to look Aiden square in the eye when he spoke, and Aiden knew he still played hockey every week on a local beer league team. Aiden would bet good money he still knocked guys around with enough force to bruise or break bones.

"Good to see you, too, Rico," Aiden said. "Mind if I join you guys?"

Rico raised an eyebrow at Jeff, who stood behind Aiden. "Sure thing, kid. Let's teach Jeff a little something about the game of hockey, eh?"

Aiden laughed, and Jeff scowled at them both.

"I'm going to regret this, aren't I?" he said.

They quickly set up, and a half hour before puck drop, they went live.

"Welcome, Spartan hockey fans, to today's broadcast, as your hometown team takes on the number ten Princeton team in the season opener! I'm Jeff Flash, here with my broadcast partner, Rico Playfair. And we've also got a very special guest with us today, senior Spartan forward, Aiden Fuller!"

"Hey everyone," Aiden said. "Thanks for having me, guys."

"Well, I think our listeners agree when I say we'd much rather have you on the ice instead of up here with us, but we're gonna have fun. Before we get into the game preview, I think everyone is dying to know what exactly happened that cost you the first five weekends of your senior season."

Aiden hesitated. "Well...I can't go into too much detail. Suffice it to say I made a really stupid decision, and now I'm paying for it."

"I'm going to assume it was a dare gone wrong," Rico said

knowingly, and Aiden winced.

"Those were a thing when you were here, too?" Aiden asked him.

"Kid, we *started* the dares."

Aiden's eyes widened, his mind churning with a thousand questions. "We'll be having a conversation about this later," he said, and Rico laughed.

"You got it. But I can tell Jeff feels left out, so let's get back to the task at hand."

Jeff, who was pouting over his exclusion from the boy's club Aiden and Rico were part of, perked up and said, "Right, the show. Normally I'd open with an interview with Coach, but it's not every day we get an actual player up here for an entire broadcast. So I want to hear from you, Fuller. How's the vibe in the locker room this season? Who are you expecting to have a breakout year?"

"I'm a firm believer that the foundation of a good hockey team is built on the back of a good goaltender," Aiden said. "And I don't think you're going to find one in the NCAA right now who's better than DeLuca. He's been a brick wall for us for years, but I think last season he really settled into his game. He led the league in shutouts, had a ridiculously high save percentage, and kept us in a lot of games when the guys in front of him made stupid mistakes, myself included."

Rico and Jeff laughed indulgently, and Aiden continued, speaking about the camaraderie in the locker room, how he and his teammates had spent countless hours in the offseason training, and the number of team building activities they'd participated in over the summer.

"We've got a tight group," he said. "We all get along really well, and we all understand what's at stake here, which I think is going to make all the difference as the season progresses."

"That's all great to hear," Jeff said. "Was it like that with your teams, Rico?"

"Yeah definitely. You have to trust each other out there. And you have to understand that when one of you wins on the ice, you all win. And when one of you loses..."

"You all lose," Aiden finished for him. "I'm not going to pretend I carry this team on my back. But I am aware that I generate a significant amount of our offensive production, and am one of the best defensive forwards in the country. Losing me is a loss for the team, but I'm confident they'll find ways to win games without me."

"Spoken like a true leader," Jeff said.

With that statement, the noise level in the arena rose as the Spartans skated out of the tunnel. The band, a quarter the size of that present at football games, began the fight song, and Aiden reclined in his seat while Jeff and Rico ran through their pregame talking points.

Badly, he wished he were on the ice instead of up here, but he could definitely think of worse ways to watch his team take on a non-conference opponent.

When Jeff pressed play on the pregame interview he'd done with Coach, and Rico sat back and withdrew his phone from his pocket, Aiden stood and stretched, looking over the ledge and across the ice to the student section.

There in the middle of the crowd, the only one wearing green in a sea of white student section jerseys, stood Kenzie, Jessica's blonde head bobbing next to her as she clapped and sang along to "Victory for MSU."

He watched as her head whipped up in his direction, and he waved a hand to get her attention.

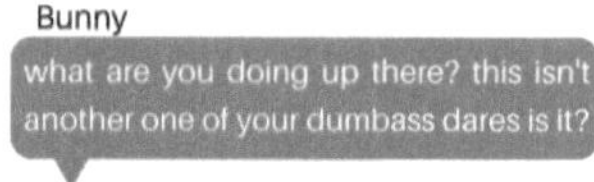

Aiden laughed as he typed his response.

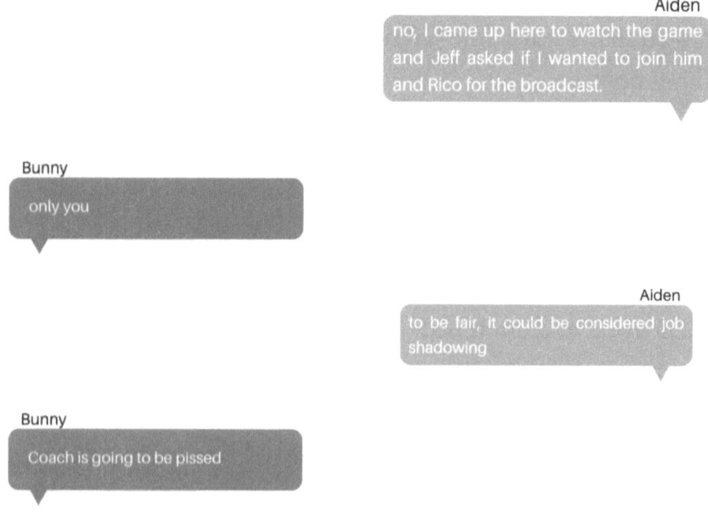

And what the hell was that supposed to mean? Aiden didn't have time to consider Kenzie's comment further, or formulate a response, because Jeff was tugging on his suit jacket, so he quickly sat and slipped his headset back on.

"Welcome back, Spartan fans! Jeff Flash here with Rico Playfair and Aiden Fuller. Puck drop is moments away."

Aiden had never given much thought to what exactly he'd do with a journalism degree after graduation if hockey didn't pan out. At least, not until Kenzie had asked what he'd do if playing was no longer an option. Broadcasting had crossed his mind as a possibility, but at some distant date, after a long, successful career. Over the years, he'd seen a lot of guys transition from players to analysts, without any formal training other than the fact that they played the game at the highest level possible, and successfully. To him, that seemed like a solid way to spend retirement.

His mother disagreed, and had wanted him to go into something practical like business or accounting, but Aiden's cocky ass couldn't imagine being stuck in some office for the rest of his days, only interacting with a handful of people. With journalism, he figured he'd at least be able to put his natural charms to good use.

Radio was so much more difficult than television. Aiden imagined it was like explaining a movie, in detail, to a blind person. But as it turned out, Aiden was a natural broadcaster. Not only because he knew the game of hockey inside and out, but because he was comfortable with a microphone in front of him. Jeff had the hard job of giving play-by-play, and Aiden was awed by his ability to easily track the puck from all the way up here, but Aiden loved when Jeff and Rico deferred to him when big plays happened. He loved describing exactly how the play had unfolded, his intimate knowledge of his teammates adding color to his analysis.

Although he missed being on the ice with his team-mates—would much rather be skating and checking and shoot-ing—he was having fun.

At the first intermission, the Spartans led the Tigers one to nothing. Aiden knew he was expected in the locker room, so he hastily bid Jeff and Rico goodbye, promised he'd be back for the second period, and hauled ass downstairs.

When he arrived, his teammates were sprawled around the oval-shaped locker room. Jack, the superstitious little shit, still had all of his gear on, even his helmet, though he had to be sweating his ass off. The rest of his teammates had shed their buckets and mitts, and reclined at their stalls.

"Where have you been?" Coach asked when Aiden sprinted into the room, no doubt noting he would have arrived sooner had he been seated in the stands and not up in the booth.

"I watched from the box," he said. It wasn't entirely a lie, and Coach didn't have to know he'd been on the radio.

"Perfect," Coach said. "Tell the boys what you saw."

All movement in the room ceased, and Aiden stilled, staring dumbfounded at his coach. "I'm sorry?"

"You had a bird's eye view of the ice. If you're not playing, the least you can do is break down the first period."

Aiden didn't move, and his coach stared at him expectantly.

Well, okay then.

Confidently, Aiden strolled to the doorway at the far end of the room and said, "Video room, now."

Without hesitation, his teammates rose and followed him to the media room, where Aiden raised the projector screen and picked up a dry-erase marker.

When everyone was seated, he began.

"Okay, so here's what I saw…"

For the next ten minutes, Aiden spoke quickly, drawing diagrams on the white board and looking to his coaches for input or confirmation that they agreed with his suggestions. His teammates sat in rapt attention, nodding in agreement, asking questions, and taking his ideas and expanding on them. They were ahead by a goal, but that lead could disappear in a moment. With Aiden's help, they had a solid game plan heading into the second period.

As everyone shuffled out, Coach blocked Aiden's exit.

"You going back up to the box?"

"Yes."

"Good," Coach said, clapping him on the shoulder. "See you next intermission."

Dazed, Aiden hurried back upstairs, joining Jeff and Rico right as the puck dropped.

"Oh!" Jeff said. "We weren't sure, but Aiden has indeed joined us for the second period. What's the energy like in the locker room right now?"

"They're hungry," Aiden said. "They know a single goal isn't going to decide this one, so we tweaked a few plays and they're hoping they can use those to generate some more solid scoring chances."

And they did. Aiden watched the second period unfold, sandwiched by Jeff and Rico, as his teammates went on to score three more goals.

In direct contrast to Princeton's goaltender, Jack had been perfect in net. Through the first forty minutes, he had faced twenty-six shots and stopped every single one. When Aiden went down to the locker room at intermission again, spirits soared.

"You guys do realize you still have twenty minutes left to play, right?" Aiden asked after he watched two freshman high five like they'd just won the conference championship.

"So we can't celebrate?" one of them asked.

"You can celebrate in twenty minutes when the game is over and we have more goals than Princeton," Aiden said.

The freshman's brow furrowed and his mouth dropped open. Aiden steeled himself to give the kid an undressing for whatever retort he was about to make, but Coach interrupted.

"Fuller is right. We celebrate when this thing is over."

Chastised, the freshman dropped onto the bench in front of his locker.

Coach turned his attention to Aiden. "Got any notes?"

"Neutral zone play looks like shit," Aiden said with a shrug.

Coach barked out a laugh, and turned to his players. "He's right. Tighten up those passes, and stop chipping it into the corners when we're not on a change."

"And stop going offsides," Aiden added. "You guys know better."

Coach nodded his agreement. "That too."

"It's our first game of the season," Asher said under his breath, and Coach and Aiden both whipped their attention in his direction

"If you don't clean up the mental mistakes now, we'll never have a shot at a natty," Aiden said.

To his surprise, the remainder of his teammates mumbled their agreement, and Aiden smiled, trying not to puff his chest out in pride.

Coach stepped into the center of the room to address the team, and Aiden stood off to the side, thinking things could definitely be worse. He might not be playing, which wasn't ideal, but surprisingly, he was having fun tonight.

And it could only get better from here.

The Spartans did indeed win by a score of four to zero, earning three points in the standings and giving Jack the first shutout of his final collegiate season. After Aiden had joined his teammates for a victory fight song in the locker room, he headed up to the concourse in search of his mom, sister, and stepdad.

When he found them, he was surprised to see Kenzie standing in their little group.

"Den!" Eloise yelled, rushing at him. In a well-practiced move, Aiden caught her mid-stride and lifted her off her feet, swinging her around as he crushed her to his chest in a hug. Her hair still smelled of that cheap strawberry conditioner she'd been obsessed with for as long as he could remember, and the scent clinging to his nostrils fortified him. She had grown so much since he'd last seen her a few months ago, but he was glad she hadn't grown out of that.

When he set her back on her feet, he studied her. Her wavy hair, the exact shade of his own, was pulled back from her face by an eclectic mix of green and white barrettes, and the jersey he'd gifted her four years ago still hung past her knobby knees.

"Who are you and what have you done with my little sister?" he asked her seriously.

"It's me, Den! I promise!"

His mom stepped toward him and wrapped her arms around his waist. He squeezed her tight, comforted by her warmth and the cloud of vanilla scented perfume that always hovered around her.

"Did you grow again?" she asked when she stepped away and looked up at him.

"I wish," he said. "But I'm still six-three."

"I think you're shrinking, honey," his stepfather said, extending a hand for Aiden to shake. "Hell of a game."

"If only I got to play," he said with a weak smile.

"Soon, sweetheart," his mother said. "Although I'm still incredibly pissed that you thought streaking in broad daylight through the busiest part of campus was a good idea."

Aiden's cheeks burned, sufficiently chastised in a way only his mother could accomplish.

Then a flash of green had him glancing up from his family in time to catch Kenzie turning away from them. But he wasn't going to let her go that easily.

"Kenzie!" he yelled, and ran the short distance after her. He caught her wrist in his hand and spun her to face him, pulling her close. "Where do you think you're going?"

"You were busy with your family," she said quietly. "I didn't want to intrude. Jess and I were going to say hi and go get dinner."

"Trust me, you were not intruding. I was hoping you'd come to dinner with us, actually."

Her eyes widened, that ocean blue practically glowing in the dim overhead lights.

"Are you sure that's a good idea?" she asked, sharing an indiscernible look with Jessica.

Aiden squinted at her, confused. "I thought we agreed we were giving this thing a real shot," he said, voice lowered.

"Yeah like last week! I didn't expect to meet your family so soon!"

"I've met your brother and sister-in-law already," Aiden pointed out.

Kenzie huffed. "That hardly counts," she said with an eye roll. "My brother is famous."

"Kenzie, please," he said, his tone an octave away from begging.

"What if they hate me?" she asked quietly, turning her head away from him.

He captured her chin between his thumb and forefinger and gently forced her to look him in the eye. "They're going to love you," he said, and lowered his mouth to hers.

The kiss was slow, sweet, the most gentle press of his lips against hers, and over way too soon. To Aiden, it felt like it had been ages since he'd tasted her, and he wanted more.

Distantly, Aiden heard Jessica say, "And this is where I take my leave."

"Fine," Kenzie said when they parted, her breath fanning over his lips. He nearly drew her back in to get completely lost in her, but he couldn't. Not with his family fifteen feet away and an arena of hockey fans emptying out around them.

"Fine, what?"

"I'll go to dinner," she said, stepping from his embrace. "But don't kiss me in front of them again."

Aiden sighed, but said, "I won't."
"Promise?" she asked, extending her pinky.
He hooked his finger around hers. "Promise."

chapter 16
Kenzie

MUCH TO KENZIE'S CHAGRIN, Aiden was right.

His family *did* love her, and she adored them right back.

Kenzie half expected there to be some sort of tension between Aiden and his stepfather, between the boy and the man who had taken his father's place. But she quickly came to realize Dan and Aiden had a wonderful relationship.

"He's never tried to take my dad's place," Aiden had said to her on the drive from the rink to the restaurant in Okemos, where they were having dinner. "He and my mom actually met in a support group for people who unexpectedly lost their spouses, and they were really good friends for a while until it bloomed into...more. But he's never tried to step into that role of father figure. He's been more like a friend than anything."

From the way Aiden spoke about Dan, she could tell he deeply respected him and appreciated what he'd done for his mother and their family in the wake of their tragedy.

And Eloise was the most perfect ray of sunshine.

"So you like Harry Potter?" she asked Kenzie at dinner, mouth half full of mashed potatoes and gravy.

"El," her mother scolded. "What have I told you about talking with food in your mouth?"

Eloise dropped her gaze to her plate and audibly swallowed, then looked up at her mom and said, "You told me it's tacky and rude."

The table burst into laughter at the pronouncement, Aiden's mom shaking her head with an exasperated grin. Kenzie had seen that same expression on her own mom's face in regards to her brothers plenty of times to recognize it for what it was: pride.

Turning her attention from her daughter, Aiden's mother leveled her hazel-eyed gaze on Kenzie. "So," she said conversationally, pausing to sip her wine while Kenzie waited for what was sure to be an interrogation. "How long have you and Aiden been sleeping together?"

"Mom!" Aiden shouted, nearly tipping over his water glass as he threw out a hand in protest.

Kenzie gasped, choking on her own spit in the process, coughing until her eyes watered.

"What?" Aiden's mom asked. "It's only a question."

"Well, we haven't slept together," Aiden told her, and Kenzie didn't miss the note of pride in his tone. "Not that it's any of your business."

"Aiden went through puberty without his father around," his mom told Kenzie. "So I had to be Mom *and* Dad. We're very close because of it."

Kenzie was unsure how to respond, unsure if the comment even warranted one. Aiden made an impatient, warning noise in his throat.

"Mom, please don't bother her about this. We've literally been on like two dates."

"That's more than you usually take girls on before you get them into bed," she reminded him.

"Oh. My. God," Aiden whined, dropping his head into his hands.

Kenzie couldn't help it; she burst out laughing.

Eloise, who had been laser-focused on her food, looked up at Kenzie's outburst and, without knowing why, joined in. Soon the entire table was folded over, mirthful tears running down their cheeks.

"Honey, stop tormenting the poor kids," Aiden's stepdad said once they'd all calmed down.

"Thank you, Dan," Aiden said. Then he leaned closer to Kenzie, his breath fanning across her cheek as he whispered, "Although I would like nothing more than to get you naked, bunny."

Kenzie shivered from head to toe, and quickly picked up her wine and gulped down several large swallows. Aiden chuckled next to her.

As the rest of the evening unfolded, Kenzie sat back and watched the family interact, coming to the realization that Aiden Fuller was an enigma.

On campus, he was a hotshot hockey player, emphasis on *hot*, with an *I'm-all-that* attitude that had females tripping all over themselves trying to get his attention. And yet, he wanted the one girl who'd openly disdained him the moment she realized who he was.

With his family, he was sweet, attentive, and jovial. Happier than she'd yet seen him. With each minute she spent in his family's company, she couldn't help the comparisons she drew between Brent and Aiden. It was clear Aiden loved his mother, and the two were extremely close. As her mother's first born, Brent had always been closer with their mom than she or Nate. Sandra Jean loved each of her children equally—or so she said—but she and Brent had always had a special connection Kenzie and Nate would never understand. On top of that, Aiden was extremely attentive to his little sister, and a pang echoed through Kenzie's chest as she remembered when she was younger and Brent had doted on her, exactly how Aiden did with Eloise.

When they were alone together, Aiden became a combination of the two personas. He was incredibly sweet to Kenzie, holding open car and building doors, holding her hand, and telling her she looked pretty. But then he'd turn that charm on her, and Kenzie's toes would curl in anticipation of what he might say next. She was always on guard around him, bracing for the next subtly sexual comment, or a touch that would have her stomach doing backflips.

Nobody had ever turned her on the way Aiden did, and all they'd done was kiss. She couldn't imagine the way she'd react if he bothered to put his hands on her body with any sort of intention. Half the time she wanted to get on her knees and beg him to do just that, but she held herself back.

She had to maintain some semblance of composure in his presence, even if she was desperate for him.

Once dinner was over, Kenzie let his mom wrap her in a hug.

"Take it easy on him," she whispered in Kenzie's ear. "He's so much happier than I've seen him in ages, but he's more fragile than he lets on."

Kenzie pulled away and gave his mom a soft smile. "I will."

Kenzie had always thought she was the fragile one in this relationship, but maybe...maybe she and Aiden were more alike than it appeared.

"Bunny!" Jack yelled when they walked in the door of the house, rushing up and scooping her off her feet. When he set her back down, he gave her a peck on the cheek. "Did you hear your boy made his broadcasting debut tonight?"

Kenzie turned to Aiden, eyebrows drawn together. Aiden's expression rested comically between irritation at the way Jack had manhandled her and bashful.

"I did," she said.

"Speaking of," Aiden said, turning to her. "What was your *you never do* text about?"

Kenzie sighed. "You're already on thin ice," she said, ignoring Asher's chuckle at the unintended pun. "I just wish you wouldn't make such a spectacle of yourself."

"Kenz has a point," Luke chimed in.

Aiden glared at each of them in turn before releasing a heavy exhale. "Fine, I won't do it again."

Kenzie rose and pecked him on the cheek. "Thank you."

Their gazes locked, tension thickening around them. Aiden bent, and Kenzie moved to meet him halfway. Right as their lips were about to collide, a pillow smacked the side of Aiden's head.

"Get a room!" Asher yelled.

Aiden groaned, but closed his hand around Kenzie's and towed her to his bedroom. When the door was closed behind them, Kenzie moved to sit on his bed, and Aiden turned the lock and immediately began shedding his clothes.

The first time she'd witnessed this particular ritual, it had been uncomfortable. She'd watched him but tried not to, and wondered if she should remind him she was in the room.

This time, she openly studied him as he stripped.

Aiden was built like a statue, and Kenzie looked her fill.. He loosened his tie and removed it, then flicked open the top button of his dress shirt. Kenzie tracked his fingers as they brushed the strong column of his throat, then his chest and stomach as he made quick work of the remaining buttons. He shrugged out of it, then tugged off the white tee beneath in that smooth, one-handed way only men could.

Each muscle of his body was perfectly defined. Kenzie traced her eyes over the slopes of his shoulders, the bulges of his biceps, and the thick, corded lengths of his forearms—the left covered in swirls of tattoos. She wanted to sink her teeth into his traps and pecs, and wondered how soft his skin would be if she ran her fingers over the ridges of his abdominals and followed them with her mouth.

As he unbuckled his belt and pulled it free from the loops, his gaze caught hers and held. Completely enraptured by this man, Kenzie didn't dare break his stare as he unzipped and dropped his pants to the floor, leaving him in nothing but a pair of blue and white checked boxers.

"Like what you see?" Aiden asked, his lips twisting into a cocky grin, but Kenzie noted with no small amount of satisfaction that his chest heaved in time with his rapid breaths, mimicking her own.

Kenzie could only nod, trapping her bottom lip between her teeth to stop herself from saying something she couldn't take back. It should freak her out, how much had changed between them since the first time she'd come here. Instead, she was simply excited for all the possibilities of what came next.

But she was in uncharted territory here, and she didn't know what the rules were going forward. They had agreed to give this thing between them a real chance, and she'd met his family. For all intents and purposes, they were dating. Right? So what was stopping her from saying and doing exactly what she wanted at this moment?

"You're beautiful," she told him honestly.

Aiden's cheeks colored, and he prowled toward her. "So are you," he told her when he reached her perch on his bed, wedging himself between her legs and placing his hands near her hips, bracketing her in.

"What are we doing?"

Aiden blinked, as though confused by her question, but lazily replied, "Whatever you want."

And what did she want?

She wanted to taste him. She wanted to press her mouth to his, to kiss that smirk off his face, to make him sigh against her when she brushed her chest against his and tunneled her fingers into his silky-smooth hair.

But she also wanted more dates, more adventures with his hand in hers, more wearing his jersey to games, more *everything*.

"I want you," she said finally, a little breathless.

"You already have me."

In the span of a heartbeat, she was on her back on the bed, Aiden hovering over her, his mouth capturing hers in a kiss that set her mind and the room spinning, blurring everything out of focus until only she and Aiden and all of the places they were connected—mouths, hands in hair and brushing across skin, chest to chest and hip to hip—remained.

Aiden's kiss was ravenous, like he'd been lost in the desert and Kenzie's lips were the first taste of water he'd had in days. And she met him with equal vigor, wanting to erase every single millimeter of space between them until she couldn't tell where he ended and she began.

Lazily, he ran his fingers across her collarbone and ghosted them over her chest, trailing them lower until he found a strip of exposed skin where her jersey—*his* jersey—had bunched up. Without warning, he slipped his arm under the material and brought his hand up to cup her breast.

"God," he mumbled against her mouth. "You are so soft."

In answer, she brushed her fingertips along the ridge of his spine. "So are you."

He moved away from her mouth, and she made a noise of protest until he pressed kisses along her cheek and jaw, nudging his nose along that sensitive spot behind her ear and nibbling at the lobe.

"Oh," she gasped.

Aiden smiled against her neck as he bent his head lower, sucked the soft skin where her shoulder sloped up, and pinched her nipple between his thumb and forefinger.

"Aiden..." she groaned.

"Yes, Mackenzie?" he asked innocently, picking his head up to stare down at her. In her lust-filled haze, he appeared fuzzy around the edges, haloed by the desk lamp behind him.

"Do that again," she begged him.

He obliged, moving from one breast to the other, this time licking a path from her shoulder to her jaw, and she nipped at his collarbone in response.

She shifted her hips up to meet him, groaning again when she was greeted by the hard line of his cock pressing against her through his boxers.

Abruptly, Aiden sat back on his heels and studied her. Kenzie was instantly gripped by panic, wondering what she'd done wrong. She resisted the urge to turn away from him, and was rewarded a second later when he spoke.

"I cannot tell you what seeing you in that jersey does to me," he said, tone low and dangerous, broadcasting to her exactly how much he was coming undone. "But I'd really like you to take it off now. Can you do that for me?"

As always, Aiden gave her a choice, ultimately letting her decide how far they went tonight. Would it always be like this? Him providing her with an escape hatch in every situation?

Kenzie wasn't a virgin, but she'd only been with a handful of guys, and each of them had been that particular brand of narcissistic in bed that seemed common in males in their early to mid-twenties. Kenzie had been a means to an end; a quick way to an orgasm. Not a single one of them had cared about what she'd wanted or needed.

But everything was different with this man in front of her. Aiden was unselfish, unhurried, and unwilling to make her do anything she didn't want to.

"I..." she trailed off, unsure how to articulate this in a way that wouldn't have him kicking her out seconds after the words left her mouth. "I think it's obvious how badly I want you."

Aiden grinned and nodded. "I want you, too, but why do I sense a 'but' coming?"

She sighed and sat up, rising onto her knees so she was face to face with him. "We've only just agreed to give this thing a shot," she said. "I've never really been in a serious relationship, at least not since high school, and that hardly counts. I'm willing to bet you haven't, either. I don't want to push our physical boundaries too far too fast."

That was the truth...but it wasn't. This man in front of her, in a few short months, had blasted through her emotional barriers. She was breaking all her rules with him and for him, falling headlong into disaster. While she still could, she wanted to keep that last wall intact, because she knew once she let him take her, once she let him have her body, those last vestiges of her heart she'd managed to hang onto would be in his hands. If—*when*—that happened, she'd never be able to get rid of him.

To her surprise, Aiden didn't try to fight her, or even seem particularly upset by her desire to halt whatever had been about to happen.

"I understand," he said, then pressed a bruising, toe-curling kiss to her mouth before fully backing away. "Do you want to crash here tonight, or do you want me to bring you home?"

Dazed, Kenzie glanced at his bedside alarm clock, and was shocked to find it was already well past midnight. As if her body realized it, too, she yawned largely, and Aiden chuckled.

"I think I'll stay here."

Aiden nodded. "Let me get you a shirt and some shorts. I've got an extra toothbrush, too, and you're welcome to help yourself to any of my skincare."

Kenzie laughed. "Skincare?"

"Don't give me that look. You think my face looks like this

thanks to genetics? Of course not. I take care of my skin."

She shook her head. Aiden continued to surprise her.

He gathered some clothes and stalked into the bathroom, rifling through drawers before emerging with a toothbrush still in the packaging.

She took her time washing her face and brushing her teeth, trying to regain a little of her composure before she went out there and had to share a bed with this boy who drove her crazy in the most delicious of ways, right after telling him she didn't want to sleep with him.

Then she stripped out of her socks, shoes, and jeans, and lifted Aiden's jersey over her head.

But she felt cold without it, and the shorts he'd given her were comically oversized. So without thinking twice, she whipped off her t-shirt and bra and donned the jersey again, folding her clothes in a neat stack on the floor by the vanity.

"Kenz," Aiden croaked when she opened the door and walked back into the room.

"Yes?"

"Tell me you at least have underwear on still."

Kenzie laughed. "Of course I do."

"What happened to the t-shirt and shorts?"

She shrugged. "They're still in there. But I wanted to wear this...unless you'd rather I didn't."

Aiden rose from the bed and walked toward her, snaking his hands around her waist and pulling her close. "I wouldn't dream of making you take that off. Unless you want to. As far as I'm concerned, you can wear it every day for the rest of your life."

She smiled at him, and he responded by kissing her, a sweet little peck that had her wanting more but knowing she couldn't ask.

"Do you have a side preference?" he asked when they pulled apart, gesturing to his bed.

"I usually sleep in the middle of my bed, so no. I'm good with whatever."

Aiden gestured for her to take the side farthest from the door, and Kenzie crawled in, laying on her back and tracking him as he double checked that the door was locked and then turned off the lamp. Surely by memory, Aiden moved back across the room and slid between the sheets next to her.

For several long moments, neither of them moved. Then Aiden said, "Can we at least cuddle?"

"Duh," she said, and turned onto her side so Aiden could scoot up behind her and wrap his arms around her, one thrown casually across her middle, the other snaking under the pillow beneath her head.

"Good night, bunny," he said quietly, his breath shifting her hair to tickle her neck.

She shivered and burrowed deeper into his embrace. "Good night, Fuller."

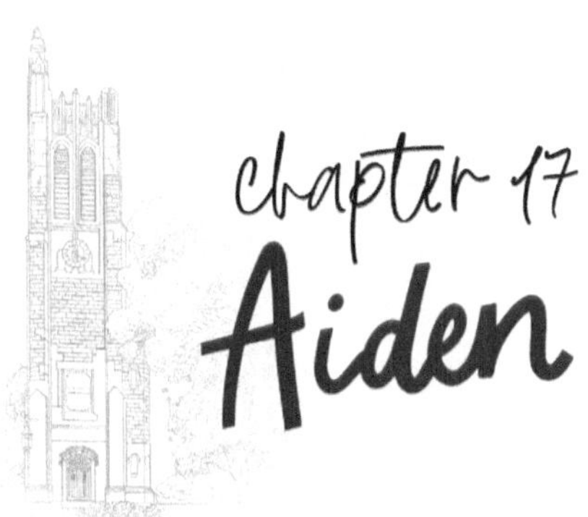

chapter 17
Aiden

"FULLER!"

His shouted last name and incessant pounding on his bedroom door jarred Aiden awake, causing him to bolt upright. Kenzie grumbled in her sleep and curled into a ball next to him.

Aiden smiled, and leaned down to press a kiss to her temple.

"FULLER!" Luke yelled again. "Morning skate! Get up and let's go."

"Go away!"

Aiden stilled, then busted out laughing at Kenzie's outburst.

"Morning, bunny," Luke said through the door, quieter this time.

"Morning," she mumbled.

Aiden leaned down and brushed his lips over the blade of Kenzie's cheekbone. "I'm sorry for the incredibly rude wake up call," he said in her ear, "but I have to get to the rink."

Kenzie rolled onto her back and stared up at him, slowly blinking. Aiden studied her and how the bright, ocean depths of her eyes had turned foggier with sleep. How her hair floated around her head, fanning out across his pillows. How the side of her tanned face was creased from lying on it all night.

"You are stunning in the morning," he blurted.

A slow, sleepy smile spread across her face. "You're not so bad yourself."

"I'm going to kiss you now," he said, leaning down and capturing her mouth before she could protest.

He shifted between her legs, and she raised her knees to bracket his hips with her thighs.

Now was absolutely not the time, but Aiden couldn't help releasing the damper on his lust for this girl, at least a little bit. He couldn't resist pressing the full length of him, from chest to hips, against her, grinning into their kiss at her gasp when she encountered his hard length. Thrusting his tongue into her mouth, Aiden lost himself in the kiss, in how soft and warm she was, how languid he felt from sleep, and how every noise, every sweep of her tongue and slide of her lips against his had him wanting to ignore her wishes to go slow and take her right now.

"FULLER!" Jack yelled this time. "I know your girlfriend is super hot and all, but you really cannot afford to be late to the rink!"

Aiden pulled away and rested his forehead against Kenzie's, both of their chests heaving. "Fuck," he whispered.

She raised her hands to shove him away, though Aiden only moved enough to tilt his head and press a kiss to the tip of her nose.

"Go," she said. "I can't have you getting in trouble on my account."

Reluctantly, Aiden rose and shuffled around the room, throwing on gym shorts and a t-shirt before hustling into the bathroom to brush his teeth.

When he emerged, Kenzie was upright on the bed, the sheets pooled around her waist, his jersey draping across her delicate shoulders. Aiden's mouth went dry, and it took all of his willpower to remain rooted to the spot instead of rushing to her for one last kiss before he left.

"Stay as long as you want," he said. "And don't worry about locking up when you leave."

He was going to get absolutely nothing done today thinking about this girl half naked in his bed.

For the first time since his suspension, he was almost glad he couldn't play.

The Spartans won again that night, sweeping their first series of the season. To celebrate, the boys threw a party.

Shocker, right?

Aiden found it difficult to muster any major enthusiasm for the task. Of course he was happy they'd won, but he would've been a lot happier had he contributed in any meaningful way. Coach had sent him to the press box again with strict instructions to *stay off the air.* Aiden did as he was told, and instead had sat with a few other hockey personnel, tasked to act as a sort of scout, where he'd report back on areas where they could improve during intermission. It was nice to be involved, but his entire body ached to play.

"I can't wait to actually see you on the ice," Kenzie said to him that night, as though she'd read his mind. She was tucked into his side as they watched a game of beer pong unfold in front of them. In comparison to his rather melancholy mood, Kenzie basked in the revelry.

He looked down at her, where her pretty round cheeks were flushed from the drink in her hand, her hair in a messy bun piled atop her head, his jersey once again hanging on her lithe frame.

Leaning closer, he whispered, "I can't wait for that, either. You won't be able to resist me once you see my skills."

Kenzie shivered, and Aiden grinned, loving how easy it was to rile her up. They hadn't discussed sexual partners or experience, and honestly, none of that mattered to Aiden now. When he got her naked and willing, he was going to ruin her for everyone else, make her forget about all the boys who had put their hands on her before him.

And with *that* image in mind, Aiden needed a distraction.

"Bunny and I call next!" he shouted into the room, and his four teammates—Jack and Asher teamed up against two freshmen—turned to stare at him.

Jack shrugged. "Okay," he said, turning his attention back to the table and immediately sinking a ball in a cup. Water splashed out—they'd stopped filling the cups with beer ages ago after one too many spills on the ancient hardwood floors—and one of the freshmen took a large drink from the cup in his hand. "Be prepared to lose."

"Aiden!" Kenzie protested, tugging on his arm so he'd look at her.

"What? Are you any good?"

"I've never even played before!" she hissed, and Aiden's eyes widened.

Stupidly, he said, "You've never played beer pong before?"

Kenzie rolled her eyes and settled them on him in a glare. "I just said that."

"What...how? You were in college before, right?"

"We didn't really do house parties in NYC, remember? Going out was easier. This," she said, sweeping her arm out at the mass of bodies gathered inside the hockey house, "is all new to me."

Aiden's brain seemed to misfire, and he had difficulty understanding exactly how this twenty-three-year-old girl hadn't yet experienced something as simple as playing a game of beer pong.

"Well, you're in luck," he said. "Tonight, we're going to change all that."

"What's that supposed to mean?"

"It means tonight, I'm introducing you to all the college party things you haven't done yet. Have you played flip cup? Done a beer bong? Shotgunned beer?"

"No, no, and no," she said, splashes of deep pink staining her cheeks.

Aiden tipped her head back with a finger under her chin and bent down to give her a quick kiss. Against her mouth, he said. "Do not feel embarrassed. It's nothing to be ashamed of. But it's time we fix it. Do you trust me?"

She nodded, emphatically and without hesitation.

"Good. Let's do this."

In the interest of giving Kenzie the best night he could, he slowed his drinking, sipping on his beer and letting her take the lead during beer pong.

Despite having never played before, she was a natural, sinking nearly as many shots as he did. After Jack and Asher had won the game against the freshmen, Aiden and Kenzie made quick work of his roommates.

When they won—on her shot, no less—she cheered and yelled into the room for the next challengers to step up and try their luck.

Aiden had different ideas.

"Actually," he said loudly. "We're done playing! Someone else can play these losers."

"One and done, Fuller?" Jack said with a head shake. "Embarrassing."

"Just trying to give my girl a good night," he said. "She's already three sheets to the wind, and we have to pace ourselves."

Kenzie had moved into the center of the adjoining living room, hands raised in the air as she swayed her hips back and forth to the beat of the Notorious B.I.G. song pulsing from the speakers. Hypnotized, Aiden stood and watched.

Kenzie had a natural rhythm about her, was in full control of her body, and Aiden couldn't help the smile that spread across his face watching his girl let loose. He knew it wasn't something she did often, and it warmed his heart that she felt comfortable enough in his house—and safe enough with him—to dance alone in the middle of the party, uninhibited.

Unfortunately, Aiden wasn't the only one who appreciated her moves. Guys around the room watched her hungrily, and Aiden's jaw tightened, the warmth in his chest replaced by ice cold jealousy.

"Okay, that's enough," he said, stalking toward her and grabbing her by the wrist, pulling her from the makeshift dance floor and toward the back of the house.

"I was dancing!" she protested, pulling her arm free.

And shit, she was even more drunk than he'd initially thought. Maybe he should've taken more of those drinks during beer pong, but it was too late to go back now. If he tried to tell her to slow down, she'd only rebuff his efforts, most likely accuse him of being exactly like her brother, and run away.

If he'd learned anything about Kenzie in their time together, it was that telling her not to do something almost certainly ensured she would.

Exactly as he'd expected, a smaller group of people gathered around a long, white folding table set up in the center of his postage-stamp backyard, a rousing game of flip cup taking place.

Aiden and Kenzie sidled up to the table, and Aiden said to the group, "Hey guys."

"Sup Fuller."

"Hi Aiden."

"You gonna play?"

Aiden nodded. "My girl has never played, though," he said, indicating Kenzie, who was staring wide-eyed at the overturned cups and upright cans spread across the table.

"Well let's show her how it's done then," one of the guys said, and people lining both sides of the table shuffled to make room for them. Aiden stood at one side and directed Kenzie to the other.

"So here's how it goes," he said to her, splashing some beer into a Solo cup and explaining the rules of the game.

Exactly as she had with beer pong, Kenzie took to the game naturally. This game required far less hand-eye coordination and much more patience, which was something she had in spades. Though they were on opposite teams, Aiden couldn't help rooting for her, cheering happily and pulling her in for a kiss when she beat him.

At that point, she was so unsteady on her feet, Aiden decided it was time to get her to bed.

"Do you want to crash here or do you want to go home?" he asked quietly.

They stood in the darkened hallway that led to his bedroom, Kenzie's weight supported almost entirely by his left arm wrapped around her waist. Thanks to his large size and high tolerance, Aiden only had a small buzz. If she asked him to, he would gladly walk her home right now. The party would be going on for several hours yet, despite the fact that it was after midnight, and he wanted her to get some rest.

"I want you," Kenzie slurred, then threw her body sideways so she was backed against the wall, taking Aiden entirely by surprise as she pulled him with her.

In seconds, he found himself with every inch of his body, from chest to knee, pressed against her. Kenzie reached up and buried her fingers in the hair at his nape, scratching at his scalp in the way that made his eyes want to roll back in his head.

She rose on her tiptoes and pressed her mouth to his, losing her balance along the way and dragging her lips across his cheek. Undeterred, she followed a path across the sharp line of his jaw and down his neck. The sound her tongue made as it scraped along his stubble was obscene, and sent a jolt to his groin that had his cock almost instantly hard.

Aiden wanted her—wanted this—badly, but not at the expense of her regretting it in the morning. She had stopped him once before when she was completely sober, and as much as she seemed to want this now, Aiden couldn't take it from her. Not when he knew better.

So when she moved her hands under his shirt and scraped her fingers over his abs, the muscles jumping in time with her touch, Aiden gripped her wrists and pulled them free, holding her arms by her sides.

"Kenz," he said, voice low and rough. He leaned down to rest his forehead against hers. "Not like this."

Aiden blinked his eyes open and pulled away to stare at her. In the dim light of the hallway, he saw her eyes widen in confusion, then narrow and blink rapidly, shining more brightly than before.

And, *fuck,* he'd hurt her feelings.

"If you don't want me, Aiden," she said, voice steadying with what he knew was embarrassment, "all you have to do is say so."

"I do want you," he said, cupping her face in his palms. "Badly. But you're drunk, and I don't want to take advantage of you."

"I'm not drunk," she said, pushing away from him and moving down the hall—away from his bedroom.

Guess she's not staying here tonight.

For someone so inebriated, she was particularly nimble, bobbing and weaving through the crowded living room until she reached the front door and stepped out onto the porch. She power-walked onto the sidewalk, turning in the direction of her apartment.

Barefoot.

Aiden sighed and hurried after her.

"Is she okay?" Sofia called from behind him.

He turned as he continued to move toward Kenzie, shooting Sofia a thumbs up. "She's just drunk," he assured her. "I'm going to take her home."

"Okay," Sofia said. "She's lucky she has you." Then she went back inside, walking right into Jack's waiting arms.

"Kenzie," he said to Kenzie when he finally caught up with her, grabbing her wrist and pulling her to a stop.

She jerked free from his grasp and continued walking. "Leave me alone, Aiden."

"No," he said, this time grabbing her and pulling her to his chest, wrapping his arms tightly around her.

"Please," she said quietly. "I want to go home."

"Then I'll take you home. But at least let me carry you. You're not even wearing shoes."

Glancing down at her feet, she let out a small sound, a cross between a hiccup and a giggle, when she realized they were bare.

Which then turned into full-blown hysterical laughter.

He had to get her off the street before East Lansing public safety came by and dinged her for public intoxication.

That was the last thing either of them needed.

Finally, she said, "Okay."

Aiden turned and let her scramble onto his back, then quickly walked the six blocks from his place to hers.

About halfway, she passed out, becoming a deadweight on his back, and he was grateful he remembered the code from the time he'd come over to study so he could get them upstairs without waking her.

When he reached her door, he was doubly grateful she'd hidden a spare key under her doormat. Thankful for years and years of training, Aiden easily squatted with Kenzie still on his back, removed the key, and let them inside.

Flipping on lights as he went, he made his way through her living room and kitchen, then down the hall to her room, where he gently laid her on the bed. The bottoms of her once-pristine white socks were now nearly black from the dirt they'd picked up over the course of the evening. Her jeans clung to her legs in an obscene way that had him wanting to peel them off her, and his jersey covered her top half.

Sleeping in jeans was about the most uncomfortable thing ever, and as badly as he wished he were undressing her for different reasons, Aiden unzipped her pants and pulled them off, tossing them into the corner of the room.

Then he moved into her attached bath and rifled through her medicine cabinet, finally finding a bottle of Advil. He shook two pills loose and carried them into the kitchen, where he filled a glass of water and grabbed a bottle of Gatorade from the fridge.

When he reached her bedside again, he jostled her shoulder, waking her. "Kenzie," he said quietly.

Bleary eyed, she blinked up at him exactly as she had that morning, though now the milky white of her sclera was marred by red veins. She mumbled something incoherent, and he smiled.

"I need you to take some medicine."

"I don't want to."

Aiden sighed, reminded of how much he hated taking care of drunk people. But he also understood that Kenzie didn't let go like this often, if ever, and he would feel even worse if he left her to her own devices and she woke in the morning with a jackhammer pounding her skull.

"I know you don't want to, but I promise you'll feel better if you do."

Gingerly, he helped her sit up, figuring if she were going to throw up, this would be the time. When she was upright on the edge of her bed, feet dangling, the color in her face remaining steady, he said, "Open up."

Kenzie did as she was told, and Aiden popped the pills into her mouth, then wrapped her fingers around the glass of water and lifted it to her mouth. She took a small sip to wash down the pills, aware even in her drunken state that too much too soon could upset the delicate balance of her stomach.

Without ceremony, she flopped onto her back, nestled into her pillows, and promptly passed back out.

Aiden couldn't help but chuckle, then set the glass of water and bottle of Gatorade on her nightstand.

Though they'd shared a bed the night before, Aiden didn't feel comfortable crawling in next to her. He had a feeling that when she woke up in the morning and realized what she'd done—throwing herself at him—and how he'd reacted—by turning her down—she'd be more embarrassed than anything. He didn't want to exacerbate the situation by forcing her to immediately confront him.

They needed to have a conversation about what came next, and as badly as he wanted to scoop her into his arms and cradle her against his body all night, he had to practice restraint. Maintain some boundaries until they could sort out the events of the evening.

So he turned away from her and flipped off the light, whispering, "Good night, honey," as he closed the door behind him.

chapter 18
Kenzie

WHEN KENZIE WOKE THE next morning, her tongue was glued to the roof of her mouth

With a groan, she rolled onto her side and waited for the throbbing at her temples to withdraw. It ebbed a little, but she still felt as though someone was hammering her skull.

Blindly, she reached for her nightstand, groping along the surface until her hand connected with the bottle of Gatorade she vaguely remembered Aiden leaving there the night before.

She groaned again. *Aiden.*

It was truly the first time she'd gotten to see Aiden in his element as a big man on campus. Though she had been undeniably drunk, she'd been acutely aware of where he was and what he was doing at all times. She'd loved watching him work the room, chirp his teammates, and effortlessly teach her the rules of beer pong and flip cup.

It had her feeling all sorts of things.

Memories returned in snatches. Him guiding her wrist as she tossed a ball across a table. Him showing her the proper technique to use in order to flip a cup perfectly onto its rim on the first try. How he'd mopped her up when she spilled half a drink down her front.

How she'd kissed him in the hallway.

What the hell had she been thinking, drunkenly throwing herself at him like that? Her cheeks burned as she remembered.

Then her mind snagged on something else: his reaction.

Not like this.

Her cheeks burned impossibly hotter.

Flipping onto her back, she threw a forearm dramatically across her forehead, like a Victorian woman dropping onto a fainting couch.

Giving this relationship a real shot had been Aiden's idea, so she knew he hadn't exactly been happy on Friday night when she'd put a stop to their tryst before they could go all the way. Still, she hadn't expected him to outright reject her when she told him she wanted him last night. What was that, anyway? Some sort of retribution for bruising his ego?

Embarrassment turned to fury in her veins, and she reached for her phone—plugged in, on the nightstand, presumably courtesy of Aiden.

And speak of the devil...

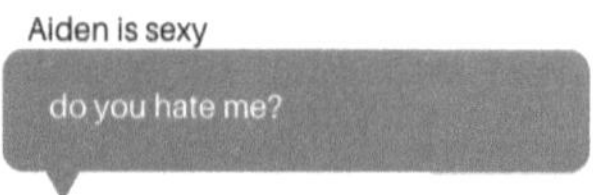

Kenzie considered his question. Did she hate him? No. But she was definitely pissed.

Get out here?

Kenzie leapt from her bed and stumbled as she got her sober legs under her, ignoring the way her stomach lurched and head pounded with the rush of blood as she ran down the hall and slid into the kitchen.

Aiden stood at the stove, shirtless, feet bare, a pair of grey joggers clinging low on his hips, directing the eye south, showcasing that perfect vee cut of his muscles.

"What are you doing here? How did you even get in?"

"Good morning to you, too, bunny. Did you forget I brought you home last night?" he said, scooping fluffy scrambled eggs out of a pan and onto a plate. He whirled and set the plate on the bar-height counter attached to her island, where it joined similar plates loaded with sausage, sliced fresh fruit, and roasted sweet potatoes.

"Did you...do all of this for me?" she asked, indicating the spread.

She didn't only mean breakfast, and he knew it.

Aiden nodded. "I figured you'd be mad at me and feeling like shit, so I thought I'd kill two birds with one stone."

Kenzie was indeed mad, but mostly at herself. She was also starving, so she climbed onto a barstool and spooned food onto her plate. A moment later, Aiden silently set a steaming mug of coffee and a glass of orange juice in front of her, and she gave him a tight but thankful smile.

The whole thing felt incredibly domestic, and it did funny things to Kenzie's resolve to be angry about Aiden's rejection.

After loading her dishwasher and wiping down her counters, Aiden sat next to her and made himself a plate. They ate in stilted silence, Kenzie painfully aware of his every movement next to her.

"You finished?" he asked after they'd both inhaled their meals. He stood and cleared their plates, rinsing them before putting them in the dishwasher.

Kenzie's brows drew together at the way he moved around her kitchen like he lived here. He'd only been here a few times, but he'd somehow managed to make himself feel at home.

She wondered if that was because it was her place, and he felt comfortable around her, or because he was Aiden, and he felt comfortable anywhere.

When he circled back around her side of the counter, he jerked his head in the direction of the living room. "Come sit with me."

Reluctantly, Kenzie rose from the barstool and trailed after him, sitting as far away from him on her sectional as she could manage.

"Why are you still here?" she asked, annoyed by her attitude but unable to reel it in.

"I wanted to make sure you were okay, and..." Aiden pushed a hand through his hair and scrubbed it down his face in exasperation.

"Well?"

"I'm assuming you remember kissing me last night."

"You mean do I remember kissing you and you pushing me away? Sure do."

Aiden grimaced, but Kenzie's embarrassment had morphed into anger, so she pressed on.

"I don't like being made a fool of, Aiden. Did I misread all the small touches and quiet moments we've had over the last couple months? Did I misunderstand when you asked me to give this thing with you a real shot? If I did, tell me now."

Aiden groaned and stood, moving over so he was sitting right next to her. As if to prove she hadn't misread anything, he placed his hand on her ankle and brushed his thumb along the arch of her heel.

"I pushed you away because I didn't want you doing something you'd regret," he said.

"And you think I'd regret that? Letting you take me to bed?"

"Well, wouldn't you? How would you have felt this morning if you woke up naked in bed next to me? Would you have been happy with yourself, or would you have run screaming?"

Honestly, she would've run screaming, and the look he leveled her with said he knew it, too.

She met his gaze, and his normally milk-chocolate eyes darkened.

"So you're telling me the only reason we didn't have sex last night is because you're a gentleman and didn't want to take advantage of me?"

Aiden snorted a laugh but nodded. "Exactly."

Emboldened, Kenzie climbed onto his lap, straddling him. "Well guess what, Fuller?"

Aiden remained still as a statue beneath her. "Hmm?" he asked, his cock already swelling against her.

"I'm stone-cold sober now," she whispered. "And I still want you."

Aiden sighed deeply and pulled her mouth down to his.

His lips were warm, his mouth tasting of bitter coffee and sweet cream, and Kenzie could've gotten drunk all over again on the feel of his tongue as it slipped into her mouth.

Aiden dove his fingers into her hair, heedless of the knots sleep had provided, and pulled, tilting her head back to expose her neck.

He nipped and sucked at her jaw, trailing his lips down to her collarbone, then running his nose along her skin, inhaling deeply.

"How is it that you consumed all the alcohol in East Lansing last night and still smell amazing?" he asked, his lips tickling her skin. "If I drank as much as you did, I'd smell like the bathroom at Rick's."

Kenzie laughed, and he dipped his attention to the valley between her breasts, still covered by his jersey from the night before.

"You have no idea how hot you are in this thing," he said, bunching the hem in his fists. "But I'd really like to take it off now."

"Be my guest," she said, raising her arms so he could lift it over her head and toss it across the room.

He ran a finger along the slope of her left breast, then unclasped her bra and latched his mouth around her nipple in one smooth motion, sucking it in and swirling his tongue around.

Goosebumps broke out across her skin, a low moan escaping her.

Anchoring her fingers in his hair, she gasped and pulled him closer. "Fuller."

She felt more than saw his grin against her skin, and before she could even ask, he moved over to the other side.

Her gasp became soft mewling, and Aiden growled in response.

Settling his hands on her hips, he gripped her tightly and pulled her down harder onto his lap, the hard length of his dick pressing against her center.

She groaned, and Aiden said, "Do you see what you do to me? How could you ever think I don't want you?"

Kenzie was almost unable to form words, except for, "Touch me. Now. Please."

Aiden needed no further encouragement and dove his hand down the front of her panties, easily parting her and dragging his fingers through her pussy.

"Fuck, Kenzie," he said, head dropping back onto the couch as he slid his pointer through her wetness. "This all for me?"

She wriggled on his lap, urging him to put those fingers to better use.

Aiden chuckled and pressed a finger into her, but only as far as the first knuckle. "Answer me," he said. "Answer and you'll get the rest. Tell me you only get this wet for me."

"I only get this wet for you," she said, voice shaking. "No one else has even come close."

"That's what I thought," he said, and pushed his finger all the way in, then added another, his thumb deftly tracing circles around her clit while he fucked her with his hand.

"If you keep doing that," she started, voice a strained whisper, and then immediately lost her train of thought when he pressed his thumb into her clit and rubbed. Her back arched, and he clasped her nipple between his teeth, the sensation only adding to what he was doing with his hand.

"If I keep doing this, what?" he asked when he let go of her nipple, voice sounding as wrecked as hers.

"Don't stop," she said. "Just...don't stop."

"Never," he whispered reverently.

And was it possible he enjoyed giving her pleasure as much as she enjoyed receiving it?

Kenzie wanted to be selfish in this moment, to bask in the sexual attention this man was giving her, but she simply couldn't. It wasn't in her nature.

"Let me make you feel good, too," she said as she reached for the waistband of his pants.

His right hand, the one working its beautiful magic on her, never slowed, but his left hand moved at lightning speed to stop her.

"You don't have to do that."

"I want to," she told him, kissing him long and slow as she slipped into his joggers and took the hard length of him in her hand.

"Mackenzie..."

God, she loved her full name on his lips.

Aiden was big. Like...ridiculously so. Even by touch, she could tell he had the biggest cock she'd ever interacted with. The thought scared her and thrilled her in equal measure.

Experimentally, she smoothed her hand up his length once, twice, three times, swiping her thumb over his head each time she did.

Aiden moaned and reflexively pumped into her touch.

"You were saying?" she asked, bringing her thumb to her mouth and sucking the precum off. His saltiness exploded on her taste buds, and she honestly couldn't wait to suck him off one day, to make him come undone with her lips and tongue and teeth.

"Just...keep doing that," he said through gritted teeth, then awkwardly shoved his pants down his hips with one hand, bearing himself fully to her, giving her unrestricted access.

She continued to stroke him, loving the velvet texture of him, so soft and smooth against her palm. But her movements were jerky, halted by his dry skin.

Desperately, she wanted to take him in her mouth, but she didn't want to give up the perfect angle of his fingers.

When she withdrew her hand, Aiden made a sound of protest in the back of his throat, his hand stilling against her sex.

"Shh," she told him, then spit on her hand and gripped him again, her hand sliding along much easier now.

Those selfish boys she'd been with before had taught her a few things.

Aiden remained still, and Kenzie squirmed, begging him to move.

"That was so fucking hot," he said, then renewed his attention to getting her off. She gave him a hearty squeeze and he gasped, his fingers twitching inside her.

After that, it was all pumping arms and whispered words of encouragement, Kenzie shifting slightly on his lap when she wanted him to change the angle, him directing her *harder* or *softer* when he wanted her to increase or decrease pressure.

When she was close, Kenzie lifted herself off Aiden, balancing her knees on either side of him on the couch cushion, giving him free rein to fuck her with his hand as hard and fast as he could, and she mirrored his movements with her own hand.

They came in unison, him with a heavy groan as he tossed his head back and spilled all over her fingers and his stomach. At the same time, that tension that had slowly built where his hand moved inside and against her released and spread, sending shockwaves along her spine and tingles down her thighs. Kenzie fell forward onto him as she shook and shivered, her hand still moving jerkily up and down his cock.

When the pulsing stopped, Kenzie lifted her head from Aiden's chest and pressed her forehead to his. Wrapping his free hand around the back of her neck, he rubbed gentle circles at the base of her skull, heaving a contented sigh.

Several long moments later, after basking as long as she felt comfortable in the post-orgasm glow, she climbed off Aiden's lap, righted her underwear, and walked topless into the kitchen to wash her hands. Then she grabbed a length of paper towel and, on her way back to the couch, scooped Aiden's t-shirt off the floor and dropped it over her head. When she reached Aiden, she mopped the cum from his stomach.

Once he was clean, and he had pulled his pants up, Kenzie had every intention of settling on the couch next to him, but he tugged her down onto his lap again.

"Do you believe me now?" he asked, once again settling his hands on her hips.

"About what?"

"Look at me," he said, and she pulled away, studying him.

Heavily lidded eyes. A sexy, satisfied smile. Sweat beading his hairline and glistening along the sharp points of his collarbones.

What was the saying? Rode hard and put away wet?

But he looked happy about it—happier than Kenzie had ever seen him.

"You look...sated," she said.

"I am," he told her, leaning forward to capture her lips in a searing kiss. When he broke away, they were both breathing hard, heart rates once again kicked up. "This is what you do to me. Rile me up and calm me down. Turn me on and get me off. I have *never* experienced this with anyone else. Only you, bunny."

Kenzie was unsure how to respond, swallowing hard around the sudden lump in her throat.

Hadn't she been thinking this same thing? That nothing about her previous relationships and entanglements had prepared her for Aiden and how it felt to be with him.

How her anxiety had never reared its ugly head in his presence, the beast never woken. How this post-hookup moment normally would've been strained and awkward, but with him, she could simply enjoy the aftermath of a mind-blowing orgasm and not worry about either of them rushing out the door in that ridiculously uncomfortable post-hookup dance.

Aiden had shared some heavy things with her, and it was time she returned the favor.

"I have really bad anxiety," she blurted.

Aiden's eyebrows drew together. "Okay..."

"I had a bit of a mental breakdown when I was a senior in high school," she said. "I just...freaked out. I had taken on too much at once, and I snapped."

The words flowed from her, and Aiden remained silent, listening. "All my life, I've tried to live up to my brothers' work ethics. I looked up to them, and how talented and successful they both were. They made our parents so proud, and I only wanted to do the same."

Aiden studied her as she spoke, his fingers laced through hers, grounding her.

"Junior year is the time you start preparing for college, you know? In the interest of making myself stand out on college applications, I kept adding more and more to my plate. On top of dance, cheerleading, and gymnastics, I was on the yearbook staff, debate team, and in Model UN. I wrote articles and photographed for the school paper, was a National Honor Society member, and volunteered at Big Brothers Big Sisters."

"That's...a lot."

Kenzie choked on a laugh. "I know. I did okay at first, but by the time December of senior year rolled around, I was drowning. It got to the point where I hardly slept, drank coffee by the gallon, and just generally ran myself ragged."

Kenzie paused, remembering the day she lost her mind.

"I was covering a girls basketball game for the paper one night that January, and two opposing players were going after a loose ball that came out of bounds near me. One of them knocked me over and I just...lost it. I was screaming nonsense, threatening to kill her, pushing and shoving and swinging at anyone who tried to come near me to calm me down. It was ugly. I don't think my parents knew how bad it had gotten until that moment.

"Of course, I became a social media sensation for all of a week until the next big scandal came along."

She didn't tell Aiden the scandal had been her boyfriend cheating on her. That wasn't the point of the story.

"I spent the last semester of my senior year at home, submitting my homework online or having my parents drop it off at school so I could graduate on time, which I did in absentia. I was too embarrassed to face anyone. Brent and Nate had been moved out for ages at that point, but they came home for my graduation *party*," she said, throwing air quotes around the word. "We had a family dinner at home, just the five of us, to celebrate me graduating high school with honors."

"Why are you telling me this?" he asked quietly. "Not that I don't appreciate the vulnerability."

"Since those days, I've found it really hard to be comfortable around people. I was a social pariah in my hometown for ages, and it got to the point where everyone I knew either made fun of me for having a mental breakdown, or they only wanted to get close to me because, by that time, Brent was an NHL standout. They all wanted something from me, whether it was notoriety by proxy, or the opportunity to make themselves feel better by putting me down. My therapist has always told me that I'd find people I could trust eventually. My family, of course. Berkley, absolutely. Their friends Lexie and Mitch. Jessica. I've kept my circle small...until now.

"I can't really explain how, or why, but I've never once felt anxious in your presence. I always just feel...calm. Protected. It's been nice, like I can finally just be myself and turn off the part of my mind that always feels inadequate.

"*You* make me feel safe, Fuller."

Aiden wrapped his arms around her and hugged her tightly to his chest.

"I promise you, Mackenzie Jean," he said against her neck. "I will always be a safe place for you."

And the scary thing was? She believed him.

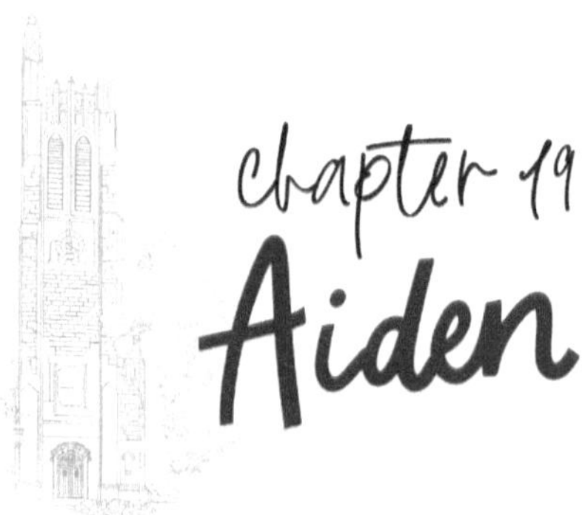

THE CLOCK ON AIDEN'S suspension ticked closer and closer to zero, and with each passing day, the itch to play grew stronger and stronger. At that point, he would gladly peel himself out of his skin if it meant getting back on the ice.

Practices weren't the same, didn't even come close to matching the adrenaline rush of game play.

And on top of keeping his head on straight for two more weekends, he now had another thing driving him mad: Kenzie.

Or rather, the incessantly looping thoughts of what they'd done on her couch last weekend, and the things she'd shared with him afterward.

It had been a long time since Aiden had let a girl give him a hand job, and it had definitely never occurred without him burying his dick inside her afterward. He was once again reminded that nothing about his relationship with Kenzie was normal.

The thought was equal parts terrifying and exhilarating, an

adrenaline-inducing phenomenon all its own. Every second he wasn't with her, he wanted to be. Every other thought was of her: what she was doing, where she was, who she was with, if she was thinking about him, too. Somehow, he'd become a possessive boyfriend, something he swore he'd never be.

To make matters worse, the Spartans were on the road the last weekend of October and the first of November, meaning he and Kenzie would barely see each other for two long weeks.

"What the hell am I supposed to do with my weekends while you're gone?" Kenzie asked.

They were on the couch in her apartment, lying side by side, decidedly not paying attention to whatever the hell Kenzie had put on the TV an hour before. Instead, they were alternating making out and talking.

"You have friends, don't you? Call Sofia or Jessica. Or both!"

"I don't want to," Kenzie whined, pressing her lips to the pulse point in his neck and sucking.

Aiden groaned. "Trust me, I would much rather be here with you than sharing a hotel room with Jack. I love the dude, but he snores like a buzzsaw."

Kenzie giggled, and Aiden nuzzled her neck, feeling the vibration of her laugh against his skin.

He skated his hands along her sides, sliding them below the waistband of her pants and cupping her ass.

"Aiden," she said, pushing him away as he tipped his head down to suck her nipple into his mouth through the thin cotton of her shirt—*his* shirt.

Ever since the weekend before, she'd taken to stealing his clothes, saying she loved the way they smelled like him.

It did wonders for his ego, seeing her walking around in his shirts, broadcasting to the world that she was his

Reluctantly, he withdrew. "What's wrong?"

"I can't..."

"Can't what?"

"Do...that," she said, gesturing between them, where his erection pressed against her thigh and he was seconds away from slipping his fingers through her sex.

"Why not?"

Kenzie heaved a sigh and said, "What is it Alicia Silverstone says in *Clueless*? I'm riding the crimson wave."

"Oh!" Aiden said, understanding dawning. "That's okay. We can cuddle and watch a movie."

"You sure?" she asked, concern lining her features.

"Of course," he assured her. "I just want to be with you."

She gave him a smile, one that started small and grew until she flashed her bright, white teeth at him. "In that case, I'll make us some popcorn."

Ten minutes later, she returned with a near-overflowing bowl of popcorn and two drinks—a bottle of beer for him, a seltzer for her. Together, they curled up on the couch, Kenzie's back to Aiden's front. After a short discussion, they turned on *Miracle*.

"Lake Placid is beautiful," Kenzie said wistfully. "It's the best in the winter, and the arena is...I get chills every time I step inside, and I've never played a minute of hockey in my life."

"I'd love to visit one day," Aiden said. "That game changed hockey in America forever. Those guys are such role models, and I loved wearing the red, white, and blue when I played in Ann Arbor."

Aiden had considered it the greatest honor to have been recruited by and given the opportunity to play for the National Team Development Program in Ann Arbor during high school. The offer to sign with them had come on the heels of the death of his dad, and though moving away from his family had nearly broken his heart, joining the team had been the best thing that could've happened for him in the wake of such a tragedy. His teammates had become like family to him, and it had made those dark days a little brighter.

He told Kenzie all of this as she trailed her fingers over the tattoos on his left arm, the touch comforting as he once again bared his soul to this girl.

"This single-minded focus I have for hockey and making it the top priority in my life isn't just because I love the game so much, or because I'm good at it, or because it makes me feel closer to my dad. Hockey saved me, and I owe the game *everything*."

"I'm assuming that's why you got this tattoo," she said, brushing a touch across the American flag rippling on a phantom breeze on his bicep.

"Exactly."

"How did you end up with a full sleeve anyway? And what do they all mean?"

Aiden laughed at the memory of his first tattoo.

"My second week on campus," he began, "we'd just finished a training session, and all I wanted to do was go back to my dorm, shower, and go get some food. Unfortunately, the upperclassmen had other ideas."

"Oh no," Kenzie said, realizing where this story was going.

"Yeah," Aiden said. "They dared all of us freshmen to get the

Spartan helmet tattooed on us somewhere."

"What possessed you to get it so big?" Kenzie asked, spinning in his arms to point at the tattoo that dominated almost his entire deltoid.

Aiden chuckled. "I figured, go big or go home," he said with a shrug. "But that's not the point. The point is, after that...it turned out I really loved getting tattoos. It's peaceful, you know?"

"I'm not sure everyone would agree with you, but I get it," she said, and he swiped his thumb over the tiny word on the inside of her right wrist.

Breathe.

"It's a reminder," she said. "A cheesy little attempt to marshal my thoughts when my anxiety is spinning them out of control. If I just breathe through it, everything will be okay."

He pressed a kiss to it. "I love it," he said against her skin.

"I love yours," she said. "I want to know the stories behind all of them."

And so he told her.

"This one," he said, twisting his arm to indicate the squiggly little star on his elbow, "is a drawing Eloise did when she was nine. That was the second one I got."

His sister's name also ran along one point of the star, as well as those of his mother and father.

He continued to catalog them all, him and Kenzie laughing at the crazy stories behind them, and how four years ago the arm that had been bare was now entirely engulfed in ink. From where his neck met his shoulder to where the lines and shapes abruptly cut off at his wrist, his skin was forever decorated with permanent mementos of the things, places, and people he loved most.

The underside of his arm, from his elbow up to his armpit, featured a man on a motorcycle, endlessly riding along a road, trees and cliffs rising around him.

"I modeled this after the Black Hills in South Dakota," he said. "My dad had always wanted to visit the Sturgis bike rally but never had the chance to go. Now he's forever riding through those hills."

"Aiden..." Kenzie said, eyes shining with unshed tears. "That's so sweet."

He gave her a watery smile in return and moved on.

"I got this one as a reminder that life is short, and to make each second count," he said, pointing at the massive clock that stretched across the ball of his shoulder, brushing against the edges of both the Spartan helmet on his deltoid and the flag on his bicep.

"You really miss your dad, don't you?"

"Of course I do," he said. "It never gets easier, and every day I walk around with a hole in my heart. But...you get used to it."

That was a lie. He would never get used to not having his father around, and he frequently experienced anger and despair in equal measure at the thought that he would never see him again. But some days were better than others, and Aiden forced himself to keep pushing forward.

It's what his dad would've wanted.

On the soft underside of his forearm was the Chicago skyline.

"To remind me where I came from," he said to Kenzie.

Above it, stretching around to the top of the skyline was a galaxy of planets and stars.

"Eloise is big into astronomy," he said to Kenzie as she traced the outline of a constellation. "The older she got, even though she doesn't remember our dad, she got this idea in her head that he's up there among the stars, waiting for us to join him."

"That is...beautiful," Kenzie said, leaning down to brush her lips over the path her fingers had taken.

"She's a smart kid."

The remaining space was filled by flowers—his mother's favorites—a hockey player shooting a puck, FULLER emblazoned on the back of his jersey, a compass pointing due north, trees, gears and rope, and a sparrow on the inside of his wrist.

"Jack dared me to get that," Aiden said when Kenzie touched it and looked at him quizzically. "He said I needed something girlie and delicate."

Aiden snorted at the memory, but Kenzie remained quiet, smoothing her fingers over the outline of the tiny bird.

"I don't think sparrows are girlie or delicate," she said, then turned her back to him and lifted the hem of her shirt, exposing the tattoo in the center of her back between her shoulder blades.

A sparrow.

"What?" Aiden said, which made no sense in context, but was the only thing his mind conjured.

"Sparrows symbolize a number of things," she said, dropping her shirt and once again facing him. "Joy, community, teamwork, protection, simplicity, hard work, self-worth. I struggle with a few of those myself, and though I can't see it, I can feel it with me always. My little wings, carrying me when I can't carry myself. Jack didn't understand the meaning behind the little bird when he gave you that dare, but community, teamwork, protection, and hard work? All of those things are you, Aiden."

She placed her hand over his heart. "They're all the good things about you, along with so many more. Neither of you may have realized what it meant, but I can't imagine a bird more fitting for you than a sparrow."

Aiden covered her hand with his and brought it to his mouth, pressing a kiss to the center of her palm. "How is it possible we have the same tattoo?" he asked against her skin.

"I guess we were destined to find each other."

Two days later, Aiden found himself on a bus heading north.

This weekend, they were playing another non-conference series against Northern Michigan University, which was located in Marquette in Michigan's Upper Peninsula.

"Okay," Coach yelled from the front of the bus, standing to address them. "How many of you have never been to the UP?"

Aiden, Jack, two of the freshmen, and all six international players raised their hands.

"Well then, you're in for a treat."

Coach moved back to his seat, and the bus rounded a corner, the Mackinac Bridge stretching out in front of them.

"We have to cross *that*?" Jack asked, eyes widening at the sight of the massive suspension bridge that spanned the five miles over the Straits of Mackinac, where Lake Huron met Lake Michigan.

Aiden liked to think he wasn't afraid of anything, but the further they drove onto the bridge, the more his anxiety spiked. For starters, the lanes were incredibly narrow, one of which was made entirely of metal grates through which one could see the churning waters of two Great Lakes below. It was truly a feat of modern engineering that they could hold the thousands of pounds this bus weighed without bending or breaking.

Aiden couldn't let himself ruminate on it too long. It was like flying; if he gave it too much consideration, he'd never be able to make it to the other side without an accompanying panic attack.

As they reached the peak of the structure, a lot of his teammates stood and started snapping photos out of the bus windows.

Aiden texted Kenzie.

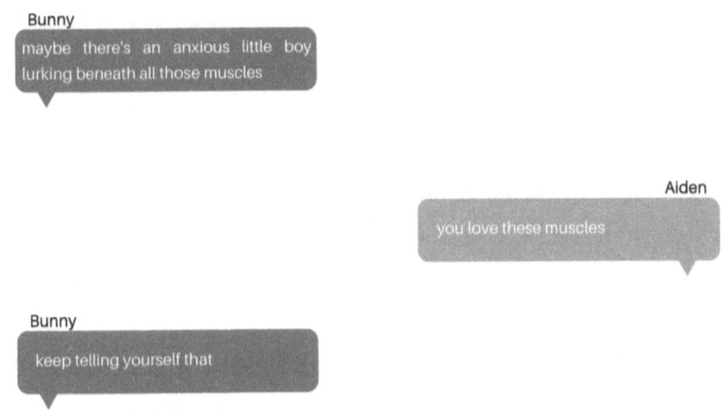

Once they were across the bridge and back on solid ground, the three hours to Marquette passed smoothly. Aiden had his laptop open in front of him, typing up an article for his blog.

As part of one of his journalism classes, Aiden had been tasked with keeping a blog all semester long, detailing his classes, homework, and other extracurriculars he participated in that pertained to his degree.

Lucky for him, he was a student-athlete who spent his days around hockey players. There was no shortage of fodder.

Today's post was about the trip to the UP, and how crossing the Mackinac Bridge was like crossing into a different world.

For starters, there was already snow on the ground, and the bulk of the landscape consisted of trees, trees, and...more trees. Everything about the UP felt more peaceful, slower-paced and quieter, as though these people weren't in any rush to get things done. Like they had all the time in the world.

Aiden's favorite part of the trip was the stretch between the cities of Munising and Marquette, which took them along the edge of

Lake Superior. It was a blustery day, with snow and sand kicked up by the wind and blown across the road. The waves on the lake were towering, white-capped swells that hit the rocky shoreline and sent sprays high into the air.

Lake Superior was cold and unforgiving, and it amazed Aiden that people lived here year-round. Chicago was a lakefront city, too, but the scenes along Lake Shore Drive were worlds away from this.

Marquette was a college town, with a feel at complete odds with the one they'd left behind in East Lansing. For starters, it wasn't only a college town. Yes, Northern Michigan University resided there, but Marquette was also full of families and young professionals in addition to the student population. It was a bustling city that stretched far beyond the reaches of campus.

Not to mention, where East Lansing was all lights and color, high-rise buildings, and guys in skinny jeans and button-up shirts with loafers, Marquette was old, beautiful architecture, people with dreadlocks and flannels, guys wearing oversized parkas and Timberlands, and girls in sweaters and comfortable yet warm-looking boots.

Finally, they arrived at their hotel, the bus dropping them at the doors then driving away to deliver their gear to the arena.

Not that Aiden had any.

As Jack keyed open the door to their room, Aiden's phone rang. He answered without checking the readout, hands full of his backpack and duffel bag.

"Did you survive your trip across the big, scary bridge?" Kenzie asked when he picked up.

"Ha ha, very funny."

"Is that Kenzie?" Jack asked, moving to stand inches away from Aiden. "Tell her I said hi!"

"She can hear you, dumbass," Aiden said, shoving his roommate away.

Kenzie laughed and said, "Hi Jack!"

"As badly as I want to talk to you right now, we just got to the room and I have some homework to finish up before practice tonight."

"That's okay," she said. "I just wanted to say hi and make sure you made it alive."

"We did," he said, smiling. "Thanks for checking."

"Bye, Fuller."

"You guys are so cute it's disgusting," Jack said when Aiden hung up and tossed himself on the bed.

"Thank you," Aiden said, though he was sure Jack hadn't exactly meant it as a compliment.

"You really like her, don't you?"

"Yes, and it scares the shit out of me."

"Why?" Jack asked as he reclined on his own bed.

"I don't know how to give my full attention to anything but hockey."

"From where I'm standing," Jack said, "you've been doing a pretty good job of it already."

"Yeah, but I'm not even playing."

"Why does that have to change anything?" Jack asked. "You're still training with the team and traveling to games exactly like you would be if you were playing."

Aiden considered that for a moment, quickly realizing he had no rebuttal. Jack was right.

Jack continued. "All I'm saying is your relationship doesn't have to change once you start playing again if you don't want it to. You're in control here."

Aiden remained silent while he considered that. Could it really be that simple?

"We've gotten a lot closer the last few weeks," he said finally. "It's been...nice. Different, but nice. I don't want to lose that."

"There's nothing that says you have to," Jack said. "Although, it's weird to see you like this with someone. But I'm happy for you."

"Thanks, man," Aiden said. "I never thought I was the relationship type until Kenzie."

"Personally, I think you've always been a relationship type," Jack told him as he scrolled on his phone. "You were just waiting for the right girl."

And wasn't that statement in the same vein as what Kenzie had said the day before? That they'd been destined to find each other?

With a smile on his face, Aiden decided to take a quick nap before practice, and instantly fell asleep.

The next night, he sat with the rest of his scratched teammates in the uppermost row of seats, directly above the visiting bench inside the Berry Events Center.

Aiden was surprised to find how...open the arena felt. Unlike Munn, where you walked off street level and right onto the concourse, street level here was a set of stairs leading up the concourse, and the rows of seats descended until they flattened at the ice. The players entered at ground level and walked right into the bowels of the building.

Not only that, but the ice was Olympic-sized, meaning the rink was about fifteen feet wider than a standard rink. It provided more room along the wings, making breakaways all the more likely.

Aiden wanted to be down there with his teammates, but he was nonetheless mesmerized.

NMU had been a perennial top finisher in their own conference the last five years, since their current head coach had taken over. Plus, they were at home, where they were used to the oversized ice and had their own fans backing them. Yoopers, as those born and raised in the Upper Peninsula were called, took their hockey seriously, and Wildcat fans were a rowdy and dedicated bunch.

Jack appeared to be having an off night, letting in two quick goals in the first period on ugly bounces he normally would've stopped. Everything else appeared to be running smoothly as far as their offense and defense went, but something was up with Jack.

At intermission, Aiden hurried down to the locker room, leaving the rest of his teammates in the dust.

"What's wrong?" Aiden asked Jack the second he laid eyes on him.

"I don't know," he said. "I'm sweating, but I'm freezing. I just...don't feel right."

Aiden stepped closer and took a good look into Jack's face. His skin was flushed, a sheen of sweat coating his cheeks and forehead. Aiden rested the back of his palm against Jack's forehead, noting the elevated temperature but reminding himself it could be the result of exertion.

"Marta!" Aiden yelled, and a brunette popped her head out of the attached training room, eyebrows furrowed. "Can you come take Jack's temp?"

"Sure thing," she said, withdrawing and reappearing a moment later, then bobbing and weaving her way through the massive hockey players, thermometer in hand.

When she reached Jack and Aiden, she pressed a button and held the device to his head, sweeping it from temple to temple.

"One-oh-one," she said a moment later.

"Fuck," Jack said.

"I'm sorry, Jack, but I have to tell Coach. You're out for the rest of the night."

She made her way back across the locker room, and Aiden watched in horror as she sidled up to Coach, told him about Jack, and sternly relayed the message that their starting goaltender was not allowed back on the ice tonight.

"Fuller! DeLuca!" Coach yelled, crooking a finger in their direction, then disappearing into the office behind him.

The two exchanged a look before obeying.

"Who the fuck got you sick?" Coach asked Jack the second they stepped in front of him.

"Do I really need to be here for this?" Aiden asked.

"Yes," Coach said. "DeLuca is going back to the hotel, and you're taking him."

"In what, exactly?"

"Go find the bus driver and tell him to bring you back," Coach said, shooing the boys away with a flick of his wrist. "Now if you'll excuse me, I have to figure out how to win this damn hockey game without my starting goalie."

The game clock in the locker room ticked closer to the end

of intermission, and Coach went out ahead of them, shouting at the backup goalie that he was in net, then yelling orders at the defensemen to tighten up their game.

Shortly after, they cleared out, leaving Aiden, fully dressed in his suit and tie, and Jack, halfway through undoing his pads, his jersey shed and tossed into the dirty laundry bin across the room.

Aiden left briefly to find the bus driver, alerting him to the small change of plans, then going back to get Jack. By then, Jack had made quick work of removing his gear and changing his clothes. He was shoving his arms into his suit jacket as Aiden re-entered the locker room.

"Let's go," Jack said, shoving an MSU hockey beanie over his blond hair. "I feel like shit. I can't wait to go to sleep."

"Yeah you look like shit, too," Aiden told him, earning a small smile from Jack. "How'd you get sick, anyway?"

"There's something going around the sorority house, so Sofia must have passed it on to me."

They went back to the hotel, and once Jack had stripped and crawled into bed, promptly passing out, Aiden walked to the gas station across the street to get him some Gatorade and cold and flu medicine for when he woke.

Then he settled on his own bed, connecting his AirPods to his phone and turning on the radio broadcast of the game.

The Spartans pulled off a comeback that evening, ultimately winning the game by a score of three to two. After Jack went down, their backup goalie—a sophomore who hadn't seen many game minutes—really stepped up, and the rest of the team did their jobs. They won the next night, too, and returned to East Lansing in good spirits on Sunday.

With that series over, only two games stood between Aiden and getting back on the ice, and it couldn't come soon enough. He hadn't minded taking care of Jack, but he would've preferred to help the team out by scoring goals and playing solid defense.

His chance to do that was coming, and he hoped to be ready for it when it did.

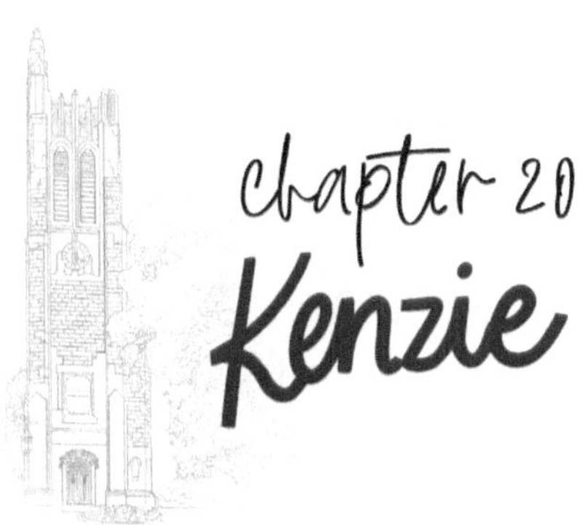

chapter 20
Kenzie

"Isn't celebrating before you even get back on the ice a little...weird?"

Kenzie didn't only think it was weird; she thought it was downright stupid, but she'd never tell Aiden that. The look on his face reminded her of children around Christmas time: his cheeks rosy, eyes glistening with joy, perma-smile stretching across his face.

"Nope," he said happily, slinging his arm across her shoulders the second they stepped out of her building and onto the street.

The first stop of the night was Harper's, which was the perfect spot to get a buzz and dance before it got too busy and they left for elsewhere, most likely Dublin, or even Rick's.

"It's a little weird," Jack said from behind them, startling Kenzie, who had momentarily forgotten he was there.

Aiden turned and shot Jack what Kenzie guessed was a glare over the top of her head. She chuckled, and he pulled her tighter into his side.

"We've never been out together like this," he said to her. "You sure you're ready?"

She shrugged. "It had to happen sometime, right? Aren't you worried how your adoring fans will react?"

She accompanied her words with a poke to his side, and he fake laughed. "I doubt anyone will even notice or care."

Up ahead, the queue for Harper's nearly reached the bottom of a tall staircase, and Kenzie hurried to join it, narrowly beating a group of girls walking down the sidewalk from the opposite direction.

Aiden and Jack reached her as the girls did, and one of them shot her a dirty look while another yelled, "Aiden!" and draped her body across his in what Kenzie guessed was supposed to be a hug.

She tried to quash the jealousy that flared in the pit of her stomach, but to no avail. The girl was tall, thin, and blonde, her short leather skirt showing off her long, tan legs, shoulders and back bared by the halter top she wore.

Kenzie glanced down at her faux-leather leggings and cropped sweater, and frowned. For starters, it was frigid out, winter finally creeping its way over the city in the form of frosty morning grass and temperatures hovering around forty. Second, the girl was stunning, and Kenzie couldn't help comparing her cozy and comfortable outfit with the girl's jaw-dropping, head-turning one.

And she didn't particularly like the way Aiden's big hand splayed across the girl's bare back, either.

"Fuller," Jack called, shooting Kenzie a wink. "Let's go."

Aiden turned back to them and followed Kenzie up the stairs. He looped his arm through hers, and when the line paused again, spun her to face him.

"You're mad, aren't you?"

"No," she lied.

"Mackenzie…"

"She's definitely mad, you idiot," Jack said. "You let that girl hang all over you with your girlfriend standing right there. If I was bunny, I'd punch you in the face and leave you to find someone hotter." Jack turned to Kenzie with a cheeky grin and added, "I fully volunteer for the job, by the way."

Kenzie laughed and stretched onto her tiptoes to kiss Jack on the cheek. "Thank you."

"Kenz," Aiden said quietly, though still loud enough for Jack to hear, if only because he pressed his head into the space between them, hanging on their every word, "if I wanted that girl, I would've had her a long time ago. But I'm a nice guy, and I'm not going to shove her off when she throws herself at me. That's just mean."

"You didn't have to look like you enjoyed it so much," Kenzie said under her breath, though she knew he was right.

Jack snorted, but Aiden captured Kenzie's chin in his hand, fingers splayed across her cheek.

"I don't want anyone but you." He stared deeply into her eyes, the chocolate depths of his melting her. "Do you believe me?"

Before Kenzie could respond, Jack cut in. "If it makes you feel better, bunny, in the entire four years I've known him, I've never seen him with anyone the way he is with you."

Kenzie's wide eyes darted back to Aiden. "Is that true?"

"Yep," he said proudly. "Now do you believe me?"

"Yes."

"Good, now let's celebrate."

And celebrate they did.

Despite the relatively early hour, Harper's was packed, and Kenzie was thankful for both Aiden and Jack's big bodies as the former led her and the latter trailed her to the bar, protecting her from the worst of the crush of bodies.

They ordered drinks, the female bartender passing them out free with a wink at Aiden.

Jack raised his into the middle of their small circle. "To bunny's boyfriend," he said, winking at Kenzie again. To Aiden he added, "I can't wait to have you back out there tomorrow."

Aiden laughed, clinked his bottle with Jack's glass and Kenzie's can, said, "Thank you," then took a long drink.

After two more drinks, Harper's became unbearably populated, and Kenzie's anxiety over the sheer number of people reached its peak. She'd never been able to pinpoint what exactly would trigger an anxiety attack. Tonight, apparently, it was a combination of things. The too-loud music. The girls screaming at each other over the volume of said music. The random guys putting their hands on her body without invitation. The level of inebriation from everyone around her. The buzz along her limbs.

Her heart was in her throat, making it difficult to breathe, pulse pounding a thousand miles a minute.

Finally, she turned to Aiden and said, "Get me out of here, please."

Aiden didn't ask questions, didn't argue or beg to stay longer. He simply set his drink on the nearest flat surface, grabbed her hand, jerked his head at Jack to follow, and led her out of the bar. When they reached the sidewalk, Kenzie sat on a low retaining wall, dropped her head into her hands, and took several deep breaths, in through her nose and out through her mouth.

"Is she okay?" she heard Jack ask quietly.

Aiden must've nodded because he didn't verbally respond, only sat next to Kenzie and placed a reassuring hand between her shoulder blades, right over her sparrow tattoo, anchoring her when lightheadedness threatened to fly her away.

"You're alright, honey," he said. "If you want to go home right now, we can."

Though he couldn't see, she gave him a grateful smile, her heart rate lowering by the fact that he was here, always keeping her safe like he'd promised.

The moment lengthened, and Jack eventually crouched at her other side, clasping her hand between his.

To passersby, it probably appeared as though the boys were comforting a drunk girl. Kenzie couldn't muster the energy to be embarrassed by the picture they presented.

Finally, she lifted her head and gave Jack and Aiden each a wobbly smile, then focused her attention on Jack.

"I have pretty bad anxiety," she told him. "I never know what's going to trigger it, and the crowd in there tonight...it was too much."

Jack nodded and reached out to squeeze her shoulder. "Do you want to go home?" he asked, echoing Aiden's earlier sentiment.

Kenzie shook her head. Now that her heart had slowed below cardiac event levels, her mind cleared and her chest loosened. "No, let's stay out."

"Are you sure?" Aiden asked.

"Very," she said. She stood and dusted her ass off with her palms, and the boys rose with her. "Where to next? Dublin or Rick's?"

Jack flicked his wrist and checked the time on his watch. "It's nearly midnight," he said. "I think it's time for Rick's, don't you guys?"

Kenzie nodded, and Aiden laced his fingers through hers. They walked hand in hand, following Jack across the street and up the block to Rick's.

Once safely inside the basement bar, Kenzie breathed a sigh of relief. Rick's wasn't the nicest bar in the city. In fact, most people would agree it was the dirtiest and dingiest. But she loved it because it was unassuming and unpretentious. It didn't try to be anything but what it was: a dive.

"Drinks?" Jack asked.

"Yes please," Kenzie said. "Vodka soda for me."

"I've got them," Aiden said. "You guys hang back here."

There was a mass of bodies four people deep between them and the bar, and Kenzie melted. Aiden was worried about her, and her heart warmed.

"You're good for him," Jack said when Aiden disappeared into the throng.

"He's good for me, too," she said.

"I'm really happy for you both," he told her, and Kenzie smiled.

"And what about you?" she asked. "Any special ladies Jack DeLuca has his eye on?"

Jack fought it, but a small, self-satisfied smile appeared on his face. It was the kind of smile that said, *I've got a secret*, and Kenzie was dying to know more.

"You do!" she accused, grinning and pointing a finger at him. "Who is she? Anyone I know? Tell me *everything*."

"You do know her, yes. But I'm not saying anything more on the subject. It's new, and I don't want to jinx it."

Kenzie desperately wanted to press him for more, but decided to let him have his secrets...for now.

Still, she couldn't help the way her mind swirled with the possibilities. It had to be Sofia, right? They'd gone on that date to the cider mill a little over a month before, and Sofia had told her in class the next week that they'd had an amazing time and she hoped to see him again. Not to mention the pair had a physical relationship before that date.

But as Kenzie considered it further, she realized Sofia hadn't been around much lately. In fact, she hadn't seen her and Jack together since that party where she'd gotten too drunk and Aiden had to carry her home.

Kenzie's memory tripped over that hockey tailgate, when they'd stepped onto the patio at Munn, and Jack and Jessica had shared that *look.* They clearly knew each other, and Kenzie had a feeling it was in a deeper way than two people who may have crossed paths on campus. Unfortunately, she had been unable to get anything out of Jessica about it, and Jack had been similarly tight-lipped with Aiden.

But she and Jessica were close—practically sisters—and Jack was Aiden's best friend. If Jack was interested in Jessica, it didn't make sense that he wouldn't just say so.

Kenzie opened her mouth to ask, but Aiden returned with their drinks at that moment, and all thoughts of anyone's relationship but her own deserted her.

She'd been staring at him all night, and had seen him in various stages of undress over the last few months, but nothing ever prepared her for the sight of Aiden. Tall, broad-shouldered, each muscle on his body perfectly defined and proportioned. Those big hands and long fingers that held her, wrapped around her, and dug into her flesh in the best ways. The wavy blue-black hair curling around his ears and the edge of his ball cap. The tight black t-shirt with a hooded jean jacket thrown over top. The dark-wash denim with holes in the knees clinging to his quads.

He was a study in perfection, the ultimate prize for straight women, and he was all hers.

The thought made her lightheaded, as though she'd become some Victorian Era heiress ready to swoon and faint at his feet.

"I have to pee," she blurted, then thrust her drink back into Aiden's hand and hurried away from them.

Blessedly, there was no line to the women's restroom, so she slipped into a stall, relieving herself quickly.

While she washed her hands, she looked herself dead in the eye in the mirror above the sink and said, "Get your shit together, Jean. You deserve him. He could have anyone he wants, and he wants you."

After a quick reapplication of her lipstick and an adjustment of her ponytail, she was ready to face him again.

When Kenzie came back from the restroom, Jack was nowhere to be found, but Aiden stood at the edge of the dance floor, unsurprisingly surrounded by a gaggle of females, all vying for his attention.

Right as one spun her back to him, clearly intending to plant her ass in his crotch and dance on him, Kenzie reached his side, and he pulled her to him. The girl bounced off Kenzie's back and whipped around to glare at her before stomping away, two other girls hot on her heels.

Aiden turned her and pulled her back to his chest, settling his hands low on her hips, gripping her tightly, his fingertips like a brand on her soft flesh.

The song changed, a throwback Fetty Wap jam replaced by a popular Tiesto song, and without thinking, Kenzie and Aiden began to sway side to side to the beat.

Kenzie tried to melt into the moment, to lose herself in the feel of Aiden's hands on her body, the way his heartbeat thumped against her shoulders in time with the bass of "The Motto." But she couldn't quite enjoy herself, couldn't ignore the way eyes tracked every move they made, the bulk of them females staring at her with open disgust.

"I don't think you understand the effect you have on women," she yelled over the music, tilting her head back to look at him over her shoulder.

Aiden ducked so his mouth was level with her ear. "The only woman I care about is you," he said, voice low and husky, sending shivers skittering across her skin. He pulled her impossibly closer, until not even a millimeter of space remained between them, the thick length of his cock pressing against her ass. "Because *this* is how *you* affect *me*. Every single second I'm around you, I'm hard. It's embarrassing, like I'm a teenager again with these uncontrollable urges. I want you every second of every day."

Kenzie spun in his arms and rose onto her tiptoes, throwing her arms around his neck and crashing her mouth to his.

The kiss was almost punishing, a way to prove to him that she felt all the things he did. That she felt connected to him in a way she never had with anyone else. A promise that she wanted him as badly as he wanted her.

Aiden broke the kiss and grabbed her hand, pulling her off the dance floor and out of the bar, then down the block until he found an alley.

He led her down it and backed her against a brick wall, then lowered his mouth to hers.

His kiss was all-consuming, and if Kenzie hadn't already had several seltzers in her, she'd be drunk on the way his mouth moved against hers, and the way their tongues tangled. How he tasted of beer but smelled like he always did—clean with a note of something that could only be described as masculine. Aiden was a pure, undiluted *male*.

"As your boyfriend," he whispered against her ear, hands skating down her sides, "I think I should know the sounds you make when you come."

"You're not my boyfriend," she croaked, the heat of his palms on her body so at odds with the chill seeping through her top from the building at her back. They hadn't actually defined their relationship yet, though she couldn't deny they'd both been seriously committed to each other in all but name for the last month. Still, she couldn't help needling him a little bit, desperately wanting to see how he responded.

Aiden leaned in and pressed a kiss to that sweet spot right below her ear. Kenzie shivered, and felt his lips curve into a smile against her skin. "I don't know about you," he said, his already deep voice growing impossibly more so with what Kenzie could only describe as desire, "but I've considered myself yours since that day you handed me my ass outside Case. I want you to be my girlfriend. And I want to be your boyfriend. Is that something you want?"

His words sent a rush of pleasure through her, amplifying the reaction he'd already elicited with his hands and mouth and sheer nearness.

"Fuller, this isn't really the time—"

"I think this is the perfect time. Do you want to be my girlfriend?"

"Aiden..."

"Answer me," he growled, and she'd be damned if she didn't get impossibly wetter at his commanding tone. "Answer me or we're going back inside right now."

She didn't like being put on the spot like this, and didn't like that her pleasure was contingent on providing an answer to what, really, should be a simple question.

And it *was* simple, wasn't it? If Kenzie were honest with herself, she had been falling for him since the moment she'd laid eyes on him. Since he'd dared her to get a free drink, then asked her to come home with him. Since she'd seen how he was with his family. Since he'd taken care of her drunk ass, then made her come undone with only his fingers and his words.

In every moment, he'd handled her with care.

All along, slowly, day by day, she'd been falling.

She wanted him. Badly. In every possible way. And the hard line of his cock against her stomach said he felt the same.

So she turned her head slightly and brushed her mouth over his, saying, "Yes. I want to be your girlfriend. Now make me cum."

Swiftly, he scooped her off her feet, and she instinctively wrapped her legs around his waist like a koala clinging to a tree as he crashed his mouth to hers.

Aiden shifted his stance so his legs were set wider, his massive thighs supporting the bulk of her weight so he could dive his hand down the front of her leggings.

Deftly, he made contact with her clit, and Kenzie dropped her head back, the slight sting when the brick bit into her skull nothing compared to the waves of pleasure already radiating from Aiden's touch.

She ground harder against him, urging him on, breathy moans she should've been working harder to silence escaping her. Aiden chuckled.

"You like that, don't you?" he asked. "Is it just that it feels good? Or is it because anyone could walk by and catch us at any moment? Who knew my little bunny was such a dirty girl?"

Spurred on by his words, Kenzie's release rolled through her, waves of exquisite pleasure blooming from Aiden's fingers and then cresting and crashing. She trembled in his arms as he applied steady pressure while she rode out the orgasm.

"Aiden..." she said, mind swirling, thoughts completely incoherent as she came down from the high. "I want you."

Even in the faint light reaching from the street to their hidden spot in this darkened alley, she saw his eyebrows shoot toward his forehead in surprise.

"Now?"

"Now," she confirmed, then reached between them and made hasty work of the button and zipper of his jeans, pushing them and his boxers out of the way enough to take him in her hand.

At her first touch, he hissed through his teeth. As she wrapped her fingers around him, she suddenly doubted her ability to take him into her body.

"Aiden," she said, her tone tinged with amazement and a little fear. "It's been like...a really long time."

Aiden, whose attention had been focused on his cock and its exposure to her touch, raised his head to look at her. The depths of his eyes twinkled like stars winking in and out of the night sky, and a slow, sexy smile—the one he only flashed when he knew he was about to do something epic—spread across his face.

"Don't worry," he said, rolling her leggings down her hips and reaching down to insert a finger into her pussy, and then another, and then a third, preparing her for a much larger appendage. "I'll be gentle. This pussy is mine now, along with everything else. I'll take good care of it."

"Yours," she agreed.

Warmth spread along her limbs, like an egg cracked atop her head that slowly leaked down and down and down. Kenzie had never pegged herself as a girl who was into dirty talk, nor had she ever been with a guy who could back up his big talk in the streets with any sort of sexual prowess between the sheets.

But she was completely turned on by everything this man did, and she felt more safe and cared for in his arms than anywhere else.

Kenzie wanted to be a different girl with Aiden, one who wasn't a slave to the whims of her own negative thoughts and unpredictable anxiety. One who wasn't afraid to take chances, who went after exactly what she wanted and didn't apologize for it.

And right now, what she wanted was *him*. She'd already given him more pieces of herself than anyone before, so what was one more?

Clutching Aiden's shoulders, she pulled him impossibly closer.

"Now," she said, and as always, he understood exactly what she was asking.

"My wallet," he said through gritted teeth.

Without asking why, she reached into his back pocket and flipped the wallet open, easily finding the condom. She wasn't entirely surprised he was the kind of guy to always have one.

She replaced his wallet and ripped the foil open with her teeth, then slowly rolled the rubber down his length and gave him a squeeze at the base that had him bucking into her hand.

The head of his cock pushing inside her stung a bit, but he paused, giving her time to adjust, before giving her more and more until he bottomed out.

"You feel *amazing,*" he said with a groan, fingers digging deliciously into her ass.

Kenzie echoed the sentiment with a moan, unsure if she could form words right now.

They fit together perfectly, like two adjacent pieces of a puzzle, like they were made for each other.

Two halves of a whole.

Kenzie knew she was ruined. The exquisite way he nestled perfectly inside her, the way she'd relaxed and stretched after that initial discomfort, how she gripped him, tight like a glove, from base to tip.

She'd never find this again, and she didn't want to.

Aiden's head dropped to her shoulder. He hadn't moved yet, and Kenzie wiggled a little on top of him, trying to elicit a reaction.

"Kenzie," he growled, tone laced with warning.

"Fuller." She said his name like a command, but tacked one on for good measure. "Move."

He obeyed instantly, pulling all the way out and pushing back in, the stroke torturously slow.

"Fuck," she said. He'd managed to hit a spot impossibly deeper than before, and she shivered.

"Aiden," she said, cupping his cheeks in her hands so he would look at her. "As much as I would love to wring this out for as long as we possibly can, you do realize we're only about fifty feet from half of East Lansing's population, right?"

"So you're saying you want it fast and rough?" he asked, one corner of his mouth ticking up into a smirk.

Slowly, he withdrew until he was poised at her entrance. Kenzie could only nod.

Aiden turned his head and kissed her hard, biting at her lower lip. "Hold on."

She wrapped her arms around his neck, burying her fingers deep in the thick waves of his hair as he began to move.

Having gotten off only minutes before, she didn't expect to do so again, content to be joined with him and let him use her in any way he needed to. She was surprised when an orgasm once again built in that spot low in her belly.

Compared to the first one, it was a slow burn, the warmth slowly crawling up her torso and along her limbs. Judging by his erratic movements, Kenzie guessed Aiden was close, too.

Confirming her suspicions, he said, "Fuck, I'm almost there."

She dug her heels into his ass, and his hands tightened on her thighs.

He adjusted his stance, changing the angle so he, somehow, hit an all new spot inside her, and Kenzie fucking loved it.

"Oh my gaahhhhh," she moaned. "Right there."

"Kenzie." Her name was a gasped plea. "How did we go so long?"

Somehow, she understood he didn't mean sex.

He meant a lifetime spent without *this*, without each other.

"I don't know," she gasped. A particularly aggressive thrust had her back slamming into the brick wall, and before she could even open her mouth to protest, Aiden once again shifted his weight and wrapped an arm around her waist, the other a bar under her ass, providing a barrier between her and further pain, but still fully supporting her weight.

He continued his frantic fucking, mumbling words of encouragement and compliments all the while, until Kenzie could feel his whole body trembling with the effort of holding himself back.

And she was *right there*, but she knew she needed him to let go before she could allow herself to do the same.

"I can't wait to fuck you in a bed," he growled.

"Fuller," Kenzie said, his name choked off as a moan escaped her lips.

"Yeah Kenz?"

She grabbed fistfuls of his hair and tugged, tilting his head back to look him in the eye. Sweat beaded along his hairline, the only outward manifestation of exactly how much work he was putting in here. Never again would Kenzie complain about how much time he spent at the rink.

"Stop talking and let go," she said.

As though she'd flipped a switch, Aiden did what she asked, coming undone with several long pulses inside her, his entire body going rigid while he rode out the orgasm.

Like a chain reaction, Kenzie followed him over the edge. She arched her back and dug her fingers into Aiden's shoulders, knowing full well she would've drawn blood without the barrier of fabric between them.

Once they stilled and their breathing slowed, Aiden pulled free, her pussy aching with the loss of him. Kenzie unwound her legs from his waist and he loosened his grip on her, letting her slide along his front until she could put her feet on the ground.

While she righted her leggings, Aiden removed the condom, tied it in a knot, and tucked it into his pocket once he pulled up his jeans.

Without warning, he backed her against the wall and kissed her.

This was more than a kiss. Aiden fucking *consumed* her. Their joining had only recently ended, and Aiden kissed her like he couldn't wait to do it again.

Fuck, she wanted that mouth so much lower.

His tongue plunged into her mouth, rubbing against her own, and she nipped and sucked in response, their teeth clashing in a way that should've seemed awkward and inexperienced, but for Kenzie only added to her infatuation with Aiden Fuller. Neither of them cared that the kiss was messy and uncoordinated; they simply needed to be connected.

Finally, they broke apart, both sensing the longer they spent back here, the more likely they were to get caught. And after his near-arrest for public nudity, Kenzie couldn't risk something similar happening again. Not when he was about to get back on the ice.

"Let's go home," she said, reaching down to thread her fingers through his and tow him back onto the well-lit city street.

"Your place or mine?"

"Mine," she said, then tossed him a saucy little grin over her shoulder. "I want more, all night, and I don't want any pesky roommates lingering outside your door like the creeps they are."

"They mean well," he said sheepishly.

"I'm sure they do," she said. They were only two blocks from her building now, and she tipped her head back, looking up at her darkened windows. "Besides," she added. "At my place, we can be as loud as we want."

Aiden pulled her to his side and tossed his arm around her shoulders, pressing his mouth against her ear. "And I'm going to make you scream."

Fuck. Yes.

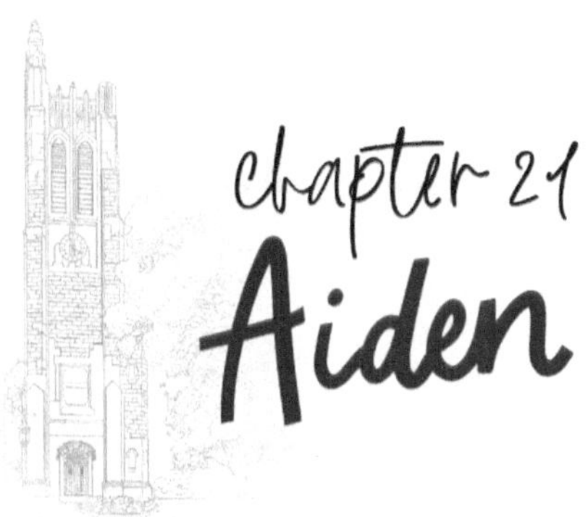

chapter 21
Aiden

"WHERE DID YOU AND bunny disappear to last night?" Jack asked when Aiden walked into their house the next morning.

"A gentleman doesn't kiss and tell," he said.

Jack smirked knowingly. "How was it?"

Aiden considered that for a moment, unsure if there was a word in the entirety of the English language that would adequately express last night's experience. So he settled on, "Mind-blowing."

Jack's answering grin was of the shit-eating variety. "Well you forgot something," he said, and withdrew Aiden's debit card from his wallet. "I squared up."

"Oh fuck," Aiden said, reaching for the piece of plastic. "Thanks."

"Sounds like you did," Jack said with a wink, then turned to go back upstairs.

Aiden smiled, remembering flashes of golden brown skin, dark brown hair, vibrant blue eyes, pink lips, soft warmth against hard heat, tongues, teeth, and endless sighs and moans of pleasure.

Leaving Kenzie's bed this morning had been a feat of Herculean strength, but Aiden had bigger fish to fry at the moment.

He got to play today.

The smile grew into a full-blown grin.

Finally.

It had been a full seven months since Aiden had suited up for a game, but he donned his gear by muscle memory, laser focused on the task at hand, his mind completely blocking out the chatter of his teammates around him in the locker room.

A sophomore by the name of Pascoe, who happened to have played on a line with Aiden and Asher last season, sat down at his stall next to Aiden's and asked, "You nervous?"

Aiden shook his head. "Nah. Just ready to get back out there."

"We're happy to have you back," Pascoe said, and Aiden gave him a tight-lipped smile.

The team had done well in his absence, going undefeated in non-conference play and splitting with conference opponents Minnesota and Wisconsin.

Tonight they took on Notre Dame, a five hundred team that hit hard and skated fast. Aiden didn't think their record reflected the whole story, and he was more than ready to get out there and bury them.

Coach entered the room and stepped to the white board in the corner, picking up a dark green dry-erase marker and scribbling out numbers. All conversation in the room ceased, the only sound the squeaking of the marker as it flew across the surface of the board.

"Lines for tonight," Coach said unnecessarily; they'd all been through this enough times.

Aiden scanned the lines, searching for his number twenty-seven.

Eventually, he found it on the fourth line, on the wing of two freshmen.

Surely, the rest of his teammates had noticed, too, and several of them shot him disbelieving looks. Aiden quickly strapped on the rest of his gear and hurried across the carpeted floor to where Coach stood with one of the trainers.

"Fourth line?" Aiden said without preamble once he reached his coach. "Really?"

Coach gripped Aiden's upper arm and pulled him out of the locker room and into the deserted hallway. When on flat feet, Aiden looked his coach directly in the eye, but somehow, even with his skates giving him two or three extra inches, the man still managed to make Aiden feel small.

"First of all, don't air your shit in front of your teammates. I guarantee you just made those freshmen you're playing with feel like shit for being on the bottom line. Second, you haven't played a game in seven months, Fuller. And I know you've worked your ass off during your suspension to stay in shape and keep your game sharp, but neither of us knows how tonight is going to go. So you're taking short shifts and playing with those freshmen until I see what I need to see to move you back to your usual line. I don't want to hear another word on the subject. Understood?"

Aiden nodded, sufficiently chastised. "Understood."

As it turned out, Coach had been right to give Aiden time to readjust, and after the showing he put on, he wouldn't be back on a line with Asher and Pascoe anytime soon.

He skated out for his first shift since April about four minutes into the first period. As he'd expected, Notre Dame's players threw their bodies around, cutting off lanes up the wings by tossing Spartans carelessly into the boards. Offense was choppy, passes that should've gone tape to tape getting cut off at the last second, the puck turned over repeatedly in the neutral zone.

Aiden knew what he needed to do. He'd played in hundreds of games—probably thousands, actually—in his lifetime.

Unfortunately, whatever synapses that sent those directions from his brain to his limbs were experiencing some sort of disconnect. Instead of feeling fast and fluid, skating and taking shots and checking opponents like it was muscle memory, he was slow and sloppy, his passes inaccurate, shots embarrassingly wide of the net.

Then there was the fact that he almost gave Notre Dame a goal because of a dumb mistake.

He'd been behind the net on a change, Jack shifting restlessly in the crease as he tended to do, keeping himself amped up in case things went sideways quickly.

And they did.

Asher came over the boards and streaked into the neutral zone, then across the blue line, and Aiden passed to him. In the same moment, a Notre Dame player came flying onto the scene, intercepted the pass, and nearly caught Jack off guard on his glove side.

Aiden came off the ice shortly after, and his line didn't take a shift again for several minutes.

Honestly, he'd never been more thankful to see the end of a period than when the buzzer sounded at the end of the first.

"What is going on with you?" Jack asked from behind him as

they padded single file down the tunnel at first intermission.

Aiden shrugged. "I'm rusty."

Jack grabbed Aiden's shoulder and spun him until his back was against the wall, their teammates streaming by, unbothered by whatever was going on between the two.

"That's not *rust*," Jack said, using air quotes around the word. "I know better than anyone there's no *rust* on your body. This is all in your head."

Aiden hated how well Jack knew him, and was embarrassed to admit how right he was.

Coach appeared then. "Problem here?"

Jack shook his head. "Just helping Fuller get his shit together."

Coach gave him a nod and continued on to the media room, where they'd review tape and make adjustments for the second period. For all Aiden's bone-headed game play, the score was luckily tied at zero.

"Tell me what's really going on," Jack said. "Now."

Aiden hesitated despite the fire in Jack's eyes and the stern expression that said he'd beat it out of Aiden if needed.

And truthfully, what *was* his problem?

He'd been prepared to have a couple growing pains after not playing for over half a year, but this was more than that. He knew it, Coach knew it, and Jack knew it, too.

"Kenzie," he said with a sigh.

Jack nodded indulgently. "I figured. Go on."

"I don't want to let her down," he said. "She's never seen me play before, and you know me. I talk big game. My stats from previous seasons speak for themselves, but...I just want her to be proud of me."

"Well she's not with you because you're a hockey player," Jack reminded him. "In fact, you being a hockey player is what sent her running in the first place. She's with you because she cares about you. But if you want to make her proud, you're not doing a very good job of it right now."

"I know," Aiden said, raising his gloved hands to his hair and awkwardly pulling at the strands. "And I feel like I'm being pulled in two directions out there. My mind is half focused on my game and half focused on what she's thinking, watching every move I make. She's not just some random girl, you know? Her brother is ridiculously talented, so she's used to watching stellar athletes. What if I don't measure up? I don't know what to do."

"Play your game," Jack said simply, as though it were that easy. "I realize it's easier said than done, but you've been playing hockey for a long time, Fuller. Long before bunny came into the picture. Stop acting like this is your first game ever. It's just another night, exactly like the thousands you've played in before. Forget about Kenzie. Forget about everything happening outside of those boards. Focus on this. Stop letting your heart do the talking and use that brain of yours. Let it go for the next forty minutes. Your game will come back."

Aiden studied Jack for a long moment, until Luke poked his head out of the media room and hollered for them to get their asses inside.

"When did you become so philosophical?" Aiden asked.

"I'm a goalie," Jack reminded him, "so if anyone knows anything about mental fortitude and shaking off a bad period or game, it's me."

Jack entered the media room ahead of him, and Aiden paused

for a second longer, inhaling deeply.

Let it go let it go let it go, he chanted to himself as he held his breath in for three...two...one...

He exhaled and stepped inside to join his teammates, turning his focus wholly to the task at hand: winning this game.

The rest of the game went about as well as the first period, which is to say Aiden continued to play like shit. He tried to compartmentalize, but every time he skated past the student section, he thought of Kenzie, and wondered what she thought of him.

It caused him to blunder a lot of plays, and the pitying looks his teammates shot his way certainly didn't help matters. The freshmen on his line who had started the game excited to play with him now avoided him in the locker room.

He'd become a pariah, an angel fallen from grace.

Everything he'd worked so hard for was firmly back within reach now that his suspension was up, and he was fucking it all up because of a girl.

Kenzie wasn't just any girl, obviously. He cared deeply about her, and it was difficult to imagine his life without her in it, despite the fact that they'd only known each other for a few months. They'd shared things with each other that they'd never been able to with anyone else, and their connection was something special.

Once in a lifetime kind of special.

"What's going on with you?" Kenzie asked when they'd crawled into bed that night.

"What do you mean?" he asked, reclining back on his pillows, arms bent behind his head, studiously avoiding her gaze in favor of watching the ceiling fan whir above him.

"You looked like shit, and somehow I don't think that's how you usually play."

"So I had an off night," he said irritably. "I haven't played in seven months, bunny. Cut me some slack."

"I think there's more to it than that."

Aiden absolutely did not want to have this conversation right now, but it wouldn't do either of them any good to hold it in.

"I…" he began, then cut off. How did he word this in a way that wouldn't upset her? "I'm struggling to compartmentalize."

"Compartmentalize what, exactly?"

"You and my game," he said, rolling onto his side to face her. "I've never been in this situation before, and I don't know how to do this. I care about you, so much, but hockey is—was—everything to me before you."

"You don't know how to do, what, exactly? Be with me and play hockey at the same time?"

"Yes," he admitted, voice barely above a whisper.

Kenzie was silent for long, tense moments, and Aiden's pulse pounded loudly in his ears while he waited.

"Do you want me to stop coming to your games? I can do that for you, Fuller, if that's what you need. Do you want me to leave right now? Do you want to…table this? Us? Until you figure your shit out?"

She didn't sound angry, or hurt; simply resigned, which was somehow even worse.

"I want to not be such a fuckup," he said finally.

"Unfortunately, that's not a solution to the problem at hand."

He wished he could see her face. Outwardly, she appeared calm, but they weren't touching, and the darkness prevented him from studying her expression. Somehow, he knew her heart was thrumming in her chest, her throat and chest probably tight with anxiety, but her voice was even.

"I think..." he said, hesitating.

"Just say it, Fuller."

"I think it would be best if you didn't come to my games anymore," he said. "At least until I'm back in a rhythm. It sounds so dumb, but I've never really had anyone to play for. My mom, sister, and Dan have been watching me play for ages. You're...new. And you're very important to me. Tonight, all I could think about was not making a fool of myself in front of you, and I ended up doing the exact opposite. I need to give my team one hundred percent, and I'm not sure I can do that if I know you're somewhere in the building, watching every move I make."

"If that's what you need, then that's what I'll give you," she said with zero hesitation. She reached out to him, settling a hand in the center of his chest. "I never want to be a distraction for you, Aiden. I *want* you to succeed, and if you need your games to be a Kenzie-free zone, then they will be."

The weight that had settled on Aiden's shoulders lifted, and he inhaled deeply, the remnants of the perfume Kenzie had put on that morning filling his nose. He caught her hand in his and lifted it to his mouth, pressing a kiss to the center of her palm. "I don't know what I did to deserve you," he said quietly, more comfortable being vulnerable in the pitch black than he'd be in the light. "But I want this to work. I want *us* to work. I promise it won't always be like this."

"I know," she said, equally as quiet. "I'm not going anywhere."

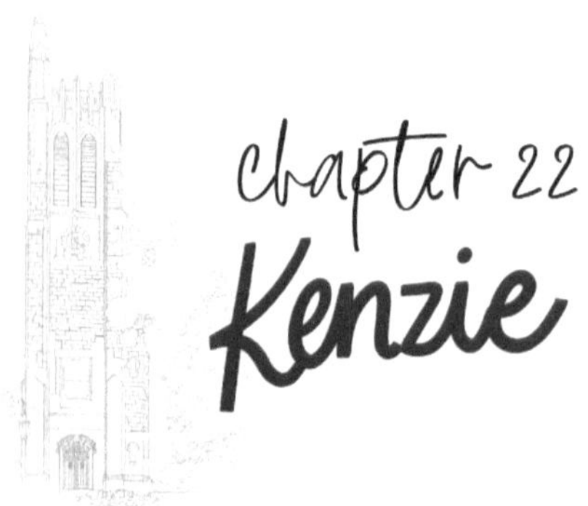

chapter 22
Kenzie

THREE WEEKS PASSED IN a blink, and suddenly Kenzie was staring down the barrel of her first end-of-semester exams at Michigan State.

It was a Wednesday afternoon in early December, and Kenzie and Jessica sat at IHOP, where they'd decided to get a late lunch. It had been a while since they'd spent any time together, Kenzie too wrapped up in Aiden and Jessica busy with student teaching and her own relationship.

"How are things with Silas anyway?" Kenzie asked when Jessica mentioned he was planning a fancy date night for their anniversary the upcoming weekend.

"Things were rough for a bit there," she admitted. "But...I think we're back on track. This weekend should help."

Unfortunately for Jessica, the words leaving her lips didn't match the expression on her face. It seemed as though she was trying to convince herself as well as Kenzie, and Kenzie's eyes narrowed. Jessica studiously ignored her, focusing her attention on her hands curled around a mug of coffee.

There was a reason Jessica had lied to her, and it definitely had something to do with a certain Spartan goaltender. But Kenzie knew pressing the issue wouldn't yield the results she wanted, so she dropped it.

With feigned enthusiasm, she said, "That's great to hear, Jess."

The compliment sounded dull, even to her own ears.

"And how about you and Aiden?" Jessica asked, clearly trying to turn the attention away from herself.

Kenzie sighed, unsure where to begin. "He's finally playing again, right? And he looked like absolute shit in his first game back. I figured it was a fluke, or something was bothering him, so I confronted him about it that night. Turns out the thing bothering him was me."

Jessica gasped, and Kenzie held up a hand to halt the tirade she was surely about to embark on. "I guess he's struggling to compartmentalize, which I don't entirely understand because he's been playing hockey for a hundred years, but whatever," she said, waving a hand flippantly.

"This is not a *but whatever* kind of conversation, Kenzie. What the hell happened?"

"He asked me to stop coming to his games."

"That little shit," Jessica said. "I'll kill him."

Kenzie laughed despite her frustration. "I told him I'd do whatever he wanted, and that was the compromise. The thing is...it seems to have worked for the most part."

"What do you mean?" Jessica asked after the waitress appeared with their platters of food.

"Despite his shitty play that Friday night, they still won, and Saturday he had a much better game. The last two weekends they've been out of town, and he scored four times and notched six assists, so he's in good shape points-wise. They've got Michigan this weekend, so I'm happy his game is coming back. But he's still been distant, despite the fact that I gave him exactly what he asked for. I've hardly seen him. Before when they traveled, he'd call me and FaceTime me all the time. Now it's like he can't get off the phone with me fast enough.

"When they got back on Sunday, I expected him to come over so we could...you know..." she trailed off.

"I get it. You wanted to fuck his brains out after not seeing him for a while."

"Precisely," Kenzie said with a chuckle. "Eventually he invited me over to the house, but nothing happened because he claimed he was exhausted, and he passed out while we were watching a movie. I feel like he's pulling away, but I can't figure out why. What happened over the last three weeks? How did we end up here?"

"I hate to state the obvious here, Kenz, but you need to have a conversation with him. Have you tried to talk to him about it?"

"No..."

Jessica exhaled roughly, clearly exasperated. "You need to."

Then she promptly dug into her food, leaving Kenzie swirling in the vortex of her thoughts.

As Kenzie walked through her apartment door an hour later, Berkley called.

"Hey Berk," she said, dropping her purse on the sideboard. "I just left lunch with Jessica."

"How is my little sister?" Berkley asked. "She never calls me anymore."

Kenzie laughed at Berkley's pouting tone. "She's good. Busy preparing for her end-of-semester evaluation. She's nervous."

"She's a great teacher," Berkley said. "She'll do wonderful."

"How about you text her and tell her that?"

"I think I will."

"I'm assuming there was a reason you called me?"

"Oh!" her sister-in-law gasped and giggled. "I totally forgot *I* called *you*. Pregnancy brain is such a bitch. Anyway, I wanted to see if you were still coming tonight?"

"Coming where?" Kenzie asked dumbly.

"Your brother's game?" Berkley said. "Your parents are in town?"

"Shit!" Kenzie said. "I completely forgot. But yes, I'll be there."

"What's going on?" Berkley asked.

"How do you know something is going on?"

"You do realize how strange it is that I just had to remind you that your own parents are in town, right?"

Kenzie snorted. "Okay, fair. It's just a little Aiden drama."

"Lay it on me," Berkley said. "I've got time."

With a resigned sigh, Kenzie repeated everything she'd told Jessica, thankful her brother's marriage had given her the sisters she'd been desperate for her entire life.

She loved her brothers, but they weren't exactly the ideal sounding boards for girl talk.

"Have you talked to him about it?"

"Your sister asked me the same question, and the answer is still no."

"You need to," Berkley said, yet again echoing Jessica's words.

"Take it from someone who knows: not communicating your feelings and worries will be the death of your relationship."

"I'll talk to him later. Tomorrow. Next week after exams." *Sometime in the future*, she thought. *Maybe never. Who knows.*

"Do it tonight," Berkley said sternly. "As a matter of fact, you should bring him tonight. You can clear the air on the drive over and he can meet your parents finally. Your mom has been pumping me for information about him, you know."

Kenzie groaned. "I'll think about it."

"Sounds good. See you later," Berkley said, then disconnected.

You should bring him tonight.

Berkley's words stuck in her brain like a popcorn kernel stuck in her teeth.

Should she? Her parents would be there, and of course Berkley, and probably Lexie and Mitch if they were in town. Nate would definitely be there if he wasn't on shift or on call. It could be a lot to throw at Aiden at once with their relationship on such rocky ground, but it could also be exactly what they needed to get back on track.

After a moment's hesitation, she called him, fully planning to talk to him about whatever was going on with him.

"Hi bunny," he said when he picked up.

"Hey you," she said. All her plans for a serious conversation went out the window when she heard his voice, that deep and low rumble that caressed her body even through a phone line, and instead she blurted, "Do you want to go to a Warriors game with me tonight?"

"It's a school night."

"Yeah but it's a free hockey game. In Brent's suite. Please? I really want you to be there. I want you to meet my parents."

Aiden was silent for so long, Kenzie was certain he was trying to come up with the best way to turn her down. Instead, he surprised her by saying, "What time are we leaving?"

"Six," she said. "I'll pick you up."

"Not a chance," he said. "I'll be outside your building at 5:45."

Kenzie rolled her eyes but didn't argue, knowing it was a fight she wouldn't win. If Kenzie had learned anything about Aiden these last few months, it was that he took being a gentleman and the conventional rules of dating seriously. It was one of the many things she liked about him. "Fine. I'll see you later."

"Bye," he said and hung up.

She'd talk to him tonight on the drive to Detroit, and hope it didn't ruin the entire night.

Exactly as he'd said he would, Aiden was waiting for her fifteen minutes before six. When she hopped into the car, she leaned across the console to give him a kiss, which he enthusiastically returned.

He shot her that panty-dropping smile and said, "You look hot."

Kenzie glanced down at her distressed jeans, the denim so dark it was nearly black, and cropped Warriors hoodie with "JEAN 22" on the back.

"Thank you," she said. "You always look hot."

Aiden laughed and reached for her hand, pressing a kiss to the back before depositing it in her lap, attention turning to the road where snow fell softly.

Had she imagined the disconnect between them over the last few weeks?

She'd had several expectations for tonight, but not a single one of them had included getting the old Aiden back. The reemergence of this fun, flirty, supremely sexy version of Aiden in his black jeans, tight black shirt, and hooded jean jacket had Kenzie ready to make him pull over so she could drag him up to her apartment and undress him.

But now was not the time.

Kenzie's mind spun. Was it even worth voicing her concerns now that he seemed to have turned back into his normal self?

Berkley's words once again echoed in her head.

Not communicating your feelings and worries will be the death of your relationship.

Resolved, she opened her mouth as they passed through Howell.

Never once had she been anxious in his presence, but now...her hands trembled in her lap, skin suddenly chilled and clammy all at once.

"Are we okay?"

Aiden shot her a quick sideways glance, the headlights whizzing by from the opposite direction setting his eyes glinting in the darkness.

"Of course," he said. "Why wouldn't we be?"

"Something is going on with you," she said. "You've been really distant these last few weeks. Basically since your suspension ended."

"I haven't been distant," he argued, and she noticed a tinge of annoyance in his tone. "I've been busy. Now that I'm playing again, I have to learn how to juggle everything."

"So now I'm something you have to juggle?" she asked, unable to help herself, hurt lacing every word. It was an overreaction.

She knew that. Mentally, she screamed at herself to chill out. It was a shame her mouth didn't want to listen. "I thought we already moved past this. You promised me things would get better. I stopped going to your games, Aiden. Because you asked me to. Because you seemed to think that would be some magical cure-all for whatever mental block you experienced."

"That's not what I'm saying. But look...I've never had a relationship like this. I've never really had a relationship at all that lasted more than a few nights. Before it was hockey, hockey, hockey all the time. And now...now there's you, too. I'm struggling to balance the two. I'm struggling to give both you and my team the time and attention you deserve."

Kenzie understood he was trying to make her feel better by confiding in her, by giving her this vulnerable piece of himself. She knew Aiden was fallible; he was human, after all. But to her, based on this conversation and the way he'd treated her and their relationship the last few weeks, she felt like she was more of a hindrance to his life than a benefit.

"If that's how you feel, why did you come with me tonight?"

Aiden didn't have a temper, at least not in any explosive way Kenzie had witnessed in their time together. He'd always been quiet and thoughtful, carefully considering each thought he had before speaking it into existence, never raising his voice to her or flying off the handle when things went sideways.

The same could not be said for her, who stewed in his passenger seat, like a vat of soup ready to bubble over.

"I don't understand what you're asking," Aiden said finally.

"You just told me you don't know how to navigate this, *us*, and hockey at the same time," she said, steam releasing from that pot inside her. "So why did you come with me tonight? It seems like you should be home focusing on your series with Michigan this weekend."

"Where is this coming from?" Aiden asked, deftly avoiding the question, which only infuriated Kenzie more.

"You've told me from the beginning that hockey is and always will be your number one priority, Aiden. I get that. My brother was the same kind of guy before he met Berkley. I have no delusions here that I'm the Berkley Daniels to your Brent Jean. So I'm asking you now: how do I fit into your life going forward? Do you even want me to?"

Suddenly, Aiden smashed the brake pedal and swerved to the side, coming to a stop on the edge of the median that separated the eastbound traffic from the west. He angrily stabbed at the button for his flashers, unbuckled his seatbelt, and turned to her.

"That's really how you feel?"

Aiden's face was illuminated by the lights of passing cars, every line of his full lips, chiseled cheekbones, sharp jaw, and long, straight nose etched in...fury.

He was *angry*? *He* was angry?

Well, welcome to the fucking club, Fuller.

"I don't know how to feel," she answered, trying to keep the lid on her rising temper. "All I know is that things the last few weeks, since you started playing again, have been weird. We hardly see each other, and I get it. I knew it was going to be an adjustment. But you told me it wouldn't affect us, and it is. You know it is."

The scariest part about this whole conversation was realizing how far she'd truly fallen for him, and how cutting him out of her life now would be removing something vital from the very fiber of her being. But she'd known from the beginning how important hockey was to him, and she couldn't ever let herself get in the way of that.

"I'm not asking you to choose here, Aiden," she said. "But to me, it feels like you already have and you're just too afraid to say it out loud."

Aiden scrubbed a hand over his head, the inky strands of his hair standing every which way. "I never planned on you," he said quietly. "I had a routine, rules. Things that would get me where I wanted to go. And you came along and threw a wrench into the whole damn thing. We're floating in space here. You have to give me time. Can you do that for me? Trust me enough to wait here with me while I figure it out?"

Could she?

Yet again, he hadn't answered her question, avoiding the actual topic at hand. But Kenzie pushed down her reservations and locked them in a box, burying them in some deep, dark, infrequently traveled corner of her mind. A problem to deal with on a different day.

Right now, Aiden wasn't explicitly saying one way or the other where he thought their relationship was going. All he was asking for was time and trust.

She could give him that.

"Yes."

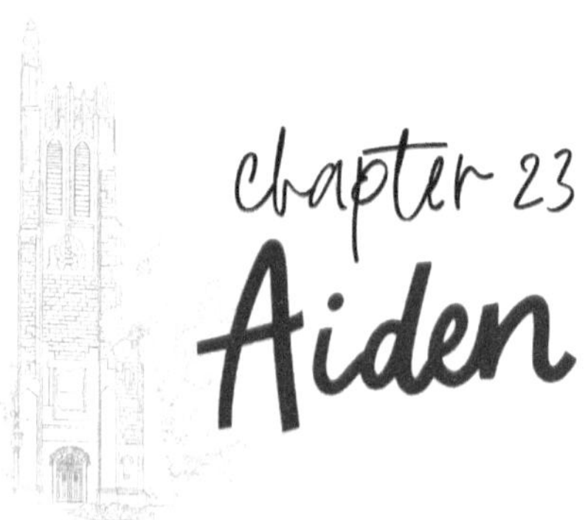

chapter 23
Aiden

AIDEN SIGHED IN RELIEF when Kenzie said, "yes," and leaned in kissing her hard, deeply inhaling her scent, branding it on his memory.

Playfully, she pushed him away when he moved his hands to the hem of her shirt, his fingers tickling the exposed skin of her abdomen.

"Aiden," she said. "We're parked on the side of 96 and we have a hockey game to get to."

"Highway and hockey game, got it," he said, reluctantly moving away and buckling himself back in, pulling back onto the highway when it was safe to do so.

"So what exactly should I expect here?" Aiden asked as they neared Detroit.

The skyline shimmered in the distance, buildings scraping the starry sky. It wasn't Chicago, but it was beautiful, and he knew he'd come to love it if he got the opportunity to play for the Warriors one day.

"My dad will probably try to break your hand," she told him. "But my mother will fawn all over you. So prepare for that emotional whiplash. Not sure how Nate will react. Could go either way."

Aiden laughed, and Kenzie directed him down the freeway, telling him to take an exit once they neared the river.

"Well Brent already tried to break my hand at that alumni dinner, so I'm used to that from the Jean family," he told her.

Kenzie gasped. "He did not!"

Aiden nodded solemnly. "Sure did. Crushed my poor little fingers in his grip. It's a good thing I had five weeks of suspension to recover."

Kenzie giggled. "Nothing about your fingers is poor or little," she said, tone indicating she remembered all the things those fingers had done to her.

And now, his dick was hard.

"Kenzie..." he warned, and she laughed harder.

"Just saying, Fuller. Your hands are magical. Perfect. My favorite thing about you."

"Really? My *hands?* What about my dick?"

"I like that, too," she said. "But your hands...I like the way mine fit into them perfectly. And when you dig your fingers into my hair and scratch my scalp. And when you run them over my body and put those fingers inside me..."

Not a moment too soon, they pulled up in front of the arena, and Aiden barked, "Tell me where to go!"

Kenzie's laughter turned into a full-on maniacal cackle. Aiden was going to pay her back later for her dirty little mouth putting ideas in his head and hardening his flesh to uncomfortable levels minutes before he met her family.

"Around back," she said, pointing up the street. "We can park in the player's lot."

Aiden followed her directions, eventually pulling up to a guard station at the entrance to a gated lot.

"Sorry sir," the guard said when he stepped up to Aiden's window. He was an older man with a bushy grey mustache, eyebrows to match, and a Warriors ball cap settled atop his salt-and-pepper hair. A deep-blue parka with the Warriors logo at the breast wrapped around his body, his large hands gloved. "This is for players and player's guests only."

"Hey Frank!" Kenzie said from the passenger seat.

"Who is that?" Frank asked, bending down and shining his flashlight into the interior of the car, illuminating Kenzie's face. "Mackenzie Jean, is that you?"

"Sure is! How're you, Frank? How are Martha and the kids?"

"Oh, everyone is great!" he said. "Joshua and his wife just had a baby girl, and Millie and her family are living with us while construction on their new home finishes up! It's great having everyone here for the holidays. I just let your parents in about ten minutes ago!"

"That's great to hear," Kenzie said, a huge smile on her face. "But we better get in there. You know how my mom gets if I'm late."

Frank huffed out an indulgent laugh. "That I do. Enjoy the game, kiddo!"

"Thanks, Frank. Merry Christmas to you and yours!"

"You as well!" Frank said, then turned and signaled his partner to open the gates.

Aiden drove through and pulled into the first spot he found, put the car in park, turned it off, and turned to Kenzie, gobsmacked.

"What the fuck did I just witness?"

"What? That back there?" she said, waving a dismissive hand in the direction of the guard station. "Frank has worked security for the Warriors for like thirty years, and my brother has been playing here nearly ten. You get to know people."

Kenzie got out of the car and Aiden followed, rushing up behind her and scooping her off her feet, pressing a smacking kiss to the side of her neck. She squealed and squirmed until he finally put her down and captured her hand in his.

"You continue to surprise me, Mackenzie Jean."

She looked up at him, giving him a small, secretive smile. "You haven't seen anything yet."

Aiden had been to the arena the Warriors called home several times during his years at Michigan State, but always as a player or a regular old ticket-holding fan.

Never as a VIP.

When they reached the side door that served as the player entrance, Kenzie greeted the security guard with a passing wave and, "Hey, Greg, good to see you!" He handed her some sort of badge, and Kenzie breezed through.

Aiden fought the urge to punch him when he stared at her ass a little too long as she marched through the security checkpoint.

They moved down the hallway situated beneath the seats of the arena until they came to a tiny, inconspicuous elevator. Kenzie held the badge up to a scanner, and the doors opened. They entered and she pressed the button for the suite level, once again scanning the badge.

The elevator jerked into motion, and Aiden grabbed her and kissed her.

When he pulled away, she was breathing hard, and he gave her a cocky grin.

"What was that for?" she asked.

"Wanted to before I have to be on my best behavior around your parents."

And then all the blood drained from Aiden's face as he remembered he was about to meet her parents.

"You just remembered what we're about to do, didn't you?" Kenzie asked with a laugh.

"Is this how you felt when you met my family?" he asked her.

"Yes. Although...no offense, Fuller, but I think this might be a little harder for you. I am the baby, after all. Brent's overprotective bullshit doesn't really hold a candle to how my dad can get if he thinks his little girl is being threatened."

Aiden froze, blood chilling. "What exactly about me is threatening to you?"

Kenzie gave him one of those *get real* looks and gestured to his...everything. "Have you seen yourself? You're sex on a stick. And you're a hockey player. Are you forgetting my parents raised one?"

"Oh god," Aiden said. "I should've stayed home."

Kenzie stepped up next to him and looped her arms around his waist. "I promise it'll be fine, Fuller. One look at how happy I am and they'll realize there's nothing to be worried about."

He studied her closely: the smooth skin of her forehead and between her brows, her full lips pulled back in a smile, eyes twinkling in delight.

She *was* happy, and that was because of him, wasn't it?

Panic rose in his chest.

What he'd told her in the car was true; he needed time to figure his shit out. He felt confident he would, but it wasn't as simple as an overnight fix.

He simply hoped she'd stick around while he settled into this new normal.

The elevator arrived at the suite level, and Kenzie towed him out of the car and down a deep-red carpeted hallway until they reached a door with a plaque next to it that read BJ 22.

"You ready?" she asked, settling her hand on the doorknob.

"As I'll ever be," he said, and she rose up to give him a quick kiss.

Then she pushed the door open.

"You're late!" a woman called the second they pushed inside, and Kenzie pulled her hand free from his as a petite woman with brunette hair enveloped her in a hug, a cloud of Chanel No. 5 washing over him.

"Sorry, Mom," she said. "Aiden drives like a grandma."

"I do not," he said indignantly, and she smirked.

Sandra Jean turned her gaze on him, blue eyes a shade or two darker than her daughters. Aiden felt like he was being assessed by a head-to-toe scanner of some kind, and he was thankful his dick had returned to its unaroused state.

"So you're the infamous Aiden Fuller," Sandra said.

"Mom!"

"It's fine, bunny," Aiden said. "I'm sure my reputation precedes me."

"Brent has told us about you," Sandra said.

"I've also told you about him!" Kenzie protested.

Sandra cut her gaze to her daughter. "Your brother is the one who showed us Aiden's little streaking video, though."

Aiden's face flamed, and he secretly prayed for a black hole to open and suck him into oblivion.

"Then I guess you're glad he's fully clothed now, aren't you?" Kenzie asked her mom. "Although...the video really doesn't do him justice."

"Mackenzie Elizabeth Jean!" Sandra shrieked, then spun and threw her hands in the air. "Ronald, come get your daughter."

"I'm your daughter, too," Kenzie reminded her. Then a man unfolded himself from a seat on the balcony and came inside to see what the fuss was about. Kenzie squealed, "Daddy!" and ran right into his arms.

Kenzie's dad set her back on her feet and held her at arm's length. "It's been too long, bug," he said. "How are you?"

"Good," she said. "This is my boyfriend, Aiden."

Aiden thrust his hand out. "Pleasure to meet you, Mr. Jean."

Staring at Kenzie's dad was disconcerting for a number of reasons, the least of which being Brent could've been his father's twin if not for the nearly thirty years that separated them.

"You can call me Ron," he said, and shook Aiden's hand. Aiden braced himself for the grinding of his bones against each other, but it never came. Ron's handshake was firm but not crushing. Aiden took that as a good sign. "Thanks for getting my little girl here safe tonight."

Aiden nodded. "Of course. Bunny is very important to me."

Ron raised an eyebrow, and Aiden realized too late he'd called her by her nickname...a truncated version of the term "puck bunny," which her father was surely familiar with.

Before Ron could bite his head off, Berkley came to the rescue.

"Did he just call you 'bunny'?" she asked, pulling Kenzie in for a side hug. Her stomach had grown since Aiden had last seen her three months ago. Now, it formed an adorable bump that on someone taller would've looked normal, but seemed obscenely large on Berkley's petite frame.

"Yep," Kenzie said proudly. "I totally hated it at first, but now I think it's cute. His teammates even call me that."

"Aww, that's so sweet," Berkley said, smiling up at Aiden. "Good to see you again, Aiden."

"You too," he said, replying with a shy smile of his own.

Another dark-haired man joined their group, and Aiden recognized him from Kenzie's pictures as her other brother, Nate.

Kenzie launched herself at him, beaming, and Aiden sensed that something about their relationship was different than hers with Brent. The two appeared more like friends than big brother and little sister. Kenzie seemed more at ease around her middle brother than her eldest. It seemed as though Nate actually treated Kenzie like the twenty-three-year-old woman she was instead of viewing her as the little girl Brent did.

Aiden liked him instantly, and after a quick handshake and introduction, it appeared Nate felt the same.

"I didn't know she was bringing her boyfriend!" Aiden heard Nate say to their dad as they walked toward the bar on the far side of the room to get drinks. "Good looking kid."

Kenzie laughed and pointed a finger at Aiden. "Don't let it go to your head," she said. "Although you are pretty hot."

Aiden raised his hands in a placating gesture. "Wasn't going to." He leaned in and ghosted his lips over her cheek, whispering in her ear, "You're pretty hot too."

When she shivered, he chuckled, then backed away when her father ambled toward them—though his hand remained possessively on the small of her back.

Ron held a beer out to him, and Nate handed Kenzie a seltzer. The two men waited for her and Aiden to open their cans, then held their own out.

"Cheers," Ron said. "To hockey bringing us all together."

Everyone echoed the sentiment and sipped from their drinks, Aiden nearly choking on his when a hulking blond man appeared behind Ron.

Ron Jean was not a small man. Like his sons, he was tall, and had passed his broad-shouldered frame on to Brent.

Mitch Frambough made him look about three feet tall.

"Uncle Mitch!" Kenzie squealed, throwing herself at yet another man tonight.

If two-thirds of them hadn't been related to her, the final one being in a very committed relationship *and* her brother's best friend, Aiden would have certainly developed a complex.

When Mitch released her from their hug, she turned to Aiden and said, "You remember my boyfriend."

One of Mitch's dark-blond eyebrows rose. "Boyfriend?"

Kenzie rolled her eyes. "Don't make it a big deal."

"Yeah, baby, don't make it a big deal," a tall brunette woman said, shoving her way into the circle.

"I just think it's interesting," Mitch said.

The brunette scanned Aiden head to toe, arms crossed over her chest, body language screaming *unimpressed*.

Aiden resisted the urge to squirm under that hazel gaze, her eyes more golden than green, like pools of honey. Her legs seemed to go on forever, and Aiden guessed she had to be close to six feet tall, with a curtain of straight, dark hair that fell all the way down her back. She was a smokeshow, and she knew it.

He'd never once been intimidated by a woman, but Aiden somehow understood that this one would eat him alive in a heartbeat if the need arose.

"Stop scaring the poor kid, Alexandra," Berkley admonished, entering their little powwow belly first.

"I'm not scaring him. I'm simply checking out the goods." She turned to Kenzie. "You did good, kid."

Kenzie grinned broadly, and Mitch groaned. "Lexie..."

Lexie turned and looked up at her boyfriend, giving him a small smile before turning a wolfish grin on Aiden. "His tone means I'm going to be punished later," she said, then added in a stage whisper. "And I'll probably like it."

"LEXIE!' Berkley and Mitch yelled.

Lexie laughed and hooked her arm through Kenzie's, towing her away from the group. Aiden heard her say, "Tell me *everything*," as they walked toward the balcony, and he bit back a grin.

"I'm sorry about her," Mitch said. "She's..."

"Lexie," Berkley supplied with a sigh, and Mitch nodded, as though that explained everything.

"It's fine," Aiden said.

"She means well," Berkley said. "She's just really protective. She doesn't have any siblings of her own, so Kenzie is kind of like the community little sister, even though I have one of my own."

"Jessica, right?" Aiden asked.

Berkley smiled brightly. "Yep, that's her. You've met her?"

Aiden nodded. "She and Kenzie came to a football tailgate the hockey team hosted back in October. Turns out she knows one of my teammates, too?"

"Jack," Berkley said, surprising Aiden. Had Jessica talked about Jack to her sister? Was there something there? Jack had been cagey lately, tight-lipped about his relationship with Sofia and steadfast in his refusal to talk about how he and Jessica knew each other.

Something fishy was going on.

Aiden didn't have time to consider it further, or press Berkley for details, because a horn sounded from outside the suite, alerting them to the impending game-starting puck drop.

Never once had Aiden watched a hockey game from this high. The vantage point was incredible, not affecting his ability to track the puck one bit. But it wasn't the same as sitting in the stands, didn't hit the same as being completely immersed in the game with all five senses.

It was easy to see why the Jean family sat up here, though. When Brent scored midway through the first period, the entire arena lost its shit, the deafening roar surely rocking the building on its very foundation. He couldn't imagine being the relatives of the man these Warriors fans looked at like a god, and the melee that would ensue if they were exposed to such a celebration.

When the first period ended, and Kenzie asked Aiden if he wanted to watch a period from the club seats in the lower bowl, he swiftly agreed.

She told her parents they'd be back for the third and pulled him from the suite. Halfway down the hall to the elevator, Kenzie abruptly stopped and pushed open a door, pulling him in behind her and flipping the lock.

"What are you do—" Aiden started, his question cut off by Kenzie's mouth on his.

"I miss you," she said against his lips, already working his zipper down and shoving her hand into his boxers.

"I'm right here," he said back, nipping at her lips before trailing them across her cheek and down her neck, moving his hands below her sweater, filling his hands with her breasts, squeezing in that way he knew would rile her up, grinning against her skin when she rewarded him with a heavy, contented sigh.

"I want you," she said. "Right now."

His pants pooled around his ankles in seconds, and Kenzie fell to her knees in front of him a moment later. She worked his boxers down and his dick sprung free, right into her waiting palm.

"Kenzie," Aiden said, voice strained as her hand caressed him. "Are you sure this is a good idea? I mean your parents are—"

"Don't bring my parents into this, Fuller," she said, stroking him harder and faster.

"I'm just saying, anyone could walk by and...oh my god," he said, his train of thought once again derailed when she put her mouth on him, sliding her tongue up and down the length of his shaft once before closing her lips around him.

She might not care about the fact that her parents were right down the hall, but she seemed to possess at least some sense of urgency, because she wasted no time by teasing or toying with him. Instead, Kenzie dove right in, giving him head with a gusto that surprised him, quickly bobbing up and down. The warmth and wetness of her mouth was a delicious combination that edged Aiden closer and closer to his release faster than he thought possible.

Then again, there wasn't a single thing he could think of about Kenzie that didn't turn him on, and when she was around, he was in a perpetual state of arousal, mere moments from blowing apart if she so much as looked at him in some type of way.

"Kenz," Aiden groaned, chest heaving, every muscle pulling taut with the effort of holding back.

He drove his fingers into her hair, intent on pulling her off, not wanting to come in her mouth when they'd never discussed if that was something she was into. Kenzie hummed around him, showing no signs of stopping, the vibrations along his dick causing him to jerk his hips, sending his head to the back of her throat. All of Aiden's good intentions went out the window, and he found himself instead pulling her closer, pushing deeper into the wet warmth of her mouth. When she gagged, the stab of guilt in his chest was overwritten immediately by her hand clamping around the base of his cock and squeezing.

Aiden let go, his release barreling down his spine and across his thighs, his legs shaking with the force of it. He came in great spurts, dropping his head back onto the metal door behind him with a *thunk*. Kenzie continued to suck him through it, swallowing down everything he gave her until he finally stilled.

With a small *pop*, Kenzie pulled away and rose to her feet, wiping her mouth with the back of her hand and stretching onto her tiptoes to kiss him.

The taste of him lingered on her lips and tongue when she brushed it against his, and he couldn't imagine anything hotter in that moment than her fruity seltzer mingling with his cum to create a heady mixture that Aiden would forever crave.

When she backed away, he bent to pull up his boxers and pants, then wrapped a hand around the back of her neck and pulled her close, pressing one more deep kiss to her mouth.

"Fuck," he said finally, clearing his throat when his voice caught. "That was…"

Her bright teeth flashed in the darkness when she smiled. She reached for his hand and he wove their fingers together, squeezing tight.

"I know," she said. "Now come on before we get caught."

Still dazed from his orgasm, Aiden followed her out, barely paying attention as they got in the elevator and took it to the concourse level. Kenzie led them to the block of seats reserved for players' friends and family. She sat and pulled him onto the chair next to her, releasing his hand so she could brush her fingers through her hair, setting to rights the strands Aiden had rearranged.

The second period had started in the midst of their tryst, but Aiden was far from paying attention.

Instead, he studied the girl beside him. To him, there was nothing in the world sexier than Mackenzie Jean. It amazed him how much had changed in such a short amount of time, how he'd started this semester with a suspension and was ending it with a girlfriend.

Cloud nine was firmly under his feet.

But it had holes.

The night had started off on a bad note and had unfolded toward this, enjoying the game he loved with the girl he loved.

And…fuck.

There was no point in denying it to himself anymore: he loved Mackenzie Jean. But loving people meant the possibility of losing them, and if he wanted to keep Kenzie, he had to find a balance between her and hockey. They both deserved his full, undivided attention, and he had absolutely no idea how he was going to make it work.

Then he remembered something Jack had said to him months ago.

You're in control here.

Up to this point, Aiden hadn't handled anything about this situation well. Now that he was playing again, his hockey routine had changed. He wasn't going out or drinking as much, spent more time in the weight room and at the rink, and had to devote more time to tutor sessions to keep up with homework.

When he'd thought nothing would change once his suspension ended, he'd been sorely mistaken. The mental fortitude he needed while playing hadn't been required during those ten games, and he'd gotten comfortable in *that* routine, the one that featured Kenzie front and center.

In the last three weeks, time with Kenzie had taken a backseat, and he didn't know how to fix it.

His work-life balance was all sorts of fucked up, and Aiden desperately needed to find a happy medium that worked for everyone.

Because he refused to give up the thing that had been such an integral part of his life for so long, but he also couldn't let go of the girl who'd stolen his heart.

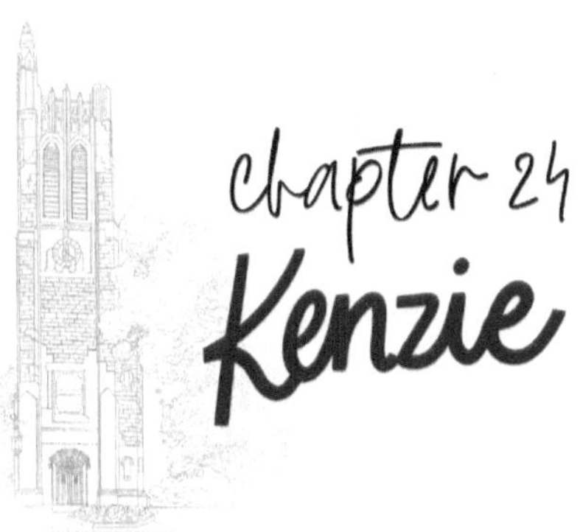

chapter 24
Kenzie

FOR A FEW BRIEF moments after Kenzie had given him head in that supply closet upstairs, it seemed as if that closeness she'd been missing with Aiden in recent weeks had returned. She'd thought they were back on track.

By bringing him down to the lower bowl, she'd hoped the new vantage point would loosen him up further after her skillful oral had started the work.

Aiden's attention was on the ice, but he didn't appear to be processing any of what he saw. When he'd first sat, a smile had played at the corners of his lips, and his eyes glinted with bone-deep contentment, the kind that only came after a really good sexual release. Now, those lips had flattened into a straight line, eyes grown weary, shoulders curving forward, as though bracing himself for something.

Something had shaken him, and the distance in his eyes told her he was off in some far away corner of his mind. At least now she knew where his head was at, knew he was having difficulty balancing her and hockey. But when her anxiety threatened to rise to the surface in that moment, when her brain attempted to turn to the worst case scenario, Kenzie quashed it, shoved it down, threw up a wall to hold it at bay.

Aiden had asked her to give him time, and she intended to do so. There was no reason to panic.

Yet.

As promised, she and Aiden returned to the suite in time for the start of the third period, and watched with her family as Brent scored his third goal of the night, the game delayed as hats rained from the stands. Even from all the way down below, the in-arena cameras managed to seek out the Jean family, broadcasting their celebration on the Jumbotron: their parents embracing, smiles stretching their cheeks high and wide, Mitch yelling at someone in the stands below to toss his hat on the ice for him, and Lexie, Berkley, and Kenzie embracing, tears streaming down Berkley's cheeks.

"I'm just so fucking hormonal!" she wailed, swiping at her eyes, smearing her mascara everywhere. "And the last time he scored a hat trick was the night we talked for the first time. It's crazy how much has happened in the last three years."

Kenzie nodded in agreement and glanced over her shoulder at Aiden, who clapped her father on the back in congratulations.

"Hell," she said to Berkley and Lexie. "It's crazy how much has happened in three months."

Lexie laughed. "You know, when we told you to get out there and find yourself again, we didn't mean hop into a relationship with the first hot guy you meet at school."

Kenzie scoffed. "You're one to talk," she said with a nod to Mitch.

"Not the same and you know it," Lexie reminded her.

This was true. Lexie and Mitch had fought tooth and nail to be together. Their love had spanned years and thousands of miles and mistakes and misunderstandings, but here they were. Against all odds, they'd made it work.

Kenzie once again looked to Aiden, and found him already staring at her. She gave him a weak smile, and he returned it, then returned to his conversation with her dad.

She knew he cared about her. And he cared about hockey. Surely, if Lexie and Mitch, two people who had so much shit between them attempting to pull them apart, could find their way back into each other's arms, she and Aiden could make this work.

If they wanted.

And that was the crux of it, wasn't it?

Did they want?

Did *he* want?

Once the game ended in a 4-1 victory for the Warriors, the group moved into the suite, cracked open more drinks, and waited for Brent to join them.

Aiden appeared at her side. "Should we go before your brother comes up here?"

Kenzie's brow furrowed. "Why would we do that?"

"It's not exactly a secret that he doesn't like me," Aiden said with a shrug. "I don't want to cause problems."

Kenzie grabbed his hand and gave it a reassuring squeeze. "He wouldn't dare with my parents here."

"If you're sure."

She rose on her toes and planted a kiss on the underside of his jaw. "I am. It'll be fine. Promise."

Brent arrived with more fanfare than usual thanks to his three-goal night. The first to reach him was his wife, who turned sideways in deference to her bump and twisted her head so her brother could plant a kiss on her waiting mouth, then settle a hand on her belly and grin widely at his family.

Kenzie found herself thinking maybe Aiden had been onto something by wanting to leave early.

Brent's reaction confirmed it.

"What is he doing here?" Brent asked, glaring daggers at Aiden.

"He's my boyfriend, Bee, and my guest."

"Like hell he is," her brother growled, and their mom raised a hand.

"Now is not the time," she warned them.

Brent's face, which had moments before been cloaked in anger, shifted quickly to blankness, like a storm cloud passing by the sun, there and gone. The only outward signs of his rage were the pinched skin around his narrowed eyes and the flat line of his mouth.

"Now that you're all here, we have some news," her mom said, stepping to her father's side and sliding a hand into his.

Kenzie's anxiety reared its head. "You're not sick, are you?"

"What? No!" her mom assured them. She shared a look with her dad, then with a beaming grin, said, "We're moving to Michigan!"

The suite became a vacuum, all sound and air instantly sucked from the room.

Brent was the first to recover. "You're *what*?"

"To be honest, we've been thinking about it for a while," Mom said. "All three of you are here, and with the grandbaby on the way, it doesn't make sense for us to be all the way across the country anymore. We want to be closer to our babies."

Kenzie's eyes filled with the happiest of tears, and she reached her parents in two long strides, throwing her arms around their necks. "That's the best news ever."

Her mother held her at arm's length, tears lining her own lashes. "We're happy you think so, bug."

Nate joined the hug next, and then Brent, squishing Kenzie in the middle of her four favorite people.

Eventually, they disbanded, and Brent asked, "When's the big move?"

Sheepishly, her dad grinned and said, "The first of the year."

"That's...soon," Nate said, mouth tipping into a frown.

"Soon?" Brent said with a laugh. "That's in three weeks!"

"We closed on the new house last week, and signed the paperwork for the house in New York before we flew out yesterday. I know it's happening fast, and it's not the most ideal time to move with the holidays coming and everything, but we couldn't miss out on the new house, and we couldn't refuse the all-cash offer we received on the New York house." Her parents shared a look, soft smiles so full of love that Kenzie's heart clenched. "Mitch has been such a huge help."

Brent whirled on his best friend, whose face blanched under the sudden scrutiny. "You knew about this?"

"Guilty," Mitch said with a strained smile. "They asked me not to say anything until it was official."

"I think everyone is forgetting to ask one very important question here," Berkley said, joining their group. "Where exactly are you moving to?"

Kenzie's mom grinned. "We found a beautiful house in this little town you might have heard of. It's called Bloomfield Hills."

Berkley gasped, and a groan escaped Brent before he could check it.

Bloomfield Hills was the Detroit suburb where they lived.

Kenzie laughed, and Brent turned to Mitch. "I'm going to kill you."

Mitch held up his hands and said, "Hey, if it makes you feel better, their house is on the opposite side of the city."

Brent considered this, then said, "Actually, it does."

"It's going to be wonderful having you so close," Berkley said, tears flowing freely down her face as she settled a hand on her bulging abdomen. "Baby boy is so lucky to have grandparents who love him so much."

"It's a boy?" Kenzie's mom asked, tears welling in her eyes. Berkley nodded, smiling widely, and she hauled her daughter-in-law in for a hug. When she pulled away, her gaze darted to her own sons. "Being a boy mom is the best."

Remember me, your daughter? I'm standing right here, Kenzie wanted to say.

It was too much. Too much changing at once. Too much of Kenzie feeling forgotten and left behind.

A hand slid into hers. Startled, she looked up at Aiden, having forgotten in all the chaos that he was here. Without doing anything more than simply holding her hand, he grounded her before her mind could spin out of control. She'd never understand how he managed to do that, but she was more thankful for it than ever.

"How do you feel?" he asked quietly.

As their gazes held, Kenzie took stock of her emotions. "I've been better," she said. "The next few weeks are going to be a lot, and I just...don't go too far."

Aiden lifted his hand and settled it along her cheek. Kenzie leaned into the touch. "I'm here with you through all of it," he reminded her, and sealed the promise with a kiss to her forehead.

Kenzie's heart swelled, and in that moment, she knew they and everything else would be okay.

Later, as the arena staff hustled them out, Berkley asked, "You're coming over this weekend to help with baby shower invites, right? We really need to get those out since we're less than two months away."

Kenzie nodded. "Yep," she said. "I don't have class on Friday, so I'll come down that afternoon."

Berkley nodded. "Thanks, Kenz. Me and this kid love you."

"Love you, too, Berk," she said.

Kenzie turned to follow Aiden, who already stood sentinel at the door, waiting for her, when Lexie caught her arm and pulled her in for a hug.

"Call if you need me," Lexie whispered in her ear. Kenzie backed away and nodded.

She didn't know how Lexie knew something was going on; she was only grateful that she had her to lean on.

The ride back to East Lansing was quiet, both of them lost in their own thoughts.

"Do you want to come over?" Aiden asked.

"I think I should go home. Tonight was...a lot. I need some time to process."

Aiden nodded in understanding. "I meant what I said earlier," he told her. "I know things have been shaky lately, but I'm here for you for all of it." He reached across the console and captured her hand. "Don't hide from me."

Kenzie nodded, knowing he couldn't see her in the dark, swallowing the lump of emotion lodged in her throat.

The silence in the wake of those words was oppressive, sucking the air from the car. When Aiden pulled up to her building, she couldn't get out fast enough, giving him a quick peck on the cheek before rushing off. She should've asked him to stay. In some deep, hopeless-romantic corner of her heart, she wished he'd come after her anyway, follow her upstairs and hold her.

But she didn't, and neither did he.

Instead, Aiden drove away, and Kenzie went up to her condo alone.

Friday evening, after she'd spent most of the day catching up on her last assignments of the semester and studying for finals, Kenzie headed to Detroit.

On the drive there, she called Dr. Mathews.

"I think it's time," Kenzie told her therapist without preamble.

"Okay, I'll bite," Dr. Mathews said with a laugh.

"I'm ready to tell Brent and Berkley about leaving FLEX."

"Really," Dr. Mathews said, sounding surprised. "What prompted this?"

"I'm on my way to their house now to help Berkley with baby shower invites and it just seems like the right time. This baby is going to be here before we know it, and I don't want to spring this on them after he's here."

When Kenzie had first learned of Baby Jean's impending arrival, she had admittedly been nervous about the shift the baby would create in the family dynamic. But over the last few months, thanks to long chats with Dr. Mathews, she'd come to realize that nothing about her relationship with her brother had to change simply because he was becoming a father. She would *always* be his baby sister; a baby wasn't going to change that.

"I think that's incredibly practical. How are you feeling about it?"

"Good," Kenzie answered honestly. "I'm going to tell Berkley first, gauge her reaction, and then together we can tell Brent."

"Seems like you've got it all figured out," Dr. Mathews said. "I know this is going to be difficult for you, no matter how you're feeling right now, but just remember that it's not the end of the world. Your brother and sister-in-law will still love you once all the cards are on the table, and you'll feel much more free without this thing hanging over your head."

It was nearly five p.m. by the time she arrived at Brent and Berkley's, and she was grateful her brother's truck was missing. She knew there would be a discussion about Aiden, and she wasn't quite ready to face the firing squad.

When she walked into the kitchen, she found Berkley at the island, her laptop open in front of her, envelopes and stacks of invites spread across the counter, a glass of non-alcoholic wine dangling from her right hand.

"Rough day?" Kenzie asked, nodding at the wine.

Berkley sighed dramatically. "I wish it was the real stuff," she said. "This kid is sucking the life out of me. He better come out ten pounds with a full head of hair like his father for all the work I'm doing growing him."

"No offense, sis, but I don't think your body is equipped to eject a ten pound baby."

Berkley looked down at her stomach, which already bulged dramatically despite the fact that she still had about three months until her due date.

"This kid is going to kill me," she said finally. "So I suppose we better celebrate him first."

Kenzie laughed and slid onto a barstool next to her. Berkley shifted her laptop so Kenzie could see the screen.

"Here's a spreadsheet of all the invitees and their addresses," Berkley said. "I've divided them into two columns, half for you and half for me. As we go, we'll just mark them off so we don't have any duplicates and so we don't forget anyone. Sound good?"

"Yep. Let's do this."

Each envelope received three things: the actual invitation, a ticket for the diaper raffle entry, and a card asking attendees to bring a book signed with their name instead of a card so Brent and Berkley could begin building Baby Jean's library.

"Do you guys have a name picked out yet?" Kenzie asked as she addressed an envelope.

"We do," Berkley said slowly. "But I don't want to share it yet. We'll announce it once he's born, so for now he's just Baby Jean."

"And speaking of," Kenzie said, figuring now was as good a time as any to discuss the thing that had been weighing on her for months. "There's something I want to talk to you about."

Berkley's eyebrows rose, her hand stilling over the envelope she was filling out. "What's up?"

"I want to step down from FLEX."

Berkley's mouth popped open in surprise. "Really?"

Kenzie nodded, swallowing hard. "I've been thinking about it for a while. I've actually always planned to do it. I just wasn't sure how to broach the subject with my brother, so I told him I wanted to take a leave of absence while I was at school to give myself time to figure it out. But with the baby coming...things are changing for both of you. I want to give us ample time to come up with a solution."

The door leading from the garage opened and her brother breezed inside as Berkley said, "When are you going to tell him this?"

Before Kenzie could respond, her brother said, "Tell me what?"

Time slowed to a crawl as Berkley shot Kenzie an apologetic look and said, "Kenzie is leaving FLEX," to Brent.

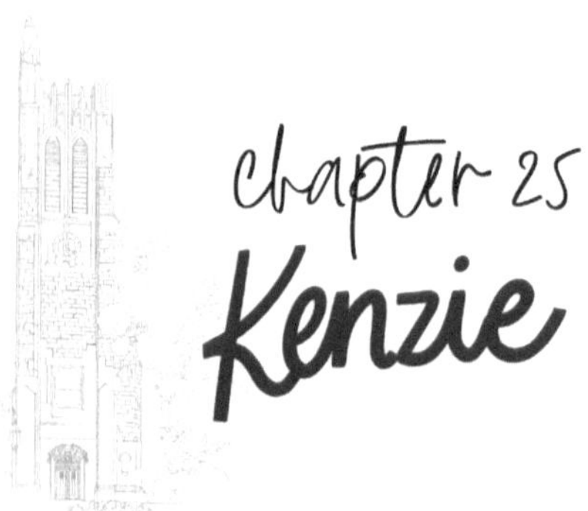

chapter 25
Kenzie

IT WAS A TRAIN wreck, the reaction from her brother instantaneous, and Kenzie glared at Berkley.

"Traitor," she muttered, then turned to face Brent, who had dropped his hockey bag on the floor and crossed the room in two giant strides to loom over Kenzie at the island.

"What do you mean you're *leaving*? You're already *on leave*."

"I mean I'm not coming back. Not when I finish school, not ever."

Despite the fact that shit was about to hit the proverbial fan, a weight lifted off Kenzie's chest, like the moment when an anxiety attack loosened, the band around her lungs cut free, and she inhaled deeply.

"I don't understand," her brother said.

"I'm just not happy," she told him. "I've loved working with you on FLEX, but I think I've outgrown my role in the company, and it's time to move onto something else."

"Like what?" Brent asked. "You're already finishing your degree to help the company."

"Actually, I'm not. I'm finishing my degree because I want to. Full stop."

"I don't even need you to have a degree," Brent said. "I need you to run the day-to-day."

"You can hire anyone for that. Someone who actually wants to be there. That's just not me anymore, Bee. I'm sorry."

Her brother stared at her...and stared and stared, for so long Kenzie was worried she'd broken him. The longer the silence stretched, the more she relaxed, thinking he was processing and would surely let this go without a fight. He'd say they could sit down right now and hash out logistics, that he supported her in whatever she wanted to do.

She couldn't have been more wrong.

"No," Brent said.

"What do you mean, *no*? You can't stop me."

"As your big brother and partner, I can, and I will. You're about to make a huge mistake, and I can't in good conscience let you go through with it."

"Brent, this isn't up for debate," she said calmly, though anger churned in her gut.

"Kenzie, this is our business. *My* business, my livelihood."

Kenzie snorted. "Oh, please. You don't need FLEX to survive. You make more playing one game of hockey than probably seventy-five percent of this country makes in a year. That's not even including what this one makes," she added, hooking a thumb at Berkley.

"The point is," her brother ground out, "you can't just up and walk away because you're no longer enjoying it. It's work, Kenzie. It's not supposed to be fun."

"Tell that to your hockey career."

"You know, your head was on a lot straighter before you moved to EL and started partying and fucking around with that Fuller kid."

Kenzie reared back as though she'd been slapped. She had given *everything* for this company, had dropped out of college and moved across the country for it. How *dare* he suggest she didn't take it as seriously as he did? How dare he speak to her like that?

Kenzie exploded.

"Don't you dare bring Aiden into this. He has nothing to do with it. I made this decision before I even met him, and I've been trying to figure out how to tell you ever since! But I was terrified, and this reaction is exactly why." She heaved a deep breath, attempting to marshal her hysteria. "I haven't been happy, truly happy, in a long time, Brent. I owe it to myself to figure out what *happy* looks like. I'm only twenty-three years old and in college, you asshole. What the fuck do you expect from me?"

Brent remained unfazed by her outburst, hip leaned against the counter, arms crossed over his chest. In her periphery, Kenzie clocked Berkley watching, eyes darting between them, mouth agape. "You know what I was doing when I was twenty-three? Playing professional hockey. Being young doesn't give you the right to be immature, or to fuck with our business."

"Yeah well not all of us are pompous, overachieving pricks like you. And for the last time, me leaving is *not fucking with our business!*"

With jerky movements, she gathered her things. What should've been a quiet weekend with her brother and Berkley, helping Berkley plan the baby shower and getting some much needed Aiden-free time, had turned into...this.

She was disgusted.

With herself, with her brother, with all of it.

As she stuffed her arms into her coat and feet into boots, she furiously blinked, using every ounce of resolve she possessed to hold her tears at bay.

"Where do you think you're going?" Brent asked. "We're not done here."

"Yes we are," she said, stalking down the ridiculously long hallway that led to the front door. Her brother's heavy footfalls trailed behind her, and she whirled on him as she reached for the handle. "I don't want to hear from you for a while. Just...leave me the fuck alone."

"We have to help Mom and Dad move next week, you brat!" he yelled at her retreating form. "You're going to have to talk to me sometime!"

Yeah well sometime *is not tonight*, she thought.

Kenzie keyed her car open and threw herself behind the wheel, started it, and backed out of the drive, Lizzo's *Truth Hurts* serving as the soundtrack for her getaway.

Once she navigated out of Brent's neighborhood and sped through the sleepy town, she got on the freeway at her first opportunity. It was only once she set her cruise that she glanced at the clock, noting it was half past six. The sun had long since disappeared below the horizon, the headlights of her and her fellow travelers' vehicles illuminating the highway lanes.

It was Friday night, which meant she had a few options at her fingertips for ways to fill her suddenly wide open social calendar.

She could call Jessica, and they could hit the bars, stumbling back to her apartment sometime in the wee hours of the morning after their usual detour to get drunk fast food.

She could go home, crack a bottle of wine, and wallow in self-pity over the fact that she and her brother were in a fight the likes of which the Jean family had never seen before.

On a normal Friday night, she'd be with Aiden, but he had a game tonight.

Wait...*Aiden.*

A few taps on her phone screen confirmed the start time and the opponent, and a few more had her GPS fired up and ready to go.

They'd agreed that she wouldn't attend any of his games, but what he didn't know wouldn't hurt him.

Twenty minutes later, she pulled into the parking lot of Yost Ice Arena, home of the Michigan Wolverines hockey team, and hustled inside. She bought a ticket at the door, not giving a fuck where it was because she fully intended to stand the entire game, and made her way inside.

Yost was formerly a field house that had opened its doors in 1923 and had been converted into an ice arena in 1973. For a building that had been standing for a hundred years, Kenzie expected it to be dingy and worn, showing the signs of its age. Much to her chagrin, the arena was beautiful, with bench seating, exposed brick, and soaring windows at one end that had earned the building the moniker The Cathedral of College Hockey.

Kenzie reached the edge of the concourse and set her sights on the ice, glancing at the Jumbotron hanging from the center of the ceiling to find she'd only missed five minutes of the first period.

Kenzie had been to enough hockey games in her lifetime to understand the nuances of the game better than most men ever would, so she stood at the railing, attention captured entirely by the vicious dance unfolding on the ice below.

As it stood entering that night's game, the Spartans were behind the first-place Wolverines in the conference standings by two points.

A win tonight would catapult them into the top spot over their in-state rivals.

The game was fast and physical, full of hard hits and spectacular scoring chances that had fans rising from their seats only to drop back down with groans.

Both goalies guarded their respective nets like brick walls. Kenzie had never paid particular attention to Jack DeLuca, too concerned with where the puck was to focus on anything else during games, but she was impressed. His reflexes were quick, his ability to move from post to post fluid. He stopped shots that lesser men would've let in, and Kenzie found herself cheering loudly for him, much to the annoyance of the Michigan fans in her vicinity.

Aiden and his teammates scored a goal early in the third, but ultimately fell to Michigan by a score of four to three. Kenzie knew he would be in a bad mood and want a distraction. Whatever was going on with them, no matter the strain their relationship had experienced recently, she wanted, *needed*, to see him tonight. Wanted his arms wrapped around her, needed to take him into her body and lose herself in bliss.

As she made her way out to her car, she texted him.

While she waited for the car to heat up and for Aiden to text back, she mindlessly scrolled her social media.

Finally, her phone buzzed.

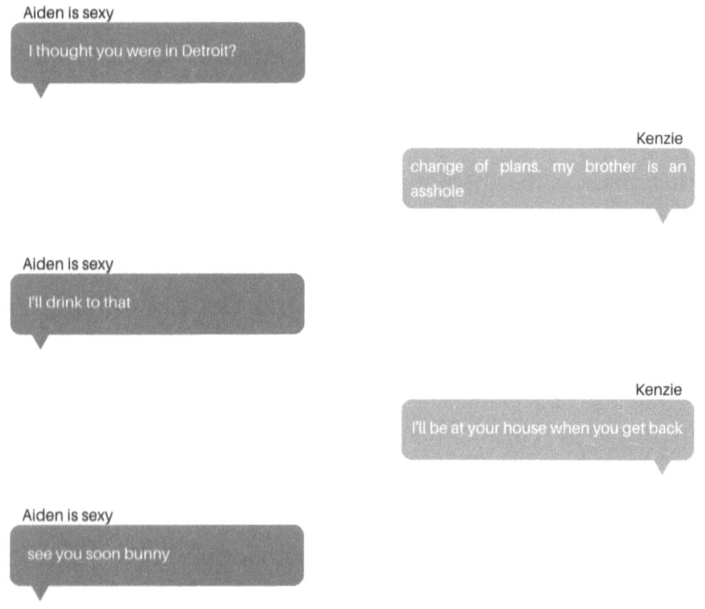

She took her time traveling back to East Lansing, knowing it would be a while before Aiden and his roommates arrived. Before getting back on the freeway, she took a detour to the Briarwood mall, where she wandered in and out of boutiques and cosmetics stores, ultimately returning to her car with a few wintry outfits from H&M, new jeans and panties from American Eagle, and mascara and a new lipstick from Sephora.

The fight with her brother seemed years away now, her anger

dissipated by some retail therapy and thoughts of Aiden.

When she reached the outer edges of Lansing proper, she swung through Meijer to stock up on seltzers, knowing full well she wouldn't want to drink anything the boys had in the house. Then she headed to Aiden's, dropping her alcohol and duffel bag off before heading home quickly to leave her car in the parking garage. The walk back was brisk, but it fully cleared her head.

When the boys rolled in some indeterminate amount of time later, half of their team following closely behind, and a hoard of people showing up in pairs not long after, Kenzie had already drunk enough to generate a nice buzz. Her cheeks warmed, lips tingled, limbs loosened comfortably.

Desperately, she wanted to have a good time, but it was obvious Aiden was miserable, so after witnessing one of his teammates sock him on the shoulder and tell him to get a grip one too many times, she intervened.

"C'mon," she said. Breaking through the wall of hockey players gathered around his perch on the couch, she reached for his hand.

Without any shift in facial expression, Aiden let her pull him to his feet and tow him to his bedroom, where she removed the key from around his neck and let them in, locking the door again behind her.

She pushed Aiden across the room until his knees buckled at the edge of the bed.

"What happened with your brother?" he asked quietly.

Kenzie heaved a sigh and walked around to the other side of the bed—what she'd come to consider *her* side—and crawled on top, curling into a ball against the mountain of pillows Aiden had stacked there.

As if sensing she needed him close, he moved next to her and scooped her up so she curled against him, her legs slung across his lap, her head on his chest, his arms wrapped tightly around her.

"I finally told him I'm leaving FLEX," she said.

"I'm assuming that didn't go well."

Kenzie let out a derisive laugh. "No, it didn't. He said my head isn't on straight, and he accused me of wasting all my time partying and fucking around with you," she said quietly, embarrassed. "And the worst part is, he's not wrong."

Kenzie *had* been partying, and she *had* been fucking around with Aiden. Both of those things were true. But, as she'd told her brother, she was only twenty-three and in college; she was *allowed* to do those things. And he didn't control her life, as much as he wanted to. Without a shadow of a doubt, she knew leaving FLEX was the best thing for her in the long run. She only hoped her brother would come to see her side of things.

"Kenzie," Aiden said, sifting his fingers slowly through her hair. "That's bullshit and you know it."

"He just can't see past the success of the company to realize how unhappy I've been the last year. I was fully prepared to sit down with him and Berk and figure everything out tonight. But then he started screaming at me and I told him I didn't want to hear from him for a while and stormed out. Of course, he reminded me we're helping Mom and Dad move next week. Asshole."

"Well, I'm happy you're here," he said, pressing a kiss to the top of her head.

"Your turn," she said, tilting her head to look up at him. "What's going on?"

"I'm struggling to get my game back after being off for so long," he said. "And I'm worried that my off-ice antics are going to cost the boys a potential championship run and me a rookie contract."

Kenzie's heart seized. Aiden never spoke so candidly about hockey and all the ways he felt solely responsible for the team's success or failure. When he did, she felt compelled to remind him of a few things.

"Aiden, the success of this team does not weigh on your shoulders. You know that, right?"

"Logically, yes," he said. "But I've worked my ass off to become one of the best players in the country, and when I'm not performing my best, everything is off. We lost tonight because I wasn't at one hundred percent."

"That's bullshit and you know it," she said, echoing his earlier words.

He rolled his eyes. "Hockey is my entire life, bunny."

"Ouch," she said jokingly, but still, the comment stung more than she wanted to admit.

He wrapped his arms tighter around her. "You know what I mean."

"Yeah yeah," she said, rolling her eyes and trying to turn away from him. "Hockey is your number one priority—I get it."

He was quiet for so long that Kenzie was worried he'd fallen asleep. The rumble along her back when he spoke again startled her.

"Hockey is the only connection I have to my dad," he reminded her. "He's gone, and I'm still here, and every time I step onto that ice, I feel connected to him in a way that I don't feel anywhere else. I want him to be proud of me, wherever he is. My mom tells me he is, but when I'm skating...that's the only time I actually believe it. Like he's right there with me, sitting on my shoulder and whispering words of encouragement in my ear. And on nights like tonight, when everything was going wrong, I could practically feel his disappointment."

"Oh, Fuller," Kenzie said, shifting so she was straddling his lap and holding his face in her hands. "He *is* proud of you, all the time, wherever he is. You're his son, and you're one of the best people I know. How could he not be? I can't imagine what it must be like for you to not have him, but if there's one thing I'm certain of, it's that he is so proud of you. The most proud."

Aiden wrapped his arms around her, clutching her tightly to his chest, as though she were a life raft saving him from drowning. She could've lived in that hug forever. She'd never been held like this, as though she were a lifeline for someone. And even though Aiden was drunk and vulnerable—even though they both were—she couldn't bring herself to wriggle out of his embrace and establish some physical distance between them in the wake of all the emotional intimacy.

But then Aiden said, "I'm sorry I keep hurting you. I've been struggling to balance you and hockey. I know that. And I know it's not fair to you. I don't ever want you to think you don't matter, that you don't mean the entire fucking world to me, Mackenzie Jean. You've been so fucking patient with me, but I'm terrified one day that patience will run out and you'll leave. And I can't...that can't happen." He titled his head so their gazes collided. "I love you, Mackenzie Jean, and I'm not sure I'd survive if you left me."

Kenzie gripped the sides of his face tightly, holding his stare. "I love you, too, Aiden Fuller, and I'm not going anywhere."

Aiden clung to her, his face buried in the crook of her neck.

When he eventually pulled back, she rested her forehead against his, content to simply be in this moment with him.

Then she tilted her head, lips a breath away from his, and said, "I'm going to kiss you now."

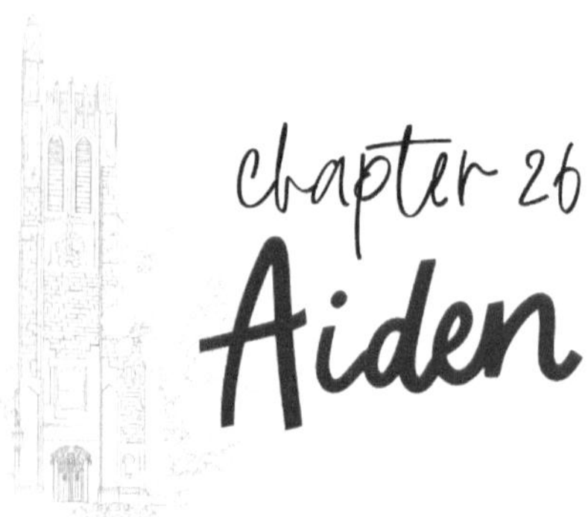

chapter 26
Aiden

THE KISS WAS A slow slide of Kenzie's full lips against his, there and gone, tentative as though she were gauging his reaction. She pulled away and whispered, "This okay?"

Aiden fisted a hand in her hair and brought her mouth back to his. Against her lips, he said, "God, of course. You don't ever have to worry about that."

To prove his point, he kissed her harder, delving his tongue into her mouth in exploratory strokes. He wrapped his hands around her rib cage, lightly digging his fingers into her back and pulling her closer, holding her tighter. In response, she ground down onto his lap, and they both groaned.

"Kenz," Aiden said as he tore his mouth from hers, chest heaving with the adrenaline pumping through his veins. He slid his lips and tongue along her jaw and down her neck. "I want you so bad."

He pulled away and stared into those eyes, thinking how he could drown in their depths. In response, Kenzie reached between them, bunched the hem of her shirt in her hands, and whipped it over her head, tossing it somewhere across the room. He reached behind her and set his fingers on the clasp of her bra, ready to remove it with her go ahead. Both of them were fragile right now, emotions rubbed raw, and all Aiden wanted to do was lose himself in her...but only if she wanted it, too.

"Then have me," she said, and Aiden pinched the material between his thumb and pointer and slid the hooks free. Softly, he trailed his fingers over her shoulder blades and up the column of her neck, then down the slopes of her shoulders, pushing the straps off so her bra fell between them.

Kenzie's breasts were...perfect. Slightly more pale than the rest of her skin, with dark-pink nipples the size of quarters. Aiden lifted them in his hands, marveling at how he could fit the whole of them in his palms.

Leaning forward, he captured one of her nipples in his mouth, grinning against her skin when Kenzie gasped above him. Lazily, he skimmed his lips into the valley of her chest and back up, giving the other nipple the same attention.

He was so hard, one touch from Kenzie would set him off like a bomb, and he wanted, *needed* to wring at least one orgasm out of her before he embarrassed himself.

In one smooth motion, he sat up and flipped them, dropping Kenzie faceup on the bed. Then he pulled his own shirt off, wanting to be skin-on-skin when he leaned down to kiss her again.

And...*fuck*. Every smooth inch of her chest and torso pressed against all the hard lines of his had Aiden's eyes rolling back in his head.

Kenzie whimpered against him, and Aiden said, "Me too, bunny."

He shifted his weight back and knelt between her legs, hooking his fingers in the waistband of her leggings and peeling them and her underwear slowly down her legs, then throwing them over his shoulder. A small crash followed, but in that moment, Aiden didn't have a single fuck to give.

Moving so he was flat on his stomach, eye level with Kenzie's pussy, Aiden said, "I'm going to kiss you now."

Kenzie let out a breathless laugh at his echo of her earlier words, which quickly turned to a moan the moment he trailed the tip of his tongue in a slow path around her clit.

"Fuck," she said on an exhale.

He'd never get tired of this, the way she melted into the bed the more he worked her toward that precipice, his tongue swirling around and around, accompanied by gentle sucking and, eventually, the insertion of two fingers into her warmth, pumping them in and out in time to the movements of his mouth. Her little gasps and moans and incoherent mumbles of encouragement. Her taste.

Her.

Aiden knew she was close when she tightened around his fingers, her thighs quaking with the effort of holding back.

"Let go," he growled, then sealed his lips over her clit and sucked hard, curling his fingers inside her at the same time.

Kenzie detonated, a cry tearing free from her throat. Her thighs clamped around his head as she arched off the bed while he continued to work her through it, loving how she pulsed around his fingers, feeling like a god with the knowledge that he could do this to her.

When she stilled, Aiden rose and shed his pants and boxers, then hooked his hands behind her knees and shifted them back and wider.

He gripped his cock at its base and dragged it through her warmth; the wetness from her orgasm coating him was nearly his undoing.

"Can I..." he trailed off, hoping what he was asking was obvious.

"After that?" she said, eyes heavily lidded, voice already wrecked. "You can have whatever you want."

Aiden grinned. "I want all of you. I want *everything*."

He lined himself up with her entrance and began to push inside. Only the tip breached before she said, "Wait!"

Aiden pulled back quickly, then leaned forward until they were face to face. "What? What's wrong?"

Kenzie smiled, raising her head so she could give him a gentle kiss. "Nothing," she said. "I just...condom, please."

Aiden relaxed, then nodded.

He reached for his nightstand, pulling open the drawer, removing a pack of condoms, and tearing one free from the rest. He watched Kenzie as he tore into the foil and rolled the rubber down his length.

"Now where were we..." Aiden said, once again lining himself up, fully prepared to push into her in one rough thrust, unsure he could hold back even a millisecond longer.

But again, Kenzie stilled him with a hand on his forearm. "Aiden..."

She gnawed on her bottom lip, then in a rush said, "Iloveyouyouknow."

Aiden grinned. "I'm sorry, repeat that?" he asked, knowing full well what she'd said but wanting to hear it again.

And again and again forever.

Kenzie heaved a sigh and dramatically threw her forearm across her face. "I love you, you know."

Aiden leaned down and captured her mouth with his, pressing his lips to hers three times in quick succession. "I love you, too, baby," he said against her skin. "And I'm going to make this so fucking good for you."

Reaching down, he gripped the base of his cock and positioned it at her entrance, sliding home in a single, quick thrust. Kenzie moaned and tightened around him.

"I'll never get sick of this," he told her, pausing for a moment to enjoy the feel of her wrapped all the way around him, squeezing him from base to tip.

"Sex?" Kenzie asked with a breathless laugh.

"*You*," he said, then began to move.

Kenzie didn't respond, simply clung to his shoulders as he drove into her, pressing her into the bed, hands braced beside her hips.

Sex in love was an infinitely more euphoric experience than sex in lust. Before, sex had always been about his release, but also about making sure the girl had a good time.

With Kenzie, it wasn't about having a good time, or chasing his release. With her, it was about making her happy, giving her everything, and being as close to her as humanly possible, feeling like they were connected on physical, emotional, and dare he say, spiritual levels.

Mackenzie Jean was an altar Aiden wanted to worship at every day.

This girl...she was it for him.

As if she'd sensed where his thoughts had turned, she dug her fingernails into his back, returning his focus to the task at hand.

"Aiden," Kenzie moaned, and he knew she was close to going over the edge.

"I know, honey," he said, dropping his head to the crook of her neck. "I know. I've got you."

Pressure built at the base of his spine, like a storm surge gathering strength, a wave reaching higher toward the sky as it rushed toward the shore.

He slid one of his arms under her back and lifted her off the bed, sitting back on his heels at the same time, still buried inside her.

Aiden hadn't even moved again and Kenzie whimpered, her pussy clenching so hard around him he knew it was only a matter of seconds before she went off. A few quick pumps and it'd be game over. For both of them.

To get a better angle, he shifted a bit, settling himself more comfortably under her, and then used an arm under her ass to lift her off him and drop her back down. Kenzie repeated the movement herself, bouncing away on top of him, and Aiden gripped her hips in his hands, holding tightly, bucking up to meet every one of her downward thrusts.

"Right there," she gasped, throwing her head back. "Don't stop."

Aiden didn't intend to, picking up the pace until the whole bed rocked under them. The party raging beyond the door became a distant memory.

Then he leaned forward and scraped his teeth against her shoulder in that way he knew she liked and bit down hard, chasing the pain away with a swipe of his tongue. She'd have a bruise there in the morning, and he couldn't wait to see the mark on her skin in the light of day, like a brand only he could give her.

In response, Kenzie dragged her nails down his back, digging her fingers into the muscles, surely drawing blood, and finally let go, moaning and gasping and shaking, muscles going rigid before she melted, wrapping herself fully around him as the shockwaves continued to pulse through her body.

In two more thrusts, Aiden followed, throwing himself off that cliff and into the deep water after her. He was drowning, torn asunder by the force of his own release. Kenzie's weight on top of him kept him from stretching out and letting the climax flow through him. Instead, it was kept closely contained so it seemed more powerful and longer-lasting than any he'd had before.

When the waves eventually ceased, Aiden pulled himself free of Kenzie and collapsed backward onto his pillows, dragging her down next to him.

"Well done, Fuller," Kenzie said, tone sleepy and content. "That was...incredible."

"Different, though, right?" he asked, shifting their bodies so he could kick the covers down and pull them back up over their naked skin. "Incredible, yes, but...different."

"In the best way," Kenzie said. "I think sex with someone you love is different. Better."

Aiden nodded, chin brushing the top of her head. "I was thinking the same thing."

"I know we still have some things to figure out," she said quietly, already half asleep. "But I want to figure them out with you. I want to do this. I'm all in if you are."

Mentally, he'd been a mess the last few weeks. But knowing she loved him, and finally telling her he felt the same...he couldn't figure out why he'd been worried.

"I'm not saying it's going to be easy, and I'm not saying I won't fuck up, but of course I'm all in."

Kenzie's only response was a mumbled, "good," before she drifted fully into unconsciousness.

Aiden tightened his hold on her and buried his nose in her hair, afraid if he relaxed even an inch she'd slip through his fingers.

"You two look awfully cozy," Jack said at the breakfast table the next morning.

The boys were enjoying a meal together before heading to the rink for morning skate. They'd face off against Michigan tonight, in East Lansing this time, and all four were eager to get on the ice and work through the mental mistakes they'd made the night before.

Aiden had woken Kenzie this morning with his face between her legs, and his scalp still stung where she'd pulled his hair as he'd made her come.

Now she sat on his lap in one of his sweatshirts, which she'd thrown carelessly over her head as they'd left his room in favor of the kitchen.

Kenzie shrugged and stuffed a piece of melon in her mouth. Aiden wrapped an arm tighter around her waist and said, "We had a good night."

His teammates smiled, and Kenzie tilted her head to kiss him on the cheek.

"I'm glad to see you guys managed to figure things out," Asher said. "We've been worried the battle between bunny and hockey would not go in favor of your relationship."

Kenzie stiffened, and Aiden glared daggers at Asher. "Really, Ash?"

"I'm just saying...it was touch and go there for a while. You've always been so dedicated to hockey. I couldn't see how you were going to make room in your life for Kenzie."

"Ash..." Luke said. "Shut the fuck up."

Asher raised his hands in surrender, digging back into his meal, completely unaware of how Kenzie had reacted to his comments.

"Seriously, we're happy for you guys," Jack said, and Luke nodded his agreement.

Aiden gave them a strained smile, and Kenzie mumbled, "Thanks, guys," before rising from Aiden's lap and padding back into his room.

Aiden rose to follow Kenzie, and as he left, Jack smacked Asher upside the head, saying, "Good going, dumbass."

When Aiden entered his room, he found Kenzie in the process of getting dressed. She'd managed to don her leggings and bra, and was stuffing her arms in the sleeves of her sweater when she looked up at him.

"I'm sorry about Ash," Aiden said. "He's an idiot."

"He's not, though."

"He is. I have been struggling, and I told you that. But I know we can make this work. It doesn't have to be all or nothing, one way or the other. I can give my everything to hockey *and* give my everything to you."

While he spoke, Kenzie's chest rose and fell faster and faster, her shaky hands toying with the frayed hem of her top. She sat down hard on his bed, and Aiden took a step toward her.

"Don't," she said, forcing the word out, the single syllable strangled.

Aiden realized what he was seeing: a panic attack.

Respecting her wishes, he didn't move toward her. All he said was, "Breathe."

"I'm trying," she whispered. "I've been trying. But maybe *trying* isn't enough. Hockey is your whole fucking life, Aiden. I don't want to be the one responsible for fucking up this one thing you want more than anything because I love you and want to be with you."

"That's not what's happening here, and you know it," he said, taking a small step forward.

"Logically, sure. Unfortunately, my brain doesn't always listen to logic."

She unsteadily shot to her feet, and Aiden reached out to catch her, his hands encircling her biceps. "Just breathe and sit with me for a second. I love you, and that's not going to change. Your brother did it, didn't he? Found a way to balance hockey and his life with Berkley? Why can't we do the same?"

Kenzie shoved away from him. "We are *not* Brent and Berkley."

Well...that stung. Not because she wasn't right. Obviously, they weren't her brother and his wife. But there wasn't anything to say they couldn't have a relationship as happy and fulfilling as theirs one day. So why was Kenzie trying to backtrack, after everything she'd said the night before? After they both agreed to be all in?

She stalked to his desk, where her keys lay on the surface next to his laptop and her bag rested on the floor nearby.

"Don't run away from me right now, bunny," he said. "Please.

I'm begging you."

She turned to face him, her usually golden skin bleached white under the excess of adrenaline and whatever mental gymnastics her mind was performing.

"I'm not running away," she said. "I just...I can't breathe right now. I need to go home. I—I love you. And I know we'll figure this out. You just have to give me some time. The last few days have been a lot, and...I'm not doing great. I need my meds and my bed and some alone time. Okay?"

Tears lined her lower lashes, and Aiden wanted so badly to go to her, wrap her in his arms, and never let her go. But he understood anxiety played funny tricks on her, and unlike that night outside Harper's when she'd let him and Jack talk her through a minor attack, she had routines in place to help her survive this bigger one. Routines that didn't include him.

Aiden settled for cupping her face in his hands and pressing a kiss to her forehead.

"Call me when you feel better, please."

Kenzie nodded. "I will."

And then she was gone.

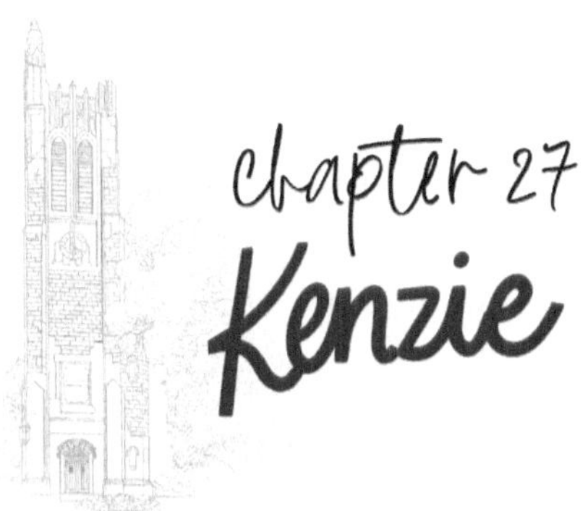

chapter 27
Kenzie

FACE BURNING WITH SHAME and embarrassment, Kenzie rushed through the kitchen of Aiden's house in the direction of the front door. When she made it outside, she sucked in large, grateful breaths of sharp, fresh air. The chill pierced her lungs, soothing some of the tightness in her chest.

Kenzie ate up the distance between Aiden's house and her building, and by the time she let herself into her apartment, she was so lightheaded she collapsed in a heap in front of her door, head bent over her lap, and breathed.

She deployed every trick in her arsenal to calm down, but after a few minutes when the blackness at the edges of her vision refused to recede, Kenzie knew she needed to call in reinforcements.

With shaky fingers, and after dropping the phone several times, plus accidentally pressing the wrong contact and awkwardly stabbing at her phone to hang up before Matt—one of her old New York friends—could answer, she finally connected to Dr. Mathews.

"Hello, Mackenzie," she said, cool as a cucumber. The even tone of her therapist's voice was a balm to Kenzie's frayed nerves, and her heart rate dropped a tick.

"Help," she managed, the word strangled.

"What's going on?" Dr. Mathews asked.

"I—" Kenzie tried, but failed to speak anything beyond that.

"I'm here," Dr. Mathews said. "You're safe. Just breathe, Mackenzie. You're okay."

Her phone clattered to the floor as her grip on it slackened, and she pressed the speakerphone button, allowing Dr. Mathews' soothing words to fill her apartment and slowly soak into her mind, talking her off the ledge this panic attack threatened to toss her over.

Some time later, Dr. Mathews said, "Did you take your meds?"

"No," Kenzie croaked. "I..." She swallowed hard and tried again. "I collapsed at the door when I got back from Aiden's. Haven't made it that far yet."

"Take your meds, Mackenzie," Dr. Mathews prodded. "And then get into bed. Once you feel safe, you can tell me what happened."

Kenzie did as her therapist asked, rising on legs that felt like jello and shuffling toward her room. Her first stop was the bathroom, where she shook out a pill and washed it down with a hefty gulp of water. Then she stripped down to a t-shirt—Aiden's, she realized—and her underwear, and crawled beneath her heavy down comforter.

"Feeling better?" Dr. Mathews asked.

"Somewhat," Kenzie said, voice stronger than it had been minutes before.

"What was your trigger?"

"I don't really know," she answered honestly. "I think it's a combination of things. My parents are selling my childhood home and moving to Michigan, which I'm so excited about, but it's very bittersweet. We'll still have the cabin in New York, but it's not the same. Then Brent and I got in a huge fight last night because I told him I'm not coming back to FLEX, and Aiden's roommates this morning were talking about how they're surprised our relationship is solid and surviving and I just...freaked out. It wasn't any one thing. Just a lot at once."

She took a few minutes to go into detail on each of these things, finding that talking it out helped ease some of the weight on her chest.

"Understandably so," Dr. Mathews said diplomatically. "Your life is undergoing a lot of change, change you can't exactly control. You can't control your parents selling their home, and losing a piece of your childhood would be stressful to even the most emotionally well-adjusted. And you definitely can't control your brother's reaction to the news that you're leaving the company. The only thing you can control there is how you respond, and since this is something you've been holding in for a long time, it makes sense that you would defend yourself. As for Aiden, you've spent a significant amount of time in recent weeks worried that you would lose him if he couldn't figure out the balance between you and hockey. His roommates were certainly aware of the issue, and they couldn't have known what that conversation would do to you. And while you may be relieved that you and Aiden are going to be okay, that release of stress, like waiting for so long to receive news of something, whether good or bad, and finally getting the good news, caused an excess of adrenaline that sent you into a tailspin."

Having Dr. Mathews explain that her reaction to all her life changes was warranted and understandable further loosened the tension in Kenzie's limbs. All at once, she was so very tired. Her eyelids became leaden, breathing blessedly slowing to a resting rate.

"I think I'm going to take a nap now," she told Dr. Mathews, not bothering to acknowledge anything her therapist had said, not having the energy to unpack it all right now.

"Call me tomorrow," Dr. Mathews said. "You're okay, Kenzie. Everything will be okay."

Kenzie drifted off to sleep with those words swirling in her brain, wrapping around her like a warm blanket on a cold winter day.

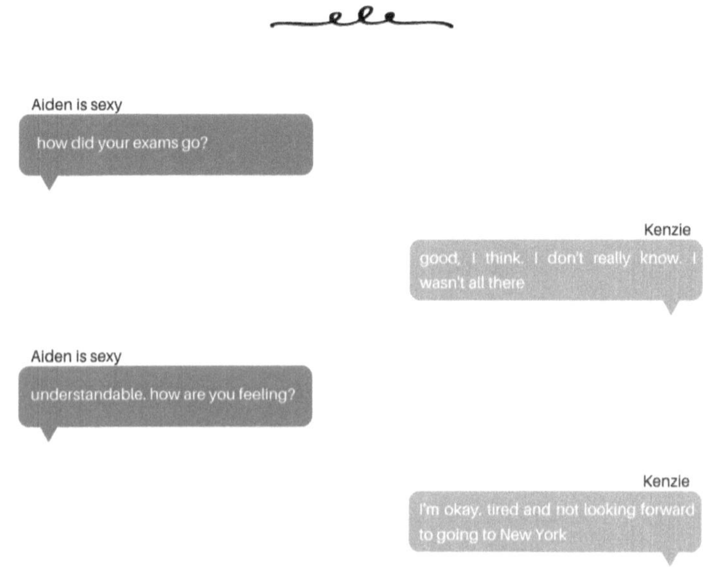

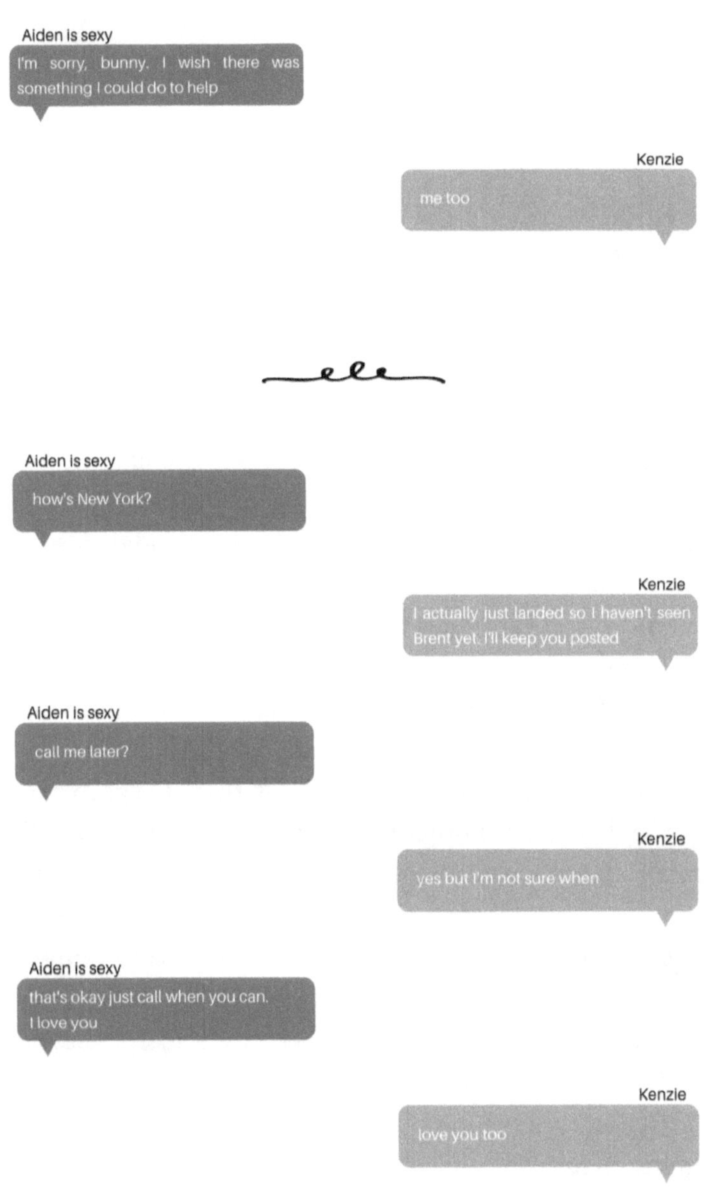
Aiden is sexy
I'm sorry, bunny. I wish there was something I could do to help
Kenzie
me too
Aiden is sexy
how's New York?
Kenzie
I actually just landed so I haven't seen Brent yet. I'll keep you posted
Aiden is sexy
call me later?
Kenzie
yes but I'm not sure when
Aiden is sexy
that's okay just call when you can. I love you
Kenzie
love you too

"Have you lost weight?" her mother asked when she picked Kenzie up from the airport.

"No," she said. "I just...had a bad weekend."

"Too much booze?"

"No," Kenzie said. "Bad couple of mental health days."

Her mom's mouth flipped to a frown. "Want to talk about it?"

Kenzie sighed, knowing her mother wasn't going to let her get away with saying nothing.

"My relationship has been a little rocky lately, and then you and dad dropped this bomb on us. I'm excited you're moving, and I think Aiden and I are going to be okay, but...it's a lot at once."

Her mother dropped a reassuring hand onto her shoulder and squeezed. "I'm sorry, bug. Your father and I never intended for this move to be a source of anxiety for you."

"It's not your fault, Mom. It's my brain that's the problem."

As she drove, her mother steered the conversation away from Kenzie's struggles and toward the plan for packing up over thirty years of memories. Kenzie was grateful for the distraction, although her parents selling her childhood home was a bittersweet milestone.

"I heard you and Bee had a fight," her mom said suddenly as she turned onto the tree-lined street that led home.

"Ugh, don't remind me, please. That's another thing that's been weighing on me."

"Well...I can't have my children on the outs with each other,"

her mom said. "You two are having a discussion when we reach the house and airing this all out. I won't have this hanging over our heads the next couple weeks, especially not with Christmas next weekend."

Kenzie groaned, but she and her brother did need to have a conversation. She supposed there was no time like the present.

The second she and her mom stepped inside the house, Brent approached her, hands in his pockets, and jerked his head in the direction of the hall, where she followed him like a prisoner being led to the gallows.

When they entered the game room at the back of the house, Brent closed the door behind them and turned his weary gaze on Kenzie.

"I'm sorry," they blurted at the same time, then burst out laughing. Brent pulled her into an embrace. She pinched his side but hugged him back, inhaling deeply, the familiarity of the cologne he'd worn since high school somewhat soothing her frayed nerves.

He led them to the couch and pulled her down next to him. As she used to when she was younger and had injured herself in some manner or another, coming to him with scuffed knees and bruised elbows, he let her curl into his side, wrapping his arms tightly around her.

With a jolt, she realized how much she'd missed this. Things between them had been so tense for so long; she couldn't even pinpoint the moment they'd stopped being brother and sister and had instead morphed into adversarial business partners.

And maybe therein laid the root of all her displeasure with her role at FLEX.

It had started to affect her relationship with her brother.

All along, her subconscious had been trying to tell her; it was only now that she finally heard it.

"I'm sorry for everything I said to you last week," Brent said as he stroked her hair. "I'm under a lot of pressure here, and it's not an excuse to treat you the way I did."

Kenzie shrugged. "You're always an ass."

"Mackenzie..." Brent warned.

With a resigned sigh, she sat up and looked him in the eye. "I'm sorry, too. I should've told you I was unhappy at FLEX sooner. I just didn't know how. We used to be so good at communicating, and somehow, by becoming partners, we forgot how."

"I didn't understand it before," Brent said, "why you wanted to leave. But I get it now. And I'll support whatever it is you decide to do next. I was just too stubborn to admit that you didn't need me anymore. That you're old enough to live your life how you choose without my constant input. It's hard to turn being a big brother off."

"You don't have to turn it off," Kenzie said. "Just reel it in. Or turn it into being the best father you can be for my nephew."

Brent grinned. "Fucking wild that I'm going to be a dad, right?"

Kenzie beamed back. "The wildest, but you're also going to be the best at it."

He ruffled her hair. "Thanks, bug. I'm also sorry for how I've acted about Aiden. I know you really care about him, and it's unfair for me to judge him based on rumors."

"I forgive you," she said easily.

"How are things with him anyway?"

"I'm not entirely sure," she told him honestly, and then launched into the whole tale of what had happened in the wake of their fight last week.

"I'm drowning a little," she told her brother. "I know he understands that and is giving me space, but I can't ask him to do that indefinitely, you know?"

"If he loves you, he'll wait as long as it takes."

In theory, Kenzie knew her brother was right. Aiden *did* love her. But she also loved him, and it was for that reason she knew she couldn't keep him waiting forever.

After she and Brent made up, the rest of the week was spent in an emotional flurry of cardboard boxes, bubble wrap, packaging tape, and unearthing memories like an archeologist on a dig. Her parents had bought the house back in early 1993, right after they found out they were pregnant with Nate. For nearly thirty-one years, Ron and Sandra Jean had made this house a home, bringing first Nate, then Mackenzie here. The Jean siblings had taken first steps, spoken first words, broken bones and had hearts broken, laughed and cried, and celebrated and mourned within these walls.

Kenzie looked forward to the next chapter of all their lives, but letting go of this place created an ache in her chest that wouldn't be going away anytime soon.

By the time Christmas morning arrived, Kenzie was mentally exhausted.

Aiden had called her bright and early, and Kenzie had to admit, his voice was like a warm blanket on a cold December night.

"Hey you," she said when she answered.

"Hi honey," he breathed. "God, it's good to hear your voice."

She smiled. "I was just thinking the same thing. I miss you."

"I miss you, too. When are you coming back to EL?"

"I'm not sure," she said. "We got a lot done last week, but there's still a ton to do since my mom wouldn't let us take down any of the Christmas decorations. And I think I'm going to drive back with them instead of flying. Classes don't start until the eighth, so it'll be nice to spend some more time with them."

"If you want, I can help move them into the new place when you get back."

"You'd do that?"

"I would do anything for you."

Kenzie's heart swelled.

A soft tapping came at the door to her childhood bedroom, now bare of everything but the bed on which she laid, the yellow walls patchy, faded around where the posters and photos she had tacked up as a teen. Those memories were now somewhere in the trash. A moment later, Berkley popped her head in, so Kenzie said, "I love you, but I have to go. I promise I'll see you soon."

"I love you, too, bunny. Merry Christmas."

"Merry Christmas," she said and disconnected.

"Are you going to have breakfast with us today?" Berkley asked.

"Maybe," Kenzie said, her voice rough from disuse.

"Your mom is worried about you," Berkley said, snaking her arm down to grab Kenzie's hand in hers. "We all are."

"There's nothing to be worried about," Kenzie said, the statement accompanied by exactly zero emotion.

A moment later, Berkley's glare landed on the side of her face like a brand, and Kenzie struggled not to squirm. It was a good thing for any potential opposing counsel in the state of Michigan that Berkley wasn't a trial lawyer, because they would lose every single time. Kenzie had found herself pinned down by that blue gaze before, and was intimately acquainted with Berkley's particular brand of persuasion.

"We understand you're going through something, Kenz," Berkley said softly. "And that's okay. But you can't lie in this bed and wallow all day, every day. Eventually you're going to have to emerge and face life again."

"I'm fine," Kenzie mumbled, though the words tasted funny, and Berkley saw them for the lie they were.

"C'mon," she said, tugging on Kenzie's wrist until she had dragged her to the edge of the bed, surprising Kenzie by the strength in that tiny body of hers.

Saying nothing of the fact that she was eight months pregnant.

Kenzie stood, towering over her sister-in-law, and studied her bulging abdomen. The reminder that her nephew was growing inside the petite body of this fierce woman doused Kenzie like a bucket of cold water over her head. If Berkley could carry her brother's giant spawn and not complain about it, Kenzie could get out of bed and stop moping about saying goodbye to her childhood home.

"Well, well, well," Nate said when she emerged from her cave. He was seated at the island in the center of the kitchen, hair mussed from sleep, black-framed glasses perched on his nose, laptop open in front of him. "Look who decided to grace us with her presence."

She flipped him the bird and said, "Shut up," making a beeline to the coffee pot, where Brent stood with his arm outstretched, a cup of coffee balanced in his hand.

"Thanks, Bee," she said quietly before taking a long, fortifying sip.

Arms wrapped around her from behind, and a cloud of Chanel No. 5 enveloped her. "Merry Christmas, my darling girl," her mom said.

Kenzie spun and gave her mom a one-armed hug. "Merry Christmas, Mama."

"Come on," her mom said, hooking her arm through Kenzie's. "Let's eat."

Reluctantly—because she hadn't exactly eaten a real meal in a couple weeks, choosing instead to survive on peanut butter M&Ms and Cool Ranch Doritos, or takeout when they paused the packing long enough to refuel—she followed her mother to the dining room, where the long table was laden with every breakfast food imaginable.

Before she dropped onto her seat, she took a moment to study her family. They all knew about her mental struggles, and she couldn't stand anyone looking at her with pity right now. Thankfully, no one seemed inclined to handle her with kid gloves.

"I know you're all aware I've been struggling," she said finally. "But I'm going to be okay. It's just going to take some time. And this," she added, tapping her temple, "has nothing to do with Aiden, so I don't want to hear a single bad word about him."

She leveled each of her brothers and her dad with a glare in turn, and each of them nodded.

The funny thing about anxiety attacks was they were like being burned, and she'd do anything she could to spare herself that pain again. Could she easily fly back to Detroit and avoid spending two or three days on the road with her parents? Of course. And did she miss Aiden? Desperately.

But she needed more time.

It had nothing to do with Aiden. It was simply her own mind playing tricks on her, and unfortunately, she now associated their relationship with that tightening in her chest, shaking in her extremities, and intrusive thoughts.

She'd spoken to her therapist a few times over the last three weeks, but the guidance had been the same every time: Kenzie had to let it go. Aiden was not the cause of this particular episode. The trigger had been a combination of a lot of changes happening in her life at once, but Aiden wasn't to blame, and she couldn't keep doing this to him.

Now that the attack had passed and she'd had some distance from it, she was more embarrassed than anything. Aiden loved her, sure. But distance had spared him from the worst of her more recent episode. How would he react when he had to watch it unfold in real time and could do nothing to help her? These were the things that kept her up at night, and compounded by the move and the fight with her brother, Kenzie was barely hanging on.

After breakfast, they opened gifts, and then spent the rest of the day in the living room, marathoning their favorite Christmas movies.

"You know, honey," her mom said during a short intermission between the first two Home Alone movies, when everyone dispersed to stretch, use the restroom, or refill on snacks and beverages, "I've been thinking about you a lot, and I had an idea."

Inwardly, Kenzie groaned.

"What's that, Mom?"

"I was thinking you should go up to the cabin for a week or so. It'd be a nice opportunity for you to relax, clear your mind, and refocus your priorities before the new semester starts."

Kenzie was...surprised. That hadn't been in the same universe of things she'd expected her mom to say, but now that the idea was out there, it quickly lodged in Kenzie's brain, taking root and spreading until she couldn't see any reason why she *shouldn't* head to the cabin for a week.

"You know what, Mom," Kenzie said. "That's an excellent idea."

Brent, ever the fun-sucker, chose that moment to insert himself into the conversation. "Are you sure it's a good idea for her to be up there by herself?"

Their mom shrugged. "Why not? It's safe and secluded. The cabin has an excellent security system—you would know, you paid for it," she reminded him. "There's Wi-Fi and full cell reception. If something happens to the house, your fancy little app will alert you right away."

"Plus," Kenzie cut in, reminding them that she was standing right there. "I'm twenty-three and perfectly capable of spending a week alone. I'd only be a half hour from Lake Placid, and like Mom said, you guys will only be a phone call away."

"Not exactly," Brent said. "Albany is still two and a half hours away."

"Brent!" their mother yelled in a rare moment of exasperation. "I'm the parent here, and if I say Kenzie can go to the cabin, she can go to the cabin! End of story."

At the outburst, everyone else in the room fell silent, the only sound the quiet whirring of the projector mounted to the ceiling.

Brent, who had always been the golden child and thus rarely had their parents raise their voices at him, sank down onto the nearest plush leather chair, twin splotches of red appearing on his cheeks.

"Sorry, Mom," he mumbled.

Their mom ignored him, turning her attention fully to Kenzie. She clasped her daughter's hands in her own and said, "You deserve this break, kiddo."

Throat clogged with emotion, Kenzie could do nothing but wrap her mother in a hug.

Leaving her family home and the chaos of packing for the quiet Upstate New York cabin was like stepping through a door into a magical universe. Kenzie's mental clarity sharpened, her surroundings more crisp and clear, the air cleaner, the snow whiter, the noises of civilization nonexistent.

Kenzie parked her dad's truck, which she'd driven up from Albany, in the driveway, snow crunching under the tires in the most satisfying way. She could make one of those ASMR videos of that sound alone, and she guaranteed it would go viral on TikTok.

She stepped down from the cab and closed the truck door, taking a moment to pause and study the front facade of their once-humble-turned-mammoth lake house.

It was less *house* and more *mansion*.

To be fair, when her parents had inherited the property from her grandparents, the cabin could barely fit the two of them, let alone them and three kids, two of whom were oversized men. And then Brent married Berkley, who had a big family of her own, and Kenzie had become grateful for all that extra space.

The dark-stained logs, which usually gleamed in the sun, were frosted over with snow, the roof covered in a blanket of powder. Upstate New York had received several feet of snow already, and thankfully one of their neighbors—who lived here year-round—had come over and plowed the driveway after a phone call from Brent.

Speaking of her brother, if he were here, he'd be spending his days outside: fishing, clearing the ice and skating lazy laps around, showing off for the neighbors, maybe taking the snowmobile out on the nearby trails.

Kenzie would be doing none of that, save *maybe* venturing outside to take a walk around their little neighborhood when she felt inclined to get some fresh air and cardio.

No, Kenzie would be spending her days catching up on all of the filthy Kindle Unlimited romances she hadn't had time for during the school year.

The little hamlet that served as the town for their cabin was named Hawkeye, which seemed appropriate to Kenzie given the fact that its hawk population was certainly higher than its human one. They didn't get mail here, but in case of an accident, they needed an address where they could direct emergency response teams.

When she arrived, it was midday, and all Kenzie wanted was to curl up on the couch with a book.

First, she turned the heat up. They kept it on during the winter months, only high enough to prevent the pipes from freezing and causing a burst when no one was here to notice. Then she donned her thickest pair of fuzzy socks, an oversized hoodie that had once belonged to her brother Nate, and turned the gas fireplace in the living room on full blast.

Now that she was alone, Aiden consumed every one of her thoughts.

Although he'd never been to the cabin—actually, he didn't even know this place existed—she could easily picture him here. In the easy chair across the room, those favorite dark-grey sweatpants of his clinging to the sculpted muscles of his quads and calves. Except he'd never sit that far away from her. Aiden always had to be touching her, and it was one of the many things she loved about him.

From the very first moment they'd met, Aiden had an innate ability to see right through all the walls she'd built up around herself. Unlike anyone else, he had truly seen her. Better than even her family ever had.

And she'd seen him right back.

Kenzie wished he were here. And she knew if he didn't have games in the middle of the week, he would come if she called.

For a moment, she considered inviting him anyway, but ultimately didn't. She didn't want that possibility hanging over his head when he had a tournament to win.

Besides, she needed this time to reset, and she couldn't do that if he were here, stealing her heart and all of her attention.

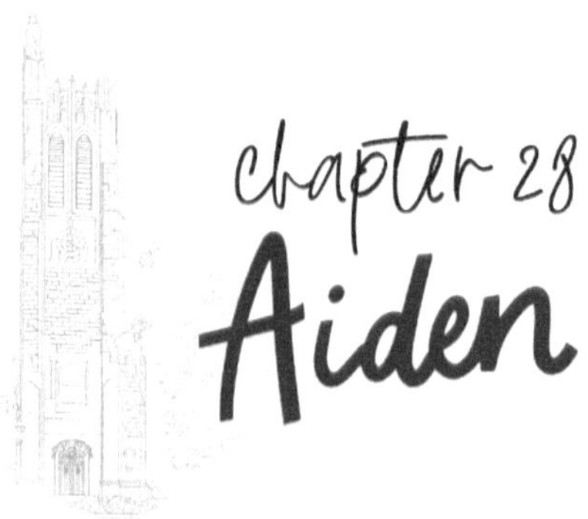

chapter 28
Aiden

THE SPARTANS WERE GREAT Lakes Invitational champs for the first time in fifteen years, and Aiden should have been celebrating.

Instead, he sat at a table in the hotel bar of the Renaissance Center, a beer dangling from his fingertips, watching as his teammates got caught up in the revelry around them. Spartan fans poured in from the streets and their rooms upstairs to celebrate with the hockey team.

"Fuller," Jack said, walking over to him and thrusting a shot of something golden into his hand. A sniff told Aiden it was something strong, and he almost told Jack to piss off, but *strong* was exactly what he needed right now.

Without waiting for Jack to salute or make some ridiculous toast, Aiden downed the liquor, relishing the burn that lit the lining of his stomach a moment later.

"Dude, snap out of it!" Jack said, fist socking Aiden's shoulder to punctuate his demand. "Kenzie ran away from you. And we get it. Anxiety and mental health struggles are nothing to thumb your nose at. But you're miserable, and I'm sure she is, too. Why are you sitting here with us when you should be with her?"

"Go away," Aiden said sullenly.

"Fuck that," Jack said, ignoring Aiden's request and pulling a chair up next to him. "What do you want, Fuller? It's your birthday tomorrow, and we just won the GLI for the first time since Obama was president. Both of those things warrant a celebration, and your bad mood is making the rest of the boys feel like shit."

"I don't care," Aiden said, rising to his feet. "I'll go upstairs then."

Jack reached out and placed his palm flat on Aiden's chest, shoving him back down into the chair.

"Asher, Luke!" he called over his shoulder, and at once their roommates joined the little powwow.

"You guys," Aiden said, leaning forward to drop his head in his hands. "Now is not the time for this."

"Now is *exactly* the time for this," Asher argued. "We're your friends, and we want to help you."

Aiden whipped his head up and leveled Asher with a glare. "Don't you think you've helped enough? You're the reason she had a panic attack in the first place!"

Asher opened his mouth to protest, but Jack cut him off.

"He has a point, Ash," Jack said, and Asher sulked. "That doesn't explain why you're still here, though, Fuller. You and bunny are good, right?"

"Yes. I think. I don't know."

Luke huffed out a laugh. "Well it's pretty fucking obvious you miss her, so I think you need to go see her. Make sure you're good. Tell her you love her. All that lovey-dovey bullshit."

"You fuckers are the reason I'm in this mess," Aiden said under his breath. He leveled Asher with a cold, hard stare. "Especially you."

Asher opened his mouth to protest again, but Jack shoved him out of their circle.

"So you agree it's a mess," Jack said, nodding sagely like a therapist might with a patient having a breakthrough. "That's the first step."

"Fuck you, DeLuca," Aiden said, the words lacking any real malice.

"Look, we get it," Asher said. "You're pissed at us for the dare. But to be fair...you're the one who turned a single date into a full-blown relationship."

Aiden opened his mouth to respond, then clapped it shut.

Asher was right: he was as much, if not more, to blame for this predicament.

Asking Kenzie out on a dare—*agreeing* to the dare in the first place—had been the catalyst that had set every single moment of the last three months in motion.

Well, besides his suspension; *that* had been all him.

And partially Jack. But mainly him.

And while he'd given Kenzie the time and space she needed to get her head back on straight, he had to admit he was fucking miserable without her.

Enough was enough, right? Why weren't they together right now? Where even was she? Had she come back to Michigan and not told him? Was she still in New York?

It seemed insane that he didn't know where his own girlfriend was.

Over the course of the last three months, he'd gotten used to her constant, steady presence. The way she quietly hummed to whatever music played on her AirPods while they studied side by side on her couch. How she always knew exactly what to say to him in high-stress situations to bring him back to Earth.

How she tasted. How she smelled. How smooth her skin felt beneath his fingertips. How perfectly they fit together.

"I can practically see those wheels spinning, Fuller," Jack said, narrowing his gaze at Aiden. "What're you thinking?"

"I miss her."

"No shit," Luke said. "So go get her!"

"How the hell am I supposed to do that?"

"You could start by calling her," Asher suggested.

Aiden hopped up from his seat, startling Asher so badly he fell off his chair. Ignoring Jack and Luke, who devolved into fits of laughter, he moved to a quieter corner of the lobby and pulled his phone out of his pocket.

He pressed the call button on Kenzie's contact info and waited while it rang.

And waited.

And waited.

"Hi, you've reached Kenzie. Leave a message."

"Fuck," he breathed, then turned to his friends. "No answer."

"Let me try," Jack said, withdrawing his phone from his own pocket and dialing Kenzie's number, then tapping the speakerphone button and holding it in the center of their group.

Aiden wasn't surprised when it went to voicemail.

Without comment, Aiden stalked across the lobby and down the hall toward the elevator bank, his teammates' footsteps landing heavily behind him as they raced to catch up.

"Where are you going?" Jack asked as he skidded to a stop beside Aiden.

"Upstairs to pack."

"Why? The bus doesn't leave until tomorrow morning."

"I don't give a fuck about the bus," Aiden said as the elevator reached their floor, dinging as the doors slid open. "I'm leaving tonight. I'm going to see Kenzie."

"YES!" his teammates cheered, then piled into the elevator with him.

Ever the practical one, Luke said, "But she's not answering her phone. How are you going to find her?"

"I'll call her brother, or Berkley, or Mitch, or literally anyone who might know where she is."

"I can call Jessica," Jack offered.

Aiden locked eyes with his goalie. "Yes, do that. Please."

Jack dialed Jessica's number as the elevator spit them out on their floor. The four of them rushed to Jack and Aiden's room, where Aiden keyed them in.

"Hey, Jess," Jack said as they stepped into the room, then pulled the phone away from his ear and put it on speaker.

"What do you want, Jack?"

"Aiden needs to know where Kenzie is."

"Please, Jess," Aiden begged. "I need to see her. Is she in Detroit? Back in EL? Where is she?"

The line was silent for several long, tense moments. Finally, Jessica sighed and said, "She's still in New York."

"Like...the city? Albany? Where exactly? It's a big state."

"Her family cabin," Jessica said. "But I've only been there once and I have no idea where exactly it is. Somewhere in the middle of Upstate."

"Okay, Upstate New York. That's a start. Thanks Jess."

Aiden was already turning away from the phone, but he didn't miss the way Jack said, "I'll call you later."

Nor did he miss Jessica's, "You better," before she hung up.

Aiden raised an eyebrow at Jack, who opened his mouth to give some sort of explanation. Unfortunately, Aiden didn't have the time, and brought a hand up to stop him. "We're not even going to talk about whatever the fuck you've got going on with Jessica Daniels right now. One relationship problem at a time."

Bag packed, Aiden tossed it over his shoulder and moved to the door, turning to survey his teammates as he reached for the handle.

"If I forgot anything, bring it home, please," he told them.

"What are you going to do?"

"I don't really know," Aiden said. "Get on a plane and figure it out as I go, I guess."

"Godspeed, my friend," Luke said solemnly.

"May the odds be ever in your favor," Asher quipped.

"Good luck," Jack told him.

He gave the three of them a grateful smile and exited the room, rushing downstairs as fast as the elevator could carry him. When it landed on the main floor, he once again hustled across the lobby and to another elevator bank that would take him down to street level. That elevator reached the ground floor and Aiden stepped out, slamming into a body so hard it may have been carved out of stone.

"I'm so sorry—" he started, but cut off as he looked into the face of who he'd collided with. "Fuck."

"Fuller," Brent Jean said, voice laced with venom. "Where are you off to in such a hurry? Shouldn't you be upstairs celebrating with your teammates?"

"I've got something more important to take care of."

Brent raised an eyebrow, as though he'd guessed what that thing was, but was unwilling to help Aiden in any way when it came to his sister.

Finally, Aiden broke the stalemate. "Where's the cabin?"

"Why should I tell you?"

"Because I need to see her!" he yelled. And fuck it all, he threw caution to the wind, unloading on this guy who didn't even like him. "I know you hate me, and you don't think I'm good enough for her, but I think she's the love of my life. And I am all in on her and our relationship. I'd like the chance to prove that to her. I haven't seen her in three weeks, and I'm going crazy. Please, Brent. If you love your sister and want her to be happy, *please* help me."

Brent considered him, that steely-blue gaze that matched his sister's perfectly sweeping over his body like an X-ray machine. Aiden struggled to remain still, to not squirm under that intense scrutiny.

Instead of responding, Brent withdrew his phone from his suit jacket and tapped the screen a few times, then lifted it to his ear.

"Hey kid," Brent said, and Aiden knew it was Kenzie on the line.

"Look, I know I haven't exactly been the kid's biggest supporter in the past, but I'm staring at your boyfriend right now and he looks like shit. Says he wants to see you. I'm calling to make sure it's okay to give him the cabin's address."

A tinny sort of squawking floated to Aiden from the phone, but he couldn't make out any of what Kenzie was saying.

"I'm just saying, Kenz...you've been pretty unbearable, too."

"I HAVE NOT!"

Aiden definitely heard that, and bit back a smile.

"Do whatever you want, I guess," Brent told her. "I'm just saying you might regret it someday if you don't fight for this one. If I hadn't fought for Berkley, you wouldn't be becoming an aunt in a few months."

So now Brent was comparing Aiden and Kenzie to him and Berkley? Hadn't Kenzie explicitly told him she was *not* the Berkley Daniels to his Brent Jean? Maybe she'd been wrong. Maybe they both had been. And if her brother was using his own relationship as a model for theirs, Aiden wasn't about to complain. Brent could say whatever the fuck he wanted if it ended with Kenzie back in his arms.

"Okay, fine," Brent said, then hung up.

"How'd you reach her?" Aiden asked. "She's not answering my calls."

"Called the landline at the cabin," Brent said, then stared at him expectantly, waiting for something.

A moment later, Aiden's phone dinged, and he dropped his bag on the floor to fish it from his coat, shoulders sagging in relief when he found a text from Kenzie.

The message itself had no words, no explanation at all.

There was only a location pin.

"That's where she is."

"Thank you," Aiden said, reaching out his hand. Brent shook it, and the second they broke contact, Aiden rushed outside, ran three blocks away from the Detroit River to where city traffic was thicker, and hailed a cab.

In that moment, Aiden could've sworn something had shifted between him and Kenzie's brother, but he'd figure out what it was later.

Right now, he had to get to his girl.

"Airport, please," he told the driver.

Seven hours later, after a long and torturous two-hour layover in Boston, Aiden landed in Lake Placid, New York. According to his Google research on the cab ride to the Detroit airport, it was as close as he could get by plane to the cabin. Having checked no luggage, Aiden beelined through the terminal, right to the rental car line.

"I'm sorry, son," the middle-aged man working told him. "You're not old enough to rent a car."

Fuck. Aiden had forgotten about the stupid age limit on car rentals.

"Look, Otis," Aiden said with a quick glance at the man's name tag, "about three weeks ago, my roommates said some things that kind of freaked out the girl of my dreams and sent her into a panic attack. She left my place, and I let her go, and I haven't seen her since. I've been fucking miserable without her. I came all the way from Michigan, and now I have to drive to some place in the middle of nowhere just to get my girl back."

Aiden heaved a deep breath, refilling his lungs after his ramble while the rental guy stared at him open-mouthed.

"And did I mention it's my birthday?" Aiden gave him a sheep-ish grin.

"That is without a doubt the most romantic thing I've ever heard," Otis said. Then he pulled a clipboard from a drawer under his desk and pushed it in front of Aiden. "Today is your *twenty-fifth* birthday, correct?"

The guy winked at Aiden, knowing full well from the driver's license he'd flashed minutes ago that Aiden was only twenty-four.

"Yes, it is," Aiden said, quickly filling out the rental form, easily fudging his birth year before the guy could change his mind.

"Good luck," the man said. "And drive safe. Looks like we're getting some snow."

"Thank you," Aiden said. "I appreciate your help."

Aiden scoffed as he stepped outside, noting the itty-bitty snowflakes falling like dandelion fluff on the wind. He clicked the lock button on the rental key fob, surprised to find the man had upgraded him to an SUV, free of charge. Either he'd been really moved by Aiden's story, or he was really concerned about the weather.

It was only about a half hour from the airport to Aiden's final destination. As he came within five miles of the cabin, snow began slanting across the road, nearly blotting out his vision, and he regretted being so cavalier about the weather earlier.

"In three hundred feet, turn left," his GPS droned in that creepy robot voice.

"I would if I could fucking see anything!" Aiden yelled uselessly.

"Turn left. Turn left. Turn left."

Aiden couldn't see more than twenty feet in front of him, his blinker useless thanks to the necessity of his flashers. He crawled to a stop, sent up a silent prayer that nobody was coming to T-bone him, and turned left. For a moment, the snow lifted, a street sign appearing in the dim, early-morning light.

Bingo.

"Continue on Richards Road for half a mile. Your destination will be on your left."

Aiden slowly crept down the road, the wall of white in front of him making it impossible to orient himself. At this point, he navigated purely based on the satellite image his phone showed. Up ahead, the road appeared to bend itself into a U shape, and in another hundred feet, he came upon a drive marked by a tall wooden placard.

JEAN FAMILY CABIN

Well, well, well. Aiden navigated up the drive, ultimately coming to a stop in front of a stunning log cabin. Through the snow, which seemed to be lightening, smoke curled into the air from a stone chimney. Beyond, a frozen lake stretched out, begging to be shoveled and skated on.

One thing at a time, Fuller.

A single light illuminated the front porch, and Aiden made his way through the snow, his shoes and the hems of his pants instantly soaked. Briefly, he debated whether or not he should knock, but ultimately decided to barge right in. He was fucking freezing and, despite having come all this way, he didn't entirely trust Kenzie not to leave him out in the cold.

With a shaking hand, he turned the knob and stepped inside.

"Kenzie?" he called, kicking off his shoes, then his soaked socks.

He padded further into the house, barely registering his surroundings as he hunted for the one and only thing he wanted to see.

Finally he found her, fast asleep, curled up under a mountain of blankets on a large sectional, a fire diminished to faint flickers in the hearth across from her.

Aiden knelt at her side and brushed an errant lock of hair from her cheek. At his touch, she stirred, slowly blinking her eyes fully open.

"Fuller," she said finally, her voice rough with sleep. "You're here."

"I'm here. I'm sorry it took so long."

With a deep sigh, Kenzie lifted herself into a seated position and patted the couch next to her.

"I'm all wet," he told her, gesturing to his pants.

"So take them off."

Aiden had a feeling she wouldn't be telling him to strip if she were more lucid, but he wasn't about to argue. He made quick work of removing the wet joggers, then crawled onto the couch next to her.

Without preamble, Aiden pulled her onto his lap and pressed his mouth to hers.

He couldn't wait any longer to breathe her in, to taste her; he'd gone too long without a hit of pure, undiluted *Kenzie*. For a moment, she stiffened, but melted into him seconds later, kissing him back with a vigor that matched his own.

"I love you," he whispered between kisses. "I'm so sorry for everything. But I love you, Mackenzie Elizabeth Jean, and I'll spend forever proving it to you."

Too soon, she pulled away and rested her forehead against his. "Aiden," she whispered.

He pulled away and looked at her, her blue eyes glowing like sapphires in the low, flickering light of the fire. "What? Whatever it is, I'll do it."

"I love you, too." A grin split his face and he leaned forward to capture her mouth again, but she pressed a finger to his lips, stalling him. "I...the last few weeks have been awful. And you have nothing to be sorry for. I'm the one who should be sorry. I hurt us both by letting this drag on so long. I just...I was so embarrassed after that day, I couldn't bear to find out what you might think of me. Being out of town was a convenient excuse to avoid you.

"This was never supposed to happen. I've always told myself I'd never date a hockey player, and I would certainly never fall in love with one. Having one for a big brother is bad enough, and I never planned on anyone getting close enough to make me want to break that rule. But I never planned on you.

"*You*, Fuller, make every rule worth breaking."

Aiden loosed a breath, the band wrapped around his chest snapping, freeing his lungs, his heart. He leaned in so his forehead rested against hers. "I'm sorry I didn't come for you sooner. Whatever you've got going on up here," he said, tapping her temple, "I love every bit of it. I love all of you, and I can't have you hiding from me when things get bad. Talk to me. Let me hold you. Let me do whatever I can to help you through it. That's what couples do, right?"

Kenzie nodded. "I missed you so much."

"I missed you, too."

Kenzie pulled away and hopped to her feet, hands raised to her head. "Oh my god, Fuller."

"What?" he said, standing and taking her hands in his. "Are you okay?"

"I'm fine," she said. "I just can't believe you spent the first eight hours of your birthday traveling!"

Aiden shrugged. "I wanted to see you. I wanted to be with you. I can think of nowhere else I'd rather spend today than right here."

She stepped into his embrace and wrapped her arms around his waist, tilting her head back to look up at him. He snaked his own arms around her hips and slid his palms down to cup her ass, the ends of her hair tickling his forearms.

"Happy birthday, Fuller," she said.

He kissed the tip of her nose, then her forehead, then moved to her mouth, pausing a breath away. "Thank you, my love."

They soon lost themselves in each other, their discarded clothing scattering around the sitting area at warp speed. Kenzie pulled her blankets off the couch and spread them on the floor in front of the fire, where they spent hours making love—sometimes long and slow, sometimes frenzied, but every second of it the most perfect birthday present Aiden had ever been given.

This love was a true gift, something he'd never allowed himself to hope for, and he'd spend every day from now on treasuring it.

epilogue

Kenzie

"Aren't WAGs supposed to sit in suites or something?" Jessica asked as Kenzie led them down to the stairs.

"It's his first professional game," Kenzie said. "I want to be close enough that he can see me when he scores."

"*If* he scores," Jack said from behind Jessica, and Kenzie shot him a glare over her shoulder.

"Don't be jealous, DeLuca," Luke said.

Jack scoffed. "Why would I be jealous? It's not like I'd be scoring if I was playing right now. I'd be preventing that."

Kenzie laughed when Luke opened his mouth to protest, then clamped it shut when he realized Jack was right.

She led the group, the rear of which was brought up by Asher, to their seats about ten rows up from the glass and slightly left of center ice.

They filed in, the five of them a mass of red and white, the shirts hastily made using Jessica's Cricut because the team obviously didn't have any merch with Aiden's name and number on it yet.

Right as they sat, the PA guy's voice blasted through the arena. "Who's ready for some Assassins' hockey?!"

Cheers rose, the volume deafening, the stands beneath Kenzie's feet vibrating with the force.

"And now for tonight's starting lineups."

Kenzie took in the scene as the announcer listed the starters, for the first time realizing exactly how surreal it was for her to be seated here.

Aiden had put up impressive numbers the second half of the season, finishing third in the entire NCAA in points and leading his team to a Final Four appearance. The Spartans had made it to the championship game, but ultimately lost to the University of North Dakota.

Immediately after the conclusion of that game, practically before the sweat on their bodies had even dried, Mitch called Aiden with an offer.

Aiden had signed without hesitation.

He'd spent the better part of the last two months in Toledo with the Warriors' ECHL team, but last weekend, he got called up.

So here they were, in Grand Rapids, where Aiden was making his first professional start for the Warriors' American Hockey League team, the Assassins.

After their reunion on Aiden's birthday, he and Kenzie had been inseparable, only spending nights apart when Aiden was out of town. If such a thing was possible, their relationship had only gotten better and better over the last few months, and Kenzie looked forward to what this new chapter of hockey, and their summer and life beyond that, would look like for them.

When she'd returned to Michigan before the start of the new semester, she, Brent, and Berkley had sat down and discussed at length plans for FLEX and Kenzie's exit from the company. Eventually, they'd decided to hire a new Chief Financial Officer and a Chief Operating Officer. Brent would remain as CEO and the figurehead of the company, maintaining controlling interest and final say in any and everything FLEX did going forward—but he would no longer be as hands on as he'd been up to that point. Kenzie retained stock, but sold half of her shares to Nate. Berkley had passed the handling of the company's legal matters to a colleague in preparation of leaving the practice and the birth of her son.

Brooks Austen Jean was born on March 24th and was quite possibly the most perfect baby boy Kenzie had ever laid eyes on. He'd arrived kicking and screaming, with a full head of that dark Jean hair and his mama's blue eyes. He had his parents, grandparents, aunts and uncles, and pretty much anyone who met him wrapped around his tiny little fingers.

Kenzie still had another year of school to finish before her degrees were complete, but she'd been spending a lot of time picking Lexie and Sofia's brains about influencing, and thanks to her smoking hot boyfriend, connection to a major activewear company, professional athlete brother, and fun, thrifty style, she'd grown her social media presence exponentially in the last few months.

A degree wasn't necessary to be an influencer, but this time Kenzie was finishing what she'd started. Eventually, she'd like to branch out into working directly with companies not only as a brand ambassador, but as a marketing exec, helping them choose the best campaigns and product placements to achieve their goals.

But all that would come with time. For now, she wanted to sit back and watch her man play his first professional game.

"There he is!" Jessica squealed, pointing and smacking Kenzie on the arm.

Kenzie grinned widely, and lifted her phone to snap pictures of Aiden on the ice. He played beautifully, blocking shots, making crisp passes, and seeming to transition smoothly into playing with new teammates, on new ice, in a new offensive system.

He even had the secondary assist on the game-winning goal.

Kenzie had never been more proud, and Jessica and the boys shouted themselves hoarse alongside her.

After the game, they remained in their seats, waiting for Aiden to fulfill media obligations and shower before they headed out for a night on the town.

They had a lot to celebrate.

When he appeared from the tunnel and saw them all waiting for him, his face split into a grin and he rushed up to meet them. His former teammates and roommates attempted to stop him for hugs and claps on the back, but Aiden made a beeline for Kenzie.

He scooped her off her feet and spun her around, finally stopping so he could kiss her, harder and longer than was probably appropriate for being in public.

Kenzie didn't care.

"You were amazing," she said against his lips, and his answering smile was so wide that their teeth clacked together when he kissed her again, their makeout devolving into a fit of laughter.

He put her back on her feet and turned to his friends, who stared at them with varied expressions on their faces. Jessica, moony-eyed. Jack, a shit-eating grin. Luke, an indulgent smile. And Asher, borderline disgust mixed with something that looked dangerously like jealousy.

Kenzie's phone vibrated in her pocket, and she withdrew it to find a text from Jessica.

"What is this?" she asked, unlocking her phone and opening the message.

"You two are disgustingly photogenic," Jessica said by way of explanation as Kenzie thumbed through the photos she'd taken.

Aiden whistled low. "We are pretty hot."

Kenzie studied the photos, finally selecting one, applying her favorite filter, then opening Instagram.

Jessica had caught them in their embrace, Kenzie's face hovering over Aiden's, both grinning stupidly, eyes shining with what could only be described as nothing other than pure, undiluted love.

It might be Kenzie's favorite picture ever.

First of many, she captioned it. *And I can't wait to see what happens next.*

acknowledgements

As ALWAYS, I COULD not do this without the love and support of my mom, dad, and sister.

To Granny J and Grandpa Vic: thank you for always cheering me on, especially Granny. I know you don't like the language I use, but I love you more than I could ever say for reading my books.

To Grammy and Grumpy: I miss you. Thanks for keeping an eye on me from up there.

To Mer: where do I even begin? I could write an entire book on what your friendship means to me, but it would really just be full of inside jokes, Joey B thirst traps, and endless streams of unanswered texts. Truthfully, though, THANK YOU. Thank you for talking through ideas with me before I ever put them on paper—or after I do and realize they suck. Thank you for reading dark romance books before me so I know if I'll like them or not. Thank you for being my favorite buddy read, for making sure I never post a stupid reel or TikTok, and for literally everything forever.

To Jen, Abigail, Allyson, Alyssa, Amanda, and Kenna (damn that's a lot of A names!): thank you for being the most amazing beta team, and providing the feedback that made Kenzie and Aiden's story so amazing. I appreciate you all so very much.

To Samantha: I say this every time we do this, but thank you times infinity for giving me the cover of my dreams. You are truly a miracle worker. I'm not sure what I did to deserve you, but I could not be more thankful for you, your talent, or your friendship.

To Meg Jones, the creator of the "dicktionary," for letting me include one in the back of this book, and to Hailey Dickert for the "spread your" pages wording. Appreciate you both so much!

And lastly, to my readers. THANK YOU FOR YOUR SUP-PORT. I couldn't keep writing books without y'all, and your constant posts, stories, reels, and general screaming into the void about my stories makes this all worthwhile.

about the author

AMANDA CHAPERON REALIZED HER passion for books, and for writing, at a young age. Growing up, she was rarely found without a book in her hands, a hobby she carried into adulthood. After joining bookstagram in 2020, she felt the pull to try her hand at novel writing. She writes what she loves to read: messy, relatable characters, lots of steam, and always a happily ever after.

She currently lives in Michigan's Upper Peninsula with Gryffin, her Golden Retriever. She loves all things romance, fantasy, young adult, and thrillers that keep her up at night. You can follow her on Instagram, Threads, and TikTok at @achaperonwrites.

Dicktionary

My dear sweet reader, please use this guide to avoid (or seek out) the spicy scenes, which can be found in the following chapters:

Chapter 18
Chapter 20
Chapter 23
Chapter 26

Spread those pages, my friend.